Discover the series y

'If you like your conspiracies t
and your heroes impossibly
– the Ben Hope series is exactly what you need'

Mark Dawson

'Deadly conspiracies, bone-crunching action and a tormented hero with a heart . . . Scott Mariani packs a real punch'

Andy McDermott

'James Bond meets Jason Bourne meets *The Da Vinci Code*'

J. L. Carrell

'Non-stop action – this book delivers'

Steve Berry

'Full of authentic detail and heart-stopping action – a real thrill ride'

Ed Macy

'Scott Mariani is an awesome writer'

Chris Kuzneski

‘Packed with dark intrigue, danger around every corner, bullets flying, sexual tension, and an endless assault of nasty villains . . . everything a thriller should be and more’

Joe Moore

‘If you’ve got a pulse, you’ll love Scott Mariani; if you haven’t, then maybe you crossed Ben Hope’

Simon Toyne

‘The action comes thick and fast and is choreographed with Mariani’s trademark skill and authenticity. The modern master of mayhem’

Shots Magazine

‘Fans of Dan Brown will love this’

Closer

‘Edge-of-the-seat excitement . . . I am hooked on this series’

5* Reader Review

‘Gripping adventure, superbly written’

5* Reader Review

‘Cinematic style, fast pace and, above all, fabulous characters’

5* Reader Review

HOUSE OF WAR

Scott Mariani is the author of the worldwide-acclaimed action-adventure thriller series featuring ex-SAS hero Ben Hope, which has sold millions of copies in Scott's native UK alone and is also translated into over 20 languages. His books have been described as 'James Bond meets Jason Bourne, with a historical twist'. The first Ben Hope book, *The Alchemist's Secret*, spent six straight weeks at #1 on Amazon's Kindle chart, and all the others have been *Sunday Times* bestsellers.

Scott was born in Scotland, studied in Oxford and now lives and writes in a remote setting in rural west Wales. When not writing, he can be found bouncing about the country lanes in an ancient Land Rover, wild camping in the Brecon Beacons or engrossed in his hobbies of astronomy, photography and target shooting (no dead animals involved!).

You can find out more about Scott and his work on his official website:

www.scottmariani.com

By the same author:

Ben Hope series

The Alchemist's Secret
The Mozart Conspiracy
The Doomsday Prophecy
The Heretic's Treasure
The Shadow Project
The Lost Relic
The Sacred Sword
The Armada Legacy
The Nemesis Program
The Forgotten Holocaust
The Martyr's Curse
The Cassandra Sanction
Star of Africa
The Devil's Kingdom
The Babylon Idol
The Bach Manuscript
The Moscow Cipher
The Rebel's Revenge
Valley of Death

To find out more visit **www.scottmariani.com**

SCOTT MARIANI

HOUSE OF WAR

avon.

Published by AVON
A division of HarperCollins*Publishers* Ltd
1 London Bridge Street
London SE1 9GF

www.harpercollins.co.uk

A Paperback Original 2019

First published in Great Britain by HarperCollins*Publishers* 2019

A catalogue copy of this book is
available from the British Library.

ISBN: 978-0-00-823598-7

Set in Minion by Palimpsest Book Production Limited, Falkirk, Stirlingshire

Printed and bound in UK by
CPI Group (UK) Ltd, Croydon CR0 4YY

HOUSE OF WAR

PROLOGUE

Syria, 2015

The two men were the last ones still inside the ancient temple as the invasion force closed in. They had been racing against time in their desperate last-minute bid to rescue as many of the treasures as they could, but they'd been too slow, too late, and their efforts were futile. Nobody was there to help them. Everyone else had fled hours earlier, when the first death knell of artillery fire sounded in the distance and the terrifying rumours became reality. Now the battle was lost and the government forces trying to hold onto the ancient city in the face of withering attack had fallen into full retreat.

These preserved architectural splendours had graced the desert oasis for two thousand years, dating back to when the thriving city had been one of the major centres on the trade route linking the Roman Empire with Persia, India and China. Here the worlds of classical and Eastern culture had melded and blossomed for centuries. Right up until the present day, their noble heritage had remained as a source of beauty and wonder for the thousands of travellers who flocked there each year to marvel.

And now, on this terrible day that would be remembered

for a long time, the ancient city was about to fall into the hands of the destroyers.

The two men knew the end was near. Even though their hours of labour had succeeded in moving the majority of the priceless artifacts to a nearby hiding place where they hoped they could survive, there was still so much to do, so many treasures to try to save. It seemed a hopeless task.

'We must hurry, Julien,' said Salim Youssef to his younger associate. 'They'll be here any minute.' He was trying to lift a magnificent Greco-Roman bust from its plinth to place it on a trolley and wheel it outside to the already overloaded truck. But the artifact was far too heavy for his seventy-four-year-old arms to handle. He gasped and wheezed, but he wouldn't give up. For the last forty years the Syrian had been devotedly in charge of the preservation and cataloguing of the priceless antiquities in this place, which for him was as sacred and holy as a site of religious worship.

His companion was a Frenchman named Julien Segal, twenty-five years his junior, who had been closely involved in Salim's work for over a decade. He was based equally in Paris and the Middle East, and spoke Arabic fluently. A man known for his elegant dress style and cosmopolitan chic, he wasn't looking his stylish best at this moment, as he struggled and sweated to drag a six-foot Akkadian alabaster statue across the flagstone floor towards the archway near to which the truck was parked. Even inside the relative coolness of the temple, the August desert heat felt as though it could bake a man inside his skin.

'It's no use, Salim. We'll never make it. Everyone else has run for it, and we should do the same while we still can.'

'You go, Julien,' Salim wheezed, clutching his chest. 'I'm

staying. I won't abandon these treasures, no matter what. This place is all I know and care about.'

'But they'll kill you, Salim.'

'Let those lunatic butchers do their worst,' the old man said. 'I'm not afraid of them. I have lived my life and don't have many years left. But yours is still ahead of you. Go! Save yourself!' He pulled the truck keys from his pocket and tossed them to Julien Segal.

The Frenchman was about to reply, 'I won't leave without you.' But the words died in his mouth as he turned to see the sight that froze his blood.

They were here.

Nine men had come into the temple's main entrance and now stood in a semicircle, watching them with detached curiosity. All were bearded and clad in dusty battledress, armed with automatic weapons. Their leader stood in the middle, with four of his soldiers each side of him. He wore black, in accordance with his rank as an ISIL commander. A holstered pistol and a long, sheathed knife hung from his belt.

That was when Julien Segal saw that three of the men were also clutching heavy iron sledgehammers in addition to their weaponry. He opened his mouth to speak, but his throat had gone dry.

Salim spoke for him. The old man stepped away from the bust he'd been trying to manhandle, and advanced towards the invaders, fists clenched in anger. 'You are not welcome here! Leave now!'

The commander in black stepped forward to meet him. He gazed around the temple's interior, looking at the statues and other artifacts that Salim and his colleague hadn't yet been able to remove to safety, and the vacant plinths of those that they had. His voice echoed in the stone chamber as he spoke:

'I am Nazim al-Kassar. You must be Salim Youssef, the curator. Tell me, old man. This place is looking quite empty. Where have you hidden the rest of these idolatrous pieces of trash you call art?'

'So you have come here to destroy them,' Salim said defiantly.

'This house of blasphemy, along with everything inside it and all that you have vainly tried to rescue,' said Nazim al-Kassar. 'It shall be razed to the ground, inshallah.'

'You will not! You must not!'

The commander smiled. 'These are the idols of previous centuries, which were worshipped instead of Allah. They have no place in the new Caliphate that will now rule this country for the rest of time. Allah commands that they be shattered and broken into dust.'

'Savages! Vandals! What gives you the right to erase history? You think you're doing Allah's bidding? Where does the Qur'an make such a command? Nowhere! I am also a Muslim, and I say that you bring shame and disgrace upon our religion!' The old man was seething with fury. Cringing behind him, Julien Segal was too terrified to utter a word.

The commander's voice remained calm as he pointed a black-gloved finger at Salim and replied, 'Old man, I will ask only once. You will lead me to where you have hidden the idols of this false divinity, so that the soldiers of the Caliphate may consign them to the past, where they belong.'

'Then I belong there with them,' Salim said. 'I will die before I allow you to wreak your unholy destruction in this place.'

'So be it,' the commander said. 'What you ask for, you will receive.' He nodded to his men. Four of them stepped forwards, seized Salim and Julien Segal each by the arms, and forced them down to their knees on the flagstone floor.

The Frenchman knelt with his head bowed and shoulders sagging. Next to him, the older man refused to break eye contact with his tormentors and remained straight-backed, chin high.

The commander reached down to the hilt of the long, curved knife that hung from his belt, and drew out the blade with a sigh of steel against leather. Salim wouldn't take his eyes off him for an instant, even though he knew what was coming.

Julien Segal let out a whimper. 'For God's sake, Salim. We have to tell them. Please.'

'I'm sorry, Julien. I will not go to my grave knowing that I betrayed my life's work to these maniacs.'

The commander stepped around behind Salim.

Salim closed his eyes.

What happened next had Julien Segal burying his face in the dirt and crying in unbearable anguish. But the old man never made a sound. He faced his death with the same steely resolve that he'd shown throughout his life.

Moments later, Julien Segal felt the thump of something hitting the floor beside him. Followed by a second, heavier thud as Salim's decapitated body slumped forward to fall on the floor next to where the commander had tossed his severed head. Segal couldn't bring himself to look directly at it, and instead watched in horror as the blood pool spread over the floor, trickling into the cracks between the flagstones and reflecting the light from the arched window.

'Now it's your turn,' said the man called Nazim al-Kassar.

Chapter 1

The present day

It was a cold, bright and sunny October morning in Paris, and Ben Hope was making a brief stop-off in the city on his return from a long journey. The trip to India hadn't been a scheduled event, but then few things in his life were, or ever had been, despite his best efforts to lead the kind of peaceful and stable existence he might have wished for. It seemed that fate always had other plans for him.

All he really wanted to do now was put the experience behind him, move on from it and get home. Home being a sleepy corner of rural Normandy some three hundred kilometres west of Paris, a place called Le Val, and he couldn't wait to get there. First he had some business to attend to in the city, which he intended to get sorted as quickly as possible, partly since it was a rather dull chore that he'd put off for too long.

The first thing he'd done when his plane had landed at Orly Airport the previous evening was to call Jeff Dekker, his business partner at Le Val, to say he was back in the country and would be home by early next afternoon. Jeff was pretty well used to Ben's frequent impromptu disappearances; all he said was 'See you later.'

Ben's second action was to call a Parisian estate agent he knew to talk about finally selling the backstreet apartment he'd owned for years and never used any more. Back when he'd worked freelance and lived a nomadic existence, the place had come in handy as an occasional base camp in the city. It had never been more than a bolthole for him, and he'd made little effort to furnish or decorate it beyond the absolute basics of necessity. The pragmatic nature of military life was an ingrained habit that refused to die in him, though he'd been out of that world for quite some years.

Whatever the case, the apartment had long since become surplus to his requirements. Though every time he'd been on the verge of putting the place up for sale, as had happened on several occasions, another of those bolts from the blue would arrive to yank him off on some new crazy mission or other. Which, as he was all too aware, was just a reflection of the broader reality that whatever kinds of plans he had in mind, some new crisis would invariably loom up to divert him right off track.

Such was life. Maybe, after another forty years, he'd get used to it.

But that wasn't going to happen this time, he told himself. This time he was going to bite the bullet, put the place on the market, go home to Le Val and get back down to running his business. The eternally patient Jeff, his longtime friend and co-director of the tactical training centre they'd founded and built together, might appreciate Ben's actually being around sometimes. Instructing the world's top law enforcement, security and close protection services in the finer points of their craft was a dirty job, but someone had to do it.

It was just after eight a.m. At ten-thirty he was due to meet with the property agent, a nervous-mannered chap called Gerbier who, Ben already knew, would spend an hour hemming and hawing about the difficulties of selling the place. First, because despite its theoretically desirable central location it was all but totally secreted away among a cluster of crumbly old buildings and its only access was via an underground car park. Second, because even at its best it had never looked like much on the inside, either, and needed decoration work to appeal to any but the most Spartan of buyers. And third, because right now wasn't a good time for the Parisian property market in general.

Ben had to admit the guy might have a point about that. For months the city had been locked in increasingly turbulent civil unrest, boiling with constant anti-government protests that had sparked off over a long list of political and social grievances and seemed to grow more serious and violent each passing day. There had been mass arrests, the cops had started deploying armoured personnel carriers and water cannon in the streets, and there were no signs of things cooling down any time soon. Now the troubles had spread across the city into Ben's normally quiet neighbourhood. He had lain awake for some time last night, listening to the screeching sirens and loud explosions of the latest pitched battle between rioters and the police. It had sounded like both sides meant business.

'Who can tell where this will end?' Gerbier had fretted over the phone. 'The city's falling into anarchy. Nobody's buying any more.'

How justified was Gerbier's pessimism, only time would tell. Ben had been up with the dawn that morning, as always. He'd laboured through his usual gruelling pre-breakfast workout of press-ups, sit-ups and pull-ups, taken a one-minute tepid shower, pulled on fresh black jeans and a denim shirt, scanned a few latest news headlines online, meditatively smoked a couple of Gauloise cigarettes while gazing out at the non-existent view for what might be one of the last times if he got lucky finding a buyer soon, then turned his thoughts to eating breakfast. Dinner last night had been a sandwich wolfed down on the hoof at the airport, and he was starving.

That was when Ben had realised that there wasn't a scrap of food in the apartment. Worse, much worse, the bare kitchenette cupboards contained not a single coffee bean.

And so here he was, heading briskly along the street, his scuffed brown leather jacket zipped against the chill and the third Gauloise of the day dangling from his lip, in the direction of a local coffee bar where he could get some breakfast and a much-needed fix of the black stuff. It was a five-minute stroll, but when he got there he discovered to his chagrin that the coffee bar had had its windows smashed in last night's disturbances and was shut.

The owners weren't the only local traders to have suffered damage from the latest round of protests. All up and down the street, storekeepers were resignedly sweeping up broken glass, nailing plywood sheets over their shattered windows, hauling out buckets of hot soapy water to try and scrub away graffiti that had appeared overnight. Ben stopped for a brief conversation with Habib, who ran the little Moroccan grocery store and tobacconist's where he'd often bought his cigarettes. Habib expressed sympathy with the protesters but worried that his insurance premiums would sky-rocket if these riots kept up. Ben offered his commiserations, wished Habib good luck and walked on in search of breakfast. He still had plenty of time to kill before meeting Gerbier.

The signs of last night's troubles were all around. Though it hadn't rained overnight the roads and pavements were slicked wet, small rivers created by police water cannon trickling in the gutters and pooling around washed-up garbage that choked the drain grids. A recovery crew with a flatbed lorry were removing the burnt-out shells of three cars that had been torched by the protesters. Barriers and cones had reduced the traffic to a crawl as cars and vans and motorcycles threaded their way along streets still littered with riot debris and spent tear gas canisters.

As Ben walked along, he spied one rolling in the gutter and picked it up to examine it, just out of curiosity. It was the strong stuff, the real McCoy. Then again, France's riot police never had mucked about when it came to dispersing violent demonstrations. The warning on the empty canister said, in French: DANGER – DO NOT FIRE DIRECTLY AT PERSON(S) AS SEVERE INJURY OR DEATH MAY RESULT. Ben had seen from the online news headlines that a couple of civilians had already been accidentally killed that way as the protests mounted. There was a good chance of more fatalities to come. One serious casualty among the police, and the government would probably send in the army.

Ben continued on his way, thinking about Gerbier's words and wondering where, indeed, it was all going to end. As he'd grown older and wiser he had come to understand that history was the key to predicting what lay in the future. As the saying went, those who failed to learn from the hard lessons of the past were doomed to repeat them. Paris had seen more than its fair share of revolutionary unrest in its time, and none of it seemed to have done much good. The big one of 1789 had kicked off much the same way as was happening now – and look how that ended, eating itself in an orgy of blood and severed heads and giving rise to the Napoleonic empire and rather a lot of even bloodier wars, followed eventually by a new monarchy to take the place of the old. Then had come the July Revolution of 1830, the one portrayed in the famous Delacroix painting that used to be on the old 100-franc banknote, depicting the topless Liberty wielding tricolour flag and musket as she led the people to victory, this time against the royal regime of Charles X. Same dubious result. Then just eighteen years later they'd been at it again, with the populist uprising of 1848 that had spilled enough blood in the streets of Paris to tear down the establishment once more and trigger the foundation of the Second Republic, which lasted exactly three years before the Second Empire turned the country back into a de facto monarchy.

And on, and on, through the ages and right up to the present. Round and round we go, Ben thought. An endless cycle of inflamed passion leading to disappointment, and resentment, and blame, simmering away and slowly building up to the next outburst. And for what? So much suffering and destruction could only deepen the rift between nation and state, while calls for reform would largely go unheeded and life would ultimately carry on just like before. Sure, go ahead and protest about overinflated taxes and rising costs of living and the insidious encroachment of the European superstate and police brutality and human rights infringements and loss of personal freedoms and privacy and anything else you feel strongly about. All fine. Angry mobs ripping their own beautiful city apart, looting and pillaging, harming small businesses, traumatising innocent citizens, not so fine. Unless you really believed that a violent street revolution was the only possible way to change things for the better.

Well, good luck with that.

Those were all the things on Ben's mind as he walked quickly around the corner of Rue Georges Brassens and collided with a young woman who, quite literally, ran into him without looking where she was going.

He didn't know it yet, but fate had just launched another of those bolts from the blue at him.

Chapter 2

The woman crashed straight into Ben with enough force to knock the wind out of herself and send her tumbling to the pavement. It took Ben a moment to recover from his own surprise.

Though it hadn't been his fault, he said in French, 'Oh, I'm so sorry,' and went to help her to her feet. He'd become skilled at languages back during his time with Special Forces, learning Arabic, Dari, Farsi and some African dialects, along with various European languages. He had now been living in France long enough to virtually pass for a native speaker.

As she picked herself off the pavement he saw she was more stunned than hurt. She was maybe twenty-five years old and slender, wearing a long camel coat over a white cashmere roll-neck top and navy trousers. Her hair was sandy-blond and her face, if it hadn't been flushed with shock, was attractively heart-shaped with vivid eyes the same blue as Ben's own. She didn't look as though she weighed very much, but it had been quite a collision. The little leather satchel she'd been carrying on a shoulder strap had fallen to the pavement and burst open, scattering its contents.

'Are you okay?' Ben asked her. She seemed too flustered to reply, and kept looking anxiously behind her as though she expected to see someone there. A couple of passersby had paused to gawk, but quickly lost interest and walked on. Ben said, 'Miss? Are you all right?'

The woman looked at him as though noticing him for the first time. Her blue eyes widened with alarm. She backed away a couple of steps, plainly frightened of him. He held his arms to the sides and showed her his open palms. 'I mean no harm,' he said jokingly. 'You're the one who ran into me. Maybe you should look where you're going. Here, let me help you with your things.'

He crouched down to pick up her fallen satchel. Her purse had fallen out, along with a hairbrush, some hair ties, a book of Métro tickets and a little black plastic case that said GIVENCHY in gold lettering. The contents of women's handbags had always been a bit of a mystery to Ben. He was also aware of the delicacy of the situation as he quickly scooped up her personal items from the pavement. She paid no attention while he retrieved her things, apparently too distracted by whatever, or whoever, she seemed to think was lurking in the background. When Ben stood up and offered the satchel back to her, she reached out tentatively and snatched it from his hands like a nervous animal accepting a titbit from a strange and untrusted human.

So much for being a knight in shining armour.

'You're bleeding,' he said, noticing that she'd scuffed the side of her left hand in the fall. 'Doesn't look too bad, but you should put some antiseptic on it.'

Still the same terse silence. She turned her anxious gaze behind her again, scanning the street as though she thought she was being followed. Pedestrians walked by, paying no attention. The traffic stream kept rumbling past in the background. A municipal cleaning crew was slowly working its way along the street towards them, gathering up last night's wreckage. A couple of pigeons strutted and pecked about among the debris in the gutter, seemingly unbothered by whatever was frightening the woman. Then she quickly looped the strap of her satchel over her shoulder and hurried on without a word or another glance at him.

Ben watched her disappear off down Rue Georges Brassens, walking so fast she was almost running, still glancing behind her every few steps as if someone was chasing her.

He shook his head. Some people. What the hell was up with her? The way she'd acted with him, anyone would think he'd been about to attack her. And who did she think was coming after her?

Maybe she was an escaped lunatic. Or a bank robber fleeing from the scene of the crime. Perhaps some kind of political activist or protest organiser the cops were trying to round up and throw in jail along with the other thousand-odd they'd already locked up.

Ben looked around him and saw no squads of gendarmes or psychiatric ward nurses tearing down the street in pursuit. Nor anyone else of interest, apart from the usual passersby who were all just going about their business, the majority of them deeply absorbed in their phones as most people seemed to be nowadays, doing the thumb-twiddling texting thing as they ambled along and somehow managed to avoid stumbling into trees and signposts. It seemed to him that those without digital devices to distract them from their present reality were walking somewhat more briskly than normal, a little stiff in their body language as if trying hard not to take in too much of their surroundings and dwell at any length on the signs of the battlefield that their city environment had become.

One way or another, though, the Parisians had far too much on their minds to be worrying about some panic-stricken woman running down the street blindly crashing into people.

Ben shrugged his shoulders and was about to move on when he saw that the young woman had dropped something else on the ground. She'd been so distracted that she had failed to notice that her phone had bounced off the kerbside and into the gutter, where it was lying among the washed-up debris and broken bottles the cleaning crew hadn't yet reached.

He picked it up. A slim, new-model smartphone in a smart black leather wallet case. The leather was wet, but the phone inside was dry. There was no question that it hadn't been lying in the gutter for long, and that it belonged to the woman. He could feel the residual trace of warmth from where it had been nestling in her bag close to her body. In an age when people's phones seemed to have become the hub of their entire lives, she must have been in a hell of a preoccupied state of mind not to have noticed its absence.

Ben stood there for a moment, thinking what he should do. Further along the street he could see the striped red and white awning of a café-bistro that had obviously escaped damage and was open for business. His mouth watered at the thought of coffee and croissants and he was torn between the temptation of breakfast and the notion of going after the woman to return her phone. She was well out of sight by now, and could have turned off onto any number of side streets. He decided on breakfast and slipped the phone into his pocket.

The place was bustling and noisy, but there was a table free in a corner. Out of habit, Ben sat with his back to the wall so he could observe the entrance. A hurried waiter took his order for a large *café noir* and the compulsory fresh-baked croissant.

While he waited for his order to arrive, Ben sat quietly and absorbed the chatter from other customers. Predictably the subject of the day, here as everywhere in the city, was the riots. A pair of middle-aged men at the next table were getting quite animated over whether or not the president should declare martial law, order the rebuilding of the Bastille prison, stuff the whole lot of troublemakers behind bars and throw away the key.

When his breakfast arrived Ben gave up eavesdropping on their conversation, took a sip or two of the delicious coffee and tore off a corner of croissant to dunk into his cup. A Gauloise would have rounded things out nicely, but such pleasures as smoking inside a café were no longer to be had in the modern civilised world. He went back to thinking about the strange woman who had bumped into him. What was she so frightened of? Where had she been running from, or to? He had to admit it, he was intrigued. And sooner or later, he was going to have to do something about the phone in his pocket.

Curiosity getting the better of him, he took it out to examine more closely. If the screen happened to be locked, there might not be much he could do except just hand it in to the nearest gendarmerie as lost property. But when he flipped open the leather wallet he soon discovered that the phone wasn't locked.

Which left him a number of potential ways to find out who the woman was and where she lived, allowing him to return the item to her personally. Ben was good at finding people. It was something he used to do for a living, after he'd quit the SAS to go his own way as what he'd euphemistically termed a 'crisis response consultant'. A career that involved tracking down people who didn't always want to be found, especially when they were holding innocent child hostages captive for ransom. Kidnappers didn't make themselves easy to locate, as a rule. But Ben had located them anyway, and the consequences hadn't been very pleasant for them.

By contrast, thanks to today's technology, ordinary unsuspecting citizens were easy to track down. Too easy, in his opinion.

Feeling just a little self-conscious about intruding on her privacy, he scrolled around the phone's menus. There were a few emails and assorted files, but his first port of call was the woman's address book. She was conservative about what information she stored in her contacts list. There was someone called Michel, no surname, and another contact called 'Maman/Papa', obviously her parents, but no addresses for either, and no home address or home landline number for herself. But the mobile's own number was there.

Ben took out his own phone to check it with. Damn these bloody things, but he was just as bound to them as the next guy. He'd got into the habit of carrying two of them: one a fancy smartphone registered to his business, the other a cheap, anonymous burner bought for cash, no names, no questions. Its anonymity pleased him and it came in handy in certain circumstances. But for this call he used his smartphone. He punched in the woman's mobile number. Her phone rang in his other hand. You could tell a lot about a person from their choice of ringtone. Hers was a retro-style *dring-dring*, like the old dial phone that stood in the hallway of the farmhouse at Le Val. Ben liked that about her. He ended the call and the ringing stopped. So far, so good.

Next he used his smartphone to access the whitepages.fr people finder website, which scanned millions of data files to give a reverse lookup. When a prompt appeared he entered the woman's mobile number and activated the search. Not all phone users were trackable this way, only a few hundred million worldwide. Which was a pretty large net, but still something of a gamble. If it didn't pay off, he still had other options to try.

But that wouldn't be necessary, because he scored a hit first time. In a few seconds he'd gained access to a whole range of information about the mystery woman: name, address, landline number, employer, and the contact details of two extant relatives in the Parisian suburb of Fontenay-sous-Bois a few kilometres to the east. If he'd been interested in offering her a job, he could run a background check to verify her credentials and see if she had any criminal record. If he was thinking of lending her money, he could view her credit rating. As things stood, he only needed the basics, which he now had.

Piece of cake.

Her name was Mme Romy Juneau. All adult women in France were now officially titled *Madame* regardless of marital status, since the traditional *Mademoiselle* had been banned for its alleged sexist overtones. But her parents' shared surname matched hers, suggesting she was unmarried. Some traditions still prevailed. Ben guessed that the phone contact called Michel was probably a boyfriend. She worked at a place called Institut Culturel Segal, ICS for short. The Segal Cultural Institute, whatever that was, in an upmarket part of town on Avenue des Champs-Élysées.

More important to Ben at this moment was her home address, which was an apartment number in a street just a few minutes' walk from where he was sitting right now, and in the direction she'd been heading when they'd bumped into one another.

It seemed safe to assume that she hadn't been going to work that morning. Maybe she had the day off. Whatever the case, it was a reasonable assumption that she'd been making her way home. From where, he couldn't say, and it didn't really matter. If she was heading for her apartment, there was a strong likelihood that she'd have got there by now, considering the hurry she'd been in.

Ben scribbled her details in the little notebook he carried, then exited the whitepages website and punched in Romy Juneau's landline number. As he listened to the dialling tone, he thought about what he'd say to her.

No reply. Perhaps she hadn't got home yet, or was in the bathroom, or any number of possibilities. Ben aborted the call and looked at his watch. The morning was wearing on. He needed to be thinking about finishing breakfast and heading over to see Gerbier at his offices across town. Romy Juneau would have to wait until afterwards.

He was slurping down the last of the delicious coffee when his phone buzzed. He answered quickly, thinking that Romy must have just missed his call and was calling him back. His anticipation soon fell flat when he heard the unpleasantly raspy, reedy voice of Gaston Gerbier in his ear.

The estate agent was calling, very apologetically, to cancel their morning appointment because his hundred-year-old mother had started complaining of chest pains and been rushed off to hospital. It was probably nothing serious, Gerbier explained. The vicious old moo had been dying of the same heart attack for the last thirty-odd years and false alarms were a routine thing. Still, he felt obliged to be there, as the dutiful son, etc., etc. Ben said it was no problem; they could reschedule the appointment for next time he was in town. He wished the old moo a speedy recovery and hung up.

There went his morning's duties. Ben couldn't actually say he was sorry to be missing out on the joys of Gerbier's company. And never mind about the apartment. It wasn't going anywhere. With a suddenly empty slate and nothing better to do, he decided now was as good a time as any to play the Good Samaritan and deliver the lost phone back to its owner in person. Given the nervous way she'd acted around him before, so as not to freak her out still further by showing up at her door he'd just post it through her letterbox with a note explaining how he'd found it. And that would be that. His good deed done, he could wend his way back to his apartment, jump in the car and be home at Le Val sometime in the afternoon.

Ben munched the last of his croissant, paid his bill and then left the café and set off on foot in the direction of her address. The sky was blue, the sun was shining, the day was his to do with as he pleased, and he felt carefree and untroubled.

He had no idea what he was walking into. But he soon would. He was, in fact, about to meet Mademoiselle Romy Juneau for the second time. And from that moment, a whole new world of trouble would be getting ready to open up.

Chapter 3

Romy Juneau lived in a handsome 1920s period apartment building near the end of a busy little street called Rue Joséphine Beaugiron, fifteen minutes' walk away, flanked by a travel agency and a corner bar-restaurant called Chez Bogart.

Like Ben's own neighbourhood, the street hadn't survived last night's riot completely unscathed. The quaint old antiquarian bookshop opposite Romy's building had taken a hit, and like Habib the grocer its owner was surveying the damage with a sour look of disgruntlement as two carpenters fitted a sheet of plywood over the broken window. Why anyone would attack a specialist book store filled with nothing but a bunch of dusty old tomes by dead writers, Ben couldn't say. Maybe the rioters were intent on procuring some edifying literature to alleviate the boredom of throwing firebombs at the police.

Romy's building had an art deco archway, once grand, now slightly grungy, on which someone had recently sprayed an obscene slogan about the president. It had tall carved double doors, firmly locked, with a smaller inset door, also firmly locked. On the wall by the door was a buzzer panel with twelve buttons, one for each apartment, each with a corresponding name plate with the initial and surname of the resident. R. Juneau was in apartment 11.

He pressed the button for apartment 6, labelled J. Vanel, waited for some guy's voice to crackle 'Qui est-ce?' out of the speaker grille, and said he had a delivery for Vanel that needed signing for. A moment later the buzzer buzzed and the inset door clicked open, and Ben pushed through into a brick foyer that led to a small interior courtyard. A short, stumpy concierge lady with curlers in her hair was sweeping the floor and barely glanced at Ben as he walked in. The hallway walls were streaked with dirt and a row of wheelie bins smelled of mouldy garbage. Not the best-kept apartment building in Paris, but not the worst either, not these days.

To his left was the door to the concierge's ground-floor apartment, to his right a spiral stairway with a worn antique banister rail. Set into the centre of the stairway was an original period cage lift apparently still in service, all ornate black wrought iron. A Gothic death trap, to Ben's eye. On the opposite wall were fixed twelve separate grey steel mailboxes, one for each resident, marked with their names. He took Romy's phone from his pocket, along with his notebook and pen. He wrote a brief note to the effect that he was returning her property, signed it, folded it inside the phone's leather wallet and was about to pop it into her mailbox when he noticed that two of the other boxes had had their locks forced open with something like a screwdriver, the grey paint scratched through to the bare metal.

Hardly the most confidence-inspiring level of security. The building was obviously a little too soft a target for thieves, unlike Ben's place which had a hardened steel security door you'd need a cutting torch to break through. He didn't want to have gone to the trouble of returning Romy's phone to her, only for it to be nicked by some light-fingered opportunist punk before she could get to it. He decided to hand it to her in person, face to face. She'd surely realise she had nothing to be frightened of, if he smiled a lot and acted his usual charming self. If she asked how he'd found her address, he'd admit the truth and advise her to erase her own number from her contacts list because it made her far too easy to track online. There were too many suspicious characters around these days to be taking risks.

Choosing the stairs over the Gothic death trap, he started to climb. The stairs were worn and creaky with age, spiralling up around the central lift shaft. The first-floor landing had apartments numbers 1 to 3, the second floor numbers 4 to 6. By his reckoning that made number 11 the middle door on the fourth floor, right at the top of the building.

As he headed towards the third floor, Ben heard the rattle and judder of the lift descending, sounding like it was going to shake itself apart and bring the whole building down, and he was glad he'd taken the stairs. Through the wrought-iron bars he saw the lift's passenger, a lone man making his way down from an upper floor. Ben gave him only the briefest of glances, but his eye was trained to notice details. The guy was standing with his back to Ben and his face turned away. He was broad-shouldered and well built, about Ben's height at a shade under six feet. He wore black leather gloves and a long dark coat, quality wool, expensive, with the collar turned up. His hair was short and black, silvering in streaks. Ben caught a whiff of aftershave. The man didn't turn around as the death trap rattled on its way downwards.

Ben watched the lift disappear below him between floors, then kept on climbing the stairs. A strange, vague feeling had suddenly come over him, as though something at the back of his mind was needling him. He had no idea what it was, and quickly forgot about it.

Moments later he reached the top floor. As he'd guessed,

apartment 11 was the middle door of the uppermost three apartments. He paused on the landing for a moment, thinking of the most innocuous way to introduce himself. Honesty and openness were the best policy. She would soon realise he was the friendliest and least menacing guy on the planet. At any rate, he could be that guy when he wanted.

He removed the handwritten note from her phone case, since he'd no longer need it. Then raised his hand to ring the doorbell with a knuckle. Force of habit. In his past line of work, leaving fingerprints often wasn't a good idea.

Then he stopped. Because he'd suddenly noticed that her door wasn't locked. Not just unlocked, but hanging open an inch. He used his fist to nudge it gently open a few inches more, and peeked through the gap. The apartment had a narrow entrance passage papered in tasteful pastel blue, with glossily varnished floorboards. There were four interior doors leading off the hallway, one at the far end and one to the left, both closed, and two more to the right, both of which were open though Ben couldn't see into the rooms from where he stood.

He called out in French, 'Hello? Anybody there? Mademoiselle Juneau?' He hoped it wasn't being too sexist to assume her marital status.

There was no reply. Ben tentatively stepped inside the hall passage. He felt uneasy about doing it, since a lone male stranger didn't ideally want to be seen to be lurking in the apartment of a young single woman.

The first odd thing he noticed was the smell of something burning, which seemed to be coming from the nearer open door on the right. The second was the little stand in the passage that had been knocked over on its side across the middle of the hallway floor. A pretty ceramic dish lay smashed on the floorboards, various keys scattered nearby. The camel coat Romy Juneau had been wearing earlier looked like it had been yanked down from a hook by the entrance and was lying rumpled on the floor.

Ben moved a little further up the passage, stepped past the coat and the fallen stand, and peered around the edge of the first open door on the right. The door led to a small kitchen, clean and neat, with worktops and cupboards the same pastel blue as the hallway and a table for one next to a window overlooking the street side of the building. The burning smell was coming from a coffee percolator that had been left on the gas stove. It had bubbled itself dry and was giving off smoke. Ben went in and took the coffee off the heat, using a kitchen cloth because it was hot. Then he quickly flipped off the gas burner with a knuckle. Force of habit, again.

Whoever had been in the middle of making coffee had taken a carton of non-fat milk from the fridge and a delicate china cup and saucer from the cupboard and laid them out ready on the worktop next to a little pot of Demerara sugar and a tiny silver spoon. All very dainty and feminine. Ben presumed that someone was the apartment's occupant. So where was she, and what was all the mess in the hallway?

By now the alarm bell was jangling in the back of his mind. Something wasn't quite right. He stepped back out into the hallway and called again, a little more loudly, 'Hello? Mademoiselle Juneau?'

Still no reply. He nudged open the closed door to the left, which was a bedroom. Romy Juneau evidently had a thing for that shade of blue. It was everywhere, the bed covers, the curtains, the walls. But she wasn't in the room.

He stepped up to the further open door on the right, which he now saw led to a salon.

It was inside the salon that Ben now saw Mademoiselle Romy Juneau for the second time.

It would be the last time.

Chapter 4

As far as Romy Juneau was concerned, she would only ever have met Ben on the single occasion they'd bumped into one another in Rue Georges Brassens. She was oblivious of their second encounter, and always would be, because she was lying sprawled on the Persian rug inside her living room with a broken neck. That much Ben could tell at a glance from the unnatural angle of her head to her body.

He stood frozen in the doorway for an instant. He had seen many dead people before now. But never quite in such circumstances. His shoulders dropped and something tightened inside his throat at the pathetic sight of her lying there. The leather satchel she'd been carrying earlier had been emptied and left lying along with its contents on the rug a few feet away.

He went over to her and knelt next to the body. She was very still, with that special quality of inertia that only death can confer on a person. If there had been any blood, it would have been easy to see against the white cashmere top she was wearing. It looked as though a single strike to the neck had killed her. Ben looked around him for any kind of impact weapon, but there was nothing. A very strong man could have done it using his bare hands, but it would have taken a blow of tremendous force.

Her eyes were open and staring sightlessly straight at him, the vividness of their colour faded like the wings of a dead butterfly. Ben reached out and laid two fingers on the side of her throat. He had expected no pulse and found none. Her soft skin was still warm, also expected, because this had happened to her only minutes ago. While she'd been waiting for her coffee to brew.

Her death touched Ben deep, though he didn't know why. It was as if he'd known her, somehow. As if part of his mind was trying to reconnect with an old scrambled memory lost somewhere in the murk of the dim and distant past. It was a strange feeling.

He lingered next to her body for a couple more seconds, then stood up and walked grimly to the living-room window. It was the archetypal Parisian floor-to-ceiling iron window with the ornate knobs and designer rust, flanked by gauzy white drapes. It overlooked the same side of the building as the kitchen. He looked out at the street below. The carpenters had finished fixing the plywood to the bookshop window. Cars, vans, bikes were passing by on the road, pedestrians strolling along the pavements, normal city life going on as usual.

And up here on the floor behind where Ben was standing, a young woman with a snapped neck.

He was about to turn away from the window when he saw a man emerge from the building and step towards the edge of the kerb. About Ben's own height, though it was hard to tell from the downward angle. He was wearing a long dark coat. Quality wool, expensive. Black leather gloves that matched his shiny black shoes. He was well built with broad shoulders. Black hair, streaked with silver.

The man from the lift.

He stood at the kerbside with his back to the building

and looked down the street as though he was waiting for a taxi to come by. Ben couldn't see his face, but now he was seeing him again there was something oddly familiar about the guy – and not just from their fleeting brush a couple of minutes ago. Ben felt a weird tingle up his back, like a knife blade drawn along piano strings.

Just then, the man turned and craned his neck to look straight up at the window of Romy Juneau's apartment. He was in his early forties, with the olive skin that hinted at Mediterranean ethnicity. He could have been taken for anything from Italian to North African to a Middle Easterner. His features were strong and square, not unhandsome, and his eyes were dark and clear and intelligent. They found Ben's and stared right at him through the window.

And the tingle up Ben's back turned icy cold. That was when it hit him. It couldn't have hit him harder if the man down in the street below had pointed a gun and shot him. Because in that dizzy moment Ben realised what it was that his mind had been trying to reconnect just now. It wasn't Romy Juneau who had triggered a distant memory from the past. And the strange feeling he was getting had started *before* he'd set foot in this apartment.

It was the man in the lift who had set it off.

The man now standing staring up at the window.

Ben now realised that he knew this man. And as the memories were suddenly unlocked and rushed into his mind, he was able to pinpoint exactly when and where he knew him from, and why they had met before, and what had happened on the last occasion they'd crossed paths.

None of the memories were good ones.

For just the briefest instant, Ben closed his eyes. He was suddenly transported back in time. He flashed on another face. A very different face, one with deep dark eyes that looked into his. And he thought, *Samara*.

As the instant ended Ben opened his eyes and was brought back to the present. The man in the black coat was still looking up at the apartment window, frowning as though similar thoughts were going through his mind, too. Then a silver Mercedes Benz saloon pulled sharply up at the kerbside next to him with a screech of tyres. Its tinted driver's window slid down and another olive-skinned, swarthy-looking guy inside started gesticulating and beckoning. Ben couldn't make out the words, but it was obvious the driver was urging the man in the black coat to get in the car.

The man hesitated for a second, as though he was thinking about turning back and returning inside the building. Ben wished he would. But then the man changed his mind and hurried around to the car's passenger side, yanked open the door and flung himself into the seat, and the door slammed and the driver hit the gas and the Mercedes took off with another squeal of tyres, accelerating hard away down the street.

By then, Ben was already racing from the apartment. He jumped over the body of Romy Juneau, sprinted through the hallway and hammered down the stairs and slid down the spiral banister rail to descend the last two floors more quickly. Reaching the entrance foyer he burst out of the inset door into the street.

But the silver Mercedes was already long gone, and the man in the black coat with it. All that remained in his wake was the memory of his name, who he was and the things he had done.

And the fact that he was supposed to have been dead years ago.

Chapter 5

Ben didn't return upstairs to Romy Juneau's apartment. There was nothing more he could do. He had left no trace of his visit; it was as though he'd never been there at all.

He was burning up inside with anger and confusion and frustration. But he kept his pace slow and measured as he walked up to the end of Rue Joséphine Beaugiron and went inside the bar-restaurant called Chez Bogart. The interior was all decked out with framed posters and stills from old movies. Whoever owned the joint was obviously a big Bogie fan. And doing good business, too. Most of the punters were the late breakfast crowd, noisily enjoying their brioche French toast and buttered baguettes sprinkled with grated chocolate and bowls of *café au lait* while defenceless women got battered to death just down the street.

It was still a little early in the day for hard drinking, even for him, but Ben was willing to make an exception. He ordered himself a double shot of Glenlivet at the bar, no ice, no water, and carried it over to a corner table beneath a giant blow-up still from *Casablanca*, the classic image of Bogart in white tux, loitering by the piano as Dooley Wilson sang 'As Time Goes By'. He took a long drink of his scotch and thought about peculiar coincidences and the return of figures from the past whom you'd never thought you'd see again.

Of all the gin joints, in all the towns, in all the world.

Ben knocked the whisky down fast and soon felt the alcohol go to work to settle his nerves. Then he set down his empty glass and headed for the men's room. It was empty, which was what he needed because he wanted no witnesses. And quiet, which was also good, because when anonymously reporting a murder it was generally preferable to leave no clues as to where you were calling from. He took out his phone, the prepaid burner this time. This was exactly the kind of purpose it served. He dialled 17, police emergency, got through quickly, and just as quickly gave the call handler the necessary details. Victim's name and address, but not his own. He had no desire to spend the next two days being grilled by police detectives about what he was doing in her apartment around the time of her death.

Ben could easily have told them the name of the man he'd seen leaving the scene of the crime, but he held that information back too. There would have been no point. Whatever identity the guy had used to enter France would certainly be fake. Ben strongly doubted that his real name would even come up on the INTERPOL crime database, except in certain classified files to which regular cops would have no access. Any one of a variety of aliases Ben could have given them might have triggered a response. The kind that would have the whole street and surrounding area closed down by paramilitary forces armed to the teeth, searching door to door and stopping cars with K9 units on standby.

But that would have been just as pointless. They wouldn't stand a chance of catching the guy. He was far too good for them. And if they somehow did succeed, it would probably be the last thing they ever did.

Ben cut off the police emergency call handler's questions and left the restaurant through a tradesmen's back exit that led into an alleyway. He lit a Gauloise and slowly walked back around the corner, crossed the street and made his way along Rue Joséphine Beaugiron as far as the antiquarian bookshop opposite Romy's building, from where he could monitor events at a discreet distance. He finished his cigarette outside the shop and then wandered inside and spent a while browsing the shelves of dusty old books.

Fourteen minutes later he heard the police sirens screeching to the scene. By then he'd picked out a handsome old deluxe volume of the collected poetry of Charles Baudelaire. A present for his friend and colleague Tuesday Fletcher at Le Val, possibly the only ex-British Army sniper in the world with a taste for nineteenth-century French poetry. Ben ambled up to the front desk with the book in hand. The sirens were growing loud outside, filling the street. He said to the shop proprietor, 'What's happening now?'

'God only knows,' the guy grumbled. 'This whole city is going to shit, if you ask me.'

The two of them stood in the shop doorway watching as a pair of marked cars and a gendarmerie van screeched to a halt across the street, a team of uniforms scrambled out looking highly purposeful and disappeared inside Romy Juneau's building. Just regular police, responding to a regular incident. If only they'd known who they were really dealing with.

'Dear me, I hope nobody got hurt,' Ben said. The bookshop owner just grunted, threw up his hands in resignation at the terrible state of the world and returned to his desk. If only he knew, too.

The cops would soon call in the coroner and start asking questions up and down the street in search of potential witnesses to the incident. It was time for Ben to be moving on. He paid for his purchase, tucked the book under his arm and left the store at a relaxed pace, nice and easy, drawing no attention from anyone. The best way to disappear in a crowded city was to go underground. He headed for the nearest Métro station, joined the fast-moving crowd heading for the tunnels, and caught a packed train that took him on a winding, circuitous route back towards the safehouse.

His original plan had been to lock up the apartment, jump in his BMW Alpina and set off for Le Val. He'd have been enthusiastically greeted by Storm, his favourite of the pack of German shepherds that roamed and guarded the compound. To stretch his legs after the drive, he might have pulled on his running shoes and gone for a cross-country five-miler around the woodlands and fields, with the dog trotting happily along behind him. Later, dinnertime would have seen him sitting at the table in the big country kitchen with Jeff and Tuesday, the three of them digging into some delicious casserole provided by Marie-Claire, the local woman employed at Le Val to feed the troops and ruin everyone's waistlines with her indecently tasty French rustic cooking. Then after dinner he'd have relaxed in the company of his friends by the fire, Storm curled up at his feet; maybe a game of chess with Jeff, a glass or three of ten-year-old Laphroaig, a haze of cigarette smoke drifting pleasantly overhead as he told them about his India trip.

But that cosy future would have to be put on hold for a while. He now had other business to finish before he could go home. Business he'd thought had already been done and dusted back in August 2016. Apparently not, it seemed. Which begged a lot of questions to which Ben now needed the answers.

The name of the man Ben had crossed on the stairs and seen leaving the apartment building was Nazim al-Kassar. He was, in the plainest terms, a terrorist. Or had been, many years earlier when he and Ben, then a newly promoted officer with 22 Special Air Service, had first crossed paths in Iraq. Ben found it hard to believe that Nazim could have changed tracks since that time. Men so single-mindedly committed to an ideology of warfare, terror and destruction didn't just lose interest and switch career paths.

And Nazim had been one of the most committed of all. Meaning one of the worst, most viciously ruthless, and most lethally dangerous individuals out of all the long list of such men Ben had ever come across.

Ben was the only man who had ever been able to catch him. Nazim's capture had come at a heavy cost in terms of lives lost, on both sides. For all that, he hadn't remained a prisoner for long. Ben recalled clearly the events of the day when Nazim al-Kassar had got away from him, never for the two men to meet again.

Until this day, sixteen long years later.

Chapter 6

The story began with one Abu Musab al-Zarqawi, a Jordanian Muslim born in 1966. From an early age al-Zarqawi had been a committed jihadist, dedicated like his millions of fellows to the cause of spreading Islamic fundamentalism worldwide with the ultimate goal of creating a global Caliphate that would banish and eradicate all false religions, in particular Christianity and Judaism.

At the age of twenty-three, al-Zarqawi had travelled to Afghanistan in the hopes of joining up with the jihadist Mujahideen in their struggle against the Soviet troops who had, in their view, invaded their country. In fact, the Russians were there by invitation, having come to the aid of the pro-Soviet Afghan government in 1979 to help against the rise of rebel militants generously funded and armed by the CIA. America's financial and military support of the Islamist rebels would ultimately prove disastrous to the West, but back then Communism was the bogeyman and the Carter administration, followed by that of Reagan, were each too blind to see the future nightmare they were sleepwalking into.

The Islamists, with their own agenda, were only too happy to grab the guns and money and get stuck in, favouring hit-and-run guerrilla tactics against the Russians. The word 'Mujahideen' in Arabic meant simply 'those who fight', in the sense of jihad or holy war. And fight they did, hard and relentlessly. The cruel war of attrition had lasted more than nine bloody years, ending with the withdrawal of the battered, miserably defeated Soviet troops in early 1989. It had been Russia's own Vietnam, and it crippled their economy so badly that it became a factor in the fall of the USSR.

Arriving on the scene that same year, the young al-Zarqawi was dismayed to find the war all wound up and his chances of dying gloriously in the name of jihad dashed, at least for the moment. Undeterred, he soon began looking for new avenues into which to channel his religious zeal. Among the various contacts he established was a certain Osama Bin Laden, the son of Mohammed Bin Laden, a Jeddah property development billionaire with close ties to the Saudi royal family. Bin Laden Junior had inherited some $30 million following his father's death and left the business world behind to pursue his own interests, with a little under-the-table help from the CIA, who at that time still naively regarded him and his fellow jihadists as useful assets in the fight against Communism. While the war against the Soviets drew to a close and victory appeared imminent, Bin Laden had already started forming plans for the future. He had a vision to expand his operations on a grand scale, and to this end co-founded a new outfit called al-Qaeda, meaning 'the Foundation', a subtle reference to the worldwide Islamic Caliphate he wanted to create.

But this was still the early days, and Bin Laden was looking out for keen young talent to help him grow his operation. As plans developed, he later donated $200,000 to al-Zarqawi, with which to build a large jihadist training camp in Herat, Afghanistan. Many of al-Zarqawi's fellow Jordanians came to join him there, and he happily set about building an army of fierce fighters ready and willing to die for Allah.

From the start, al-Zarqawi had been known for his extreme views – so extreme, in fact, that even Bin Laden considered him somewhat radical. He took a rock-hard line against other Muslims whom he considered too soft on nonbelievers and thereby heretical – such as all Shi'ites, who he felt ought to be wiped out en masse. He despised the Jews even more strongly, as he had been taught to do from childhood; but his most rabid loathing was reserved for the Western oppressors of the Muslim world, the UN and America.

In 1999 al-Zarqawi's little army became officially known as *Jama'at al-Tawid wal-Jihad*, or JTJ for short. Its name meant, in Arabic, 'The Organisation of Monotheism and Jihad', which sounded deceptively academic compared to the brutal reality. Al-Zarqawi had founded his merry band of cutthroats with the main intention of leading it back to his homeland and toppling the Kingdom of Jordan, which he considered an example of heretical un-Islamic leadership. He was then still based in Afghanistan, which for the last three years had been largely controlled by its own Islamic Emirate, a.k.a. the Taliban. It was a safe haven for jihadist terror groups like the JTJ, which continued to thrive and attract new membership.

However, that all changed when al-Zarqawi's former associate Osama Bin Laden orchestrated the September 11, 2001, attack on US soil that sparked the 'War on Terror' and a whole new era began. As thousands of American and British troops flooded into Afghanistan and started ferociously attacking Taliban enclaves and training camps, al-Zarqawi decided things were getting a little hot for him there and moved his operation instead to Iraq. There he met and befriended a loyal new disciple, one Nazim al-Kassar.

Nazim was thought to have been born in Ramadi, Iraq, in either December 1977 or January 1978 depending on whichever intelligence source would later prove correct. Little was known about his family background, or what kind of formative experiences and upbringing had prompted him to embrace radical ideology with such enthusiasm in his late teens and early twenties. In common with his like-minded peers he believed devoutly that one day, thanks to the heroic efforts of warriors in this holy struggle against the infidels, the *kuffar*, Islam would rule over every corner of the world.

By the time he became a keen young disciple of Abu Musab al-Zarqawi, Nazim al-Kassar was already utterly devoted to the cause and ready to do whatever it took to show his allegiance both to his mentor and his faith. When al-Zarqawi travelled to Syria to oversee the training of Islamist fighters there, Nazim accompanied him and took a leading role in the expansion of their army, proving a strong leader of men as well as a highly proficient warrior himself, as skilled with the AK-47 rifle as he was with pistol and knife. He underwent training in strategy, counter-intelligence and explosives, and learned to speak English perfectly. He was also deployed to different countries to assist in missions and assassinations at his master's behest, one of which was the murder of an American diplomat in Jordan. Before his twenty-fifth birthday, Nazim already had infidel blood on his hands, and he was ready for more.

It wouldn't be long in coming.

In 2003, two years after invading Afghanistan in reprisal for the 9/11 World Trade Center attacks, the Americans along with their coalition of Western allies launched the second major wave of their so-called War on Terror. This time, the target was Iraq. The objective: to complete the job left unfinished in the First Gulf War and bring down the regime of Saddam Hussein, believed to be plotting further terror attacks on the West.

It was at this point in history that Nazim's path was set to cross for the first time with that of his deadly enemy, Ben Hope.

Chapter 7

In Ben's opinion, back then and still to this day, the US-led invasion of Iraq had been one of the most hideous strategic blunders in military history. The Americans and their allies had apparently learned nothing from the humiliating lessons of Vietnam, or the tribal revolts against the British occupation of Iraq in the 1920s that led to high casualties on both sides. One does not go blithely marching into these countries, gung-ho and flags-a-waving, without inviting a bloody disaster.

The Iraq war would ultimately drag on for nearly as long as the Soviets had doggedly clung onto Afghanistan, and prove every bit as badly counterproductive in the long run. Ben had predicted that outcome back in 2003, and he'd been around to watch it unfold all around him when his SAS unit was deployed into the heart of the conflict that spring. But whatever his personal misgivings about the wisdom of the whole endeavour, it was his job to do what he had to do.

On the night of March 17, Ben was among the men of SAS D Squadron who strapped themselves into the folding seats of several Chinook CH-47 troop transporters ready for takeoff from Al Jafr airbase in southern Jordan. Their destination: the township of Qu'aim over the border in Iraq, which according to intelligence reports was a strategic site from which Saddam's army were planning to launch missiles laden with chemical weapons into Israel.

This was Operation Row, a highly classified Special Forces mission taking place an entire twenty-four hours before the British government had actually voted whether or not to join the invasion. The SAS force consisted of sixty men, who had just spent the last three months on secret bases in Jordan and Saudi Arabia, training and preparing for the big push everyone knew was inevitable.

Even though Parliament hadn't officially sanctioned their mission, most of the men had already written their 'death letters', to be read by family and loved ones in the event that they did not return alive. Ben was one of the few with no family or loved ones to write to, but he hadn't been immune to the mixed feelings of fear, anxiety and excitement as the Chinooks took off into the night. The deafening roar of the turbo-prop engines filled their ears and the powerful upward surge pressed them into their seats. They exchanged glances and nervous grins in the darkness. The journey into war had begun.

D Squadron's LZ was 120 kilometres over the Iraqi border. The passage into enemy airspace had been smoothed in advance by American Little Bird helicopters, but the very real possibility of surface-to-air missile attack had never left the minds of everyone aboard. After an uneventful flight the Chinooks touched down in the barren wastes of the Iraqi Western Desert. Shivering with cold, the SAS troops disembarked and unloaded their weapons along with their transport, the open-top 'Pink Panther' Land Rovers bristling with machine guns and rocket launchers that would carry them overland to Al Qu'aim.

The Chinooks departed the LZ and thundered away into the night as the soldiers, dug into defensive positions, waited tensely for any sign of enemy attack. None came. They spent March 18 hunkered down behind their weapons, waiting for another sixty troopers of B Squadron to join them at the LZ before the combined SAS force boarded their Pinkies and set off across the rough, rocky desert terrain.

By the time the SAS were approaching Al Qu'aim, the British Parliament had finally voted in favour of joining the invasion. Operation Row was now a legitimate mission. That night, the troopers reached the outskirts of the township and began probing the perimeter of an industrial plant that intelligence reports had tagged as a likely site for chemical weapons storage.

What they found instead was an ambush. They had walked straight into a hornet's nest of resistance as waiting soldiers of the Iraqi Republican Guards lit up the night with ferocious gunfire. Ben and a small team of his men found themselves pinned down between buildings as enemy rounds peppered walls and vehicles. The crew of one of the SAS Pinkies ran for cover as the Land Rover was riddled with bullets. Ben ordered it to be destroyed with a rocket, lest their radio fall into enemy hands. The heat from the blast seared them, but provided enough cover for them to break away from their precarious position and press forward. They fought until the barrels on their machine guns glowed red hot, and the ground was covered with spent shells.

The battle raged into the night and into the following day as the Republican Guards kept up their spirited defence. The SAS had come prepared for stiff resistance, though this exceeded their expectations. Ben was crouched just yards from an SAS sniper when a bullet struck the barrel of his .50-calibre rifle and shattered it into pieces. Despite being badly hurt by the shrapnel, the sniper grabbed another rifle and fought gamely on. Inch by inch, street by street, the troopers clawed their way towards the industrial plant as gunfire hammered their positions. It finally became clear that only a targeted air strike would break the defending forces' grip on their stronghold. It was duly radioed in. Ben watched from behind cover as the stunning power of 2,500 pounds of high explosive payload from a Coalition Forces bomber tore the plant apart in a ground-shaking blast and effectively ended the battle.

It was an impressive fireworks display, but nothing in comparison to the awesome bombardment of Baghdad that Ben was to personally witness just weeks later, when his unit was deployed to the west of the city.

The fall of Baghdad, coming less than a month since Ben had arrived in Iraq, marked the end of the first phase of the war. It should all have been over then, but the real conflict was just about to begin – just as Ben had feared it would. With Saddam Hussein's army in tatters it now became all about counterinsurgency as a diverse multitude of Islamic militant groups joined in to harass the invading troops to the best of their considerable ability, using all the guerrilla warfare and terror tactics the Mujahideen had honed to perfection fighting the Soviets in Afghanistan, and then some. The SAS's orders were simple: to continue seeking and neutralising threats to the Coalition Forces. Of which there were so many, it was virtually impossible to keep track of them all.

One such group, and one of the most formidable, was Jama'at al-Tawid wal-Jihad, or simply JTJ, who fast became a prime target for Special Forces. As the SAS soon discovered, JTJ were the perfect model for all terrorist organisations. The use of suicide bombings, often involving car bombs, the planting of roadside improvised explosive devices to catch unsuspecting army patrols, and the launching of guerrilla rocket and sniper attacks were some of their favourite tactics. But they delighted most in the taking of hostages, whom they would line up on their knees in the sand and coolly decapitate with long knives. Getting captured alive by these guys was not an option. Exactly as Ben had anticipated, this war had already begun to deteriorate into a hellish bloodbath.

But it was also exactly the kind of combat environment in which his regiment thrived, operating covertly, usually at night in SAS tradition, and often out of uniform. Bearded, swathed in local civilian garb and deeply tanned by the desert sun, they could pass more easily for ragged sand-hoboes than crack troops. Which was precisely the desired illusion. As the months went by, they operated in Ramadi and Fallujah, and remote parts of Al Anbar Province where, in one raid, Ben and his unit were directed to a farm thought to be a stronghold for radical insurgents. After another spirited firefight, fifteen dead bodies dragged from the wreck of the farmhouse were identified as known members of JTJ. However one of their most notorious fighters, a bloodthirsty terrorist by the name of Nazim al-Kassar, still eluded capture. The young warrior was already responsible for dozens, if not hundreds, of killings, he had recruited multiple suicide bombing volunteers and (or so it was thought) even personally strapped them into their explosive vests.

Ben didn't know it yet, but he was destined to meet Nazim very soon. The day would be September 20, 2003.

Chapter 8

The broad parameters of the SAS's mission in Iraq gave them latitude to work together with United States Special Forces. Back then, however, international SF ops were yet to become fully integrated and it would be some time before the British and American elite units would be officially joined at the hip, sharing the same intelligence and serving the same common purpose. In those early days of the war there were still some tensions between them. As Ben was about to learn first-hand when, that September, his unit was deployed in a joint mission with elements of the US JSOC Joint Special Operations Command, comprising members of Delta Force, 75th US Army Rangers and DEVGRU, otherwise known as SEAL Team 6.

Operation Citation, as the mission was designated, called for the joint Special Forces unit to be divided into twelve-man teams and inserted deep into specific, pre-selected enemy positions in the north and west. By now the whole country had exploded into insane violence as the disparate factions and tribes started fighting not only the Coalition invaders but each other as well. The war had sparked off a lot of old grudges. Against this backdrop of absolute chaos the dedicated jihadist groups were flourishing and becoming ever more effective at disrupting military efforts to stabilise the country.

Of these, the group that had become known as JTJ was one of the most active, and its key players were now top targets. The main purpose of Operation Citation was to take as many of them as possible off the table. Dead, or preferably alive, because dead men couldn't be persuaded to rat on their friends.

Ben was in command of Task Force Red, the codename of his twelve-man team consisting of four SAS men including himself, and the rest operatives from Delta. Task Force Red's objective was to proceed to a remote village in the desert some twenty miles west of Tikrit, which US intelligence had reason to believe was being used as a meeting place for key JTJ personnel including Nazim al-Kassar and several of his top aides. Their orders were simple enough: scout the location, take up position, identify the threat and move in for execution.

It had been an unlucky mission right from the start. The most senior of the Americans was a Delta Master Sergeant called Tyler Roth, who made it obvious that he felt he should have been made Team Leader rather than this Brit guy, Hope. Roth took every opportunity to challenge Ben's command, and Ben often felt that the Americans had their own agenda in the mission. All of which compounded the sense of mistrust and division that already existed between the SAS and US troopers. Ben could only rally his team together as best he could, in the hope that they'd focus when it was most needed. He also had to hope that the American intel was right, which it frequently wasn't.

Before dawn on September 20 the heavily armed task force took up their positions around the remote village, little more than a cluster of ramshackle stone dwellings at the centre of a rocky basin. The place appeared completely desolate and abandoned, and at first it seemed to them as if they'd been sent on a wild goose chase. But then, in the blood-red hue of sunrise they spotted a line of four vehicles approaching from the west, and another three incoming in single file from the south-east, each convoy sending up a plume of dust.

As they watched and waited, the vehicles converged on the buildings and all parked up together in a great dust cloud. Through binoculars Ben counted twenty-seven men getting out of their vehicles and entering the largest of the buildings. They were clad in the familiar rag-tag garb of insurgents, most with heavy ammunition bandoliers draped around their bodies, some with chequered headscarves, all of them armed with the usual mixture of mostly Soviet weaponry. Among them, about Ben's height, well built and handsome, wearing a combat jacket and cotton knit cap, was the notorious young jihadist who was rapidly rising up the ranks and of whom there was only one known photograph, Nazim al-Kassar. The man himself, in the flesh.

As Ben had worried, the American intelligence report was somewhat off the mark. Twenty-seven men was a much larger force than they'd anticipated. It would make capturing the leaders much more difficult, since they were sure to put up a fight. One of Ben's SAS troopers, a Yorkshireman called Jon Taylor, was equipped with a launcher loaded with stun grenades. If Taylor could punt two or three of them in quick succession through the building's window, there was a decent chance of incapacitating enough of its occupants to be able to storm the place and bring off a clean mass arrest. If not, the task force might have a hot morning's work ahead of them.

The soldiers waited for all the men to enter the building, then for thirty minutes longer, for whatever strategic discussions they were engaged in to get well underway in a sense of security. Then the signal was given to move in and commence the assault.

And that was when it all went horribly bad. Taylor was twenty metres from the building and on the verge of launching his first grenade at the window when Ben saw an incoming RPG round streaking towards them from the edge of the rocky basin. Before he had time to yell a warning, the rocket-propelled warhead blew a crater right under Taylor's feet, killing him instantly. Within instants, the air was thick with heavy machine-gun fire coming at them from all sides, and Ben knew the American intel had been even worse than previously thought. Task Force Red had been misled. A third contingent of militants had been en route to the meeting when they'd spotted the soldiers and opened fire from hidden positions all around the rim of the plateau.

Under aggressive attack, Ben's unit found whatever cover they could and fired back. But then several of the insurgents inside the house came swarming out, shooting as they came. The task force were pinned between two enemy factions, with no longer any option but to fight their way out.

The battle was brief, intense and frenetic. In the midst of it Ben saw another of his SAS guys go down, hit in the thigh. Two of the Delta troopers were less lucky, one blown to pieces by another RPG round and the other fatally wounded in the throat by a rifle bullet fired from the house.

Then out of the corner of his eye Ben spotted Nazim al-Kassar and four of his men breaking from the entrance and running for the dusty black SUV in which they'd arrived. He fired on them, punching holes in the side of the vehicle. The SUV took off, wheels spinning in the dirt. Ben kept firing until his rifle was empty, shattering the windows and perforating the bodywork like Swiss cheese.

The SUV went into a wild skid and crashed into a low

wall. Its driver burst through the windscreen in a spray of broken glass and blood, his face mangled to a pulp, his body sprawling lifelessly across the bonnet.

Ben drew his pistol and sprinted for the wrecked car, ignoring the bullets flying past him, intent only on stopping al-Kassar before he got away. He wrenched open the car door. Al-Kassar was in the back seat with blood on his face, clawing a pistol from his belt. Ben lunged inside the car, smacked the gun out of his hand and knocked him unconscious with three vicious strikes from his pistol butt. The elusive Nazim al-Kassar was now a prisoner.

Less than three minutes later, the fight was ended. The unseen attackers retreated from the edge of the plateau and into the surrounding hills, never to be seen again. The smoke cleared from the butcher's yard of the village to reveal eleven dead insurgents on the ground, three more dead inside the building, and two critically injured. The rest had thrown down their guns and surrendered, evidently not quite so willing as all that to lay down their lives for Allah.

The task force had lost three men, Taylor and two of the Delta guys, as well as sustaining two further non-fatal casualties. Ben radioed in a CASEVAC chopper and the injured were airlifted from the scene along with the wounded prisoners. A grim death toll, to be sure. Ben was deeply upset about Taylor, and furious with the misleading US intel that had dropped them in the soup like that. But the task force had succeeded in its mission to snatch al-Kassar and several of his top aides. JTJ had just suffered a major defeat.

Or so Ben thought, as he returned to base that day with a truckload of prisoners in tow.

War and politics made for a terrible combination, yet the pair were inseparable bedfellows. As a commanding officer Ben was in possession of a secret British Ministry of Defence memo ordering the SAS under no circumstances to allow Iraqi prisoners to be handed over to the US Joint Special Operations Command, for fear that they might be whisked away by the CIA to some covert facility where they would be subjected to torture. The Abu Ghraib prisoner abuse scandal was still fresh, and the suits in Whitehall wanted no part of any dirty dealings – at any rate, that was the official pretence.

So, on their return, Ben was careful to hand the prisoners over to a regular US Army unit. This caused a major dispute with the Delta guys, because Delta were in effect the military arm of the CIA, under the shady umbrella of its Special Activities Division. Hence, the D-boys had their own dark agenda and secret orders. And now Ben was the party pooper. Tyler Roth was so incensed by his decision that the two of them very nearly came to blows following an angry argument that night.

Two days later, the politics of the situation came back to haunt Ben with a vengeance. Unaware of just who they had in custody because of the shroud of secrecy surrounding Special Ops missions, the regular army grunts holding al-Kassar and the other top-level JTJ prisoners slipped up on security discipline. Ben was having breakfast with a group of other SAS guys when he heard the news that Nazim al-Kassar and six of his associates had managed to escape while being transferred between military camps. Al-Kassar would never be captured again, and many more people would die while he ran free.

People like Samara.

Ben had smarted over the incident for a long time afterwards, wishing that he hadn't followed his orders and instead let the Yanks do whatever the hell they wanted to Nazim and his henchmen. The incident had been one of the rotten experiences that drove a wedge between him and the military bureaucracy above him. Ultimately, it would be one of the reasons why he quit the regiment under something of a cloud, thoroughly disillusioned with the whole business and ready to move on.

But the memories were hard to let go of. Even after he'd left the military, he'd kept track of the exploits of JTJ. In 2006, the same year that Nazim's mentor Abu al-Zarqawi had been killed in a US air strike, JTJ got itself a new leader and a new name. Along with much-expanded aspirations and confidence in its achievements it now became known as ISI, the Islamic State of Iraq.

Eight years after that, the name changed again. Henceforth the organisation would be called the Islamic State of Iraq and the Levant. ISIL, for short. A name that became very well known indeed to folks in the West. And the rest was history: the bombings, the killings, the mass abductions, the media storms surrounding the filmed beheadings of hostages streamed across the internet.

All those years, Ben had always secretly wished that he might one day have the opportunity of running into his old friend Nazim al-Kassar again. Over time, he'd become resigned to the unlikelihood of that ever happening. Then the deal had been sealed in August 2016, when Ben had heard through the grapevine that Nazim al-Kassar was among a group of ISIL commanders blown to bits in a US air strike in Iraq.

To have seen him dead would have been preferable. But to hear him dead was good enough. Ben had been relieved that the world was now free of one more lunatic murdering scumbag.

And now here he was again. Walking about and looking very much alive after all.

Ben couldn't believe it. Nazim al-Kassar, back from the dead and for some bizarre reason resurfacing in Paris, of all places. What could be the connection between him and a young woman like Romy Juneau?

That was a mystery Ben intended to solve. And if fate had chosen to cross his path with Nazim's once again, it would be for the last time. Because only one of them was walking away from this alive.

Chapter 9

One thing was for damn well sure: the 2016 intelligence sources proclaiming Nazim al-Kassar's demise were wrong. Badly wrong. It felt like history repeating itself once again. Ben needed to know how that could have happened, and why the hell a supposed dead man was walking around a European city leaving bodies in his wake.

Ben was deep in thought as he rode the subway train the long way back towards the safehouse. He could think of very few people with the right kinds of connections to help shed light on the questions in his mind. In fact, when he boiled the list right down, it came to just one man. Tyler Roth, the Delta Master Sergeant from Task Force Red.

Through the same grapevine that had fed him the inside track on ISIL activities, Ben happened to know that Roth had gone on to greater glories after Operation Citation. Promoted to captain, he'd served another twelve years with Delta. His long career had hit a peak in October 2013 when, as part of the Juniper Shield operations in North Africa, his undercover team had successfully captured Abu Anas al-Libi, a senior al-Qaeda member on the FBI's Most Wanted Terrorists list, in Tripoli. Then a couple of years later, in May 2015, Roth's unit had carried out a raid on Deir Ezzar in eastern Syria, targeting the financial operations chief of ISIL.

The target had been killed in the ensuing firefight, but Roth's guys had captured his wife along with a cache of ISIL operational records and plans that had proved a goldmine for the intelligence spooks.

Or so Ben had heard, at any rate. Like the SAS, Delta worked so much in the shadows that nobody really knew anything about their activities, or couldn't talk about them if they did.

One thing Ben was fairly certain of was that the Deir Ezzar job had been Roth's last hurrah with US Special Ops. Shortly afterwards, having survived a decade and a half at the top of his profession without having taken so much as a scratch, he'd quit. Not to spend the rest of his life golfing in Florida, nor to retire to Italy to grow tomatoes like Ben's old SAS comrade and mentor Boonzie McCulloch. Instead, Roth had opted for the path that many men of their level of training and expertise took, and slipped into the murky world of PMC. Which was short for Private Military Contractors.

In one word, Roth became a mercenary. Still employed, for the most part, by the same US government he'd served in his previous career, but working for much bigger pay cheques. The real money was in fighting wars so dirty and secret that nations like America and Britain wouldn't even involve their blackest, most covert SF operators for fear of getting caught in the middle of an international flap.

He had heard nothing of Roth in years. As far as he knew, though, the American was still in the PMC game – if he hadn't met a bullet in some squalid little conflict nobody was supposed to know about.

Ben picked up some Lavazza coffee beans on the way home, and when he reached the safehouse he threw a handful in the grinder, brewed himself a cup of dark roast, lit a cigarette and got on the phone. His first call was to Jeff Dekker at Le Val, to say something had come up and he'd be delayed getting back. Jeff didn't ask what, and Ben didn't need to explain. Jeff was like that. But Ben knew that if he'd asked, his friend would have been ready to drop everything and join him without hesitation.

Jeff was like that, too.

Ben's second phone call was to a guy he knew in London, with whom he hadn't spoken in a long, long while. The guy's name was Ken Keegan, and he was the director of a small but strangely lucrative firm called Simpson Associates Ltd, based in Canary Wharf. Needless to say, no real individual by the name of Simpson was, or had ever been, involved in the business. The company acted like a talent agency, fielding top-dollar PMC assignments and farming them out to the operatives best suited for the job, in return for a hefty commission. Keegan was a wealthy man, and worked eighteen hours a day. For years after Ben left the SAS the guy had constantly been pestering him with offers of lucrative contract work in Sudan or Sierra Leone or whichever high-risk hotspot happened to be attracting soldiers of fortune like sharks to blood that week. Ben had turned them all down, and eventually the phone had stopped ringing.

Keegan answered his direct line in less than two seconds, all eager and raring to go. Ben said, 'I like to see a man who's happy in his work.'

'Fuck me. If it ain't the one and only Ben Hope.' Keegan spoke in the piping, breathless voice of the seriously fat. Which he was. Probably the largest man Ben had ever seen, on the one occasion when they'd eaten out together at a pub in London and he'd watched in morbid fascination as the guy consumed a steak and kidney pie the size of a wagon wheel. That was at least ten years ago. Keegan was probably twice as big now.

'Still not dropped dead of a coronary, then,' Ben said.

'Take more than that to stop me, mate. So what brings you sniffing around my door? Let me guess, had enough of the soft life and feel like doing some real work for a change?'

'I need something from you,' Ben said.

'I don't like the sound of that.'

'Relax. Just a number, that's all I'm after.'

Keegan sounded suspicious. 'Okay, but whose?'

'You still in touch with Roth?'

Keegan was quiet for a few moments. Ben could hear him thinking. He was waiting for more, but Ben felt no need to offer specifics. Especially not the mention of the name Nazim al-Kassar. Keegan would just think he was nuts.

Keegan said, 'You're not the only one who'd like to talk to that fucker.'

'Why? What did he do?'

'Fucking went and retired on me, that's what he did. Just when I had all kinds of plum jobs lined up for the ungrateful sod.'

'I'm sorry to hear that,' Ben said. 'I might have had something for him myself.'

'Anything in it for me?'

'I guess we'll never know now, will we?'

Keegan gave a high-pitched wheeze that sounded tubercular. 'Bastard. Anyway, I thought you were well out of all that, years ago. What's the sudden interest?'

'So do you have a number for him, or not?'

'Come on, mate. Quid pro quo. This ain't bleeding directory enquiries, is it?'

'How about as a special favour to an old friend?'

'How about in return for you taking on a job for me? I've

got more work coming in than I got guys to delegate it out to. Matter of fact I have one here on my desk that'd suit you down to the ground. Ethiopia. In and out, eight days tops, big money.'

'Let me think about it,' Ben lied.

'Yeah, well, don't think too long. Client's breaking my balls something terrible. I need this yesterday.' Keegan broke into another whistling, hacking cough, like a cat with a hairball in its throat. He went silent for a long moment, and Ben thought maybe he'd slumped dead at his desk. Then Keegan said hoarsely, 'Okay, I'll see what I can come up with. Roth's a right awkward bugger to contact, even at the best of times. Gone all reclusive and paranoid in his old age. Easier to have a conversation with the fuckin' Duke of Edinburgh.'

'I appreciate your help, Ken. Really. I don't care what they say about you.'

'Who? What?'

'You don't want to know.'

'Fuck you very much too. And don't keep me waiting on that Ethiopia job, will you? Yes or no. I'm down to the sodding wire on this one, mate.'

What an enchanting character, that Keegan. Ben ended the call, put away his phone and took out the one that had belonged to Romy Juneau. He gazed at it for a moment, getting his thoughts straight.

Somewhere, there had to be some clue as to how and why she'd got herself hooked into the world of the likes of Nazim al-Kassar. It couldn't be a coincidence that he'd turned up at her place to murder her, much as he enjoyed killing women. And from her nervous behaviour that morning it had been clear she was afraid of something, or someone. It was just as clear that Nazim hadn't been working alone, but had at least one accomplice, the getaway driver in the silver Merc.

Had they been following her in the street earlier that morning? Had she been on her way somewhere, maybe to work, when she'd noticed them tailing her, become frightened and doubled back towards home where she felt safer? If so, it hadn't done her much good. But it also meant that she must have known the identity of the man, or men, following her.

Which suggested she was definitely involved with them somehow. Ben found it hard to believe that someone like Romy Juneau could be knowingly mixed up with terrorists. But then, what did he really know about her? He had barely even met her. For all he knew, she was a top operative for ISIL. Or maybe a CIA field agent they needed to eliminate. Which seemed just as unlikely to Ben, but you never could tell.

Whatever she might have been involved in, he doubted whether her phone would reveal much. But with so little to go on, he had to start somewhere.

Turning the device on he felt none of the self-conscious pangs he'd felt earlier. Now that she was dead, things were different. It would no longer seem like prying into someone's personal affairs. In any case she was no longer in a position to resent the intrusion.

He stubbed out his cigarette, drank some more coffee and got to work.

Chapter 10

The first time Ben had gone through Romy Juneau's phone he'd gone no further than her address book, which had told him all he'd needed to know at that point. Now it was time to delve a little deeper.

He began with the call menus, starting with sent calls. There were plenty of them for him to sift through. Some were identifiable as names from her contacts list, like her parents, whom she seemed to call often, her workplace and the person called Michel Ben had noted earlier, whoever he was. She'd called Michel frequently over a period of a few months, though the phone correspondence seemed to have stopped a month or so ago, with the exception of one brief call two days ago and another even briefer one just that morning. The last call had happened just minutes before Ben's encounter with her in the street.

Ben wondered if the call had had something to do with the fact that she seemed so distraught. Out of curiosity he used his burner phone to call Michel's number, but got no reply and didn't leave a message. Then he listed the other numbers she'd called that weren't stored in her address book, and called each in turn. There was a television repair man, a home insurance company and other assorted useless stuff that he crossed off his list one by one until there was nothing left.

Moving on to received calls he went through the same process. The mysterious Michel had also phoned her often, though not in the last month or so. Her parents phoned her from time to time, less often than she called them. The rest of it was just as inconsequential. This kind of detective work was seldom very exciting.

Next, texts and emails. Which were all work-related and concerned various dull administrative matters that Ben couldn't make head or tail of. The outgoing mails bore an automatically added text at the foot of the message, which said 'R. Juneau, Research Development Officer, ICS', with the Institute's address in the eighth arrondissement of Paris. A fairly swanky location, even though it was probably knee-deep in riot wreckage these days.

Ben keyed the Segal Cultural Institute into his search engine. It was a private organisation founded in the early nineties and run by a top French archaeologist called Julien Segal. Ben had never heard of him, though there was no reason why he should have. The Institute's website described its mission as the preservation and protection of ancient art treasures, specialising in the ancient Middle East. They were one of the leaders in the development of new technologies to digitally reconstruct art treasures damaged by war, natural disaster or the ravages of time, and restore them using 3-D printing.

Middle East. War. Ben thought, *Hmm.*

Then he thought, *Middle East. War. Nazim al-Kassar. ISIL.*

Hmm again. Tantalising. Not exactly what a detective would consider hard evidence of an actual connection. But enough to make Ben curious to know more.

The website featured a little 'About Our Founder' bio of Julien Segal. A small photo showed a man in his early fifties, with a full head of silver hair and a craggily handsome face with striking, penetrative eyes like a hawk's. He had spent decades travelling the world and been personally responsible for the rescue of countless ancient artifacts that otherwise would have been lost. He supplied museums, private and corporate collections, gave lecture tours and worked closely with international cultural heritage groups such as UNESCO and ECCO, the European Confederation of Conservation Organisations.

Ben dialled the Institute's number on his burner phone and was put through to a female receptionist. He could tell right away from her tone of voice that the police must already have been in touch. She sounded as if she'd been crying, and might be about to burst into tears again at any moment.

Ben asked to speak to Monsieur Segal. The woman replied, 'I'm afraid he's currently out of the country. He travels a great deal. Can I be of any—?' She'd been about to say 'assistance', but before she got that far her emotions got the better of her and she choked up. It took her a few moments to regain her composure. 'Please forgive me. We've just received the most awful news. In fact the Institute is closing early for the day. One of our colleagues was found dead this morning. It's . . . it's just so heartbreaking. Romy was so loved by everyone here. She had only recently returned from a field trip overseas. And now . . .' Her voice trailed off with a sigh.

'That's shocking. My sincere condolences. I'm so sorry if I called at a bad time.'

She'd sounded at first as though she wanted, or needed, to talk, which Ben was pleased about because the more information he could fish for, the better. But now the woman seemed to compose herself and tighten up, as though suddenly conscious that she was blurting out her heart to a total stranger. 'I'm afraid I didn't catch your name.'

'Dubois,' Ben said. 'Bernard Dubois. And you must be—?'

'Jeanne.'

'Of course, that's right,' he said, bluffing like hell. Sometimes you could win them over with a little charm. 'Jeanne, I wonder if you can tell me when Monsieur Segal is expected back in the country?'

'Not for several more days at least.'

Ben didn't know whether she was telling the truth or giving him the brush-off. She sounded as though she wanted to get off the phone, so he pressed a little harder. 'Is there another number I could reach him on? It's really rather important.'

'No, I'm sorry, I can't help you there. It would be better to call back in a few days.'

'I'll do that, thanks.'

She sniffed and said, 'I really must go. Everyone here is very upset.'

'Just one more question, Jeanne. Was Romy expected at work today?'

She hesitated, obviously finding the question weird. The information would help Ben piece together Romy's movements that morning, which might come in useful as he learned more. But Jeanne wasn't taking the bait. 'I'm sorry, but who exactly are you?'

'Don't worry about it. Apologies for having called at this difficult time.'

Ben ended the call before she could say more. So much for winning them over with charm.

He went back to examining Romy's phone. Address book, call records, texts, emails; he was running out of options and didn't have much to show for it so far. All that remained for him to check out was the folder containing image files.

Lots of folks went about snapping anything that moved, subscribed heavily to the selfie craze and had thousands of photos crammed into their phones, but Romy wasn't one of those people. She had only five files stored in the images folder. They were arranged in chronological order. Ben opened the oldest one first, dating back to January.

The image was a self-taken shot of Romy and a young guy about the same age as her, slightly built, who looked like he might be Moroccan or Algerian. Ben wondered if this was Michel, the boyfriend. They were hugging each other and grinning cheesy grins for the camera on a cloudy beach somewhere, maybe the north coast up near Calais. They were dressed for winter, hats and coats and woolly scarves, and the sea breeze was blowing her hair across her face. She looked happy. The young guy, too. It was a sad picture, in retrospect.

The next photo had been taken three months ago, inside what appeared to be a bar. Ben could see tables covered with glassware and bottles, and red vinyl bench seating and other people in the background. Another image taken not long afterwards the same day showed the two of them posing outside the bar, pulling silly faces. Ben could see the faded lettering painted on the bar window that spelled out backwards the words LE GERONIMO.

Ben laid down Romy's phone for a moment and tried Michel's number again on his burner. Still no reply.

He returned to her phone. The fourth photo was a blurry shot of an older couple, taken in the dining room in a middle-class family home a couple of months ago. It looked like someone's birthday, though the older couple didn't seem to be having a great time. They both bore a faint resemblance to Romy: her parents, he assumed. Her father had the pasty complexion of a chronic cardiac sufferer and her mother looked like an uptight sort. They were centred at the end of a table bearing a cake festooned with candles, the smiling, goofy faces of some other people peering in at the edges of the frame. Romy wasn't among them, so Ben assumed she'd been behind the camera. Photography hadn't been her greatest talent in life, that was for sure.

When he tried to open the fifth and most recent picture file, just three days old, he discovered two things about it. First, that it wasn't a picture file at all but a much larger video clip. Second, that it was encrypted.

A window popped up requesting a PIN number. Beneath that was a prompt asking him 'Forget your passcode?' When he tapped it, the phone asked him for a security question. Which could be anything in the world, and after a couple of failed attempts the whole phone might lock itself up. He didn't even bother trying.

Now why would Romy have encrypted the video file when she hadn't made any attempt to protect the rest of her phone data? That fact alone singled it out as an item of particular interest, and Ben's curiosity was piqued. It could be all kinds of things. Something private, obviously. Possibly something very personal that Romy didn't want anyone to see.

Which left open the possibility that the clip could be something more pertinent to the questions Ben was trying to answer. He needed to get into that video file.

He was no expert on how to access inaccessible digital data. But he knew someone who was.

Chapter 11

Thierry Chevrolet wasn't named after a famous American automobile marque. His surname was derived from an old French word meaning a goat farmer. But goat farming wasn't how Thierry made his living, either.

Back when Ben had operated as a freelance kidnap and hostage rescue specialist, his work had taken him to many different countries and necessitated a number of false identities. Passports, driving licences, ID cards and other official papers all had to be perfect to avoid unnecessary entanglements with the authorities and allow him to slip about under the radar. He'd gone to a couple of dodgy characters in the forgery trade, one in London, one in Amsterdam, before he'd found the then twenty-nine-year-old Thierry working out of a tiny apartment in Paris. He was a nervous, skinny guy with a bush of Afro hair and a reedy moustache, and talked in a whispery voice owing to the fact that he only had one lung. Hardly the archetype of the master criminal. But after seeing a sample of his work Ben had hired him on the spot to produce a variety of false papers. He'd been more than pleased with the results.

Now and then things would get hot and one of Ben's fake identities would have to be ditched and replaced, so he had been able to offer Thierry a steady stream of work. The pair had got to know each other well. Ben had discovered that in addition to being an excellent forger, Thierry was also a wizard with anything techno-orientated. On a few occasions he'd employed him to hack emails, raid computer files and unlock phones 'confiscated' from associates of kidnappers. If Thierry couldn't hack and crack his way into it, you might as well toss it in the bin.

And now Ben had a new assignment for him.

Last time they'd had dealings was years ago, before Ben had retired from freelance work, moved to France full-time and joined up with Jeff Dekker to set up the tactical training centre at Le Val. He had no idea whether the guy was still active.

Ben levered up the loose floorboard in the safehouse's bedroom, dug around in the cavity below and pulled out a padded envelope sealed with tape. Inside were a couple of examples of Thierry's artistry, a British passport in the name Paul Harris, and a French one for the fictitious Vincent Fournier. Each had served him well on a few occasions.

Wrapped up with the fake passports was a dog-eared old notebook in which Ben had kept lists of contacts in those days. Thierry's number was marked just by the letter T. He dialled it, but there was no answer. Maybe it was a long shot. Thierry could have changed his phone, or emigrated, or gone straight and got a job, or died, or been caught and sent to jail. Any of which possibilities would leave Ben in a tricky situation. The issue wasn't finding someone else who could unlock the encrypted video file. It was finding someone who wouldn't ask questions about what Ben was doing with a phone belonging to the victim of an unsolved murder. Petty crooks often greased the wheels of their good fortune by acting as police informants on the side. Thierry, by contrast, was far too honourable a criminal to ever rat on a client.

Ben ruminated on his problem by brewing up another pot of Lavazza. In his experience, solutions often presented themselves just by virtue of drinking more coffee. There was no such thing as too much.

And experience proved right when, halfway through his second cup, the phone buzzed with Thierry's number on the screen.

Ben answered, expecting to hear the forger's familiar raspy, whispery tones. But it wasn't Thierry calling. It was a woman, and she sounded pissed off. Even more so when she heard Ben's voice.

She said, 'Shit. I thought it was him.'

'Thierry?'

'You a friend of his? Because if you are, tell him Abby wants his fucking junk out of her fucking place, or she's gonna torch the lot of it. Okay?'

Ben presumed he was talking to Abby. It sounded like Thierry's life had gone through some changes since Ben had last been in touch. No girlfriend had ever been mentioned before.

Ben said, 'You don't know where he is?'

'No, I fucking don't know where he is. Who're you, anyway?'

'My name's Ben. I need to find him.'

'I get the picture. You're one of them. Well, if you're gonna fuck him over, just make sure he clears his junk out of my place first, okay? It's so jam packed in here you can hardly fart.'

Abby was evidently a classy sort of gal. Ben asked, 'Is Thierry in trouble?'

She paused. 'Would you be asking me that if you were one of them?'

'I'm not. Cross my heart and hope to die.'

'Thierry *is* trouble,' she sighed. 'Story of my life.'

'What happened?'

'Same old, same old. Except this time he went too far. I told him, "Thierry, you get in debt to those people, you'll regret it." Did he listen to me? Did he ever?'

'Who did he borrow from?'

Abby made a grumphing sound. 'The kind of people who break your arms and fuck up your knees up with hammers, if you don't pay them back pronto, with interest.'

'How much does he owe?'

'Enough to piss them off that he hasn't repaid a cent of it.'

'So now he's hiding from them.'

She paused to take a noisy drag on a cigarette, then grumphed again. 'Skipped out two weeks ago. Not heard from him since. So fucking typical, you know? That's it this time. We're finished. You tell him that, if you see him. And I want—'

'His junk out of your place. I get that. Listen, Abby, I really do need to find him. Maybe I can help him.'

'I don't give a shit if you can help him or not. He's got it coming.' She sucked on the cigarette again, and seemed about to hang up the call. Then she blew out an exasperated sigh and said, 'You could try that slimeball Pierrot. They hang out together. He might be lying low there. I don't want to call, because Pierrot is *such* a creep. The way he pervs on me makes me want to fucking puke.'

She gave Ben an address for the creepy slimeball. He wrote it down, thanked her and promised to remind Thierry about the junk. She said, 'Whatever,' and hung up.

Ben slugged down the last of his coffee, grabbed his car keys, locked up the apartment and was on his way.

Chapter 12

Paris is divided up into twenty *arrondissements* or municipal districts each with its own number, which to the casual visitor seem to be scattered randomly about the city but are actually arranged in a rather quirky helix pattern, spiralling out from the centre to form something like a snail shell within the rough circle of the Boulevard Périphérique, Paris's ring road. The address that Thierry Chevrolet's ex-girlfriend had given Ben was situated on the border of the tenth and nineteenth districts, where the helix unwound itself towards its outer edge in the north-east of the city, about one o'clock on the clock face of the circle.

Ben cut across the city in the Alpina and drank in the many changes since his last visit of any duration to the place. He hacked along Boulevard de la Chapelle, following the path of the raised viaduct Métro line, and reached the Place de la Bataille de Stalingrad, where Abby's directions told him to head further north-east up Avenue de Flandre, parallel with the river. Everywhere beneath the Métro viaduct were migrant camps, spread out like a post-apocalyptic settlement of makeshift tents and shanty dwellings, with garbage choking the pavements, washing lines strung up between trees and signposts, bits of outdoor furniture scattered here and there. Hundreds of Afghans occupied one stretch near the Stalingrad Métro station; further up along the street were the Sudanese and the Somalis, the Eritreans and the Ethiopians, all clustered into their own separate camps. So much for multiculturalism. The scene was about as far from the picture-postcard tourist image of Paris as it was possible to get. The government could send in the troops to clear the place up, as it had done before and no doubt would do again, but the tents would soon return, over and over.

Welcome to the new Europe, Ben thought. These were problems that couldn't easily be fixed, and he was glad that wasn't his job.

Thierry Chevrolet seemed to have landed himself with a problem that wouldn't easily be fixed, either. Ben didn't know who he'd borrowed money from, or how much, or why, but it didn't sound good. And if Thierry had been in hiding for two weeks already, there was a decent chance the bone-breakers might catch up with him any time. In which case the job Ben had come here to do might turn suddenly unpleasant, too.

The earlier sunshine had disappeared behind grey clouds. It began to rain as he headed up Avenue de Flandre, passing high-rises and shops, a lot of them with shuttered, grafitti'd windows. After a couple of blocks he spotted the side street where Thierry's buddy Pierrot lived. He found a parking space for the Alpina and walked the rest of the way to Pierrot's building, which made Romy Juneau's place look like the Luxembourg Palace by comparison.

On his way Ben noticed the chunky black Audi SUV parked in front of the building, which looked much newer and shinier than most of the other cars along the kerbside, including his own. He didn't think it belonged to Pierrot. This could be a bad sign.

He pushed inside the building, checked his notebook for

Pierrot's apartment number and climbed the dirty staircase checking doors as he went. Pierrot's door was third on the right along a hallway on the second floor. Standing outside it was a definite confirmation of the bad sign parked in the street below.

The two very large men were leaning against the wall either side of the doorway, like two bouncers flanking a nightclub entrance. The one closest to Ben probably tipped the scales at about seventeen stones, which was three stones heavier than he was. From the guy's shape, it looked like most of that bulk was lean muscle, cultivated through countless hours in the weights room. The one on the right was larger still, but he'd invested his time differently and was as fat and round as a baby orca. Both of them were standing to attention with their thick arms folded across their swollen chests. Both staring at Ben as he walked towards Pierrot's door. Neither showing any degree of friendliness. They were white, with some kind of Mediterranean ethnicity like Greek or Armenian. Black hair razed to a stubble, dark trench coats, leather gloves, shiny shoes. They looked like a couple of extras auditioning for parts in a new *Godfather* movie. And their presence outside Pierrot's door left Ben in little doubt that Thierry's creditors had indeed already managed to track him down.

Ben didn't slacken his step as he walked up to them. He stopped, standing about five feet from the door, making a triangle with the muscleman on his right and the baby orca on his left. Each was a couple of inches taller than Ben, who measured just a fraction short of six feet. They stared. He stared back. He would have offered them a nice smile, but they didn't seem in the mood for pleasantries.

Ben said in French, 'Salut les gars.' Hi, guys. Bright and affable. There was no reply. He couldn't hear any sounds of hideous torture coming from the other side of the door, just some muffled conversational voices. It was hard to say how many of their associates were inside the apartment. He'd find out soon enough.

Ben pointed at the door. 'I've come to see my friend Pierrot. How about stepping out of the way so I can go inside?'

'Fuck off,' the muscleman said. Ben hadn't really expected much more in the way of eloquence.

'You know, this doesn't have to go badly,' he said. 'Whatever Thierry Chevrolet owes, I'm happy to settle the debt.' He patted his leather jacket, where his wallet nestled inside. 'Then we can all go about our separate business like the good-natured gentlemen we are. Now, I'm guessing you two aren't exactly the heads of the operation. So maybe you should open the door and let me talk with your boss inside. Okay?'

The muscleman exchanged glances with his monstrous pal. The two of them managed a brief grin, then turned the dead-eyed stare back on Ben.

He shrugged, as though he didn't really care either way, which in truth he didn't. 'No? That's a shame. Then I'll have to open it myself.'

Ben took a step towards the door. Which put him within reach of either guy, and technically in danger of getting hit. But that much weight, whether composed of muscle or lard, had a lot of inertia to overcome before they could properly start moving. They would be slow, and he was fast. If a punch launched towards him, he could casually take out his cigarettes and light one up before it arrived. And he already knew that it was the muscleman, as the actual or self-declared superior of the pair, who would move first.

It happened exactly as Ben anticipated. As he moved

towards the door, the muscleman peeled himself away from the wall and a big knuckly fist flew towards Ben's chest. A lot of drive behind it, no question. The guy had probably hit a lot of people before now, considering his line of work, and he had some crude understanding of how to inflict significant bodily damage on mostly unsuspecting, untrained victims.

But the rib-cracking blow never landed. Ben watched the big knuckly fist float towards him, then reached up with one hand as though he was catching a tennis ball gently lobbed his way. He caught the guy's fist *smack* in his palm and deflected and twisted it at the same time.

It was the most basic of Aikido wrist locks. Ben brought up his other hand to trap the guy's hand against his own. His fingers flowed over the guy's wrist like water. It took barely any strength to lever the joint so painfully that the muscleman was forced down on one knee, letting out a grunt of surprise and agony. That was what these bodybuilder types didn't seem to understand. You can spend a decade pumping your muscles up to the size of wholemeal bread loaves, but behind that suit of armour your sinews, ligaments and joints remain just as fragile and vulnerable to attack as when you were a skinny, pencil-necked fifteen-year-old.

Then Ben stepped casually around to the guy's right, taking the trapped wrist with him, and drove him all the way down to the floor with his arm levered up behind his back. It would only have taken a couple more pounds of pressure to break the joint. Ben pushed it through all the way until he felt the crackle and snap. At which point the muscleman would have started screaming, if Ben hadn't already been standing on his neck and crushing his face into the tiled floor.

By then the baby orca was stepping towards Ben,

reaching inside his trench coat for what Ben knew was hidden in there. Ben trampled over the fallen muscle guy and put an elbow in the fat one's solar plexus while sweeping his legs out from under him with a scything kick. The orca hit the floor with a crash that must have shaken the whole building. Ben kicked him in the throat, not hard enough to do any fatal damage, but plenty enough to make him concentrate more on breathing than anything else for the next few minutes. He lay there gasping like a landed fish, clutching at his huge neck, eyes popping. Ben reached down inside the guy's open trench coat and quickly found the item he'd been about to pull out. It was a 9mm Glock, black and boxy, fitted with a stubby sound suppressor. Not the most elegant weapon, but highly effective. He stuck the pistol in his belt.

The fight, if it could have been called such, had lasted just seconds. Ben could still hear the muffled voices coming from inside Pierrot's apartment. Someone laughed. However many people were in there, they obviously hadn't realised what was happening outside.

The bodybuilder was curled up on the floor holding onto his broken arm and moaning in agony. Ben flipped him over, frisked him and found an identical Glock in a concealed shoulder rig under his coat. Fully loaded, fifteen rounds in the mag plus one up the spout. Ben took that one for himself, too, but didn't stick it through his belt. He was going to need it, because he was about to make his entrance.

Ben grabbed the bodybuilder by his broken arm, levered him savagely up to his feet, propelled him forward and used his head to ram open the apartment door.

Chapter 13

The door burst inwards with a juddering, splintering crash. Ben stepped through the open doorway, still holding onto the muscleman, who was half unconscious and bloody from the impact.

And now Ben could see the five other men inside the apartment. First and foremost was Thierry Chevrolet, the man Ben hadn't been alone in hoping to find here. The second was the apartment's tenant, Pierrot, looking as if he strongly regretted having let his buddy crash at his place. The two chums were sitting side by side on a pair of mismatched chairs, with their wrists tied behind them, their ankles bound to the chair legs, and gags tightly stretched across their mouths. Their faces were pallid with terror, their eyes wide and staring at Ben as he appeared in the doorway. Until just a second ago they'd been looking up at the third, fourth and fifth men in the room, who were standing in a loose semicircle in front of their victims.

The three gangsters simultaneously turned to face the door as Ben appeared. The ones on the left and right were just as large as the pair who'd been posted outside on guard duty, and pretty much carbon copies. Dark hair buzzed close to the scalp, dark trench coats, shiny shoes. The one in the middle was very different, and not because he was the only one not wearing the standard-issue gangster trench coat.

He stood less than five feet in height, but his eyes blazed with a fierce intelligence lacking in any of his much larger accomplices. Ben instantly took him to be the boss man of the operation, about twice as hard-boiled and three times as psychopathic as his underlings, as though all that aggression and violence had been concentrated into a smaller, meaner, undiluted package. If he'd been a dog he'd have been a wiry terrier-cross mongrel ready without hesitation to rip into Rottweilers six times his size. He was wearing a double-breasted suit that would have fitted a twelve-year-old, expensively tailor made. He had no hair at all, and like a lot of bald guys it was hard to pin an age on him. He could have been thirty, or fifty. A sickle-shaped scar distorted his left cheek, from the corner of his mouth to his earlobe, and accentuated the sneer of hatred that he was turning on Ben at this moment.

Ben was more concerned about the curved sabre clenched in the little hard guy's fist. So, judging by the looks of utter terror on their faces, were Thierry and Pierrot. It seemed that he'd been about to take a swing at one of them when the door had burst open and interrupted him. Presumably, first to get the chop would have been Pierrot, before the little guy decided what to do about Thierry. Which probably depended on Thierry's ability or otherwise to pay his debts, and whether the little guy considered it worth trying to get him to cough up the money or just make an example of him by slicing and dicing him into small, bloody pieces.

But all that was a secondary consideration now, as the stranger joined the party. The little guy's scarred face hardened like iron. It took him only a fraction of a second to get over his surprise at Ben's entrance, and fly into the attack.

Being small and light on his feet, he was also exceptionally fast. He came at Ben whirling the sabre, the curved blade whistling as it sliced the air in a downward diagonal, right to left.

Ben propelled the stunned guard forwards to meet the savage strike, like a human shield. The little guy could do little to halt the momentum of the swinging blade, and it chopped into his own man's left shoulder, sinking deep. Trapezius muscle severed, collar bone cleaved in half, probably a lot of other irreversible damage as well. Blood sprayed from the wound. The guard sprawled to the floor, twitched and lay still. The little guy stared down at him, then back up at Ben, eyes burning with fury.

Meanwhile the two big men either side of him reached into their trench coats and pulled out their guns. Two more identical Glocks, each fitted with the same kind of long silencer. They could have unloaded all thirty-two rounds into Ben and none of the neighbours would have heard a thing.

Ben wasn't going to let that happen. But he wasn't going to kill anyone, either. He'd seen enough death today already.

So instead he shot each of them through the foot, in such quick succession that the muted coughs of the silenced 9mm in his hand sounded like one ragged, elongated report. The big guy on his left got it in the left foot, and the one on his right got it in the right foot, the copper-jacketed bullets punching straight through the shiny leather of their shoes, and straight through the flesh and muscle inside. Before pulling the trigger Ben had already decided that the floorboards were likely thick enough to stop the bullets, to prevent anyone downstairs from getting hurt. Health and safety were important considerations at such times.

The two big guys simultaneously dropped their guns and collapsed like sacks of washing, howling in pain as they clutched their perforated feet. Before they'd even hit the floor, Ben had the Glock pointed towards the short guy's face.

Ben said, 'Do yourself a favour, little man.'

The sabre remained suspended in the air for a few instants, during which the psychopathic dwarf looked as though he was seriously considering taking another swing. Ben lowered his aim to point the pistol at his groin. His finger tightened on the trigger. He said, 'Really?'

The little boss man relented, lowered the sabre and let it drop with a clatter to the floor, though the snarl of ferocious hatred never left his face. He spat.

Ben said, 'What's your name?'

'Paulo Fraticelli,' the little guy growled.

'Never heard of you.'

Fraticelli's eyes gleamed. 'You will. Make no mistake about that.'

Ben shook his head. 'I don't think so. You're in the wrong job, Paulo. Go back to picking pockets or smuggling cigarettes, or whatever pissy little racket you came from. Messing with my friends is bad for your health.'

'You're a fucking dead man walking.'

'At least I can walk,' Ben said, pointing at Fraticelli's associates on the floor. The little guy glanced down at them too. Only for a second, but a second was long enough a distraction. Ben stepped towards him and kicked him savagely in the balls, plenty hard enough to squash them flat. Fraticelli let out a screech and doubled over forwards, with perfect timing for Ben's knee to ram him brutally in the face and knock him out cold. He hit the floor with much less of a crash than his henchmen.

The muscleman still wasn't moving. Ben didn't think he was dead, but he was certainly losing a lot of blood from the gaping slash in his shoulder. Before long it was going to start dripping through the ceiling of the apartment below. Meanwhile his two colleagues with the perforated feet were making an awful lot of noise. Ben said, 'Enough of the racket, guys. People live here.' He stepped over to one of them and kicked him in the head, and the noise level in the room dropped by half. Then he stepped over to the other. Same job. The apartment was suddenly much quieter.

'Peace at last,' Ben said. He stuck the silenced Glock through his belt next to the other. Thierry and Pierrot were boggling at him from their chairs. He went over to them and pulled off their gags, Thierry first, then his friend.

'Hello, Thierry. I have a message from Abby.'

'Who the hell are you?' Pierrot gasped. He was about the same age as Thierry, with receding greasy hair, close-set eyes and a weaselly way about him. To Ben's eye the guy had the look of a small-time drug dealer. He would happily have left Pierrot for Fraticelli's boys, under different circumstances.

Thierry shook his head in amazement. 'I can't believe it's you, man,' he said in the whispery voice. 'Christ, you haven't aged a day.'

'Wish I could say the same about you, Thierry. You look like shit.' Which was harsh, but true. Time had not been too kind to the forger since Ben had last seen him. He looked weary and worn down and gaunt, and the bush of hair had mostly disappeared.

'Abby sent you?' Thierry asked ruefully.

Ben picked up Fraticelli's sabre and ran his thumb lightly along the edge of the blade. It was razor-sharp. He moved around behind Thierry's chair and started cutting him free. 'She says she's going to burn all the junk you left at her place. She also seemed to think you might have got into a little trouble. Wonder how she got that idea.'

'We're in a shitload more of it now. I was handling things just fine before you turned up.'

Gratitude was a wonderful thing. Ben said, 'Oh, I could see that.' The rope holding Thierry's wrists fell loose. He slashed his ankles free and then started working on Pierrot.

Thierry stood up stiffly and rubbed his wrists, frowning anxiously at the unconscious bodies on the floor. 'I'm serious. We're totally fucked, man. Do you know who you just worked over? These guys are Unione Corse. Fraticelli's a made guy. Now there'll be a thousand of the bastards looking for us. And you, too.'

Unione Corse was the Corsican mafia. *The kind of guys who'll break your arms and fuck your knees up with hammers.* And then some. Abby had no idea of the kind of nasty characters her boyfriend had been borrowing money from. This bunch had moved on from breaking arms and legs well before they got into their teens.

'Then maybe it's time to get out of town,' Ben said. 'Your buddy here as well. But first, there's something I need you to do for me.'

Thierry brightened a little. 'You mean, like, a job?'

'You look as though you could do with one.'

'It's been a while. Work's kind of thin on the ground lately.'

'Are you up for it?'

'You bet. Just like old times, huh?'

Ben said, 'Then let's talk. But not here.' He finished freeing Pierrot and told him, 'Pack your stuff. One small suitcase. Leave the rest.'

'This is my place,' Pierrot whined.

'Not any more, it isn't. When your downstairs neighbours see the blood coming through the ceiling and call the cops, it's going to get a little crowded around here. You can't come back any time soon. So hurry it up.'

Pierrot didn't look too thrilled about abandoning his rathole apartment, but Thierry was looking more pleased by the second. 'Oh, Ben?'

'Yes?'

'Thanks for, uh, you know, saving us.'

'I needed the exercise. Now let's go.'

The fat guard outside in the corridor was showing signs of recovery, so Ben knocked him out properly and dragged his corpulent bulk inside the apartment by the ankles. Then they pulled the door shut against the shattered frame and hurried downstairs, out of the building, past the Corsican boys' Audi and up the street to where the Alpina was parked. Ben tossed Pierrot's case in the boot, and they took off.

Thirty minutes later they were back at the safehouse. Pierrot was still sulking and hadn't spoken another word. Ben ignored him, brewed up more coffee, then sat Thierry down at the table in the living room and told him what he needed.

'Whose is it?' Thierry asked, frowning at Romy's phone.

'You don't need to know,' Ben said. 'You just need to unlock that video file. Think you can do that for me?'

Thierry spent a few moments fiddling with the phone, deep in concentration. 'Yeah, I reckon I can.'

'How long?'

'Twenty minutes, give or take.'

'You're still my guy,' Ben said.

Thierry Chevrolet might have seen better times and lost his sparkle, but the kinds of skills he possessed didn't fade with age. Ben left him alone to work, and went over to smoke at the window while Thierry hunched over the smartphone at the table. Pierrot was still lurking, silent and morose, in the background. Ben would gladly have sent him out on some errand just to get rid of him, if he could have trusted the idiot wouldn't return with half the Corsica mafia on his heels.

Eighteen minutes and three more cups of coffee later, Thierry leaned back in his chair, looked over at Ben with a sly grin and whispered, 'We're in.'

Chapter 14

'Don't get too excited, chief,' Thierry said as Ben went over to see. 'It isn't exactly what you'd call cinema quality.'

Pierrot was suddenly all interested. 'What is it? Porno?'

Ben gave him a look that made him stay in place and keep his mouth shut. Turning back to Thierry he asked, 'Did you see any of it?'

'You're the client. It's none of my business what's on there. I only looked at the first few seconds. Long enough to see what it isn't.' Thierry handed over the phone. Ben took it and sat at the table to look.

The video was less than a minute long. That made each second of its duration seem all the more precious, assuming the clip was of any value at all. After the first five seconds, Ben's heart was beginning to sink, because he could hardly make anything out. Everything was dark and jerky, just a confusion of shapes and shadows. All that was clearly visible was the purple time and date stamp in the bottom left corner of the screen, which just confirmed the date on the file label, from three days ago.

Seven seconds in, something appeared on the right-hand edge of the frame, and moved inwards to fill a third of the screen. It was the vertical edge of what appeared to be a concrete wall, pitted and craggy. The camera's focus sharpened on that, making the background even more blurry and indistinct. All Ben could glean from what he was seeing was that the person doing the filming – presumably Romy herself, though he had no way to be certain – was shooting the video clip in a furtive, clandestine way from behind the wall, not wanting to be seen. She, if it was her, seemed to be trying to angle the camera past its edge, around the corner, to film something happening further away. But the lighting was just too dark to see what.

Ben said, 'This is terrible.'

Thierry shrugged. 'You get what you get, man.'

As bad as the visual quality was, the audio was even worse. All Ben could hear through the phone's tinny speaker was a lot of white noise. The phone mic was picking up all kinds of background sounds. He was sure he could hear Romy's breathing, which was restrained, like someone trying to remain undetected, but fast and urgent, like someone very afraid of getting caught. He thought back to the one and only time he'd seen her alive. She'd been frightened then, too. Clearly terrified of whoever she thought was following her.

Had Romy witnessed something, Ben wondered. *What were you doing? What did you see?*

Somewhere in the middle of the white noise, barely audible, was the sound of muffled voices. Two of them, Ben thought. Both men, judging from the low-range tones. He strained his ears to catch what was being said, but it was impossible to make out.

'Is there anything you can do to make the sound clearer?' he asked Thierry.

'Hey, I'm a genius, not a bloody magician. You might be able to clean it up a little, but not without access to some decent audio editing software. Even then, no guarantees. You can't bring out what isn't there to start with.'

Ben said nothing, and went on watching what he couldn't see and listening to what he couldn't hear. Then, eighteen seconds in, Romy must have shifted position slightly because the vertical edge of the wall suddenly slid out of shot towards the right. The camera's autofocus was suddenly able to latch onto more of the background and suck more light from the murky shadows. The audio was still bad, but now Ben could make out more visual detail.

The scene had taken place inside some kind of warehouse or industrial building, or it could have been a cellar: a large, dimly-lit space with concrete pillars holding up the roof. Ben realised it was another of the same pillars, not a wall, that Romy was hiding behind to film the clip on her phone. She was doing her best to keep the camera steady, but the picture kept jerking and wandering and made it hard to see. Ben started freeze-framing the clip to get a better look.

At the far end of the warehouse, or cellar, rows of strange whitish objects were lined up against a wall. Some seemed to be covered with shrouds or tarpaulins, others were more clearly visible. Ben realised that they were statues. Old ones, he guessed by the look of them. Some were human figures, others of animals and mythical beasts. Some smaller in size, others so tall and large that they loomed up towards the ceiling of the warehouse. Ben let the playback roll for a few more seconds, then paused it again to catch a clear view of a massive stone creature that appeared to have the head and face of a man, the body of an elephant. Or maybe a bull. Either way it was an enormous piece of sculpture that stood nearly as high as the rafter beams, several metres tall.

It looked oddly familiar to him. Where had he seen something like it before? He thought back, then flashed on a memory of the one time he'd ever visited the Louvre museum, right here in Paris, years ago, and seen similar exhibits on display. Those had dated back several millennia, he remembered. Brought to France within the last couple of centuries, from some ancient part of what was now the Middle East.

Then Ben recalled a more recent memory, of his conversation with Romy's colleague Jeanne at the Institute, and Jeanne telling him that Romy had recently returned from a field trip overseas. He wished he knew more about where she'd gone. He could only guess that, since her work involved the preservation of ancient works of art like these, her field trips might take her to places where such objects were kept warehoused between being salvaged from their original homes and being relocated to museums in Europe and elsewhere. That much made sense – but what didn't make sense was why she was filming this so secretively, as though she wasn't supposed to be there. Who was she hiding from?

Ben unpaused the image and let the video play on. Nearly half a minute into the clip the image shifted again, panning a few degrees to the left. Ben realised that Romy was keeping so carefully hidden behind her pillar that she couldn't actually see what she was trying to film, and was just taking pot luck at aiming the camera. The picture went wildly jerky for a few moments, then steadied again.

And that was when Ben saw the two men whose indistinct voices he could hear garbled in the background. It was just a brief glimpse, and he had to pause, rewind and pause again until he was able to freeze the frame just right. The pair were standing about midway between where Romy was hiding and the statues lined against the far wall. The angle of the shot captured them both in profile, side-on to the camera. From their body language it was clear that the conversation was intense and serious. One man was taller and darker than the other, but they were too small to make out their faces.

He asked Thierry, 'Can I zoom in on this?'

Thierry tutted at Ben's lack of expertise. 'How can a guy be so damn good at some things, and so completely hopeless at others?' He leaned over and showed Ben how to make the image bigger.

The zoomed-in shot of the two men was a little blurry, but clear enough.

The shorter man on the right was older, thicker around the middle and wearing the sort of light-coloured suit that well-to-do Europeans used to wear in tropical countries. He had a full head of silver hair and a craggy face, deeply tanned. Ben recognised him from his photo on the Institute website. It was Julien Segal, the archaeologist, Romy's employer.

Which still didn't explain why Romy was hiding from him and filming the conversation in secret. But the identity of the man on the left explained a great deal.

Taller, more powerfully built, dressed all in black and seemingly doing most of the talking, the man on the left was Nazim al-Kassar.

Chapter 15

Ben stared at the small, frozen image in his hands. And so now, at last, the first pieces of the puzzle were lining up together. What connection existed between a reputed antiquities conservation expert and a notorious terrorist, he couldn't begin to understand. Just the fact that Segal was talking to Nazim at all was a glaring red alarm beacon. And here they were, caught on camera together, only days ago.

Little wonder Romy was hiding. She must have known what kind of trouble she'd have been in if they'd spotted her. What suspicions had alerted her to sneak into the warehouse and film their conversation?

Ben badly needed to know, just as he eagerly wanted to hear what they'd been talking about. He let the video run on once more, holding the phone close to his ear and straining as hard as he could to sift their dialogue from the mess of the audio track. Nearly all of it was just too garbled and muffled to catch. But here and there he was able to pick out a word. They were talking Arabic, which it made sense for Segal to be able to speak, in his line of work. Ben thought he caught the word 'shuhna', referring to a 'shipment'. A moment later Nazim pointed towards the statues and Ben heard him say something about 'humula', which Ben recognised as the Arabic word for 'cargo'. Then there were a couple of passes of dialogue that he couldn't catch a word of, before he heard Segal mention 'almakan almaqsud', meaning 'destination'.

Then the conversation was over. Ben watched as Nazim turned away from the older man and started walking towards an exit off-camera, with Segal sheepishly following. Their path was going to take them straight past Romy's hiding place. The picture, already shaky, now scrambled into nothing as she darted back around the edge of the pillar to avoid being seen. Ben could hear the sharpness of her breathing, caught by the sensitive mic. He could almost smell her fear.

An instant later, the video clip ended. All fifty-two seconds of it.

Ben laid the phone down on the table and lit another Gauloise. Was Romy's employer doing some kind of deals with Nazim al-Kassar? What was the shipment? From the little that Ben had understood of their conversation, it looked as though the cargo they'd been talking about consisted of the old statues stored inside the warehouse. Since when was a murdering fanatic like Nazim in the antiquities export and import business? It seemed insane. Especially considering that Segal's business partner was supposed to be dead.

Romy must have thought it was insane, too. Ben tried to picture her movements after the two men left the warehouse. Waiting there, hidden, terrified, until the coast was clear. Sneaking out unseen, hoping she had left no trace that could bring suspicion on herself. He wondered what she must have been thinking as she travelled back to France, perhaps sitting on the plane right next to the man she'd covertly filmed and whose secret plans she'd somehow stumbled into learning. The fact that she'd kept the video clip encrypted on her phone had to mean that she was intending to use it somehow.

As leverage against Segal? Blackmail? Or to expose him? Whatever her idea had been, she'd been too slow, or too careless. Somehow they'd found her out. And she'd paid the price for it.

Ben could answer none of the questions that buzzed in his mind, without knowing more.

'If we can clean up the audio quality,' he said to Thierry, 'I'll pay you two thousand euros. That's on top of the thousand for what you've already done. Plus expenses. Make me a shopping list of whatever kit you need. I'll see to it you have everything you want.'

Thierry shrugged. 'I owe you for getting me out of the shit, but I won't say I couldn't use the cash. I'm flat broke and I've got to get out of Paris.'

'We'll take care of that. Meantime, you can lie low here. The Corsicans will never find you.'

'I appreciate your help, chief.'

'Just like old times,' Ben said. 'And there's something else I need you to do for me.'

Across Paris, Nazim al-Kassar was preparing to meet with his elder superior, Ibrahim al-Rashid, in a few hours' time when the old man's plane landed. Nazim feared few things in this life, and even fewer people. But though he appeared outwardly calm, he was nervous about the meeting for which al-Rashid was flying in specially from his current base in Pakistan. It was a rare event for the venerable, wise Imam to leave his protected haven, underlining the critical importance of their plan. With so much at stake and the date of the shipment fast approaching, Nazim had a great deal on his mind.

Nazim's driver in the silver Mercedes was an associate named Muhammad, as many were, in their different spellings.

After leaving the woman's apartment they had sped across the city to the expensive hotel where Nazim had a luxury suite under the false name of an Omani businessman called Khalil Alfazari.

Nazim had instructed Muhammad to wait downstairs in the lobby, and gone up to his room alone. The first thing he did upon entering the suite was to wash his hands very carefully and thoroughly. This was required after touching an infidel woman, for they were considered unclean in the sight of Allah and the dictates of Nazim's faith strictly forbade him from taking part in prayer unless he were first cleansed.

Once that important duty was done, he had stripped off the tainted clothes that would not be worn again, and stepped into the marble shower. He'd washed himself all over and let the hot water pummel his broad, muscular shoulders as he reflected on his morning's work. He was glad to have taken care of the Juneau woman personally. It would have taken only a snap of his fingers to have had one of his trusted associates do it for him, but Nazim believed strongly that cleansing the world of another filthy, shameless infidel whore would bring him closer to Allah. Moreover, she had posed a serious threat to their plans. Her elimination had been ordered without a second's hesitation.

While pleased with his killing of the unclean whore, he was annoyed with himself for having failed on other counts. The wiretap that had been placed on her landline phone had indicated that soon after her return from Tripoli she had attempted to make contact with a woman called Françoise. That was all the information they had on her, no surname. But the phone message that Romy Juneau had left for her suggested that the woman was someone with whom she was keen to share information. A reporter or journalist, maybe. Which made her potentially highly dangerous to their plans, if their suspicions about Romy Juneau were correct. The wiretap on the landline have yielded nothing more, which implied that Juneau might since have been in contact with this Françoise by mobile phone, whether spoken or texted.

Hence Nazim's intention, while inside Romy Juneau's apartment that morning, had been to obtain her mobile phone in the hope that it might lead them to Françoise. Who would then, naturally, need to be eliminated too. But to Nazim's deep annoyance, he'd been unable to find her mobile anywhere in her apartment. It wasn't in her handbag, or any of the other places he'd searched. The dirty infidel bitch must have hidden it. Nazim knew he had made a tactical mistake in killing her without first forcing her to hand it over.

That wasn't the only troubling matter on Nazim's mind. Of even more concern to him than the missing phone was the issue of the man he'd seen at her window immediately after the killing, as he stepped out into the street.

Nazim was absolutely certain that nobody else had been inside the apartment during the few minutes of his visit. He had carefully checked every room, not just in search of her mobile phone but also in case he needed to kill anyone else he found there. There was no doubt in his mind that the man at the window could *only* have entered the apartment after the Juneau woman was already dead and he, Nazim, had left. But the time gap had been very close, no more than a couple of minutes while Nazim rode the lift from the top floor and exited the building.

Thinking back, Nazim recalled the person he'd crossed on the stairs on his way down. He had deliberately kept his back turned, just in case, so as to avoid any potential witness giving his description to the police. Another mistake, one Nazim couldn't entirely blame himself for. Others, however, might be less forgiving.

But what perplexed and bewildered Nazim far more – left him so stunned that he'd hesitated to get into the getaway car and been virtually unable to speak all the way back to his hotel – was that he knew this man. He was sure of it. Rock-solid positive. Unquestionably, they had met before, in another country, far, far away and long, long ago.

Nazim had often thought about this man over the years. He still sometimes had vivid dreams when he relived the moment of his capture by the commander of the enemy Special Forces assault team who had raided the village near Tikrit that day, September 20, 2003. The one time in Nazim's career when he'd come perilously close to being defeated. On escaping, he'd made two vows to himself: the first, that he would never let himself be taken again; the second, that he would one day find this man who had so humiliated him and almost been his downfall.

He had tried, in vain, to find out the man's name. He'd learned that the operation had been a joint British and American venture, but the identities of SF soldiers were an impenetrable secret even for top ISIL spies.

Nazim had always believed that he would one day meet up again with the man without a name who haunted his dreams. He would never forget his face, not even if fifty more years went by before their next encounter. From the way their eye contact had locked and held tight for those few instants that seemed like minutes, he was convinced that the man remembered him, too.

Nazim now deeply regretted not having made Muhammad wait at the kerb while he returned upstairs to confront him. A third mistake, even more painful than the first two.

The burning question was, what was the man doing there? Why would he, an enemy soldier Nazim had encountered on the battlefields of Iraq all those years ago, suddenly reappear in this way? To Nazim, the answer was clear. The foreigner must be working as an agent. Like so many of his kind, who, after fulfilling their evil service in the cause of murdering the faithful to Allah, joined the military intelligence services in order to carry on their nefarious scheme by other means.

Which, in turn, had to mean that the plans being hatched by Nazim and his associates might be known, or at least partly known, to the enemy. And now Nazim was certain why he'd been unable to find the Juneau woman's phone. She must have given it to the foreigner, along with whatever information it contained, and whatever else she might have passed to him. It was a deeply worrying development. Something had to be done about it, before the whole plan came apart.

The man with no name must die, and soon.

Nazim al-Kassar dressed, returned downstairs to the hotel lobby and rejoined Muhammad, and the two of them walked to the silver Mercedes to meet with Ibrahim al-Rashid.

Chapter 16

Next, Ben had some expensive shopping to do. To fulfil his requirements Thierry had asked for a high-spec laptop computer, a laser printer and a laminating machine. The specialised sound editing software for cleaning up Romy's audio recording could be downloaded online.

Ben set off with his list, and returned to the safehouse two hours later with boxes that Thierry helped him bring inside and set about unpacking, along with some junk food and soft drinks for his temporary houseguests. He had additionally purchased some extra items he would need for himself, namely a charcoal-grey single-breasted suit, a white cotton shirt, a plain, sober navy-blue tie and a pair of black patent leather shoes not unlike the ones that the Corsicans had been wearing earlier that day. He went into the bedroom to change, and scrutinised himself in the mirror. By no means his usual attire, but he looked the part reasonably well enough to carry out the next phase of his plan. He changed back into his civvies and set the new clothes aside for later.

While Thierry finished setting up his equipment and got down to work, Ben took the opportunity to fill in the time with a little tourist sightseeing. His destination was the Louvre Museum, where his instincts told him he might find out more about the kinds of ancient art treasures he'd glimpsed in Romy's video clip.

Despite the light rain pattering from a slate-grey sky, the usual crowds of tourists thronged the entrance to the vast, palatial museum. After having to wait in line for a ticket, Ben made his way inside through the inverted glass pyramid, which he still thought was a hideous blot on the landscape, whatever anyone said. From there he cut a path through the exhibits, not pausing every few steps like the dawdling crowds of other visitors to drink in the magnificence of the collections, but instead following the guidebook and map he'd bought at the ticket desk to head briskly towards the Near Eastern Antiquities section on the ground floor. Those were housed in the Richelieu Wing, one of the museum's three main sections, and the least congested as it contained fewer of the big-name crowd pullers like the *Mona Lisa* or *Venus de Milo*.

Ben skirted without a second glance the wondrous apartments of Napoleon III, not one but two beautiful sculpture gardens, centuries of French, Dutch, Flemish and German paintings, and arts of Islam, until he found what he was looking for in the Mesopotamia section.

Mesopotamia: literally, 'the land between two rivers', the Tigris and the Euphrates. Soil that Ben had set foot on personally, as the ancient country had once covered most of what was now Iraq and Kuwait, as well as parts of Saudi Arabia and Syria. Known as the cradle of civilisation, through its long history it had been home to the Babylonian, Assyrian and Akkadian empires among other ancient kingdoms, been the scene of countless epic battles and seen its territories change hands through conquest after conquest as entire civilisations rose and flourished, then were invaded and put to the sword.

Some of that history Ben had studied as a young theology scholar at Oxford, in another life, before any notion of a military career had ever formed in his mind. It had been during that period, many years ago, that he'd first come here to the Louvre to visit the exhibits along with some college pal whose name he'd long since forgotten. On that first ever trip to Paris as a kid of nineteen he could never have dreamed he would later return under such different circumstances. Then again, most things about the course his life had taken could not have been easily predicted.

He made his way through the Mesopotamia section, passing ancient and priceless relics to his left and right. There was the seven-foot-high Babylonian stone tablet called the Code of Hammurabi. A lion frieze from the palace of Nebuchadnezzar. Everything but old King Neb's fabled golden idol. All highly impressive, but not what he'd come here to see.

Soon afterwards, Ben found what he was looking for.

Flanking each side of a tall archway stood a pair of massive statues that looked very similar to the biggest of the artifacts Romy Juneau had caught on camera while spying on her boss's conversation with Nazim al-Kassar. Ben had been sure he'd seen something like them before. His guess had been right: it had been right here in this very spot, all those years ago. They were giant winged bulls with the heads of men, over four metres in height and length. According to the exhibit label the huge sculptures, called 'Lamassu', had been carved from solid blocks of alabaster more than two and a half thousand years ago, during the reign of Sargon II. They had been excavated from the remains of the Assyrian king's citadel at Dur Sharrukin, now Khorsabad in Nineveh Province, northern Iraq.

Ben spent a moment in reflection. He had never seen Khorsabad itself, but nearby Mosul, just fifteen kilometres away, had been a site of strategic bombings and Special Forces ops prior to its capture by Coalition troops in April 2003. Later it had become the scene of multiple suicide attacks and assassinations as the militants refused to be defeated. Persecution of Assyrian Christians by the Islamics had lasted for years, and eventually ISIL had taken over the city in their Northern Iraq Offensive, with disastrous consequences for its inhabitants.

Returning to the present, Ben had to marvel at the craftsmanship of the two Lamassu. The expressions on their human faces were benevolent, almost kindly, with eyes that seemed to return his gaze. Each had curly beards cut off square at the ends, and prominent noses below thick eyebrows. On top of their heads each wore a crown or tiara, either side of which sprouted bull's horns. Their huge bodies seemed to ripple with living muscle, and had been cleverly sculpted with five legs instead of four, creating an optical illusion that made them look as though they were standing to attention when viewed from the front, but walking when seen from the side. Ben's guidebook explained that such androcephalic, or human-headed, bulls were a characteristic feature of the decoration of Assyrian palaces.

Having seen all he needed to see, he left the museum wondering how many more Lamassu must remain hidden among the ruins of ancient undiscovered palaces beneath the sands of Iraq and its neighbouring countries, waiting for archaeologists to come and unearth them. Not to mention their cultural value, their monetary worth must be inestimable. It was little wonder that people like Julien Segal spent entire careers scouring some of the world's most dangerous places in search of such treasures.

Except members of Julien Segal's profession didn't, as a rule, frequent known terrorists, nor do mysterious deals with them that somehow resulted in the deaths of innocent employees.

Ben returned to his car deep in thought about the warehouse in the video clip. Was this Segal's own storage facility? It made sense for someone in his position to own or rent secure spaces where artifacts could be kept protected while in transit from their home countries to wherever they were destined to end up. More than ever, Ben wished he'd managed to find out from Jeanne at the Institute where Romy's recent field trip abroad had taken her. Then he might be able to discover where Segal's meeting with Nazim al-Kassar had taken place. Which might not tell him much, but right now a little knowledge was worth a lot to him.

Perhaps Bernard Dubois could have another go at finding out. Getting into the car, Ben pulled out his burner phone and dialled the Institute's number again, but the offices were now closed and all he got was a voicemail message asking him to leave his name and number. He put the burner away and checked his other phone, with a pang of annoyance that Ken Keegan in London hadn't yet been in touch with a contact for Tyler Roth. Blocked at every damned turn.

He was about to put that phone away too when it started burring in his hand. It was Thierry, calling from the safehouse.

'Got something here to show you, chief.'

Ben was surprised. 'You finished working on the audio already?'

'Not quite done there. I've uploaded the video file to the laptop and grabbed the software I need from the web. The audio cleanup might take me a while. But the other thing you asked for is ready to rock.'

'Fast work.'

'That's why you pay me the big bucks.'

'I'm on my way.'

Chapter 17

Back at the safehouse, Thierry proudly showed Ben what he'd cooked up for him. And as far as Ben could tell, it was indistinguishable from the real thing. The master forger had proved his worth yet again.

The laminated ID card featured a red, white and blue diagonal stripe across one corner, across its centre the official header of the French Ministry of the Interior and the words DIRECTION GENERALE DE LA POLICE NATIONALE. The mugshot of Ben in suit, tie and slicked-back hair had been snapped earlier with a phone camera and artfully fiddled to look like a passport photo. For the purposes of the fake police ID his new name was Inspector Jacques Dardenne. Ben had come up with the name off the top of his head and wasn't sure that he liked it, but it would do fine.

'If I'd had more time I might have been able to rustle you up a proper badge,' Thierry said ruefully. 'The card alone will only get you so far.'

'This is excellent, Thierry. More than enough for what I need.'

'I'm not even going to ask what you want it for.'

'You never asked me before.'

'And that's the way I like it.'

In truth, Ben wasn't happy about what he had to do next.

He'd mulled it over long and hard before coming to the reluctant decision that he had no choice. By mid-afternoon he was driving across the city to the commune of Fontenay-sous-Bois in the suburbs to the east. The 'bois', or woods, in the name referred to the nearby Bois de Vincennes, which was the two-thousand-acre park and former hunting grounds of the kings of France. But Ben wasn't interested in taking a scenic tour of the famous botanical gardens or the Château de Vincennes. His purpose was grimmer and darker, and he was feeling like shit about it before he even got there.

Romy Juneau's parents lived in a modest middle-class home in a pleasant, tranquil street that felt like a million miles from any of the disturbances that had been affecting the city of late. All except one. Several hours would have gone by since the police had informed them of their daughter's death. Their grief would be raw and Ben felt he had no business intruding on them at a time like this. He drove past the house twice, hating himself, and very nearly turned back, before he finally willed himself to park outside their front gate.

The police had probably spent some time with the family that morning, but were gone now and the coast was clear. Ben straightened his tie in the rear-view mirror, anything to delay the moment. With a sigh he stepped out of the car and forced himself to push open the creaky garden gate, walk up the flower-lined path to the house and ring the doorbell. Facing a vicious and determined enemy with a gun in your hand was nothing next to this.

The house was small but well cared for, with ivy growing around the front door and wooden shutters on the windows. He stood on the doorstep for nearly two long, uncomfortable minutes before he heard sounds of movement from inside, and the front door slowly opened a few inches wide on its security chain. The face that peered out at him through the gap was one he'd seen before, in the birthday photo on Romy's phone. Madame Juneau hadn't looked especially great in the picture, but now she looked like death. She was in her late fifties but at this moment could have passed for fifteen years older. Her face was gaunt and streaked with tears, her dyed blond hair was a mess and her eyes were puffy and red from crying.

Ben opened his wallet to show the police ID. 'Madame Juneau? I'm Inspector Jacques Dardenne from the Prefecture of Police. I'm very sorry to disturb you, but may I have a moment, please?'

Romy's mother blinked several times and stared at him as though she didn't understand. She barely glanced at the fake ID. Then she managed to croak, 'What do you want? The police were already here earlier. Can't you see we're grieving? My only child died today.'

Ben wasn't being insincere as he repeated his deepest apologies for the intrusion. 'I just need a couple of minutes of your time, Madame Juneau. Is Monsieur Juneau here?'

'He's in bed. My husband is not a well man. This will be the end of him, I'm sure. You can come in, as long as it's quick.'

'I promise.'

She unlatched the chain and Ben, feeling like he was drowning puppies in a sack, stepped inside the hallway. The wallpaper was flowery, like the furniture inside the chintzy living room into which she showed him. The air was so thick with unspeakable grief that he could smell it. He could also smell the booze. Madame Juneau was halfway through a large gin and tonic. Not her first of the day, judging by the unsteadiness in her gait. He couldn't blame her. If something like this had happened to his son Jude, he'd have been on the floor by now, surrounded by empty bottles.

Madame Juneau was gamely holding it together, though. She offered him tea, which he courteously declined, and perched on the edge of the flowery armchair opposite his. 'How can I help you, Inspector, ah—?'

'Dardenne. I'm in charge of the investigation. Please accept my sincerest condolences, and my promise to you that I will do everything in my power to catch this man and bring him to justice.' Ben wasn't lying about that part.

She sniffed, wiped an eye and nodded sadly. 'Thank you. But I'm a little confused. I thought that Detective Boucher was in charge. Valérie. Such a nice lady. Said I could call her any time, day or night. Are you working with her?'

'I am,' Ben said solemnly, mightily glad to have learned that Detective Boucher was a she, or else he might have put his foot in it. 'She sent me here to fill in a few details.'

'Whatever I can do to help. Although I don't know what I can tell you that I haven't already told the others. It's obvious who did this. I always said to Romy that no good could come of hanging around with filthy Arabs.'

Lovely. There was nothing like emotional distress to bring out the best in people. Ben wondered what filthy Arabs in particular she was referring to. He measured his words and asked, 'Are you saying you can identify the perpetrator?'

'Of course I can identify him,' she replied, her sorrow flaring into anger that flushed her cheeks. 'Didn't I always tell her that boy was no good for her? No good for anything, just like all his kind. He doesn't even have a proper job. But she fought me and fought me. Wouldn't listen. Said her salary was enough to support them both until he found decent work of his own. Said they were going to move in together and get married. I told her, "You have a child with that filth, I won't have it in my home. I won't see it, and I won't acknowledge it."'

Madame Juneau was growing more charming by the second, but Ben had to play along. Let her get it out, he thought, if that's what helps her deal with her pain.

'I was happy when she finally saw sense and dumped him. I thought she would be free of him then, free to find someone new and worthy of her. But how wrong I was. Because now he's killed her,' she said in a hollow and ghastly voice, her eyes clouded with brimming tears. 'She jilted him and he murdered her for it. Our baby, taken from us. Just like that. Thanks to that scum. How is that right? Tell me how that's right.'

The depth of her agony was so overwhelming that Ben found it hard to look at her. He asked, 'Are we talking about Michel?'

Hearing the name made her flush even more angrily. 'Michel Yassa,' she said, her face twisting as though it tortured her to utter it. 'He's the filthy Arab who killed my daughter.' She pushed herself unsteadily from her armchair and teetered over to a framed picture that sat on a sideboard. Picking it up, she brought it over to show Ben. The photo was a few decades old and showed a man in French military uniform, who Ben presumed must be her husband. Madame Juneau croaked, 'If poor Henri wasn't so sick he would hunt him down like the animal he is and give him what he deserves. Henri was in the army, like his father. He shot an Algerian.'

'Henri shot an Algerian?'

'No, his father did, in the war over there in '61. But Henri would have shot that bastard Yassa. So would I, if I could.' Madame Juneau put down the picture and crumpled into the armchair, melting into floods of tears.

Ben could have told her that Michel Yassa wasn't the killer, but that would have been inviting too many questions about what else he knew. And he couldn't discount the possibility that Michel Yassa was somehow mixed up in this. There could be more going on than Ben had realised.

He waited a few moments for her tears to subside, then asked, 'How did Romy and this Yassa meet?'

She wiped her eyes and shrugged bitterly. 'How on earth should I know? At some party or nightclub, I suppose. She just started mentioning him one day. We never asked, because we didn't want to know. He's just a deadbeat. A degenerate. Probably spends most of his time hanging out with other deadbeats and degenerates just like him. What does it matter? All I care about is that the police will be onto him now, and justice will be done.'

'You said he doesn't have a proper job. What does he do for money?'

'He works part-time in that awful bar. Cleaning toilets, probably. Who would trust scum like that with any kind of responsibility? She was often there with him, drinking, dancing, God knows what. I told her a nice, respectable young lady doesn't go to a place like that.'

Ben's memory flashed back to the picture on Romy's phone that showed her and Michel standing outside the bar. 'Le Geronimo?'

Madame Juneau frowned. 'Yes, that's the name. I'd forgotten it, or else I would have told Detective Boucher.'

'That's not a problem. I'll tell her myself. Did you happen to give her an address for Michel Yassa?'

She shrugged and shook her head. 'No, I don't have it. But I told her I know he lives in one of those terrible housing projects in Saint-Denis. That's where they all live. Like rats in a hole.'

'Did Romy go to visit him there often?'

'I told her it wasn't safe there. No decent French girl in her right mind would go near that place. Those that do are always getting attacked and raped. But she wouldn't listen to me. She never listened. Always going off to dangerous places, and we'd warn her against it, and off she'd go anyway. Last time it was Tripoli, in Libya.'

Ben realised that she was talking about Romy's recent field trip. This was the information he needed. 'That would be for her job with the Institut Segal, yes?'

'She went there with the director. Otherwise I'd have been terrified. You hear all these stories about what happens to white girls travelling in those countries.' She gave a bitter laugh. 'Except nowhere is safe now, is it?'

'Tell me more about her trip to Libya. Do you know the dates she went there and came back?'

Madame Juneau didn't need to think about it, because the memory was very recent. 'It was only last week. She came home just a couple of days ago. Why are you asking? I don't see the point.'

So Romy had been in Tripoli when the video clip was taken, three days ago. Which also meant that the meeting between Segal and Nazim, which she'd secretly witnessed and caught on camera, had taken place there. Then Romy had returned home to Paris the following day, when she'd called Michel for the first time in weeks. If Ben told her mother that Romy's last phone contact with her ex-boyfriend had been just that morning, not long before her death, it would make Michel look even more like a suspect in her eyes.

Ben replied, 'Just gathering information, Madame Juneau. One more thing. Did Romy speak Arabic?'

She looked at him as though it were a strange question. 'I don't know. Maybe. She might have been learning it for her work. That's not important, is it? All I care about is catching that filth. I thought the police were already hunting for him, instead of coming round here asking me more questions. I've been sitting here waiting for the phone to ring, telling me that they've got him. I hope he tries to run, so they shoot him in the legs before they drag him to prison. I want him to suffer for what he's done.'

Ben could see she was becoming more and more agitated. He stood up and said, 'Madame Juneau, I've troubled you enough. Again, please accept my condolences for your loss, and my apologies for disturbing you at this difficult time.'

'Just find the animal who murdered my little girl,' she said, and started crying again.

Ben touched her arm. 'Make no mistake, that's exactly what I'm going to do,' he replied, and left.

Chapter 18

Ben drove fast away from Fontenay-sous-Bois, as relieved to have escaped from the pressure cooker of a mother's grief as he was focused on what he had to do next.

His imperative now was to track down Michel Yassa before the police did. If there was any connection between Yassa and Nazim al-Kassar, the former's arrest for Romy's murder would be certain to drive his accomplice deep underground. Ben had no idea what that connection might be. There probably wasn't any. But if there was, he would find it. And if there wasn't, it still didn't hurt to find out more. Why had Romy suddenly called him twice after weeks of no contact, the last time just minutes before she died? If the guy knew anything at all that could shed light on this thing, Ben wanted to know it too.

He stopped for fuel, then pulled up in a layby near the filling station and left the motor running while he checked his phone. Still nothing from Keegan about Tyler Roth. No word from Thierry, either. But Ben didn't have time to feel frustrated. He took out Romy's phone and looked again at the photo of her and Michel outside the bar. Le Geronimo was a lead that Detective Valérie Boucher didn't have, and with that he gained a tactical advantage over her.

A quick web search using his own phone threw up the

address of the bar, which turned out to be in the same area that Romy's mother had said she thought Michel lived, Saint-Denis. Which meant the cops might have a rough idea where to find him, but no specific location to begin searching.

Ben slammed the Alpina into gear and took off. Saint-Denis was to the north of Paris, about twenty-five minutes' drive from where he was now, less if he put his foot down. He picked up the A3 Autoroute and stormed northwards, keeping a watchful eye out for traffic police, then hit the A1 and veered west towards his destination.

As one of the most important historical centres of France, Saint-Denis was named after the great medieval basilica at its heart, whose tower Ben could see dominating the skyline as he approached. He was no historian, but he knew about the treasures that the cathedral housed, like the crown of Charlemagne and the relics of the third-century bishop who would go on to become the patron saint of Paris. The Basilica of Saint-Denis had been a place of pilgrimage through the Middle Ages, and home to the tombs of French royalty dating back to the sixth century, including some of its most notorious players like Louis XVI and Marie Antoinette. Another of its famous incumbents was the Frankish king Charles Martel, 'the Hammer', who crushed the advance of the invasion force of the Umayyad Caliphate led by Abdul Rahman al-Ghafiqi at the Battle of Tours in 732.

But for all its rich cultural heritage, Saint-Denis was far from being a popular tourist spot. Mention its name to most Parisians and the typical response was a frown or a sigh. The place's reputation for crime and danger had been further tarnished by the terror attack that had claimed the lives of 130 victims in the nearby stadium a few years earlier. The surviving perpetrators of the atrocity had shot it out with the police at a Saint-Denis apartment building. All of which contributed sadly to the negative attitude taken by people like Romy Juneau's mother against the whole area.

Outside the cathedral the market square looked more like a souk than a European street market, filled with colour and bustle, and as Ben filtered through the crowded neighbourhood he could easily have believed he was in Marrakesh or Istanbul. A little further on stood social housing projects that might have appeared fresh and modern and optimistic back when they were first thrown up to accommodate the waves of immigrants coming in, but now they came over as sad and stained. He wondered if Michel Yassa lived in one of them.

The Geronimo bar where Yassa hung out was just a couple more blocks away, on the corner of a cobbled street opposite a halal butcher's shop. Around the side of the bar was a narrow alleyway choked with empty crates and wheelie bins. Ben parked the Alpina near the entrance to the alleyway and walked inside the bar.

The bar's interior was long and narrow, and not busy. The tall buildings opposite blocked out most of the light, so that what little of it filtered through the dirty windows made for a dim, murky ambiance. It had looked pretty basic in the photos on Romy's phone, and wasn't any better in real life. Not quite spit'n'sawdust, but not far off it.

Ben's plan was to scout the place, ask around, get talking to people and pretend to be someone who owed Michel Yassa money and had come to pay, in the hope that he'd be pointed in the right direction. The best place to start in such cases was generally the bar itself, where the lone barman was busy washing up glasses. Ben would buy a drink, pull up a bar stool and start the conversation by asking casually whether Michel was working today.

But he never got that far, because luck was already with

him. Glancing around the dim room Ben noticed a young dark-haired guy sitting by himself at a table near the back, near a doorway with a sign pointing towards the bathrooms. He was wearing faded jeans, white trainers and a G-Unit hoodie, and bore a striking resemblance to the fellow in Romy's photos.

Evidently, the police hadn't caught up with him yet. Michel Yassa didn't appear to be expecting them to. He showed no appearance of being a man on the run. In fact he was going nowhere at all, and clearly hadn't moved for some time. He was slouching low on a red vinyl bench seat, apparently lost in a world of his own as he gazed at the bottle of beer in front of him with a vacant look that Ben guessed might have something to do with the five more empties on his table. It looked as if he'd bought them all at once and been working his way steadily through them.

Yassa didn't look as though he was planning on leaving any time soon, but Ben kept an eye on him as he went over to the bar and bought a single measure of a blended brand that was the only scotch Le Geronimo stocked. He carried his drink over to a table a distance away from Yassa's and sat watching him. The barman didn't seem to give a damn, so Ben lit up a Gauloise. Just like old times.

Four minutes later, Michel Yassa hauled himself up from his seat and began making his way a little unsteadily towards the doorway leading towards the toilets. Ben set down his empty glass, stubbed his cigarette into it, stood and followed.

By the time he reached the doorway, Yassa had disappeared through it. Beyond was a long, dingy corridor with a bare brick outer wall that he guessed ran parallel with the alleyway outside. The men's toilets were off to the right. Ben entered and found Yassa at one of the urinals, standing with his back to him and one hand pressed against the tiled wall for support. He was weaving on his feet.

Ben let him finish and get zipped up. Yassa turned to leave without bothering to wash his hands, and only then did he register Ben's presence. He hesitated, then went to push past Ben towards the doorway.

Ben said, 'Michel.'

Yassa stopped. 'Do I know you?' He blinked. Stared, confused at first. Then his bleary eyes focused into a look of terror, and the drunken haze receded like a gale force wind ripping into a blanket of North Sea fog. He backed away from Ben with his arms outstretched and his palms raised. 'No! No! Please! Don't kill me!'

Ben had no idea why Michel Yassa thought he was going to kill him. But he worried that the guy was about to start yelling and screaming for help, which might draw all kinds of attention Ben didn't want. This was meant to be a private conversation.

So he knocked him out with a punch to the jaw, caught him as he fell, and bent low and scooped his unconscious body up over his shoulder. Back out in the corridor, he found a fire escape door with a panic bolt. As he'd guessed, it led outside to the alleyway. He could see the Alpina parked at the mouth of the alley.

Ben carried Michel Yassa past the stacked crates and rows of bins, and out into the cobbled street. One or two people were around, but either they hadn't noticed anything unusual or kidnapping was just daily routine in this neighbourhood. Ben opened up the car boot, dumped Michel Yassa inside, then slammed the lid, got behind the wheel and took off.

Moments later, he passed an incoming fleet of police cars with lights and sirens going. The cavalry had finally arrived, and were headed towards the social housing buildings up the street. He watched them screech to a halt and clamber from their cars. A small but hard-looking female plain-clothes officer with shoulder-length fair hair jumped out of the lead vehicle, wearing an open jacket that showed the sidearm on her hip, and marched towards the building with a look of fierce determination. Detective Boucher, personally leading the troops to bring Romy Juneau's killer to justice.

Ben smiled to himself as he drove past them with Michel Yassa in the boot. 'The early bird gets the worm, Valérie.'

Chapter 19

When Nazim al-Kassar arrived at the Georges V, one of Paris's most exclusive hotels, the venerable Ibrahim al-Rashid was sitting quietly on a sofa in his suite with several of his retinue around him, as well as his personal bodyguards and a number of other members of their group.

Al-Rashid was surrounded by an aura of great authority and commanded the deepest of respect. Nobody knew exactly how old he was, but his long beard was as snowy white as his turban and the traditional *thobe* robe that draped around his tall, slender, slightly stooped frame. To his devotees, one of the many proofs of the man's infinite wisdom was the fact that he had never been charged, or even questioned, in connection with any jihadist organisation or act. This was the ultimate demonstration of *al-Taqiyya*, the art of dissimulation, whereby the Qur'an provided detailed guidance on those circumstances under which the faithful could disguise their true ideology in order to deceive and protect themselves from the infidel. For nearly forty years al-Rashid had orchestrated his terror operations from behind a curtain of calculated secrecy, while maintaining the outward appearance of a saintly and humble man of peace. As a result he was able to travel freely around the world with no need for the aliases and false identities his soldiers required to stay one step ahead of the infidel intelligence services.

One of the means by which he preserved his anonymity and freedom was the swift, unhesitant elimination of anyone he suspected even slightly of treachery. Another was his strict avoidance of any form of modern communications technology. He would have nothing to do with telephones, let alone texts or emails. All discussion was to be carried out face to face, and even then only in utmost secrecy.

Nazim wasn't armed, but let al-Rashid's stern-faced bodyguards frisk him before he was allowed to approach. One of them swept him with a hand-held scanner to check for wires or microphones. Normally Nazim would not have submitted to such indignities, but he said nothing.

Once that was done, the old man waved him across and remained seated as Nazim walked over. They exchanged warm greetings in Arabic, and then al-Rashid reached out with a bony hand and patted the sofa cushion next to him. 'Come, sit and talk to me.'

Nazim accepted the honour of sitting by him, and gave his report on the morning's events – or at any rate those he felt inclined to share. Ibrahim al-Rashid smiled at the news of the Juneau woman's killing. It had been he himself, trusting nobody, who had ordered them to place the phone tap that had alerted them to her treachery. He was happy to hear that his precaution had brought results and the potential threat to their plan had been eliminated.

'Allahu akbar walillahi'l-hamd.' *Allah is great and to Allah we give praise.*

'Mashallah,' replied Nazim. *Allah has willed it.*

'There remains the matter of the other infidel female,' the old man said, with a certain air of disgust as though even referring to her left a bad taste in his mouth. 'If she too poses a threat, then she too must be dealt with.'

Al-Rashid was talking about the woman called Françoise, still untraced and at large, and an unknown risk factor although one could never be too careful. Nazim assured him that all efforts were being made on that front. 'We will find her and do whatever is necessary. She will not be a problem.'

The old man seemed pleased. 'Now, tell me how things progress with the shipment.'

'My meeting in Libya with our Parisian associate left me in no doubt that the plan will proceed smoothly, thanks to his connections. He has seen to it that the export permits and other administrative matters are all in order. The cargo departed from the Port of Tripoli aboard a MAERSK container ship two days ago. Transit time is seven days, if the passage is smooth, God willing.'

'Mashallah. Our associate is indeed a useful asset. Did he personally travel with the cargo?'

'No, but we have a man aboard the ship, overseeing the safety of the cargo. When the vessel reaches the Port of Le Havre our associate will be there to meet it. From there it will be transported by road to its final destination. I will be personally seeing to the distribution arrangements.'

The language both men used was deliberately vague, but everyone in the room knew exactly what was being discussed, and what the plan aimed to achieve.

'Excellent,' the old man said with a smile. 'It sounds as though nothing can stand in our way. I am proud of you, Nazim. This new strategy will drive a knife deep into the belly of the infidel and bring the House of War to its knees, inshallah.'

'I am but a humble slave of Allah,' Nazim replied piously.

The old man nodded. '"Fight them and Allah will punish

them by your hands, lay them low, and cover them with shame,"' he said, quoting from the Qur'an. '"Therefore smite them on their necks and every joint and incapacitate them. Strike off their heads and cut off each of their fingers and toes. He will help you over them, and we will fight them until there is no more disbelief and all submit to the religion of Allah alone."'

From around the room came murmurs of reverence at the sacred words they had all known since boyhood. 'Now let us have some tea,' said al-Rashid, gesturing over to one of his men who stood by a sideboard with a silver tray filled with cups and saucers, 'and we will talk more.'

The tea was served, and while they drank the old Imam seemed to be watching Nazim with a curious eye. After a time he observed, 'You appear troubled, my son. What is the matter?'

Nazim was afraid to tell him what was on his mind, about the man he'd seen at the window of the woman's apartment that morning. Even more afraid to have to confess that he'd allowed the man to go free. Such errors would not go unpunished. So Nazim just smiled and said, 'Forgive me if I seemed distracted. I was just going over the details of the plan in my mind.'

'Be at peace, Nazim,' the old man reassured him. 'Remember the message with which our Lord inspired the angels: "I am with you. Give firmness to the Believers. I will terrorise the unbelievers. And for those who believe and do good deeds will be gardens; the fulfilment of all desires."'

Soon after, it was time for the Asr, or afternoon prayer. All in the room prostrated themselves facing east towards Mecca, to symbolise the unity of the Islamic Ummah. The wise old man led the recitation of the four rakats that offered their devoted service to Allah.

Once their prayers were done, Ibrahim al-Rashid and his retinue made to leave for the airport. There were smiles and handshakes and warm assurances that they would all meet again, in this world or the next. The bodyguards checked the corridor, then the old man was escorted from the suite and left.

One of the men left inside the suite was a younger member called Sarfaraz Baqri. He was a loyal soldier who had been involved with a number of operations in France. He was strong on the technical side and knew a lot about chemicals and electronics, and his reputation as the techno-whizzkid of the gang was the reason Nazim now wanted his advice. Sarfaraz was talking to another trusted associate named Mohammed when Nazim took them aside and said he wanted to speak privately.

Without confiding too many details, he told them about the man who had involved himself in their affairs and whom they must now track down. Sarfaraz listened without comment, then asked, 'How do we find him, if we don't know his name or where he lives?'

'I'm certain that he has the Juneau woman's phone. If we can locate its whereabouts, it can lead us to him. Can you do that?'

Sarfaraz shrugged. 'Sure, no problem. All we'd need is the number.'

'I can find that out with one phone call.'

'Okay. Once you have it, we can feed it into a GPS phone tracking app, and we can find him, easy.'

'Even if it's not turned on, or not connected to the internet?'

Sarfaraz found the older man's lack of technical savvy amusing, but allowed himself only a slight smile out of respect. After all, Nazim al-Kassar had been engaged in heroic jihad when Sarfaraz was still barely out of nappies.

'Used to be, it was just governments and agency spooks who had the means to do stuff like that,' the young man explained. 'But not any more. I just need to get back to my place and get my kit. Then as long as he's still got the phone it'll take me just seconds to pinpoint him to within a metre.'

Nazim said, 'Then get to it. I want this man dead.'

Chapter 20

Ben didn't have to travel far to have his private conversation with Michel Yassa. Just half an hour's drive to the east from Saint-Denis lay the Forêt de Bondy. Once upon a time the deep, dark, sprawling forest had encircled the whole eastern side of the city and provided a notorious refuge for brigands and cutthroats. Now it was given over mostly to drug dealers and tourism, though there were still enough woodland trails and secluded areas for Ben's purposes.

He found a track wide enough for the car to negotiate and pushed as deep into the forest as he could, until he came to a lonely clearing in the middle of thick oaks and beeches, golden with the colours of autumn and fast shedding their leaves. This was as good a spot as any. He killed the engine and got out. The carpet of dead leaves and moss was spongy and soft underfoot as he walked around to the back of the car and opened the boot to reveal his prisoner curled up inside, blinking at the sudden light and looking fairly traumatised. The effects of Michel Yassa's daytime drinking session had all but worn off.

Ben said, 'All right, now let's talk. Where's al-Kassar?'

'I . . . I don't . . . I thought . . .'

Ben reached behind his hip and drew out one of the Glocks he'd appropriated from the Corsicans earlier, minus its cumbersome silencer. He pointed the muzzle in Michel Yassa's face. 'Are you going to lie to me, Michel? Because I don't have a lot of time for liars. You're going to tell me where I can find your associates, or I'm going to leave you here in the woods.'

'If you're here to kill me, then stop playing games and get on with it. I don't care. But you didn't have to hurt her, you bastard.'

Now it was Ben's turn to be confused. He lowered the pistol. It had only been a bluff anyway, since he was all but certain that Michel had nothing whatsoever to do with Nazim al-Kassar. But that was the only certainty in his mind. 'Why do you think I'm here to kill you?'

Michel Yassa stared up at him. His eyes were wide and crazed with fear and grief. 'You work for them, don't you? How much did they pay you to kill her?'

Ben stared back at him, then said, 'Get out of the car, Michel.'

Michel slowly, warily climbed out of the boot and looked around him. Ben could tell that he was thinking of bolting off into the trees. 'Go for it,' he said. 'I'll only catch you and drag you back here, and I won't be so gentle this time.'

'Shoot me, then, you piece of *merde*.'

'I'm not going to shoot you, Michel.'

'Then what the fuck do you want from me?'

'To talk. That's all.'

'You have a gun. You pointed it at me.'

'It was a test. You passed.'

'If you're not here to kill me, then who the hell are you?'

'I'm your friend,' Ben said. 'Maybe the best friend you've got right now. Everyone else seems to think you murdered her.'

Michel's face twisted in pain. 'I wouldn't have hurt a hair on her head! I loved her!'

'I know you didn't kill her,' Ben said. 'I was there just moments after it happened. I saw the man who did it. His name is Nazim, and he's not a very nice person. You don't look surprised to hear that, Michel. Because you were expecting someone bad to come knocking, weren't you? Why else did you think I'd come to kill you?'

Michel fell to his knees in the dirt and dead leaves, sobbing like a child. 'Why'd it have to be her? Why couldn't they have just killed me instead? She didn't deserve to be punished for what I did.'

This wasn't making sense. 'Punished for what, Michel?'

But Michel just went on weeping, tears pouring down his face and dripping off his chin. 'They slaughtered my family, now they've come for me. But killing me wasn't enough for those sick, cruel bastards. How did they find her? How?'

Ben crouched down in front of him and gripped his quaking shoulders. 'Michel. Stop crying. Get it together and speak to me.'

It took a while, but Michel managed to calm himself, and then a little while after that he began to talk.

Michel explained that he was from Egypt, and had immigrated to France in 2015 along with the huge wave of new arrivals into the country that year. Though he was a Coptic Orthodox Christian, he'd had to fake being Muslim to get into France, since he claimed that the immigration authorities were turning away Christian minorities from Middle Eastern countries for fear of offending the Islamic majority. He hadn't come to France by choice, but been forced to flee Egypt after his family, like many other Christians there, were persecuted by Sunni extremists of the Muslim Brotherhood. Officially they were considered terrorists by the Egyptian government, but Michel believed that the authorities secretly supported them. The situation there was getting worse every year.

'What happened to your family?' Ben asked.

Michel struggled to contain his emotions as he talked. 'My parents were kidnapped from our home and beheaded. My sister and I ran away, but she was caught, forced to convert to Islam and marry a Muslim man. When she rebelled against him, she was stoned to death in the street by a mob. I only heard about it afterwards, because I was in hiding. I took a gun and went to the house of my dead sister's husband. When he answered the door I shot him in the gut, then ran. Later I found out that he didn't die. As much as I hated him for what he'd done, I thanked the Lord for not letting me become a murderer like the people who wiped out my family.'

Michel took a deep breath, then went on, 'Then I had to escape from Egypt. I had a small amount of money, but the trafficking gangs who bring you into Europe, they rob you of everything. Eventually I managed to reach France. I thought I was safe here. I was trying to make my way, and forget about the bad things that had happened back home, even though I couldn't forget. I had a rough time of it at first, arriving in Europe with no money, nowhere to live. A week after I got to Paris I got caught shoplifting for food. I thought I was going to be deported. But then things got better. I found the job at the bar and worked hard. Then I met Romy, and we fell in love. I never told her about my past. It seemed like my life was starting to go well. But I was always afraid that the Brotherhood would come looking for me one day, out of revenge. I thought they might murder me, or kidnap me and take me back to

Egypt to be tortured and executed. They have people everywhere. White guys too.'

Now it was clear to Ben why the young guy had acted so terrified of him. 'You believe they hurt Romy to punish you for what you did, and you were next. And I understand why you think that, Michel. But you're wrong. This isn't your fault. The man who killed her is an Iraqi, not an Egyptian. And he's way too high up the chain of command to be running errands for the gangsters who harmed your family. Something else is going on.'

It wasn't easy telling someone that he and his dead family were too small fry for the real bad guys to bother about.

Michel looked at Ben through swimming eyes full of confusion and anguish, fear and anger all mixed up. He said, 'If it's not about me, why would those men go after Romy? What has she done to them?'

Ben replied, 'I don't know that yet. But I believe it's connected with her work somehow. Romy recently accompanied her boss on a business trip to Libya. While she was there, she overheard and managed to secretly film a conversation between him and the man I told you about, Nazim al-Kassar.'

'What conversation?'

'Something to do with ancient statues, art treasures stored in a warehouse in Tripoli waiting to be exported, possibly to Europe though I can't say for sure. The two of them were discussing a plan of some kind. Whatever it was, Romy was troubled enough by it to stay hidden. And she was right to be. Whatever's going on, her boss has been in cahoots with some very bad people.'

'Oh, Jesus Lord.'

'I believe that's the reason she got into danger. Someone

found out that she knew, and they silenced her before she could tell anyone.'

The colour had drained from Michel Yassa's cheeks. 'How do you know all this? How are you involved?'

And so Ben told him everything.

Chapter 21

Michel listened in hushed silence as Ben laid it all out, from the beginning. How he'd bumped into Romy in the street, the way she'd appeared anxious and had been distracted enough not to notice that she'd dropped her phone. He described how he'd traced her address, and gone there to return her property. Everything except the history between himself and Nazim al-Kassar.

Then he took out her phone to show Michel, and let him see the video clip. Silent tears ran down Michel's face as he handled the phone. He ran his fingers over it as though he thought he could touch her through it. Smelled it as though it might retain a trace of her scent. He said nothing as he watched the video, then reluctantly handed the phone back to Ben.

'Does it mean anything to you?'

'Nothing. I'm sorry. I never asked her a lot about her work.'

Ben said, 'The call records show that you and she hadn't spoken much by phone in the last few weeks. But they also show that she called you twice since she got back from her trip, two days ago and then again this morning. What did she say to you?'

'I was surprised to hear from her. Like you say, we hadn't

spoken for a while. We'd split up, you know? All because of her mother. That evil racist old snake badmouthed me to Romy so much, she managed to convince her to break up the relationship. Can you believe that?'

'I've met Madame Juneau,' Ben said. 'She is what she is.'

'So when Romy called two days ago, at first I was so happy to hear her voice after all those weeks. But she sounded scared. I asked her what was wrong, but she wouldn't tell me much over the phone. Just that she thought she was being followed. Said these guys had been tailing her in the street since she got back. Two or three of them, at different times.'

'What kind of guys?'

'Middle Eastern or North African, she said. It freaked me out, because I was suddenly thinking that the Brotherhood must have found me. I'd never, ever thought they would target her to get to me. I pleaded with her to come and stay with me for a few days. I told her she'd be safe there. Told her I'd look after her. But I think she thought I was trying to get back together with her or something. And maybe she was right. I still loved her. But most of all I just wanted her to be safe.'

A tear rolled out of Michel's eye and he wiped it. He went on, 'I guess I pushed too hard. Suddenly she's getting all cagey with me, like she regretted calling me and only did it to get it off her chest. Said forget it, she could handle it, and there was someone else who could help her.'

This was something new. Ben said, 'Someone else?'

'A woman. I think Romy said her name was Françoise.'

'Françoise who?'

'Romy didn't mention a second name.'

'Who is she? How could she help her?'

Michel shook his head. 'That's all I know.'

'Okay,' Ben said with a sigh. 'Tell me the rest.'

'Afterwards I was really anxious, pacing up and down, not knowing what to do and thinking I should go over to her place and make sure she was okay. But I didn't want to push her, you know? I had to respect her space. God help me, if only I'd listened to myself, I might have been able to keep her safe.'

'Then she called you again, just this morning.'

'She sounded even more terrified. She'd been on her way to catch the Métro to work when she saw this other guy following her in the street, really close and menacing. That's when she phoned me, all in a panic.'

'Did she describe him?'

'She was breathless and didn't say much. A guy in a long black coat. That's all I remember. She said she'd seen him before and she was certain he was coming for her.'

Ben thought, *Nazim*. Of course she knew him. She'd seen him in Tripoli just three days ago. 'What else did she say?'

'She said she was doubling back towards home, and that she was going to lock herself in her apartment. I told her I'd come straight over, and she said, "Get here fast, okay?" She was so frightened. I dropped everything and ran. But I don't have a car. I was too slow getting there.'

Michel's eyes became wet and his voice started breaking up as he went on, reliving the moment. 'By the time I reached her place, the street was full of *flics*. I watched from a distance. I knew something terrible must have happened. I was about to call her number to ask if she was okay, but just then an ambulance arrived. Then . . . then I saw them bringing her down and loading her into the ambulance. I mean, I just knew it was her. She was covered under a sheet. I almost died myself. I turned and ran and didn't stop running. I can't even remember how I got back to Saint-Denis. I just felt numb, like it was all a dream. Next thing

I was at the Geronimo, wanting to drink myself into a hole that's so deep I never come out. But I don't even have the money to do it.'

Michel broke down and his body heaved and rocked as he wept bitterly. Ben let him cry for a minute, then asked, 'Why didn't you stay and tell the police what you knew?'

'Because I was scared they'd start asking all these questions, and next thing my criminal record would come out. Wouldn't take much for them to start suspecting me, would it? As you can tell, seeing as they apparently already think I did it.' Michel stared at his hands, which were shaking. Then made a fist and punched himself in the face, again and again, as though he hated himself as much as he hated the man who had murdered her. 'Why? *Why* couldn't I have got there sooner? *Why* couldn't I have saved her?'

Ben thought Michel was going to break his own nose. He grasped his wrist and held it tight to stop him from hitting himself. 'We can't always save the ones we love, Michel. That's just how it is.'

'I don't understand why she didn't call the police after she called me.'

'She'd dropped her phone, remember?' Ben said. 'Even if she'd realised before she reached home, she was too scared to do anything except keep running until she got there. Then she probably needed something to settle her nerves. She'd put on some coffee. She might have been planning on calling the police on her landline phone after she'd drunk a cup or two. Only she never had the chance, because Nazim al-Kassar got to her first.'

'But she must have locked her door. How did he get in?'

'Maybe she answered it thinking it was you,' Ben said. He regretted the words the moment they were out of his mouth.

Michel sank his head into his hands. 'Oh, God.'

'You wouldn't have stood a chance against him, Michel. You'd be dead too.'

'I wish I was.'

Ben put a hand on his shoulder and could feel his dreadful pain. 'I can't bring her back,' he said softly. 'I wish I could, but I can't, and I'm truly sorry. But I intend to make it right, for her sake, and for yours, as much as something like this can be made right.'

'By doing what?'

'By making sure that Nazim al-Kassar never hurts another innocent person. This stops, now.'

'I want to help. Let me team up with you.'

Ben shook his head. 'You don't even know me.'

'But I can tell you're the kind of guy who can handle trouble.'

'And you're not. Not this sort of trouble.'

'I know how to pull a trigger. I've done it once, I can do it again.'

'No offence, but it's a little different when they're shooting back at you.'

'What the hell more have I got to lose? You think I'm scared of getting killed?'

'Of course you are,' Ben said. 'So am I. Only a lunatic isn't scared of getting killed. But whether you are or not, it doesn't affect the outcome. And if something happens to you I can't have that on my conscience too.'

'Then what am I supposed to do? If everyone thinks I killed Romy, that means the cops are after me, right? So I can't go home.'

'You've been a fugitive before,' Ben said. 'You know what to do.'

'I have no money, nothing. I have no idea where to go.'

'I can help you get out of the city,' Ben said. 'This place isn't getting any safer for anyone.'

Chapter 22

Ben drove Michel Yassa to the RER rail station in nearby Bondy, gave him all the cash he had so he could take a train as far away as possible and have some living expenses once he got there, then wished him good luck and drove off.

Michel was on his own now. The best Ben could do for the guy was catch the real killer before the police caught up with him and shot him full of holes.

Ben was driving away from the station, still feeling exhausted and depressed after their painful conversation, thinking about what he'd learned and what to do next, when he got a call.

He'd been expecting either Ken Keegan to phone him, finally passing on a contact for Tyler Roth, or Thierry, preferably to say he was finished working on the audio and you could now hear every word of the recording as clear as a bell. But the call was from neither of them. The phone ringing was Romy Juneau's.

Ben pulled into the side of the road and answered.

The voice on the line was a woman's. She sounded hesitant and perplexed that a man had picked up the call. 'This is Françoise Schell. I'm responding to a voicemail message I received two days ago. Is this the right number?'

Françoise. The mystery woman who Romy had said could

help her. 'Romy Juneau called you,' Ben said. 'This is her phone.'

'The name she gave was Jane Dieulafoy. But I figured that was a fake. I get that a lot, in my line of business.'

'Which is what?' Ben asked.

'I'd actually rather speak to . . . what did you say her name was? Romy Juneau. Is she available?'

As they talked Ben was whipping out his own phone and running a web search on Françoise Schell. He found her right away. She was an investigative reporter and the top search result with her name on it had three lines of metadata that contained the title of an article she'd written. It was called HOW THE ANTIQUITIES TRADE FUNDS TERROR.

And a light bulb lit up inside Ben's head. He said, 'Please don't hang up. This could be very important.'

'Why would I hang up?' she asked, sounding as though she was arching an eyebrow.

'Because you can't talk to Romy Juneau.'

'I see. And why is that?'

'Because she can't talk to you. She was murdered this morning.'

'I'm hanging up.'

'Don't do that,' he said. 'Talk to me instead. You're the reporter she tried to call. She thought you could help her.'

'I can't talk to you if I don't know who you are.'

'My name's Ben Hope. I was Romy's friend.'

'As in boyfriend?' The way she said it sounded jaded and cynical. But then, in Ben's experience seasoned investigative journalists were generally a jaded and cynical bunch.

'Just a friend.'

'She was killed only this morning, but you don't sound like you're exactly paralysed with grief.' Direct, too.

'I express emotion in other ways,' he replied. In the

middle of talking he clicked open the article Françoise Schell had written and quickly scanned the text. It was from a few months earlier. There was a photo image of her beside the title. It showed a thin-faced woman with long blond hair and intense, intelligent eyes, maybe forty or a little younger.

Below that was another picture embedded into the article, featuring a group of masked men in black robes with AK-47s and lump hammers, busily smashing up what looked like a collection of ancient statues not too unlike the ones Ben had seen in Romy's video. The rest of the article was full of information about the involvement of terror groups like ISIL in the illegal trade of old Near East and Middle East treasures. It was too much for him to take in at a glance, but there was no question that the author had delved deep into that world. Ben was certain she could potentially offer valuable insights into whatever dirty kind of business Julien Segal and Nazim al-Kassar were mixed up in together.

'What happened to her?' asked Françoise Schell. Ben could picture her at her end, tapping computer keys to look up Romy now that she knew her name. Before he could reply, she said, 'I found it. Looking at it now. Found dead at her home in Paris. Suspect has been identified. Police are launching a manhunt. Oh, right, she worked for ICS? Hmm. Interesting.'

ICS. Institut Culturel Segal. Ben said, 'But the police are after the wrong person.'

'You're not going to tell me you did it, I hope.'

'No, but I know who did.'

'Why are you telling me this, and not the cops?'

'Why did you wait two days before you replied to her message?'

'I get a lot of crank calls. Ninety-plus per cent of them lead precisely nowhere. I was in two minds whether to even call back. Answer the question.'

Ben replied, 'There's no point telling the police. In fact it's doing them a favour not to tell them. If they went after the real killer, he'd slaughter anyone they sent and then just disappear for ever. They're out of their depth dealing with someone like him.'

'I see. And you would know all this how, exactly?'

'Because I'm privy to certain insider information that's very hard to come by. I might be prepared to tell you about it.'

Françoise Schell paused, and he could sense the wheels turning in her mind. She said, 'I feel my journalistic antennae twitching. Are you trying to dangle me a story here?'

'I'm looking at your article about the antiquities trade. Are you still interested in that kind of material?'

'I'm a reporter. I have an endless appetite for all that's dark and ugly. So do my readers. Let's say it's an ongoing research project.'

'Good. I have reason to believe there's a connection with what happened to Romy, and I think that once I show you what I've got, you'll agree. I'd also like to know more about why she thought you could help her.'

'The real Jane Dieulafoy was a French archaeologist who died in 1916. Like I said, a lot of people give me fake names on the first contact. Usually it's because they're either full of crap or they're clinically insane, but either way they don't have anything interesting to offer me. Now and then, I get one who hides their real identity because they actually have something to say, hence they're scared shitless. Your Romy was one of those. Something in her message caught my attention. One thing, in particular. That's why I eventually decided to return the call.'

'Then it sounds like we can help each other,' Ben said. 'We each have information to trade. Are you based in Paris? I'm headed back towards the city and I have time on my hands right now, if you do.'

'I'm not giving out my address.'

'I'm not asking for it. We could meet at a public place. Somewhere crowded and busy. Then you've got nothing to worry about. If you think I'm full of crap or clinically insane you can just get up and walk away.'

She fell silent again, hesitating before answering. 'Okay, then, I'm interested in hearing what you've got. But it had better be good.' She named a popular café on Boulevard du Montparnasse, in the sixth arrondissement. 'Do you know it?'

'I know where it is.'

'One hour,' Françoise Schell said.

Meanwhile, Nazim's men had moved fast. Sarfaraz, the whizzkid, had been whisked back to his place by Muhammad in the silver Mercedes, along with their other colleague called Mohammed. While they were still on the road Nazim had called his Parisian associate and demanded the Juneau woman's mobile number. His associate had little choice in the matter.

Once he had the number, Nazim phoned Sarfaraz, who duly fed it into his GPS phone tracking app. Sarfaraz called back within five minutes.

'Okay, I nailed him for you, just like I promised. He's on the move. A flashing red dot on my radar screen, and I can follow him wherever he goes.'

Nazim felt his blood stir. Modern technology might be

generally considered haram by Islamic purists, but it certainly had its uses. 'Where is he now?'

'About ten kilometres north-east of the city centre, incoming.'

'I want you to follow him. Don't use the silver Mercedes, he's seen it.' Paris was full of silver Mercedes, but Nazim knew how observant the man with no name was. All his kind were trained to notice details.

Sarfaraz said, 'I have another car. It's a Mercedes too, but it's black.'

'Take Mohammed and Muhammad with you. See where he goes, and report back to me.'

'Do we need to bring anything with us?' Sarfaraz was referring to armament.

'Bring plenty. I want this dealt with fast, efficiently and as soon as possible. When the job is done, take whatever phones he's carrying and deliver them to me personally.'

'No problem, boss. On our way.'

Nazim ended the call and smiled to himself. The man with no name was already as good as dead. It was just a question of time.

Chapter 23

Ben arrived at the rendezvous five minutes early, to find that Françoise Schell had beaten him to it. He recognised her from her picture. She had taken a seat next to the full-height café window that overlooked Boulevard du Montparnasse, and was attacking an espresso coffee as though she lived on the stuff. She was well dressed in a no-nonsense skirt suit topped with the kind of fashionable neck scarf that only French women can carry off successfully. Her hair was a different style from the photo, and she was wearing noticeably more makeup. Next to her on the seat was a tiny handbag. Ben wondered how many of them you could make out of a single crocodile.

Françoise Schell looked sharply up at him as he approached. 'Not quite what I imagined,' she commented. 'Younger, thinner and better looking.'

He put out a hand. 'Ben Hope.'

She took it. Her grip was dry and hard, like the look in her eye. 'Enchantée. Françoise Schell.'

'My pleasure. May I?' He pulled up a chair.

'Please do. You're English? Your accent had me puzzled. You speak French *almost* like a native.'

'Half Irish,' he said. 'But I live in France now.'

'How nice for you. Tell me all about yourself.'

Not the most subtle way to pump him for information. But as he was discovering, Françoise Schell didn't waste time on subtlety. A waiter scooted over and Ben ordered coffee, a larger version of the same thing she was drinking. When they were alone again, he said, 'Now the formalities are over, let's dispense with all the getting-to-know-you stuff. You said there was something in particular about Romy's phone message that caught your attention. What was that?'

One corner of her mouth curled up in a wry smile, and she waggled a finger at him. 'Not so fast, Buster. First you need to lay your cards on the table. What do you have for me?'

'No cards,' Ben said. 'Only this.' He took out Romy's phone, slid it across the tabletop towards her, and directed her to the video clip file.

'I can't see anything,' she complained as she began to watch. 'The picture's all dark and out of focus.'

'Let it run,' he said, and waited while she went on watching, holding the phone close to her chest like a poker player. When the artifacts came into shot, he knew it by the curious look she fired at him.

He said, 'This was taken three days ago in Tripoli.'

'It looks like a warehouse.' She paused, watched for a few seconds longer, then said, 'Now I'm seeing two men.'

'The older, shorter one is Julien Segal, whom you might recognise since you know about ICS. You won't know the other, but you've heard of the people he works for. They go by the Arabic name *al-Dawla al-Islamiya fi al-Iraq al-Sham*, Daesh for short. Most people know them by the quaint little acronym "ISIL".'

Françoise Schell narrowed her eyes at the mention of the name. Just then the waiter scooted back over with Ben's coffee. She paused the video playback and waited for the waiter to be gone again. Glancing about her as though to check nobody was listening in on their conversation, she said in a lowered voice, 'Are you serious? Segal is one of Europe's most respected archaeology experts. His name came up again and again during my research for the article I wrote. You're suggesting he's in contact with terrorists?'

Ben tried the coffee. Excellent. 'I'm not suggesting it. The only possible way to avoid that conclusion would be that Segal didn't know who he was talking to. Which is beyond improbable. Plus, it gets better. The second man is Romy Juneau's killer.'

She was looking at him intently. 'And you know that for a fact.'

Ben nodded. 'I saw him at the scene. No question. I'd recognise him anywhere.'

'Which suggests you know him.'

'Knew him. A long time ago.'

She frowned, arching a suspicious eyebrow. 'This is where we get to the insider information part. You're not just some friend of Romy Juneau. Who are you, really? What were you doing at the scene of the murder?'

Ben pointed at the phone in her hands and said, 'Go on watching.'

Françoise Schell was visibly simmering with questions as she resumed the playback. 'What are they talking about?' She held the phone close to her ear, and shook her head. 'The sound is terrible.'

'We're working on it.'

'We? You're part of a team?'

'I wouldn't call it that, exactly.'

She let the clip play through to the end, then turned off the phone and laid it back on the table. 'Okay, you have my attention. Am I to assume that Romy Juneau filmed this?'

'She was in Tripoli with Segal when she witnessed this conversation. I'm pretty sure this is Segal's own warehouse, used to store artifacts for export back to Europe or elsewhere. As you can see, they didn't know she was in there. She must have sneaked in after them.'

'The other man, did she know who he was?'

'The fact that she was hiding suggests that maybe she had a pretty good idea of the kind of people her employer is mixed up with. Once the audio is cleaned up, it might tell us what she overheard them talking about.'

'Why do you have her phone?'

Ben replied, 'I came into this situation by accident. Literally. We bumped into each other in the street, she dropped her phone and I was trying to return it.'

'Do you actually expect me to believe that?'

'It's the truth.'

'And yet it just so happens that you had a prior acquaintance with the man who killed her.'

'Coincidence.'

'I don't believe in coincidences.'

'Then maybe it was fate,' Ben said. 'He and I have unfinished business, going back.'

'Going back to when and where?' She studied him for a moment. 'I get it. We're talking about Daesh here. Radical Islam is to war and conflict what whipped cream is to strawberries. So you're some kind of military person on the other side. You certainly have the look. And you speak Arabic pretty well, which makes you no ordinary soldier type. So maybe you're from military intelligence. There's an oxymoron if ever there was one.'

'You show me yours, and I'll show you mine,' Ben said.

She smiled another of her cynical smiles. 'That sounds like a fun game.'

'Meaning, tell me what Romy said in her message, and I'll tell you all about my acquaintance with the charming Mr Nazim al-Kassar.'

'That's his name? Al-Kassar?'

'Don't bother looking him up. You won't find anything on him. Now, the message?'

She studied him for a moment longer, still not trusting him. Then replied, 'All right. Let's play.' She reached into the tiny crocodile leather handbag next to her, took out her phone and spent a moment twiddling and scrolling to bring up her voice messages. She held the phone out to Ben.

'Here. Listen.'

Chapter 24

Romy Juneau's voice in her phone message sounded nervous and flustered, and she was talking so fast that she was almost tripping over her words.

'*Hello, my name is Jane Dieulafoy and I'm reaching out to you because I read an article you wrote and I have information. I work in the antiquities business and I have evidence of something bad happening within my company. A criminal enterprise. A conspiracy. I don't even know what to call it.*'

Then there was a pause before she went on, sounding even more agitated: '*What they're planning is terrible. I don't know what to do, and I'm desperately hoping that you can help me. Something has to be done to stop the shipment. Please call me as soon as you can. I believe I'm in a lot of danger. I think they know. Please, I'm desperate for your help.*' Romy finished the message by giving her landline and mobile numbers.

'I tried the landline first,' Françoise Schell said. 'That was the phone she called me on. But there was no reply. Now I know why, of course. So then I called the mobile, and you answered. But I still don't get it. Why didn't she go to the police? Why come to me?'

'You heard her,' Ben said. 'She didn't know what to do. She was scared and confused. Maybe she felt she needed to gather more information before making any move. Maybe she wasn't completely sure that her suspicions were right. Maybe she respected her boss too much to want to believe he was capable of trafficking with criminals. She saw you as someone with knowledge and connections that might be able to help.'

'Maybe. But that doesn't tell us what she overheard.'

'A shipment,' Ben said. 'That's the key to understanding this.'

She nodded. 'That was the thing that caught my attention, too. The rest of it is just run-of-the-mill stuff that I hear all the time, conspiracies, paranoia, people convincing themselves of all kinds of crazy delusions. But crazy people rarely mention anything this specific.'

'It has to have come out of the conversation she witnessed. Or else it was what made her suspicious enough to sneak into the warehouse to listen in. Either way it's obviously part of this criminal conspiracy she's talking about. A shipment of what?'

She shrugged. 'Ancient artifacts, I suppose. The objects you could see in the background. I can't see what else it could refer to, can you? If we had a consignment number I could probably run a trace on it. I know some people.'

Ben shook his head. 'Segal doesn't need Nazim and his connections for that. Exporting recovered historic art treasures from those parts of the world is what he's been doing for years. That's his whole business. And in any case, what could be less threatening and sinister than a cargo of old bits of stone? Museums are full of them.'

'Then what makes this shipment so special?' she asked. 'Why would it have to be stopped, according to her?'

'You're the one who's researched all this,' Ben says. 'You tell me.'

'All I've researched is what's in my article. I expect you've already read it?'

'It's been a busy day.'

'It wouldn't hurt for you to have a basic grounding in what we're dealing with here.'

'Walk me through the main points.'

Across the other side of Boulevard du Montparnasse, the three men were watching from their black Mercedes parked a little further up the street, a few cars behind the metallic blue BMW Alpina they had followed there. Mohammed sat at the wheel, Muhammad in the back and Sarfaraz in the front passenger seat holding a camera with a telephoto lens, through which he'd observed the man Nazim had described get out of the Beemer, cross the street to the café and go inside. It was just after five in the afternoon.

'It's definitely our guy,' Sarfaraz was saying. 'He's not alone. Turned up a few minutes ago to meet a woman.'

Nazim al-Kassar was on the other end of the hands-free phone plumbed through the car's stereo system. 'Describe the woman.'

'White bitch, blonde, fortyish, kind of skinny but still worth raping if she had a bag over her head. She's sitting right by the window. He's sitting across the other side of the table. Doesn't look like they know each other well, from the way they're acting. They shook hands when he arrived. Like business colleagues who just met.'

'She must be the same one the Juneau woman called,' Nazim's voice said over the car speakers. 'The reporter, or whatever she is. What are they doing now?'

'He showed her something on a phone. Photos, or a video. She seemed to be looking at it with a lot of interest. Then they talked, and then she showed him something on her phone. Now they're back to talking again. Looks like an intense conversation.'

'They're swapping information,' Nazim said. 'It's these phones. I knew it. We need to stop them, right now, before it goes any further. Take them out. Immediately.'

There was no hesitation about obeying the order. 'We're on it.'

'I want a picture of them dead, and don't forget to get those phones. Got it? Call me when it's done.' Nazim ended the call.

Sarfaraz put down the camera. He turned around to look at Mohammed at the wheel, then Muhammad in the back. They both nodded. Muhammad had a large attaché case next to him on the back seat. He popped open the catches and raised the lid. Nestling inside were three Škorpion submachine pistols. Czech weapons, the professional badman's weapon of choice for messy, up-close-and-personal hit-and-run assassinations ever since they were invented in 1959. Muhammad handed one to each of his companions and took the third for himself.

There was silence in the car for a few moments, except for the metallic sounds of magazines being checked and slammed back into place, actions being cocked, folding stocks being extended, selector switches being set to fully automatic fire, safety catches being clicked off.

'Allahu Akbar,' Sarfaraz said. Mohammed and Muhammad repeated the same holy words in reply.

Then they looped their weapons' black fabric slings around their necks and shoulders, stepped out of the car, looked left and right, waited for a gap in the traffic and began walking across Boulevard du Montparnasse in the direction of the café.

Chapter 25

Françoise Schell leaned her elbows on the table. 'Muslim terror groups, in particular Daesh, or the Islamic State, ISIL or ISIS or whatever you want to call them, have been taking an unhealthy interest in ancient antiquities for years,' she explained. 'It started for purely ideological and religious reasons, a quest to destroy the relics of pre-Islamic cultures as being something idolatrous, meaning the worship of supposedly false gods.'

'I do know what idolatrous means.'

She shrugged. 'These acts of deliberate cultural vandalism date right back to the earliest days of Islam. In fact it goes all the way back to the Prophet Muhammad himself, with his treatment of the pre-Islamic religious idols that were kept at the holy Kaaba in Mecca, in 630 AD. These represented ancient Arabian deities like Hubal, who were worshipped by the Quraysh tribe and others. Muhammad had decided to seize the Kaaba for his own purposes and turn Mecca into a place of Islamic worship. He could have asked the pagan worshippers to remove their idols to some other place where they could carry on their religion in peace. Instead he and his followers went in and violently smashed them to smithereens, all 360 of them, with the aim of wiping out the whole religion of the Qurayshi people. Later on he did all he could to wipe them out too, but that's another story.'

Françoise Schell gave a dark smile and paused for a sip of coffee. 'Anyhow, the Prophet of Islam's destruction of the Kaaba idols established the precedent for countless similar acts of cultural destruction throughout their fourteen hundred years of supremacist conquest. As far as they were concerned, any and all artifacts of pre-Islamic civilisation were the products of *jahiliyya*, societies of unbelievers, and had no value whatsoever. When the first jihadist naval expedition into Europe conquered Rhodes in the mid-seventh century, they came across the site of one of the wonders of the ancient world, the giant statue called the Colossus of Rhodes that had been built in 280 BC to honour the sun god, Helios. Needless to say, there was no room for such blasphemous pagan idols in any new territory falling under Islamic rule. Muawiya, the expedition commander, who later became caliph, had its remains carted away and sold off as scrap metal.

'The same treatment was dished out to victims of jihad wherever the Muslim armies went. As the conquest swept into India they spent centuries levelling Hindu temples and massacring thousands of Brahmin priests. They would break the idols, mix the fragments with the flesh of slaughtered sacred cows and hang them in nosebags around the necks of the Brahmins they kept alive as slaves. Then if anyone dared rebuild the temples, whole towns were put to the sword of Islam, women and children were taken as slaves and the chief culprits were crushed under the feet of elephants. In Keysin, Anatolia, in the early ninth century, they sacked and destroyed an ancient church said to have been constructed by the apostles of Christ themselves.

'And on, and on. The ruin of the Church of Calvary and

the Church of the Resurrection in Jerusalem in 937. The razing to the ground of the Spanish city of Santiago de Compostela and its famous shrine of St James, sixty years later. The desecration of the Hagia Sophia, the grandest church in Christendom when, in May 1453, after seven hundred years of trying, the jihadists finally got their chance to sack Constantinople, slaughter or enslave its inhabitants and overthrow what was left of the Byzantine Empire, as their prophet had vowed to do centuries earlier. Nothing outside Islam was safe as they pursued their quest to purify the whole world from idolatry.'

It was a grim historical account and it left her almost breathless. She shook her head as though she could hardly believe it herself.

'This is all in your article?'

'Are you kidding? I could write a book.'

Ben smiled. 'Perhaps you should.'

'Except nobody would publish it. They'd probably say it was "Islamophobic".' She made quote marks in the air with her fingers. 'No matter that these are documented historical facts.'

Ben said, 'I was in Iraq, during the war. I saw a lot of the ravages there.'

Françoise Schell looked pleased. 'See, didn't I guess you were the type? Well, if you were there, then you don't need me to tell you how little has changed for these lunatics. They're basically still living in the seventh century and, given the chance, will carry on exactly as always. As the Islamic State gained territory and occupied cities throughout the Middle East, killing and beheading as they went, they blew up every ancient church and synagogue they could find, as part of the same old attempt to erase Christian and Jewish heritage from history. The list includes the destruction of the Nineveh Wall in Mosul in 2015, and the lovely video footage they took of themselves merrily wrecking the Mosul museum the same year. The bulldozing of the ancient Assyrian relics of Raqqa. The attack on the ancient city of Palmyra, and all the irreplaceable art treasures they broke up there with sledgehammers. Not to mention the attacks on Shi'ite mosques like the Askariya Shrine in Iraq, or the Muslim shrines of Timbuktu that the Islamic Ansar Dine terror group were so keen to smash to bits in 2012, because the militant Sunnis despise the Shi'ites almost as much as they despise the Jews and Christians. There's more, much more. The scale and atrocity of the vandalism are simply unbelievable. Even without taking into account the appalling bloodshed and human misery inflicted over fourteen hundred years, it's without a doubt the worst litany of wanton destructiveness ever committed in the history of the world.'

Ben had the impression that she could talk about this all day, impassioned as she was.

She said, 'But somewhere along the line, something changed. The terrorists, whose leaders aren't *completely* stupid, finally started cottoning on to the fact that these things they were smashing to pieces might seem worthless and idolatrous to them, but a lot of other people in the world actually regarded them as being rather valuable. That's when they turned from simply destroying ancient art treasures to trading in them. Having bombed the crap out of a place they'd begin excavating the ruins to see what stuff they could salvage and put on the black market. After their destruction of the four-thousand-year-old Assyrian city of Tel Ajaja in Syria, 2016, it's estimated that they hauled away at least forty per cent of the relics to sell off.'

'I hadn't realised it was such an orchestrated business.'

'Oh, it certainly is that. And here's the scary part. If they were just trying to enrich themselves like any other organised crime empire, that would be one thing. But Islamic law prohibits its warriors from waging jihad for personal gain. Despite the documented historical fact that their Prophet, may Peace be upon Him, used to happily share out among his victorious troops the trophies of war from all the Jews and Christians and other tribes he'd slaughtered and beheaded, back in the early days. Thanks to a bit of theological jiggery pokery the modern militant fundamentalists decided it was perfectly permissible to sell plundered artifacts to enrich their organisations, so long as it was done purely for the jihadist cause. Just as it's allowed for them to make money from all kinds of other commodities forbidden to Muslims, like drugs, or alcohol, or improperly slaughtered meat, and so on, on condition that the loot is used exclusively for the purpose of funding holy war against the *kuffar harbi*. That is to say, the pigs, apes and other infidels who are the stated enemies of Islamic fundamentalist doctrine. People like you and me. Then Allah approves of it. Am I getting Islamophobic yet?'

'Maybe a little bit.'

'Tough shit. I just report facts. I don't deal in fiction, I don't do phobias, and nobody's gonna label me with some pseudo-psychiatric term that was invented to stifle free speech.'

'I'd imagine that the trade in stolen antiquities is worth a bit more to them than hijacking truckloads of booze and corned beef,' Ben said.

'You have no idea. It's not just millions. It's hundreds upon hundreds of millions, year on year. Every penny of which gets reinvested straight into their fucked-up tireless ideological crusade. More money means more guns, more bombs, more sophisticated communications and recruiting networks, better infrastructure, enhanced power and influence, and so on. This thing turned out to be a goldmine for them. Most of the goods are brought to the West, via networks of crooked middlemen, smugglers and the like.'

'And Julien Segal is one of those?'

'Well, it looks that way, doesn't it? He's certainly got all the right contacts, knows how the system works. Just the man to slip the merchandise into Europe under the radar. Taking a hell of a risk, but I suppose the money's good.'

'And that would account for the shipment Romy talked about, if the antiquities in Segal's Tripoli warehouse are contraband looted by ISIL,' Ben said.

Françoise Schell frowned. 'Except that still doesn't explain all that's in her message. She said they were planning something terrible. That sounds like more than just black marketeering.'

'Unless the proceeds are intended to pay for explosives for suicide bombers to detonate in any number of major cities across Europe. That's pretty terrible.'

'Agreed. But I get the feeling that I'm missing something. My instinct is generally right on these things.'

'Then we'll just have to figure it out,' he said.

She looked at him. 'We?'

'You're an investigator, aren't you? With sharp instincts and a strong knowledge of the subject. Sounds good to me.'

The whole time they'd been talking, the busy boulevard the other side of the window was an endless two-way sea of cars and trucks and bikes and bodies and faces of all colours and varieties, constant and monotonous and far less absorbing than the conversation they were deep into. Ben had tuned out completely from what was going on outside, or he might have noticed the three men who crossed the road from the black Mercedes parked down the street, approached the café and paused outside like regular prospective customers checking the place out.

Françoise Schell was looking at him with a half-smile, part amused, part surprised. 'Are you hiring me?'

'Maybe we can work together,' Ben said.

And that was when he glanced sideways out of the café window and saw the three men standing outside. All three of them staring at him. Black hair, dark eyes, olive faces, serious expressions. The one in the middle clean shaven and in his late twenties or thereabouts, the other two a few years older and both heavily bearded. Each of the three was wearing a thin black strap around his neck and shoulder, from each of which dangled a black metallic item that was not a camera. The trio were just standing there in plain sight, making no attempt to hide what they had. Pedestrians were walking by and paying no notice, serenely lost in their thoughts, their phones, their everyday lives.

But that was all about to change.

Ben lunged across the table and grabbed Françoise Schell roughly by the arm, and the two of them tumbled out of their seats as he knocked the table sideways and dragged her to the floor with him, pinning her body under his. The three mobile phones that had been lying on the table between them hit the floor. Cups flew. Coffee splashed. She screamed. A nearby waiter dropped his tray. People turned in sudden shock at the sight of the man attacking the woman at the window table.

And then the café window blew apart in a storm of gunfire from the street.

Chapter 26

The Czech Škorpion submachine gun carries a magazine payload of twenty rounds and pumps them out of its short barrel at a cyclic rate of eight hundred a minute. Multiplied by three, that made for sixty rounds firing through the café window in the space of one-point-four seconds. Just the blink of an eye, but as all hell broke loose and glass rained down and bullets raked the inside of the café and thudded into walls and tables and bodies and people cried out in terror and Ben tried to drag Françoise Schell out of the field of fire, it was the longest one-point-four seconds anyone would ever live through.

Or not live through.

And then it was all over. The last pieces of jagged glass fell from the shattered window frame. Gunsmoke swirled around the interior of the café. Ben heard people groaning and shrieking around him. He was lying on the floor beside the capsized table they'd been sitting at moments earlier, with Françoise Schell under him, and broken glass and spilled coffee everywhere. And blood. He could smell its coppery tang and feel its warmth. It was all over him.

It wasn't all his blood. He'd been quick enough to pull Françoise down out of her seat to escape the worst of the point-blank gunfire directed at them through the window, but he'd been too slow to save her from all of it. A bullet had ploughed a hole in the side of the head and gone straight through. She was dead.

Then Ben felt the pain, and knew that he was injured too. How badly, he wouldn't have time to think about until later. If later ever came. He rolled off Françoise Schell's body and scrambled for cover behind the fallen table. The face of a dead waiter stared at him from inches away, covered in blood. The gunmen had stepped over the lower edge of the window frame and were striding into the café. Crunching broken glass underfoot. Smoke trickling from the hot receivers of their machine guns. All three Škorpions were empty. The shooters let them dangle loose on their slings, reached inside their jackets and drew out pistols. One of the older, heavily-bearded ones stepped over Françoise Schell's body, glanced down and spotted the three mobile phones on the floor among the glass and the blood. His eyes lit up. He bent down to scoop them up with his free hand.

That was when Ben knew that this wasn't just any old terrorist attack on a bunch of Parisians enjoying their afternoon coffee. This was a targeted hit aimed specifically at eliminating him and recovering the evidence that someone up the food chain had obviously known, or guessed, was contained inside the phone memories.

Either way, he wasn't going to stand there and let them do it.

The gunmen began firing as they came. The snap of pistol shots filled the café and more people screamed. Ben's capsized table offered little in the way of protection. Two bullets punched through the flimsy wood and a third passed over the top of him. He was suddenly very conscious of the hard, angular shape pressing against the back of his right hip, inside his waistband, hidden under the hem of his leather jacket.

The Glock he'd captured from the Corsicans and pointed in Michel Yassa's face. He'd almost decided to leave it in the car. Which would have been a fatal decision.

Ben drew out the pistol. The butt fitted into his hand like an extension of his arm. He thrust it up and over the edge of the table and fired back at the gunmen, BLAM BLAM BLAM. The one who'd picked up the phones now dropped them again, along with his pistol, and clapped a hand over his chest and fell back among the blood and the broken glass. The other two kept on coming, focusing their fire Ben's way. The remaining bearded one was maniacally yelling the war cry 'ALLAHU AKBAR!' as he squeezed off shots as fast as he could. Ben caught him square in his gunsights and took him down with a triple-tap to the chest, three holes almost touching, like a clover leaf. As number two went down to meet with the seventy-two virgins of jannah, the last gunman suddenly seemed to realise that he was about to become the third, and wasn't ready for such a fate. He faltered, squeezed off two more shots that smacked into the tabletop in front of Ben, then turned and began to bolt towards the shattered window through which he'd come.

Ben had no problems with shooting him in the back as he tried to escape. But as he levelled his sights and pressed the trigger, nothing happened.

Even the ultra-reliable mechanism of a Glock could jam sometimes. Ben was trained and ready for it, and he cleared the jam and punched the gun back up to find its target, who was now leaping wildly through the shattered window and racing across the pavement, pistol in hand, his empty submachine gun swinging about on its sling, running for all that he was worth.

Out in the street, pedestrians were fleeing in terror. Others had thrown themselves to the pavement or huddled behind parked cars, trying to make themselves as small and invisible as possible. Some were simply rooted to the spot, paralysed with fear and shock. Ben was about to open fire on the fleeing shooter when he saw the group of frightened women and children right in his field of fire behind the target. He swore, lowered the gun and gave chase.

Sprinting across the street, the gunman almost collided with a car whose driver was desperately trying to get away from the scene. Ben headed after him in pursuit. He jumped over the dead body of the bearded terrorist who'd tried to take the phones. The guy was lying with his arms outflung, eyes staring up at the ceiling, already enjoying the promised rewards of the afterlife. All three phones were lying next to his body. Ben grabbed them and stuffed them into his pocket and kept running. He reached the shattered window and leaped through. Hit the pavement running and sprinted after the fleeing gunman, trying to get a shot at him, but the guy had reached the opposite side of the street and was ducking behind parked cars for cover.

As Ben ran into the street he was aware of the blood running down his side and wetting his shirt. His own, not Françoise Schell's. A strange chill was coming over him. But he'd been injured before, and lived to tell the tale; and at this moment his focus was too intensely locked on his target to dwell too much on his own wellbeing. Catching a glimpse of movement through the parked car windows, he debated whether or not to shoot. Innocent bystanders as well as the gunman were taking cover back there. There'd been enough collateral damage from this thing already.

Then the shooter came up again, this time with his left arm clutched in a stranglehold around the neck of a young Nigerian woman who'd taken cover in the wrong spot at the wrong time. Her face was tight with fear and she was clawing at his arm to escape his choking grip, but he was hanging on tight as he swung her body in front of his, using her as a human shield while he aimed past her shoulder and fired at Ben. A shop window shattered to Ben's rear, showering glass over the pavement. He ducked as more bullets whistled past him. Couldn't shoot back for fear of hitting the shooter's hostage.

'POLICE!' The shout came from down the street. It was too soon for the emergency response units to have turned up. Two gendarmes who must have been on patrol when they heard the shots were running towards the scene, pistols drawn. They locked eyes on the gunman clutching the hostage and pointed their weapons, but like Ben they couldn't open fire in case they hit the woman. They were both screaming at him to drop the gun and let her go. He swung the pistol their way, then back at Ben, as though panicky with indecision. Then aimed it back at the cops and fired, screaming 'DAESH! ALLAHU AKBAR!' and one of them spun around and corkscrewed to the pavement clutching his hip. The other one still couldn't shoot, and threw himself behind a car as the gunman kept on blasting at him, blowing holes in bodywork and sending up sprays of exploding glass. Ben's sights were hovering right on him, but it was too dangerous to risk a shot. The gunman ducked low and kept himself hidden behind his hostage as he hauled her kicking and screaming up the street towards a black Mercedes that was parked a few cars behind Ben's own BMW. As he raced the last few yards, he dumped the woman and let her sprawl to the pavement, then ripped open the driver's door and leaped inside.

With the hostage out of the field of fire, Ben had the green light to pump bullets into the Mercedes. Nine-millimetre holes perforated the bonnet and turned the windscreen into a mass of white cobwebs. The Mercedes roared into life, screeched out of its parking space and came veering right towards him where he stood in the road, forcing him to leap aside.

He kept firing as it sped by him. He couldn't tell what he was hitting inside. The side windows blew out, then the rear screen. The back end of the Mercedes was fishtailing all over the road. Ben aimed for the tyres and was about to try to take them out when the second cop came up from behind his cover with his gun raised. His eyes were flashing and he was all keyed up with adrenalin, and Ben could see the guy was ready to shoot anything that moved. As far as the cop was concerned, he'd stumbled into the middle of some kind of turf war shootout between rival criminal gangs, and Ben was just as much a target as the escaping gunman.

Ben lowered his pistol and ripped out his wallet, flipping it open to show the fake police ID inside and holding it up high for the gendarme to see. The cop blinked in total confusion, but held his fire. Ben yelled, 'Detective Jacques Dardenne, Police Nationale. Stand down, Officer. I'm in pursuit of a terror suspect.'

The Mercedes was speeding off fast down Boulevard du Montparnasse. Ben ran for his car, blipping the locks as he went. The gendarme was still just standing there alone. But he wouldn't be alone for long, because half the Parisian police would soon be screaming to the scene. Ben yelled, 'Multiple casualties inside the café, including two dead terrorists. Hold the fort, Officer. Backup's on its way.' Then he was behind the wheel of the Alpina and firing it up in a throaty blast of quad exhausts and stamping his foot on the gas, slamming into the car in front to knock it out of his way as he took off after the disappearing Mercedes.

This bastard wasn't getting away so easily.

Chapter 27

Ben's foot was hard to the floor as the revs mounted in a soaring howl and the acceleration pressed him back into his seat. The Mercedes had a seventy-yard lead on him but the Alpina could hit 100 kilometres per hour from a standstill in under four seconds. The boulevard became a tunnel blurred at the edges. All he could see was his prey ahead, its flaring brake lights getting closer now as the Mercedes was forced to slow for the confusion of stalled traffic further down the street. Drivers were honking horns, or getting out and craning their necks wondering what was happening, or else abandoning their vehicles and escaping on foot as they began to realise that an incident was taking place. The Mercedes ploughed a wild course between the stopped cars, hitting everything it came near and turning the confusion to panic and chaos.

Ben followed with gritted teeth, refusing to let up his speed. He intended to catch this guy and make him talk, no matter what.

The gap between him and the Mercedes had halved already. Now it closed to thirty yards. The fleeing gunman was on the edge of losing control. Suddenly a stretch bus lumbered out of a side street and slammed on the brakes as its driver saw the Mercedes rocketing straight for him.

The Mercedes flew into a squealing skid, mounted the central reservation sideways, pulverised an empty bus stop and a railing and almost overturned before it somehow righted itself and kept on going.

Just twenty-five yards behind, Ben swerved around the front of the stopped bus, knocked aside the wreckage in the Mercedes' wake, and kept on chasing. Next the gunman took a violent turn to the left, off Montparnasse and into Boulevard Raspail, screaming so wide through the junction that he almost overshot and smashed through the entrance of a corner patisserie. Ben dived into the turn right on his tail and accelerated hard after him.

Ahead, Boulevard Raspail split into a fork, with one-way warning signs flanking the entrance to the street to the right. The gunman could probably hardly see a thing through the opaque spider's web of his shattered windscreen. He sped through the signs and the wrong way up the street, and Ben had to follow. The street was narrow and shady, lined with parked cars and motorcycles, fine apartment buildings with fancy balcony railings looming high on both sides, like a canyon against whose walls the roaring engines of the two cars echoed as they sped up the middle. At the end of the street was a T-junction with a big office building directly opposite. The Mercedes was halfway there when a colourful sports bike turned into the junction at an acute angle of lean and accelerated briskly, the rider obviously too focused on his racing skills to notice the two cars speeding straight towards him the wrong way up the street.

By the time the motorcyclist saw the Mercedes coming it was already too late to swerve out of the way. The parked vehicles on both sides made it too narrow to pass. He was hard on the brakes and his suspension was compressed deep into its fork tubes. No way to stop in time, let alone get out of there. The Mercedes wasn't slowing down. The gunman clearly thought he could run straight over the top of the oncoming bike. Instants before the inevitable collision the rider threw himself off his machine and went tumbling. The riderless motorcycle stayed upright on its wheels for the last couple of yards before it collided smack into the middle of the front end of the Mercedes.

The impact lifted the car's rear into the air. The bike somersaulted violently over the bonnet and came slamming down on the road behind the car. Ben braked hard to avoid running over the wreckage. Now totally out of control, the Mercedes veered straight into a row of parked cars along the kerbside, ploughing a trail of carnage before it came to a crunching halt against a solid iron bollard.

That was the end of the road for the gunman.

Ben threw open his driver's door and stepped out of the Alpina. The road was covered in spilled fuel and oil from the smashed sportsbike. Nearby, its rider, still stunned, was getting to his feet and pulling off his helmet. He was a young guy, maybe twenty. Ben called out to him, 'You okay?', to which the young guy gave a dazed kind of nod, and Ben replied, 'Good. Now beat it,' flashing the police ID. The rider nodded again and stumbled off, with just a glance at the twisted ruin that was all that was left of his bike.

Ben could hear the wail of sirens tearing up through Montparnasse and approaching fast. In minutes, this whole place would be swarming with real police. But for the moment he was alone with the last of the three gunmen who'd just tried to kill him, and succeeded in killing a lot of innocent people in the attempt. Ben felt a pang of deep sadness for Françoise Schell. She was dead because he'd persuaded her to meet with him, no other reason.

And somebody was going to pay for that.

The Mercedes was a wreck, its front end crushed like a concertina against the thick iron bollard. The engine was dead and hot metal was ticking and a wisp of smoke was rising from under the crumpled, bullet-holed bonnet. There was no movement from inside. Ben walked towards it. He winced as a lance of pain shot through him. He could feel the blood trickling warm down his left side. He kept walking, eyes fixed on the Mercedes, gun in hand, ready for the driver's door to fly open and the gunman to come jumping out, firing as he came.

But the gunman wasn't going anywhere. Ben cautiously approached the side of the wrecked car and grasped the door handle with his free hand, and tugged it open with the gun ready.

The body of the terrorist slumped sideways out of the opened door, bloody and staring. His forehead and the top of his skull were caved in like an eggshell where they'd punched through the windscreen on impact. That might have finished him off, but the two bullets that Ben had plugged him with as he'd driven off earlier would have done for him before too long. The inside of the Mercedes looked like a butcher's slab.

Ben crouched beside the slumped corpse and frisked him. The guy was wearing a gold identity bracelet that was engraved in Arabic with the name 'Sarfaraz', but aside from that he was carrying no identification, not even a phone. Too much to hope for. His slim leather wallet contained only a thick wad of banknotes. Ben took them for himself as spoils of war, since he'd given all his paper money to Michel Yassa.

He stood up. The pain was worsening now as the adrenalin of the chase was beginning to wear off. The blood was leaking mostly from his chest, as well as various parts of his upper body. If he'd taken a bullet anywhere serious, he didn't think he'd have made it this far. Then again, he'd known men fatally shot who didn't realise it until afterwards, when they suddenly collapsed.

The police sirens were getting closer, too close. He hurried back to the Alpina, stumbling once. His driver's seat was red with blood. He got in behind the wheel, managed to squeeze past the wrecked motorcycle and the Mercedes, out of the T-junction with Rue Notre-Dame des Champs and away. By the time the first cop cars turned up, he'd be long gone.

Chapter 28

Ben drove for five kilometres across the city before the pain forced him to find a place to stop and check his injuries. He pulled into a littered back alley and clambered out of his blood-smeared driver's seat into the back of the car, where he kept a small first-aid kit and a few other essentials. After gingerly peeling off his jacket and the blood-soaked denim shirt under it, he examined the sources of the bleeding. One of the bullets that had shattered the café window to the left of where he'd been sitting had scored a crease about a quarter of an inch deep across the peak of his left bicep and the curve of his pectoral muscle. He also had pieces of glass embedded in his chest, side and shoulder from the shattered window, which were digging into his flesh every time he moved.

In other words, he'd been incredibly lucky. If the bullet had struck an inch further to the right it would have carved through his heart and at least one lung. End of story, right there.

The medical kit contained a scalpel, tweezers, antiseptic cream, butterfly sutures and a pack of special painkillers called sufentanil, heavy-duty stuff designed for alleviating battlefield injuries. He spent the next uncomfortable twenty minutes closing the lips of his chest wound and extracting as many of the shards of glass as he could find, some of which had gone quite deep and needed cutting around with the razor-sharp scalpel blade before he could get a purchase with the tweezers.

By the time he'd finished he was feeling faint with pain and his left side looked like raw steak. He swabbed himself with antiseptic and patched and dressed the wounds as best he could before swallowing a couple of sufentanil. He sat back with his eyes closed and waited a few minutes longer for the drug to start kicking in, then decided it was time to move on. His old green army bag contained a fresh pair of jeans and a clean shirt left over from his India travels. He put both on, used his bloodied clothes as rags to clean up the mess on the car seat, then bundled them up and dumped them in a nearby bin.

'You'll survive,' he muttered to himself. 'You've had worse.' Which was definitely true. Once healed, the scars would be a minor addition to the collection he'd already accrued over the years.

He got back behind the wheel and drove off. But where to go? Nazim al-Kassar could be anywhere in Paris, if indeed he hadn't left the city by now. He'd soon realise that his hit had failed. Then he'd simply disappear into the shadows for a while, planning his next attack. There was no way to anticipate where or when that might take place.

Ben connected his phone into the in-car system and called Thierry to check on his progress with the audio recording. The reply was disappointing.

'Not much joy so far, chief. I've cleaned up as much of the background noise as I could and boosted up the voice frequencies hoping you might be able to hear what these two guys are saying, but it's like polishing a turd. Whatever you do, it's still a turd.'

'Keep trying,' Ben said, and ended the call.

Still nothing from Keegan. It was one bad break after another.

Ben lit a Gauloise and pondered his options as he drove. He'd just run from the scene of a major crime incident where he'd impersonated an officer, which only complicated an already problematic situation. There was a decent chance that the cop he'd spoken to had taken down the Alpina's registration. That would lead them straight to Le Val. Jeff would know how to handle things if the police turned up there. Which would buy Ben some time, but meanwhile he'd need to take the necessary precautions to avoid unwanted attention from the law.

Afternoon was turning into evening by the time Ben pulled up in the junk-filled forecourt of Fred's car-breaking plant down by the river. While the city's industrial areas were shrinking in the face of ever-expanding gentrification, Fred and his domain of scrap metal and rust, walled in like a fortress behind mesh gates and guarded by France's most vicious cur of a junkyard dog, were among the last of the holdouts. Selling dodgy cars for cash, no questions asked, was one of Fred's specialities that Ben had made use of in the past. Another was illicit firearms. All Ben needed from him today, however, was a set of scrap number plates to switch for the Alpina's.

Fred was only too happy to oblige. For a fistful of the cash Ben had lifted from the dead terrorist, he fitted the car with plates from the rusted-out corpse of a Paris-registered Peugeot that was destined for the crusher next morning. For another hundred euros Ben could have driven away with the sawn-off twelve gauge Fred wanted to sell him too, but he could live without one of those.

From Fred's place, Ben headed across the river into the

Latin Quarter, to a Franco-Lebanese food bar he knew in the fifth arrondissement. The evening was turning cold and rainy. He spent more dead man's cash on a pile of falafel with tabbouleh and lemon-marinated chicken *en brochette*, and took them back to eat in the car. He hadn't eaten all day, and needed the energy for what was promising to be a long night ahead.

Because by then, Ben had decided on his next move. If he couldn't spring a surprise visit on the hideout of Nazim al-Kassar, he could at least try to locate Nazim's business partner, Julien Segal. He wasn't going to achieve much by calling the Institute again in the morning. But there were other ways to gain information.

The offices of ICS were situated off Rue de Rivoli, not far from Place de la Concorde on the Champs Élysées and a stone's throw from the north wing of the Louvre Palace where Ben had been that morning. As he arrived in the vicinity, he saw the flashing lights illuminating the night sky above the rooftops, and soon discovered that the streets for blocks around were swarming with police and riot troops. A fresh round of disturbances was already getting underway as thousands of protesters in yellow vests braved the rain to kick up a storm against the police. From a distance it looked pretty serious. Ben could hear the roar of the angry crowds and the popping of tear gas grenades. Maybe this time, if the marchers could breach the security cordons and make it up past Place de la Concorde, they might even have a crack at the Presidential palace. Though without a doubt, the little guy himself was tucked far away from any danger.

For Ben, the rioting was the perfect cover. He left the Alpina far enough away to be safe, turned up the collar of his jacket, pulled on a woollen beanie hat and a pair of thick leather gloves, and slipped up Rue de Rivoli on foot, keeping to the arcades. Emergency vehicles howled by but they had much more to worry about than a lone figure who just happened to be wanted in connection with that afternoon's terror incident.

Segal's Paris headquarters was a handsome three-storey building, in keeping with its upmarket address. The front entrance was a solid affair and the windows on the street side were barred with iron. But skirting around the side, Ben saw that a walled garden extended from the rear of the Institute, and that only the ground-floor windows on that side were barred.

Thanks to the bad weather and the drama unfolding just blocks away, the street outside ICS's offices was unnaturally deserted. There was nothing Ben could do about the CCTV cameras. Paris was full of them these days, though public surveillance was still only a fraction of what UK citizens had to endure. He glanced left, glanced right, then quickly scaled the wall and dropped down the other side of it in the Institute's gardens. He crossed a small lawned area, with a pathway and some ornamental shrubs in large ornate pots, and slipped into the dark shadow cast by a mature elm tree that stood close to the rear of the building. Peering up through the foliage Ben singled out a balconied first-floor window that was just a short leap from the tree's branches.

Moments later he was there, swinging over the ornate balcony rail and ducking down by the window. There was nothing but darkness inside the building. The window was securely locked. There was little point in messing around with locks, since the moment he ventured inside he was sure to set off the alarm system anyway.

He used the butt of his pistol to break the glass. As expected, the alarm instantly went off. He wasn't concerned about it being heard from the outside, with a riot in full swing nearby. But a building like this, the security system was certainly hi-tech enough to be internet-connected straight to the police. Ben reckoned he had about ten minutes, maximum, before his presence drew a response.

He crawled in through the broken window, took a small pencil torch from his pocket and shone it around, and saw that he was in a conference room with a large table surrounded by chairs. He made his way quickly into a corridor, along which were rows of offices. The alarm shrilled more loudly in his ears as he made his way deeper into the building. He glanced at his watch. Seconds counted. He came to a stairway. If Julien Segal was like any other CEO in the world, his personal office would be on the top floor. Ben raced up the stairs.

One minute gone.

He came out on a landing with another corridor leading off both ways. *If in doubt, turn right.* He followed the corridor to its end, checking the little nameplates on the doors as he went. The carpeting underfoot was expensively thick, and fine antiques and paintings adorned the spaces between doors. But none of the nameplates was Segal's.

The alarm kept screeching. Ninety seconds. Ben was calm. His focus was complete. He turned and walked quickly back the other way, and found Segal's office right at the far left end of the corridor. The door was locked. He crunched it open with his boot, walked in and cast his light around. It was a plush corner office with satin-draped windows overlooking the gardens on one side and the street on the other. The room smelled of furniture polish and leather. Segal had a large and fancy antique desk and a big green leather swivel chair, resting on a Persian rug that had probably once graced some Middle Eastern palace. The walls were covered with prints of ancient artifacts, and display cabinets housed items from Segal's own collection.

But Ben wasn't here to admire works of pottery and sculpture. Two minutes and counting. The alarm shrilled on.

Ben strode over to the desk. Segal was one of those guys who kept their desktop assiduously tidy, nothing on it but a phone, a closed laptop and a silver-framed photograph of himself with an attractive middle-aged woman whom Ben presumed to be Madame Segal. The desk had nine drawers, of which three were locked. Ben didn't have a crowbar, but there were other means of getting into locked drawers, if you weren't worried about noise and damage. He drew the pistol back out from his belt, took the silencer tube from his pocket and screwed it to the threaded end of the muzzle, then pressed it to each lock in turn and blew it out, keeping his other hand over the ejector port to catch the spent cases which he put in his pocket.

Three drawers, three muted gunshots, a lot of splintered wood, a fine piece of old furniture comprehensively vandalised. He was as bad as the wreckers of ISIL.

He unscrewed the silencer, put the gun away and started rifling through the contents of Segal's desk. He started with the middle drawer and worked his way outwards and downwards, scanning their contents with the thin beam of his torch. Three and a half minutes gone. The alarm jangling and screeching as loud as ever.

Ben stayed calm as he worked his way through all nine drawers. The locked ones contained confidential business documents like financial statements, invoices and receipts, tax returns, import licences and employee contracts, Romy Juneau's among them. The other six were stuffed with less sensitive material. Letters from museum curators, transcripts of talks Segal had given, cuttings from magazines and newspapers in which he'd been interviewed, and other assorted folders and envelopes in which Ben came across nothing concerning a mystery cargo of ancient Near Eastern artifacts from Tripoli. Nor could he find any trace of the other key piece of information he was looking for, namely Julien Segal's home address.

As he finished sifting through the ninth and last drawer's contents, his heart was beginning to sink. Nothing. Coming here had been a waste of time. Of which he was running out. Six minutes gone. Time to get out of here.

He slid the drawer shut. Then pulled it open and shut it again. Something was preventing it from closing properly, but he couldn't see what. It was only when he lowered himself right down and shone the torch towards the back of the drawer that he noticed the thick manila envelope that had been hidden in a recess of the desk, like a false bottom. It must have got shunted out of place during his search of the drawers, or else he'd never have found it. He said, 'Hello,' and reached inside and pulled it out.

Nearly seven minutes gone. But when Ben examined the documents inside the envelope he realised he'd got lucky. *Bingo.* He took the sheet he needed and folded it into his jacket pocket.

Less than a minute later, he was back in the conference room downstairs. Heading for the window. Stepping out onto the balcony into the cold night air. The rain was still spitting down. The sky over Rue de Rivoli and the Champs Élysées was red and blue with flashing lights. He could hear the ongoing whoop of sirens in the middle distance; so far they weren't coming for him. Closer by, the other side of the wall of ICS's gardens, the street was still empty.

Ben stepped up onto the balcony rail and made the leap back to the tree. The jump sent a sharp jolt of pain through him from his wounds, but the leather gloves mercifully saved his hands from getting torn up by the rough bark of the beech branches. He scrambled back down until he was six feet from the ground, let go and landed softly on bent knees and made for the wall. Seconds later he was back out in the street and heading back the way he'd come, towards the car.

Just under nine minutes, in, out and gone. Mission complete.

On Rue de Rivoli it looked as if the police had succeeded in pushing the crowds into retreat, dispersing them with water cannon and CS as a phalanx of emergency vehicles moved up to clear the battle zone. The riot had been short lived. Another night's drama now coming to a close.

While, by contrast, Ben's evening was just getting started.

Chapter 29

Ben hurried back to the car. He was feeling the painkillers wearing off, and so popped two more before he headed for his next stop.

The document in his pocket was a page of a recent bank statement, one of many pages that had been carefully stored inside the manila envelope Segal kept hidden in his desk. The envelope was addressed to the ICS offices but the statements were for a personal savings account showing a balance of over a million euros, which suggested to Ben that this was where he was keeping his ill-gotten gains from the business he was doing on the side with his jihadist cronies. The subterfuge also made Ben wonder if Segal wasn't hiding assets from his wife. Men were known to do that when they were secretly planning on running out on their beloveds. Maybe when Segal hit the two or three million mark he'd be off to Monaco or Switzerland with his mistress.

Segal's financial and marital affairs were of little interest to Ben. But the man's home address was very much so – and there it was, crisply laser-printed at the head of the bank statement sheet.

It took Ben forty minutes to get there, by which time the rain had stopped and the clouds had peeled away to reveal a bright moon. Montfort L'Amaury was a picturesque little commune that nestled by the foot of the hills north of the Rambouillet Forest. The archaeologist's home, a modestly proportioned chateau in a secluded location, stood within a wooded park surrounded by a high stone wall. Ben drove slowly by the gates and saw the big house all in darkness at the head of a long, sweeping driveway. The surface of a private lake glistened under the moonlight.

He circled the property's perimeter for several hundred metres until he came to a leafy track running up its side, and turned in. A little way up the track, he parked the car under the shadowy canopy of a stand of oak trees and waded through the bushes towards the wall. It was high, but its craggy stonework was easy to climb. Ben scrambled up and over, and landed stealthily on the other side among the shrubbery of Segal's country park. Invading the same man's property for the second time in one night. This was getting to be a habit.

He still wasn't convinced that the woman he'd spoken to at ICS had been telling the truth about Segal being out of the country. He obviously travelled a lot, but having only just returned from Libya it was odd that he'd leave again so soon.

Whether true or not, up closer the chateau looked as dark and empty as it had from the road, with not a single light in any of its windows. If Segal was genuinely away on business, he'd either taken Madame Segal along for the ride or she was having an early night. Ben reached the edge of the encircling lawn and crossed a gravelled courtyard, past an ornamental stone fountain that could have belonged to the Palace of Versailles, and crept silently up to the house. Its walls were thick with ivy and the neoclassical columns on its facade gleamed white in the moonlight. As he skirted the side of the building an automatic light came on, and he retreated into the shadows for a few moments, listening and watching. The light went dark again, and he moved on, in search of an easy and discreet way to get inside the house.

When he found the little side door set into an ivy-framed recess in the thick stone wall, he realised that he wasn't the first uninvited visitor to have turned up recently with the idea of breaking into the Segal home. The hasp and padlock securing the door had been ripped loose. The splinters and flakes of paint on the ground at its foot hadn't been there long.

Ben slipped the pistol out from under his jacket and slowly, cautiously, made his way inside the house. He stood immobile in the darkness for a long time, listening, barely breathing. There was total silence, and a feeling of emptiness that told him it was safe to use his torch. The side entrance led into a utility area, comprising a laundry room and a back kitchen, then a short passage took him into the large main hallway. The floor was polished marble and gilt-framed paintings hung on the walls. An eighteenth-century longcase clock sonorously chimed the hour as he passed by. Ten p.m. but the house felt like four in the morning. The illuminated digital panel of an expensive home security system glowed dimly near the front entrance. If nobody was at home, they'd gone out without arming the alarm. Just a little odd, in Ben's experience.

It was a very big house, and it would take him some time to explore all of it. The salon was grand and huge, the dining room even more so. A music room displayed a collection of antique instruments. A library contained ceiling-high bookcases filled with leather-backed classics of literature, poetry, history and philosophical works. Every room Ben looked inside was a treasure trove of art and beauty, and yet nothing at all seemed to have been disturbed.

Whoever had broken into the house before him was either the world's most respectful burglar, or they'd had other reasons for being here.

Either way, something felt very wrong. Ben kept the pistol in his hand as he finished checking the downstairs and crept silently up the sweeping marble staircase to the floor above. More valuable artwork and antiques everywhere; again nothing that seemed remotely out of place.

Not until he came to the master bedroom, swept his torch around and saw the signs that he'd been worried he might find. The empty, dark bedroom was dominated by a princely four-poster, draped in red satin fleur de lys. In the corner by a tall window stood a Second Empire marble-topped dressing table. Beside the table, a slender antique gilt chair lay knocked onto its side on the rug. A woman's hairbrush lay on the floor close by. There were some makeup items on the dressing table: a little mascara bottle with its cap unscrewed, an eyeshadow brush set in a leather case, a tube of lipstick. Ben went over, tucked his pistol in his belt and slipped off his left glove and touched a fingertip to the mascara applicator brush. Still moist. He replaced his glove, picked up the hairbrush, and shone his torch over it to see the long, silvery-blond hairs enmeshed in its bristles.

The signs were subtle, but the message they gave out to Ben was clear. He was getting a déjà-vu memory of entering Romy Juneau's apartment that morning. Because something had happened here, too. Something bad.

And his guess was that Madame Segal's absence from her home couldn't be explained by anything as simple and mundane as a trip abroad. Which would also potentially account for the fact that the burglar alarm was disarmed. If the two of them had gone off together, they wouldn't have left their beautiful home and all its fine contents unprotected. That didn't make sense.

Only one possibility did make sense.

What Ben was seeing had all the hallmarks of an abduction.

Chapter 30

If Ben was right, and whoever had broken into the chateau sometime in the last few hours had taken Julien Segal's wife away against her will, then it couldn't be a coincidence that her husband just happened to be mixed up with vicious men for whom murder and kidnap were a routine event. And it also reinforced Ben's doubts that the story of Segal's overseas trip was true, whether the staff at ICS believed it or not.

So where were the Segals? Were the couple together somewhere, captive, or perhaps dead? Had the suspicion that had fallen on Romy Juneau led Nazim to suspect his business associate of betrayal also, and take steps to eliminate not just him but his wife? Did that mean Madame Segal was in on the whole thing too? Or was she just collateral damage, another tie to be cut?

As Ben stood in the dark, empty house, the bitterness of the realisation was sharp. Knowing that the tentative, faint trail he'd been hoping might lead him to Nazim al-Kassar had just been wiped away. Knowing that he was out of alternatives. There was no Plan B. The mystery was like a fog so dense that he couldn't make out a trace of the reality behind it.

He should just give this up and go home to Le Val.

But how could he do that, knowing that Nazim al-Kassar was alive and still out there somewhere? He couldn't let go. Not with Romy Juneau's lifeless blue eyes still gazing at him in his memory. Not with Françoise Schell in the morgue.

That was when Ben's phone burred in his pocket, jolting him out of his thoughts. He was startled for an instant, unsure whether to answer. Then he fished out the phone and saw Ken Keegan's caller ID on his screen.

'You took your bloody time,' he said to Keegan.

'Prickly sod,' Keegan's voice rasped in his ear. He sounded as though he'd just finished a large dinner and washed it down with several pints of lager before moving on to the whisky. 'So what about that Ethiopia job? Made your mind up, or what?'

'To hell with the Ethiopia job,' Ben said. 'Do you recall our conversation earlier? You'd better be calling with good news.'

'And you'd better start sounding a bit more appreciative, old son. I've been busting my bollocks all day for your sake, and it sounds like I'm going to get bugger all for my trouble. Jesus H. Christ, why do I even bother?'

'You made contact with Tyler Roth?'

'Let's say I spoke to someone who spoke to someone who's in touch with him. Pulled a lot of fuckin' strings to get that far, pal.'

'I do appreciate it,' Ben said, trying to sound more agreeable. 'So do you have a number for Roth?'

There was a pause on the line, accompanied by the sound of tinkling ice and a loud slurp. Keegan smacked his lips and said, 'Forget it. He won't talk to you.'

'Why not?'

'Don't take it personally. I told you he was a funny geezer, didn't I? He won't talk to anyone. Doesn't use phones any more. He's got this crazy idea in his head that there are people listening who shouldn't be.'

'I need to talk to him,' Ben said impatiently. 'It's important.'

And it was, more than ever, now that Ben had run out of other options. If the ex-Delta operative knew anything about why US military intel had wrongly reported Nazim al-Kassar as being dead, maybe he had other information that could lead Ben in the right direction to find him. At this point, Ben didn't care if he had to scour the earth to hunt for Nazim.

Keegan said, 'I said he won't talk to you by phone. But he'll agree to a face to face. On his terms only.'

'Which are?'

'You have to go to him,' Keegan replied. And then he told Ben where he'd have to go.

'That's got to be three thousand miles away,' Ben said. Then had to remind himself that just a moment earlier he'd been prepared to travel the globe in search of Nazim.

'Four thousand miles,' Keegan corrected him with a chuckle. 'Cost of doing business.'

'What the hell's he doing in the US Virgin Islands?'

'Playing golf and fishing with all the other retired lazy bastards, I suppose. How the fuck should I know? So what shall I tell my contact?'

'Tell him I'm on my way.'

'And what about the favour you're going to do your old mate in return for all this? Quid pro quo, remember?'

'Some other time,' Ben said, and hung up the call before Keegan could swear at him.

Alone again, the house seemed oppressively dark and empty. There was nothing more Ben could do here. He retraced his steps back downstairs and outside, across the park and over the wall to the car. It was nearly eleven o'clock. Sitting at the wheel he pulled out his smartphone again, this time to check flights to the US Virgin Islands. He found one leaving Paris before seven the next morning, sixteen hours end to end, with one connection in Miami and landing at Cyril E. King Airport on the Caribbean island of St Thomas sometime early evening, local time. He was reluctant to abort his hunt in order to go running halfway around the world, but he'd already admitted to himself that he had no choice.

Whether Roth would pay off was another question, one that Ben could worry about when he got there. If nothing else, a few hours on a plane might give him time to think.

But nothing could be more stupid than to let himself get caught at the airport, if indeed the cops were onto him. That was a risk Ben couldn't afford to take, which meant he'd have to travel as Paul Harris. It also meant he couldn't book the flight with his own credit card. That was where the rest of Sarfaraz's cash would come in handy. Ben fished out the wad of notes, unrolled it and counted up what he had left. The terrorist had been walking around with nearly three thousand euros in his pocket. More than enough to pay for the return flight and expenses, with change.

Ben drove back to the safehouse and found Thierry asleep at the computer. He considered waking him up to ask how things were coming along, but already knew the answer.

Pierrot was crashed out in the bedroom, fully clothed and snoring as loud as a chainsaw. Junk food packaging was everywhere and it seemed inconceivable that two guys could make so much mess in just the space of a few hours.

Ben let them sleep while he took a shower, cleaned and redressed his wounds and changed into fresh clothes and packed some things for the trip, including Paul Harris's passport. He unloaded and stripped his pistol, and added it to the cache of weaponry he'd already hidden from his temporary houseguests. Lastly he scribbled a note saying, 'Back soon', which he left on the table along with another few euros in case they needed to send out for a pizza. The things you had to think of.

Then Ben quietly left the safehouse, returned to the car and made the twenty-five-kilometre drive out of Paris to Charles de Gaulle Airport, where he paid cash for his flight ticket, no questions, no problems. Thank God some civilised traditions still existed. Sometime after midnight he checked into his executive room at the Hilton. Sarfaraz's money might as well pay for a few luxuries while it lasted.

Ben raided the mini-bar for all the scotch he could find, and sat on the bed flipping TV channels to catch up on the latest news of the Paris terror incident. Amid all the speculation and breast-beating the media were coyly remaining politically correct as to the possible motives of the 'Allahu Akbar'-screaming attackers, while nonetheless happy to broadcast all the gruesome scenes from the aftermath of the shooting. They'd managed to get the President out of hiding from the riots to deliver an impassioned statement about bringing the perpetrators of this latest atrocity to justice, even if nobody seemed to know quite who they were. None of the regular terrorist groups had so far stepped up to claim responsibility.

Nor was there any mention of a bogus plain-clothes police detective seen fleeing from the scene, whom authorities were seeking to help them with their inquiries. Then again, you couldn't believe everything you saw on TV.

Ben turned it off, poured himself another drink and stood out on the balcony with a cigarette, watching the activity at the airport terminal across the way. Feeling suddenly very weary, he undressed and clambered into bed.

Today had been a long day. Tomorrow might be even longer, and he had no idea what it might bring.

Chapter 31

Two hours and forty-six minutes after takeoff from Miami, the Air Sunshine flight with one Paul Harris on board touched down on the runway on the island of St Thomas. Cyril E. King International airport was its own little peninsula stretching out over the ocean. From the air it looked like a grounded aircraft carrier. St Thomas was the largest of the islands, with a few smaller ones dotted around. An invisible line separated the US territory from the British Virgin Islands, just thirty kilometres across the water.

Mr Harris was travelling light, with just a single bag whose battered military appearance drew a few inquisitive looks from the customs officials. After clearing security he stepped out into the balmy early evening. The sun was beginning to set, casting shimmering hues of gold and crimson and purple over the ocean. Palm trees swayed gently in the breeze. It felt a long, long way from the cold and damp of northern France, and it was. Off-season, the island was far less packed with tourists than it might have been. The laid-back Caribbean vibe was in evidence everywhere, and under different circumstances a fellow could have been forgiven for making straight for the nearest beach bar and seeing out the glorious sunset with a rum cocktail or two. But Ben wasn't here for the scenic tour.

While he was still en route to Charles de Gaulle, Keegan had called back to say that one of Roth's 'people' would come to pick him up at the island airport. Ben hadn't been waiting long when a bright-yellow Ford Mustang screeched into the parking lot and pulled up nearby. The guy who stepped out of the car wore dark glasses, a Panama hat and a tropical flowery shirt that hung loose enough around his middle to conceal a handgun.

'You Hope?' His mouth twisted when he talked, like a snarl.

Ben nodded. 'What do I call you? Bugsy? Baby Face?'

'I'm Angelo,' the guy snarled back at him. Pulling out a phone he stabbed a number and muttered, 'He's here.' As he put the phone away Ben got a glimpse of the revolver butt sticking out of Angelo's cargo trousers.

Ben said, 'I thought Roth didn't use a phone, as a rule.'

'He don't.' Angelo motioned towards the car. 'Let's go. He's waitin'.'

Ben didn't much care for the guy's tone, or for the fact that he'd come armed. He said nothing as he got in the car. Angelo dived in behind the wheel and took off with a raspy V8 roar and a squeal of tyres. They sped out of the airport and turned out into a long sweeping coastal boulevard following the twisty contour of the shoreline with verdant forested hills rising up on one side, the shimmering golden ocean on the other. People drove on the left in the US Virgin Islands, like in Britain, despite the cars having left-hand drive.

Ben lit up a Gauloise without winding down his window. Angelo flashed him a disapproving look from behind the dark glasses, but didn't pull out his revolver. Perhaps he wasn't such a bad guy after all.

Ben asked, 'Where are we going?'

'Across the island to meet the boat.'

The sun was sinking fast. Ben asked, 'You planning to take those shades off after nightfall, or do you like to drive blind?'

'I can see just fine,' Angelo mumbled. 'Don't you worry about me, buddy.'

'Fine,' Ben said. 'Just don't let me see that gun again. Or you won't like what happens next, okay?'

Angelo fell silent and didn't speak another word for the rest of the journey. Night fell. The road skirted the islands' capital of Charlotte Amalie, then left the city behind, snaking west and north as their headlights shone through thick forest that hugged the road, now and then passing a solitary house. From what Ben had understood, Roth lived on one of the smaller islands off St Thomas.

They passed by the small town of Bonne Esperance, and continued a winding route westwards until the twisting road had gradually narrowed with jungle-like foliage encroaching on both sides. Then the trees parted and Ben saw the dark ocean filling the horizon. The car snaked down a winding cliff track that led to a tiny harbour. Angelo pulled up by an old wooden jetty, to which was moored a motor cruiser, its lights bobbing on the water that lapped at the shore.

Angelo turned on the car's interior light and nodded towards the boat. Ben grabbed his bag and got out, while Angelo remained at the wheel. Ben walked away without saying a word to him. He walked along the jetty to the waiting boat. Its pilot was a dreadlocked Afro-Caribbean guy who was smoking a cigar and greeted Ben with a smile and a 'Hail up, Pardnah,' and introduced himself as Emile.

Ben climbed aboard, and Emile cast off. The boat burbled out to sea, the twin outboards churning up a white wake behind them. The ocean was flat and smooth, but this was hurricane season and things could get rough without warning. Emile smoked and talked incessantly over the burble of the engines, speaking a form of Creole English out of which Ben caught maybe one word in five. Ben asked him where they were headed, and Emile pointed westwards and replied, 'Over deh ih Savana Island, Bahss. That's where we be goin.'

Ben peered into the darkness. 'Roth lives there?'

Emile grinned, 'Sure does, mos' defenetly.'

'The guy with the hat. Does he work for Roth too?'

Emile's smile fell away as he replied darkly, 'Angelo? Yuh cyan trust dat moomoo.'

'Thanks for the advice.'

The boat burbled on. After a few more minutes the dark silhouette of Savana Island could be made out against the night sky, a hemispherical dome rising out of the ocean to blot out the stars. Ben could make out a few faint lines by the shore, another jetty that he guessed was their destination. As they chugged closer Emile steered the cruiser towards a tiny inlet. Forested cliffs loomed high overhead. Emile cut the motors and they bumped against the jetty and lashed up. On shore, the lights of a Jeep flared into life. Ben disembarked and headed towards the waiting vehicle, where he was met by another Afro-Caribbean much less loquacious than Emile, and a burly white guy who said, 'Yo, my name's Charlie. I work for Mr Roth. Okay if I frisk you, bud?'

Ben said it was okay, and held out his arms to let him do his work. What Keegan had said about Roth's paranoia was no joke, obviously. Charlie finished patting him down and said, 'You're clean. Welcome to Savana Island.' He ushered Ben into the open-top Jeep. The Afro-Caribbean guy gunned the engine, and they took off with Charlie riding shotgun, climbing fast into the dark forested hills.

The track was steep and twisting, and badly surfaced with

ruts full of white sand that made the Jeep tyres dig in deep and spin for traction. The night air ruffled Ben's hair and shirt, thick with the warm scent of the sea mixed with palm vegetation and flowers. They bumped along for about a mile without seeing any sign of human habitation, then rounded a bend in the track and a house suddenly came into view. It stood perched high on a clifftop with big windows overlooking the ocean and a decking on stilts that jutted out over the cliff edge.

The Jeep rolled to a halt. Charlie waved towards the house and said, 'Right up there, bud. He's waitin' for ya.'

Ben got out. The Jeep pulled a tight U-turn around him, throwing up spumes of sand, then roared back off down the track leaving him standing there alone. Four thousand miles from Paris, Ben had finally reached the island hideaway of the reclusive Tyler Roth.

Chapter 32

As Ben climbed the sandy wooden steps up to the house, he could hear the ocean's steady roar and the crash of the waves breaking against the rocks below. And something else. The soft, melodic notes of a Spanish guitar drifting on the wind. He stepped up onto the wooden walkway that led around the side of the house to the decking, following the music.

The decking was bathed in warm light from the windows. Roth was sitting on a stool with his back to Ben, facing the ocean with the guitar cradled in his lap. Playing it well, with the practised air of a man who had a lot of time to devote to becoming proficient, and a depth of melancholic expression that Ben found surprising in a professional warrior whom he'd last seen with an automatic weapon in his hands. Roth seemed lost in the music, as though unaware of his visitor's presence. A tall cocktail stood on a low table nearby, along with an ashtray in which rested a long, fat cigarette that hadn't come from a packet. The faint tang of marijuana reached Ben's nose.

At the sound of Ben's footsteps on the wooden decking he stopped playing and turned to face his visitor.

'Hey, man. It's been a long time.'

'Hello, Tyler.'

Roth laid down the instrument, stood and stepped towards Ben with a broad grin and an extended hand. He'd changed a good deal in sixteen years. Leaner than he'd been in his Delta Force days, when he and his men had spent all their down time pumping iron. His military buzz cut was grown out well past his shoulders, into a mass of sandy curly hair that was starting to turn silver and loosely drawn back into an untidy ponytail. He was barefoot, in ragged jeans cut off at the knee and a well-worn T-shirt that said BEACH BUM.

They shook hands. Roth said, 'You want a beer? Or something with a little more punch, maybe.' He motioned back at the cocktail on the table. 'They got a drink on St Thomas called a Painkiller. Rum, pineapple, coconut, orange juice and a hint of fresh grated nutmeg. I just made up a batch. Heavy on the rum, blows your mind.'

Ben had already swallowed enough painkillers for one day. 'I'm good, thanks, Tyler. I came four thousand miles to talk, not to drink.'

Roth shrugged his shoulders.

'No problemo, amigo mio, whatever you say. I appreciate you coming all this way to see me. Don't get a whole lot of visitors to the island.'

'It might have been easier to talk by phone. I was a little busy to just drop everything.'

With a grin, Roth replied, 'Sorry, man. Not an option. No phone, no email, not that I get any cellphone reception out here. It's hardly even safe to talk face to face any more. Fucking NSA got their surveillance drones everywhere these days. Privacy comes at a premium, and you're looking at it.' He spread his arms wide and beamed up at the heavens.

Ben wondered if Roth hadn't gone a bit crazy in his retirement. Maybe the marijuana and the rum cocktails weren't helping. Or maybe that was the whole idea and everyone else was playing a fool's game.

'Keegan tells me you're out of the loop. How long have you been living here?'

'Oh, a while, I guess. Not much to keep me in Bowie County, Texas, any more. Not since the last Mrs Roth took herself out of my life. Bitch. Anyhow, decided after that I was done risking my ass for strangers. I'd put by a bunch of money, enough to last me out, if I don't go too nuts with it. So here we are, just me and the cat, a case of rum and my old geetar. I like it. It's kinda peaceful.'

'I can resonate with that,' Ben said. 'Who doesn't enjoy a little peace, when we get the chance?'

Roth smiled. 'But you didn't come here to inquire into the state of my health and happiness, did you? You got your own agenda, and it's important enough to drop everything and come all the way here from . . .?'

'Paris,' Ben said. 'France, not Texas.'

'Paris, France. I always wanted to go there.'

'You missed the best days. It isn't what it used to be.'

'Story of my life, bro. Ain't that true of the whole world now? Going to hell, all of us. Faster than we think.'

'Nazim al-Kassar is alive,' Ben said.

At the mention of that name, Roth's demeanour instantly changed. One moment he was the amiable and relaxed beach bum that his T-shirt proclaimed him to be; the next he was as focused as a hunting timber wolf and wearing his implacable old Delta face. 'That's an interesting piece of information. That the reason you came here, to tell me that?'

'You don't seem too surprised,' Ben said. 'Considering your government seemed so sure that they'd taken him out three years ago.'

The ocean wind was picking up and becoming blustery.

Heavy black clouds had been rolling in from the west while they talked, and now the first fat raindrop hit the decking with a thud, soon followed by another.

'Looks like we got some weather coming in,' Roth said. 'Let's go talk inside.'

He gathered up his drink, ashtray and guitar and led Ben through one of the big sliding windows into the house as the rain started hammering down with sudden violence. The furnishings were modern and comfortable. A large L-shaped sofa took up the best part of two walls, with a giant TV screen opposite. The pictures were all of wavy palm trees and ocean sunsets. Nothing anywhere to hint at Roth's military past.

'Make yourself comfortable, man,' Roth said, propping the guitar in a corner. He flopped down on the sofa, and Ben sat across from him. The incoming squall slapped the windows like crackling fire and the wind shook the house.

'Those things come out of nowhere,' Roth said.

'A bit like certain ghosts from the past, just when you'd started to forget about them.'

'You don't believe in ghosts.'

'Do you?' Ben asked him.

Roth chuckled. 'You spend enough time out here alone, you could start to believe in just about anything. But Nazim al-Kassar coming back from the dead? That's a big deal, my friend. Especially to guys like you and me, who saw with our own eyes what that motherfucker was capable of.'

'What's the current official line?'

'How should I know? I'm just a retired army veteran. I don't have those kinds of contacts.'

'Come on, Tyler. You and I both know that once you get in that deep, you're a member for life. And you were in the game even longer than I was.'

Roth smiled. 'The official line remains what it was back in 2016, namely that a 13th Marine Expeditionary Unit Harrier squadron deployed from the USS *Boxer* in the Persian Gulf on August 21 as part of Operation Inherent Resolve, and iced al-Kassar's piece of shit ass six miles northwest of Ramadi, along with nine other ISIL commanders with whom he was meeting. Delta had boots on the ground just minutes later and confirmed that al-Kassar was among the dead.'

Ben shook his head. 'If they made a positive ID, then he's got an identical twin.'

'Actually, the ID was made from a piece of his right ear. That was the only bit of the fucker they could find still intact among the ruins of the house.'

'Nice job,' Ben said. 'Nothing like reliable intelligence.'

'You said it, amigo. But why should I believe yours?'

Ben took out Romy Juneau's phone, scrolled up the video file, and tossed the phone to Roth. 'Because it's not a piece of his right ear that's walking around killing people.'

Roth fell silent as he watched the video clip. 'There ain't much to see here, man.'

'There will be. Keep watching. I'll give you a clue. The man on the left.'

Roth's face tightened into a hard frown as he did. A muscle twitched in his jaw.

'Still think I'm seeing ghosts?' Ben asked.

Roth had watched enough. He tossed the phone back to Ben. 'That's our boy, all right. One hundred per cent, no question. Where was this footage taken?'

'Tripoli,' Ben said. 'Just days ago.'

'Small world,' Roth said. He was referring to one of the high points in his Delta career, the takedown of the al-Qaeda operative Abu Anas al-Libi.

'His last known sighting was Paris. As far as I know, he's still in France, but I have no way to find him.'

'And you thought I could help?'

'I'm on my own here, Tyler.'

Roth nodded. 'All right. I can tell you that not everyone on the Delta team was confident of making a positive ID on the remains. Personally, I'd figured on fifty-fifty, tops, that it was our guy.'

'Not too solid a basis for the White House to issue a formal confirmation.'

Roth gave a shrug. 'I wasn't totally comfortable with the official story. Now I'm even less so, for obvious reasons. But certain people high up wouldn't want to lose face by admitting claims of his demise were exaggerated.'

'They might not have a choice.'

Roth pointed at the phone in Ben's hand. 'Tell me about the other asshole. The guy on the right.'

Ben told Roth what he knew about Julien Segal's involvement. He described what had happened to Romy, Thierry's efforts to extract some meaning from the video soundtrack, his meeting with Françoise Schell and the attack on the café, and how the search for Segal had so far come to a dead end.

Roth was hanging onto every word of Ben's story. 'You think they've got the wife?'

'I've been thinking about it for four thousand miles. My guess is, al-Kassar and his people are holding her to use as leverage against Julien Segal. Whatever they're up to, it's something big and they're obviously cagey about trusting him, after what happened with his assistant. And I'd say the feeling must be mutual. He's probably just as terrified of them as Romy was. Especially now they're threatening his wife.'

'Makes sense,' Roth agreed. 'Which suggests that he still has some role to play in all of this. He makes one false move, tries to cut and run, the hostage gets it. Classic ISIL tactics. But the big question is, what the hell are they planning? Something that scared the shit out of that poor woman. So it all hangs on your guy, what's his name, Thierry? Because if we could hear what these pricks are talking about . . .'

'I'm not optimistic,' Ben said. 'He's getting nowhere.'

'And you're running out of options. If he screws up or there's nothing there to begin with, you've got squat. Which is why you came here. But what exactly did you think I could bring to the deal?'

'I was hoping you might be able to shed light on where al-Kassar hangs out these days.'

'What makes you think that?'

'You were Delta.'

'And you were SAS.'

'I've been out a long time,' Ben said. 'I left the regiment under a cloud, and they don't forget that. Whatever contacts I once had are old and stale. Whereas you were the golden boy. I don't believe they didn't give you ultra-top-level clearance after you brought them Abu Anas al-Libi. Not to mention the haul of secret ISIL plans from the Deir Azzar raid.'

Roth gave a wry smile. 'Been checking up on me, huh?'

'Hearing rumours through the grapevine is one thing. Being able to go and knock on doors is another. Don't tell me you don't have a toe in the water. Maybe more than one.'

Roth made a noncommittal gesture. 'I do know people. And those people might know something.'

'Will you ask them?'

Roth said nothing for a long moment. Then, 'You must be hungry. Let's eat.'

Chapter 33

Ben sensed that he'd pushed as hard as he could for now. To be resumed. The night was young and it didn't look as though he was going anywhere as the storm kept building outside.

Roth hit the kitchen with vigour, clattering pots and pans and whistling loudly to himself. Before long the mouth-watering aroma of grilled fish began to permeate the house, and a few minutes later he emerged carrying a tray with two heaped plates on it. 'Red snapper with lemon and okra,' he announced proudly. 'Can't visit Savana Island without tasting some real Caribbean chow. You want to grab us some vino from the refrigerator?'

The wine was a California Pinot Grigio. Ben pulled a face when he saw it, but he was prepared to put aside his prejudices. They sat down at a small table to eat. Roth uncorked the bottle and poured brimming glasses with relish.

'You're quite the chef,' Ben said, tasting the fish. The wine was surprisingly good, too, and chilled to perfection.

'Try some of the escovitch sauce,' Roth said. 'Look out for the Scotch Bonnet slices, though. They kick some serious ass, but I can't resist 'em.'

'Scotch Bonnets I can handle,' Ben said. He chewed the end off one and it was like swallowing a white phosphorus grenade mid-blast. Roth seemed to enjoy watching him struggle with it.

They ate in silence as the howling gale shuddered the windows and seemed to want to tear the house off the side of the cliff. Ben had forgotten how hungry he was and devoured every scrap, hot peppers and all. The Pinot went down all too smoothly and the level in the bottle descended fast. When it was finished, Roth fetched another from the fridge. He refilled their glasses, leaned back in his seat and lit up another marijuana joint. 'Want some of this shit?' he asked. Ben declined, and took out his Gauloises and Zippo.

Roth sucked down a few puffs, then shook his head as though deep in thought and eyed Ben curiously.

'Gotta ask you something, man. Iraq was a long fuckin' time ago. What makes going after Nazim al-Kassar such a big deal to you after all these years? Your life's moved on.'

'And Romy Juneau's life came to a rather sudden end,' Ben said, as he bathed the tip of his Gauloise in orange flame.

Roth took another puff and blew out a cloud of smoke. 'People get killed, bro. Ain't fair or right, but it's always happened and it always will. You barely even knew this woman.'

'She's not the only innocent person he's harmed. He'll go on doing it until he's stopped.'

'True, but then again you're not the only one scoping for the motherfucker. Sooner or later someone will take him down. But that's not good enough for you, is it?'

Ben was quiet for a long moment. Then said, 'Samara.'

Roth raised an eyebrow. 'Who's she?'

Ben replied, 'Just someone I knew.'

'Someone Nazim hurt?'

Ben said nothing.

Roth blew more smoke and shrugged. 'Whatever, man.

Everybody's got their axe to grind. In my case, it's Carter, Tennant and Lake. My three Delta guys who died in the firefight that day.'

'I thought only two were killed.'

Roth shook his head sadly. 'Carter and Tennant were KIA right on the scene. They didn't deserve to buy the farm, but at least it was a merciful end. Gene Lake was one of the wounded we casevaced out. Poor bastard caught one in the liver. Took him nearly four months to die in agony. I was there, with his wife Sally and their three kids, when he finally passed. Long as I live, I'll never forget the looks on their faces.'

'Some things you can't forget,' Ben said.

Roth nodded. 'And some things you can't forgive. You think the rage will pass, but it don't. I'll never stop hating those fanatical sons of bitches.'

'ISIL?'

'All of them. The whole rotten bunch.' Roth's eyes blazed. 'These people are savages, right out of the Dark Ages.'

'That's what Françoise Schell said, too.'

'And she was a smart lady. It doesn't hurt to listen to smart people once in a while, Ben. There ain't a lot of them around. And very few folks willing to hear the truth.'

'The truth?' Ben said.

'The politicians know it, when they're standing up and trying to persuade us over and over that Islam's really this touchy-feely ol' religion of peace that has nothing to do with terrorism. Half of them are only saying that because they're shit scared they'll spark off a freakin' bloodbath right on their home soil. The other half are saying it because they're in bed with the Saudis, doing deals over oil and fighter jets. Meanwhile, most people in the West still have no idea what kind of an enemy we're up against. An enemy single-mindedly devoted to destroy the whole world in order to achieve our complete submission.'

Ben flicked ash and took another sip of wine. 'I don't know about that, Tyler.'

'You don't work for the Pentagon, then. It's been thirteen years since they assigned intelligence analysts to write a report examining what's driving educated young Islamic men, and even some women, to commit acts of suicide and murder. Their reluctant conclusion? That the single source of these people's motivation was the Qur'an itself. It's not a book of religion. It's a goddamn hate-filled recruiting pamphlet for a culture of conquest that openly glorifies violence against the infidel, and has no higher calling than that of the suicide bomber.'

'Have you read the book?' Ben asked him.

'Sure I have, in three different translations as well as the original Arabic, and the hadiths and sunnah that go with it. And it oughtta scare the crap out of every freedom-loving, God-fearing tolerant Westerner who isn't walking around with their eyes shut. Certainly scares the crap outta me.'

'It doesn't help that we invaded their countries, bombed and killed their people,' Ben said. 'While America led the way as usual.'

Roth looked at him. 'Uh, says the guy who was there and took part?'

Ben replied, 'I did what I did. I don't have to be happy about it.'

'Give me a break, man. We didn't declare war on them. It's the sole purpose and mission of Islam in its purest form to declare war on us and remove us from existence. "When you clash with the unbelieving infidels in battle, smite their necks until you overpower them, killing and wounding many of them. Thus you are commanded by Allah to continue carrying out jihad against the unbelieving infidels until they submit to Islam." Chapter 47, verse 4.'

'So are you just going to sit there quoting the Qur'an all night?'

Roth swallowed the last of his wine and fixed Ben with intense eyes. 'You talk about America like we're always the instigators. Do you know when our country first had dealings with Islamic terror? It was in 1784, only just after we'd declared our independence. We were a completely new nation. Other than defending ourselves against British tyranny we'd never provoked anyone, attacked anyone, offended anyone, and all we wanted to do was get on our feet as a trading nation. That's when Muslim pirates from Morocco captured an American ship, took its crew hostage and demanded ransom in return for no more hostilities. We paid over the money. And then they kept doing it, only the attacks got worse and the sums got bigger, until we were losing up to sixteen per cent of our federal revenue to pay them off. The demands were coming from the Bey of Tunis, who called himself "Commander of the Frontier Post of the Holy War". In 1786 two of our Founding Fathers, Thomas Jefferson and John Adams, met with his ambassador in London and asked him in all sincerity, "Why are you guys doing this to us? What did we ever do to you?" You know what the ambassador's reply was? That it was based on the teachings of the prophet, that it was all written in the book, that all nations who didn't submit to Islam were sinners, that under Islamic law it was their right and duty to make war on us, and that any Muslim killed in battle against us would find a place in Paradise. In the end it took two wars between the US and the Barbary states, in 1805 and 1815, to put a stop to the attacks.'

'So America declared war on them.'

'And we damned well kicked their asses. But they started it, not us,' Roth said. 'Look. It's like this, okay? In their belief system, the world is divided into two parts. One they call Dar al-Islam, the House of Islam. That's the part of the world over which they have dominion, obtained historically through military conquest, systematic repression of other religions and forced conversion to theirs. The other is Dar al-Harb, the House of War. That is to say, the parts of the world still waiting to be conquered, including your country and mine. The Qur'an is real clear on this, my friend. Right there in black and white, it creates a canonical obligation for believers to remain in a perpetual state of war against all infidels, until the whole world is either converted or subjugated under Sharia Law. "So fight them until there is no more disbelief and all submit to the religion of Allah alone." Qur'an chapter 8, verse 39. I could quote a whole bunch of verses that say much the same thing. And they take that obligation seriously. Just like they do when Allah proclaims: "I will terrorise the unbelievers. Therefore smite them on their necks and every joint and incapacitate them. Strike off their heads and cut off each of their fingers and toes." I mean, come on, man. Doesn't it seem a strange coincidence that they're reading this stuff in their holy book, and then carrying it out in real life? Can anyone actually believe their motivation isn't coming straight out of those pages? Who're we trying to kid?'

Ben had heard all this before, many times. He knew all the arguments through and through. And in some regards, Roth was right.

Chapter 34

Ben had first come across the Qur'an and its associated texts when he was a theology student, and he'd been struck at the time by the aggressive note of many of its more belligerent verses that seemed to be a direct call to arms against unbelievers. Years later, finding himself up against its followers in combat, he'd witnessed the fierceness of their zeal first-hand.

But that wasn't the whole picture for him, and he was uncomfortable with the open hatred Roth was expressing towards these people.

He replied to Roth, 'I hear what you're saying. But you're talking about the crazies. I've known a lot of Muslims who were decent and peace-loving people. You can't pretend they don't exist.'

'Those would be the so-called moderates,' Roth said. 'But what does that really mean, "moderate Muslim"? It's just a term we made up after 9/11 so as to appear culturally sensitive or some such bullshit. If you think about it, it can only mean "a Muslim who doesn't really adhere to the full message of their central religious doctrine, the Qur'an. One who just cherry-picks the verses they want to adhere to, and turns a blind eye to the many, many verses telling them to go to war, fight and die in the way of Allah." In other words, a

Muslim who doesn't really take the teachings of their prophet, or the holy book that purportedly comes straight from the mouth of Allah, all that seriously. Could you even call that person a true believer in Islam?'

'If that's what they call themselves,' Ben said. 'You have to respect it.'

'Tell that to their brethren who actually do follow the book to the letter,' Roth said. 'They would, and do, consider such moderates as vile sinners who deserve death under Islamic law, and will end up in hellfire along with the rest of us unbelievers. "If the Muslims fail in this duty, they will most surely be apprehended by the punishment of Allah." Don't take my word for it. I didn't make this shit up, you know. Their own doctrine states quite clearly that you cannot be a moderate Muslim and a true believer. It's all or nothing.'

'You can be a moderate Christian,' Ben said, 'despite what the Bible teaches. The Qur'an isn't the only book that calls for unbelievers to be killed in the name of God. Leviticus, 24:16, "Anyone who blasphemes the name of the Lord is to be put to death." That goes for gay people, too, incidentally. Meanwhile, Deuteronomy chapter 20 commands the faithful to massacre non-Christians and plunder their property, including their women. And speaking of women, Timothy 2:11 teaches that they should submit to the authority of men, just like it says in the Qur'an. But here's the thing, Tyler. Just because those verses are there, it doesn't mean we have to take them literally.'

Roth smiled. 'You know your Bible. Theology, wasn't it?'

'Long time ago,' Ben says. 'A false career start.'

'Are you a Christian?'

'A lapsed one.'

'Lapsed or not, you do agree that it ain't Christians who go around slicing the throats of disbelievers in the name of

God, or persecuting anyone in their power who holds to a rival religion, or throwing gays off tall buildings, or murdering some poor young girl who looked twice at an infidel boy and calling it an "honour" killing, or stoning a woman to death in the street because she was forced by some a-hole rapist to be "unfaithful" to her husband? Whatever wrong things we might have done once upon a time in the name of the Christian faith, we left that kind of behaviour behind us a long time ago. Not like our dear, sweet Muslim friends, who go on acting like it's the year 630.'

Ben said, 'But you admit it's possible to take or leave what it says in the book, and still call yourself a believer.'

Roth shook his head. 'You're getting it all wrong, buddy. The only reason we can allow ourselves to cherry-pick what the Bible preaches is because Christianity is weak and fading. It was already six centuries old when Islam hit the ground running, foaming at the mouth from Day One to attack, kill or enslave anyone who didn't fall down and worship Allah. Pinning yellow badges on Jews? That was their invention, by the way. The Nazis only copied it, and that's just a taste of what's to come if we let our guard down for one minute. The Islamics have spent the last fourteen hundred years fighting for one purpose only, and they're all fired up and ready for the next fourteen hundred. *Ding*, round two. Forget about the Bible. It's had its day and it's harmless now. The Qur'an is anything but.'

'Only if a crazy radical chooses to interpret it that way.'

Roth replied, 'Okay, so let's say the majority of Muslims are peaceful, law-abiding citizens who happily ignore the call to arms that's a central tenet of their religion, and have no desire to declare jihad on their neighbours and colleagues. Fine. I'm sure the vast majority of Germans in the nineteen-thirties and forties were peace-loving people too. Didn't stop the Nazis from murdering fourteen million people in concentration camps, and costing the world sixty million lives. How about Russians? Lovely folks, most of 'em, right? Didn't prevent the Soviet regime from wiping out twenty million of their comrades, and that's a conservative figure. What about China? Hell, I'd lay down my life for some of the kind and generous Chinese people I've met. And yet a tiny minority of party motherfuckers under Chairman Mao managed to slaughter forty-five million men, women and children in just four years during their so-called Great Leap Forward. You want me to go on?'

'I get the idea,' Ben said.

'The moderate majority was irrelevant in all of those cases,' Roth said. 'Say just five per cent of Muslims are your pure, by-the-book variety, or what we like to call "radicals". Islam has one and a half billion followers worldwide. That equates to seventy-five *million* hardcore jihadists who've fully digested every word their prophet told them and are willing to act out his supreme commands. They outnumber the United States military's combatant forces by fifty-seven to one. And that seventy-five million is another conservative figure, because you can't always trust that a self-proclaimed "moderate" ain't just putting on a disguise to mask their true intentions.'

'Taqiyya,' Ben said.

'You got it, pal. The Islamic doctrine of deception that authorises Muslims to hide their real beliefs, convictions, feelings, opinions, to trick the infidels into trusting them. Straight from the words of the Ayatolla Khomeini, when he said, "Allah taught man to lie so that we can confuse our enemies. Should we remain truthful at the cost of defeat and danger to the Faith? We say not."'

Ben said, 'I don't care about their ideology. All that matters to me is whether a person is trying to inflict harm, against me or someone else. Then I have to try to do something about it.'

Roth shook his head harder. 'You're getting it back to front. The ideology is the driving force behind the whole thing. The individual nutjob trying to blow himself up and take out a hundred innocent people with him is just a symptom. The real disease is the ideas inside the book. You can't just treat the symptom. You have to eradicate the root cause.'

'So you'd want to round up every existing copy of the Qur'an and burn them.'

'On a bonfire a mile high,' Roth said with conviction.

'If history has taught us anything, Tyler, it's that you can't ever hope to change what people believe, and you shouldn't even try. We all know what happens when you try to suppress faith. The best you can wish for is to control their actions, if necessary. In this case, to make sure that the craziest ones don't carry out their intentions. Then we can do whatever the hell we need to stop them.'

Roth laughed, the intensity in his expression suddenly softening. He stubbed out the remains of his joint. 'Well, I guess that'll have to do to be getting on with. We can continue this theological discussion later. It's late, I'm pooped and I'm gonna hit the sack. There's a spare room if you want it.'

'What happens tomorrow?'

'Let me sleep on it,' Roth said. 'I'll let you know in the morning.'

After Roth had gone, Ben stood for a minute watching the ocean waves heave and crash, until he felt so exhausted that he crawled off to the spare room and curled up in bed, too tired to undress, his mind swirling with thoughts that he wanted to shut out.

As he lay there he could hear the steady, soft snoring coming through the wall. Roth might be sound asleep next door, but Ben lay awake most of the night as the storm lashed at the island. Sometime before dawn, he drifted off and began to dream.

Chapter 35

It's been a long afternoon at the dusty roadside. A ragged column of civilian traffic moves slowly through the heat haze and comes to a bottleneck as it reaches the military checkpoint up ahead. A man wearing a long robe and a chequered red keffiyeh is leading a camel along on the end of a rope. A wizened older man is driving a makeshift cart with truck wheels pulled by a donkey. A group of women and children are hurrying nervously along the road, heads bowed, eyes fixed on the ground. The children are aged between about three and ten and walking single-file daisy chain with linked hands; the women are clad from head to toe in black with only their hands and faces showing. The hot, dry air is rank with the Iraqi civilians' fear and tension.

All around, as far as the eye can see, the landscape is flat and arid, baked to the same uniform colour-washed hue by the relentless sun. A few low, crude block buildings stand in the distance, where some desiccated-looking chickens scratch about in the dirt and a dog is barking.

Formations of military Land Rover Defenders and US Army Humvees flank the roadside, filmed with dirt and sand and overlooked by a battle-scarred M1 Abrams tank whose turret gunner is hunkered down behind his Browning fifty-cal, watching the scene with an indifferent expression. A mixed unit of Coalition forces are stopping the traffic and checking people's papers, inspecting cars, pickup trucks, carts and saddle-bags for anything suspicious before waving them on their way. Pedestrians have to be frisked, which is done with great caution, especially with the Muslim women and girls, so as to cause as little offence to the civilian population as possible.

The soldiers' battledress is worn from hard use, day in and day out. Their weapons are scuffed and their eyes are grim and weary. Nobody wants to be here, any more than the civilians appreciate their presence.

Observing the traffic slowly pass through the checkpoint Ben is less interested in the contents of the vehicles, more in the faces of the drivers. Weeks have passed since the escape of Nazim al-Kassar, and Special Forces are on red alert to recapture him. A small group of SAS have been directed to assist the regular troops while identifying routes likely to be used by insurgents. This checkpoint near Karbala, about a hundred miles south of Baghdad, is one of those where their sources tell them they are most likely to intercept key personnel whose capture could potentially inform them of the where-abouts of the renegade JTJ commander or one of his lieutenants.

In other words, it's a bloody wild goose chase and nobody really has a clue what's going on. Ben feels his being here is a waste of time and a poor use of their resources. Apart from anything else, word will quickly have reached any of the mili-tants who might have been considering using this route, and they will simply have altered their itinerary. There are plenty far more valuable things Ben could be doing to help find al-Kassar, but his orders have been clear.

Ben takes his cigarette pack and Zippo from a pouch of his tactical vest, leans against a low sandbag wall and lights up a smoke. He smiles to himself as one of the checkpoint soldiers has trouble hanging onto the camel's lead rope while his colleague is patting down the animal's owner. The army doesn't offer camel handling as part of its basic training programme, but maybe it should. The comic relief over, the camel guy goes on his way. The soldiers circle a dusty pickup truck and begin their next search. This will go on all day, and then some.

From one of the low buildings in the distance comes a woman. Ben notices her from the corner of his eye and watches as she begins walking slowly towards the checkpoint. Like all the Muslim women who've passed through here today, she's dressed in black, with the full hijab and niqab that cover all of her face except her eyes. From a distance it's impossible to make out any details of her, but as she gets closer, it's apparent that she's heavily pregnant and canting her upper body back to counterbalance the weight she carries up front, with her left arm clutching her belly for support. She must be almost nine months gone.

As Ben idly watches her approach he's thinking how sad it is for babies to be born into all of this misery and fear. How long will the child survive in the midst of this terrible war, and what kind of a life will it have growing up in the remains of a country shattered by endless death and pain? He has seen too many children die in this conflict, and others. He feels deep sympathy towards this poor young woman with such an uncertain future ahead of her.

The pregnant young woman comes closer. She appears to be having difficulty walking, dragging her feet in the dust as though she's sick. Ben wonders if she's okay. She seems to be on her own. Perhaps she needs help. It's not unknown for soldiers to have to help deliver a baby when a female civilian suddenly goes into labour far away from the nearest hospital. A delicate situation. He flicks away his cigarette, stubs it into the dirt with his boot heel and starts walking towards her.

Winning hearts and minds is an important part of the SAS's mission here. He believes strongly in that role. He doesn't want these people to see him as their enemy. If there's anything he can do to help, he will, including calling in a chopper to get her to a hospital.

Ben picks up his stride as she shuffles uncertainly towards the checkpoint. None of the other soldiers are paying her any attention. He's within thirty yards of her now, close enough to see the vacant look in her eyes through the slit in her black niqab. She looks hazy and unfocused as though she's drugged out of her mind. Her left hand is still clutching her distended belly. Her right hand is out of sight within the folds of the hijab. The thin cloth over her mouth is moving, as though she's mumbling to herself. Repeating the same words over and over again.

Now Ben can hear what she's saying. It's a prayer.

And it's only then, at that very last moment, that warning bells start to jangle violently in his mind like a hundred fire alarms going off at once. His blood turns to ice and his stomach twists. It's too late for anyone to do anything except take cover. A yell bursts from his lips: DOWN DOWN EVERYBODY DOWN!

But his words seem to have little effect. His voice seems to echo inside his head, as the soldiers and civilians around him appear frozen in time and unable to hear him. His own body feels immensely heavy and it takes a giant effort to move. The nearest person to him is a young British squaddie, no more than about seventeen. Ben hauls him behind the cover of one of the olive-green Defenders and drags him to the ground, covering the startled lad's body with his own.

In the next fraction of a second, the young Iraqi woman activates the plunger switch she was clutching inside the folds of her robe, wired via a detonator to the heavy bundle of C4 explosive in the hidden backpack strapped to her stomach. Almost before the blinding flash and the deafening explosion the shockwave erupts like an omnidirectional shotgun blast, only several magnitudes more powerful. The violence of the detonation is stunning. The two-ton Land Rover shielding Ben and the young soldier is rocked nearly off its wheels. They're showered by the glass of its shattered windows. A circle twenty metres across is engulfed in smoke and billowing dust.

Then it's over, but the aftermath is only about to begin. The horror. The shock. The screams of the wounded and dying. Body parts of soldiers and civilians alike scattered in the dirt. Everything that isn't on fire is spattered with blood. Ben is on his feet, heart racing, emotions numb. The boy he protected is unhurt. Many others haven't been so lucky.

Ben runs through the smoke. His senses are in a turmoil of confusion and he wants to throw up. The sounds of pain and horror are muffled and masked by the ringing in his ears. An Iraqi man is rolling on the ground nearby. He's been eviscerated by the hail of shrapnel from the bomb. He will not survive. Ben rips off his battledress jacket and covers the man with it and tries to talk to him, but there's nothing he can do. The material of the jacket is instantly soaked with blood. Ben steps back and looks around him. Soldiers are yelling wildly and sprinting in from the edges of the scene to help anyone they can. In minutes, medic choppers will be on their way and this place will become an emergency field hospital.

Ben picks a path through the carnage towards the smoking crater and looks down at the torn, smouldering figure on the ground at the epicentre of the blast. Or two figures, because the woman's body has been separated in half by the explosion. There is nothing left of her midsection. Her legs are mangled human wreckage in the dirt, peeled to the bone. The niqab has been torn away from her face, which has somehow remained untouched by the detonation. She stares up at Ben with dark, empty eyes. She would have felt nothing, experienced only a momentary white light as the explosion ripped her apart.

He wonders who she was. What was her part in all of this? Who convinced her to sacrifice herself in this cruel war that nobody can even understand?

Ben goes on looking down at the dead woman. Her sightless gaze seems to look straight back at him.

And then her eyes suddenly snap open and she opens her mouth to speak.

'Bennnnn . . .'

He awoke with a start, uncertain of where he was for a few moments, until he realised that he was in Tyler Roth's cliff house on Savana Island in the here and now, and not back in the hellhole of Iraq in 2003. His vivid dream had left him shaking and covered in sweat. He lay blinking in the darkness, breathing hard, and focused on listening to the reassuring, meditative sound of the ocean until the tension oozed from his clenched muscles and he was able to relax into the softness of the bed.

Some things you never forget.

Chapter 36

Ben had been awake for less than thirty minutes before he heard Roth getting up and the patter of the shower. He emerged from the spare room soon afterwards to find the American bustling about in the kitchen, all energy and smiles as he put on a pot of coffee. Last night's storm was just a memory and the morning sun was shining brightly over the dazzling blue ocean. Palm trees swayed lazily in the soft breeze and the sandy beach in the cove below the house was as white as snow. Another perfect day in Paradise.

Roth had exchanged yesterday's beach bum garb for khaki jeans and an old army shirt, neatly pressed. Ben noticed the packed kit bag on the floor. 'Planning a trip somewhere?'

'You asked me what happens next,' Roth said. 'I made my decision. Seeing as we both have unfinished business with Nazim al-Kassar, you ready to buddy up?'

'As in what exactly?'

'As in, I travel back with you to Paris. You said you needed my help, didn't you?'

'I thought you were a recluse who didn't like to leave his island,' Ben said.

Roth shrugged. 'Been thinking maybe I oughtta get out more. Reckon this is as good a chance as I'm gonna get. And it's worth it, for a shot at that motherfucker. I already radioed

Charlie and told him to get me on the first flight.' He looked at his chunky watch. 'Which gives us precisely twenty-seven minutes to get ready before the chopper arrives.'

Ben had come to Savana Island in the hope of gaining information. Instead he was returning with a co-partner. It was more than he'd bargained for. But it just might work out well. Nobody could doubt Roth's skills, that was for sure.

He said, 'Chopper?'

Roth grinned. 'Quickest way out of here, amigo. When I move, I move fast. Hit the shower and grab some coffee. That's Jamaican Blue Mountain. Finest in the world.'

The world's finest coffee was drained to the last drop by the time the thump of rotors sounded over the island, and Ben looked out of the window to see the bug-like light Sikorsky helicopter coming in to land. Roth pulled on a black nylon flight jacket and a baseball cap and grabbed his kit bag, and the two men went out to meet the chopper. Sixty seconds later, Savana Island was receding into the distance as they buzzed towards St Thomas.

Another ninety minutes after that, they were in the departure lounge waiting to get on the KLM flight back to Europe, via Newark. Ben had been able to exchange his return ticket and all was going smoothly, except for the fact that he'd tried four times to get through to Thierry Chevrolet, to no avail.

'Who's that, your technician guy?' Roth asked, only mildly curious.

'I wouldn't call him that exactly.'

'What would you call him?'

'Thierry's a crook who hangs out with lowlife sleazebags,' Ben said. 'But he's a talented crook. And normally reliable. Plus, he owes me. I don't understand why he isn't picking up.'

'Never trust the French,' Roth said with great authority,

and went back to reading the magazine he'd bought from a newsstand.

Then they were off again, climbing over the glittering blue waters until the islands were just green splodges far below. Ben leaned back in his seat and wondered why Thierry wasn't answering his calls. He hoped everything was all right; it frustrated him that he'd have to wait until they touched down in New Jersey before he could try again. He brooded over it a while longer, then gave up worrying about things he couldn't control. Roth was a quiet travelling companion, apparently lost in his own thoughts and not much interested in conversation. That suited Ben fine, though he noticed the way that Roth was gripping the arms of his seat as though willing the plane to go faster, a tense look in his eyes. A man in a serious hurry, Ben thought.

When they reached Newark with a few hours to kill before the next leg, Ben called Thierry's number again and got the same result. What was going on with the guy? Roth seemed vague about Ben's concerns, as though he had more pressing matters on his mind, and announced that he was going for a walk. He was gone a long time. Ben was used to travelling alone, and he was good at waiting, but Thierry's lack of response was gnawing at him.

Finally, at 18.20 Eastern Time, they were back in the air. Ben had a window seat and watched as New Jersey, framed in the porthole window, grew smaller and hazier beneath them. They were in the clouds before they reached the Atlantic coast. Roth's stroll around the airport had obviously helped him work out his tensions. His newfound relaxation marked a sharp contrast with his earlier state, and he was content to doze off with a little smile on his face. Ben soon lost interest in both Roth and the view from the window, and thought only about Nazim al-Kassar.

Just over eight hours after takeoff from Newark Liberty, the plane hit the runway at Charles de Gaulle. Two-thirty a.m. Eastern Time was half past seven in the morning, Central European Time, making it a short night. Ben and Roth disembarked, went through security separately and met up again outside. By the time Roth appeared, Ben had already tried Thierry again twice. Still no reply. His worry was growing.

'Hot wheels, man,' Roth commented of the Alpina as Ben led him across the car park. 'I had an SRT Challenger that was faster than a goddamned Hydra rocket. Never could hit two hundred miles an hour, though. I'll bet this baby's good for it.'

'I drive like a girl,' Ben said. 'It keeps the insurance premiums down.'

'I'll bet. So what's our first port of call in the City of Light?'

Ben had already decided on that. He took off towards Paris, driving like a girl, and carved his way through the morning traffic to the safehouse.

When they got there, Ben's darkest fears were half realised. Worst case scenario, he'd imagined that either the Corsicans or Nazim's people had somehow managed to trace the address and Thierry and his friend Pierrot would be lying dead in pools of blood. But that wasn't the sight waiting to greet them.

Instead, the safehouse was empty. The two men were gone. No Thierry. No Pierrot. And no laptop containing the video clip, either, because it had been removed from the table where it had been sitting before. Nothing else was missing or disturbed. The hidden guns were still where Ben had left them. He took one for himself and tossed another to Roth.

'I'm feeling at home already,' Roth said, loading up his

pistol. 'I take it these things aren't available to civilians here, right?'

'Only if they're criminals,' Ben said. 'Welcome to Europe, land of the free.'

If Thierry and his friend's disappearance was a puzzle, the missing computer was even more so. If Nazim had taken them, he'd have had good reason for taking the laptop with the incriminating file loaded on it, too. But he'd also have left men posted in anticipation of Ben's return, which meant that Ben and Roth would have walked into an ambush just now. And if the Corsicans had taken them, common or garden thugs of that variety would have had no reason to take just the laptop without ransacking the whole apartment into the bargain.

The biggest problem with either theory was that Ben's safehouse was virtually impossible to find, let alone break into. Its only entrance was inaccessible from the street and protected by a thick steel door strong enough to resist rifle bullets. There were no signs of forced entry.

To Roth, the explanation to the conundrum was a simple one. 'You said yourself, the guy's a crook who runs with lowlife sleazebags. It's obvious he's just skipped out on you, buddy. He grabbed the dough and ran, and took your shiny new laptop with him to sell for a few extra bucks. Don't sweat it. You still have the Juneau woman's phone, with the original file on it. And we have to move on. You want to hear the plan?'

'You only just got here,' Ben said. 'And you have a plan?'

'I told you, when I move I move fast,' Roth replied.

Ben looked at him. 'From St Thomas to Newark, you wanted to move fast. You could have been strapped inside a US Air Force Lockheed Blackbird going at Mach 3, and it wouldn't have got there soon enough for you. But for the second leg of the journey, you were a guy with time on his hands. Not a care in the world. Whatever you've been hiding from me happened somewhere in-between. To be precise, it happened at the airport, during your little stroll. I sense that you're not quite as out of touch as you pretend to be. Who'd you talk to?'

For an instant Roth seemed as though he was about to deny it; then he broke into a rueful grin. 'Busted. You're an observant sonofabitch, aren't you?'

'And you're a sonofabitch with secrets. I like to be able to trust the people I work with.'

Roth reached into his jacket and pulled out a small iPhone. 'What the hell. Had to come out sooner or later, so I guess now's confession time. I broke my own rule. One of my contacts came through. But one rule I'll never break is to compromise my sources, so don't ask me to name the guy, okay?'

'Don't waste time, Tyler. Tell me what he said.'

'Actually you were only half right. I talked to him twice, the first time before you got up this morning, the second time at Newark like you guessed. My guy has a source inside the GIGN and tells me they have a lead on one of the dead shooters from the Montparnasse attack.'

Ben knew all about the GIGN, the elite counterterror division of France's National Gendarmerie. He'd taught advanced close-quarter combat classes to some of them at Le Val, and was on first-name terms with one or two of their commanders. But they didn't exactly keep him abreast of all their latest black ops missions. He said, 'I'm listening.'

'The asshole in question is the one they found bled out in his car near the scene of the attack,' Roth said. 'You wouldn't know anything about that, of course, but his name was Sarfaraz Baqri and he was on their terror watchlist, along with a bunch of known associates that they've been waiting for the right moment to spring a surprise raid on. The shooting makes it the right time.'

Roth brought up an image on his phone and held it up for Ben to see. It showed a scowling African man in his late twenties, with a scrappy growth of beard.

'This here little bundle of sweetness and light is Hasan Jafari, emigrated to Europe from the dear old Republic of Sudan eight years ago, currently resident here in Paris, suspected of various involvements with al-Qaeda, Daesh and terror cells in France, never caught, but the good guys reckon they've got sufficient probable cause to greenlight the snatch. It's happening today. You never know what juicy titbits of information might come our way, after they squeeze the fucker like a tomato. It could help lead us to al-Kassar.'

'Today when?' Ben asked.

'There was some logistical delay, or it would already have happened by now,' Roth said. 'It was originally planned for dawn this morning. When I talked to my guy the second time, I found out they'd rescheduled the raid for tonight.'

'Hence the reason you went from acting so jumpy to suddenly as cool as a cucumber.'

'I was anxious to find out how the raid had gone and whether they'd got him. Now it turns out we have some clock to burn before they make their move.'

'I take it we're not officially invited to this party?' Ben said.

'No, but we're gonna be ringside when it happens. Should be fun to watch. So I suggest we hole up here in your cosy little apartment, grab some food and sleep, and prepare for the evening's entertainment.'

Ben couldn't believe Roth had managed to find all this out with two phone calls. 'Not bad contacts for a reclusive army veteran.'

Roth chuckled. 'Just keeping a toe in the water, bro.'

Chapter 37

The scheduled time was shortly after midnight, and the location was an address in the commune of Villejuif, a few kilometres south of the city. After a long, frustrating day of waiting, Ben and Roth rolled up to the scene with plenty of time to spare and found a parking space sixty metres down the street where they could observe the action.

The directions provided by Roth's mysterious contact had led them to a quiet suburban street where apartment buildings were interspersed with older red-brick houses and gardens, some in a better state of maintenance than others. Like every other modern urban setting, most walls and shutters were plastered with graffiti, and the pavements were littered. The flicker of TVs showed behind curtained windows and the soft boom-boom of music sounded from somewhere.

'Villejuif,' Roth muttered, shaking his head. 'Jew Town. Might have been true once, but now the Muslims are driving them all out. Over fifty thousand Jewish people have fled France to the States or Israel in just a few years under threat of persecution. It's the new Nazism, the one nobody wants to admit it's even happening. You know the Islamics had their own SS divisions in World War Two, to carry out genocide against the Jews in Croatia, right? Himmler loved 'em.'

Ben was in no mood for another of Roth's history lectures and said nothing, watching the street. He still couldn't believe that Thierry Chevrolet would have skipped out on him like that. What was the world coming to, if you couldn't trust an honest crook any more?

A couple of cars passed by. The only pedestrian in sight was a beleaguered-looking old guy being dragged along by a pair of yappy terriers, who shuffled past the parked Alpina without noticing the two men inside and disappeared around the corner. Then the street was deserted, but Ben's instinct told him that the GIGN assault team was somewhere close by, biding their time until the last moment.

The target of that evening's raid was a small one-storey end-of-terrace house next door to a pharmacy. The property looked like a student rental, belonging to an absentee landlord who cared little about its upkeep. A low stucco wall bounded a neglected garden of foot-high weeds and dying trees. An ancient Puch moped was tethered up on a rusty chain inside the gate. A dim light shone through the dimpled glass of the front door, and another through the crack in a curtained window.

Ben looked at his watch. Three minutes to midnight. The occupants of the house, however many there might be inside, had no more idea of what was coming than their neighbours up and down the street. When it did, the raid would be swift and efficient, stunning in its suddenness.

'Any time now,' Roth said.

Midnight came and went. Ben had spent much of his life in that still, contained state of mind that comes before an action. He was calmly experiencing it now, even though he and Roth would be no more than observers. He knew that the GIGN unit members would be going through the same mental preparation at this moment.

And then it began.

At ten minutes past midnight, a large black Renault Sherpa light assault vehicle came roaring down the street and pulled to a sharp halt outside the house. 'Here we go,' Roth muttered.

They watched as the doors burst open and men in black jumped out, swiftly entered the gate and took their positions around the front door. The GIGN had come heavily equipped in full tactical gear, body armour and tactical helmets with goggles and respirators, automatic weaponry fitted with launchers for stun grenades. In appearance they were virtually indistinguishable from an SAS, Delta or Navy SEAL assault team, and they moved with the same highly trained fluidity. The point guy was armed with a breaching shotgun, ready to take out the door with frangible buckshot if his colleague with the battering ram didn't breach it fast enough.

They were through in a heartbeat. Effortless. Smooth. Unstoppable. The black-clad figures swarmed inside the hallway. There were loud muffled thumps from the house's interior and brief flashes lit up the windows as the raiders let off their nonlethal munitions, designed to incapacitate the target with disorientating noise and blinding light.

As quickly as the assault had kicked off, everything went suddenly quiet. It looked as if it was over.

And then, even more suddenly, it was only just beginning.

A violent explosion fifty times louder than the pop-pop of the stun grenades rocked the house and blew out the windows and front doorway in a massive mushrooming eruption of flame. One GIGN team member standing by the entrance was knocked off his feet by the force of the shock-wave. His colleague who'd been a step closer to the doorway was engulfed in the fireball. The blast illuminated the street like daylight. Then most of the street-facing section of the roof of the house crashed inwards, the wall collapsed into rubble, and the explosion became a roiling inferno.

Roth yelled, 'Holy shit!'

Ben hadn't seen it coming either. And nor had the assault team. Half of them were still inside the blazing building. At least one had been buried by the collapsing wall. Several more were on the ground and not moving – stunned, dead, Ben had no idea. The ones still on their feet were in total disarray, stunned and panicked. No amount of training can prepare anyone for walking into a high-explosive-incendiary bomb ambush. Either the terrorists had known the raid was coming, or they kept some kind of home-made device on standby at all times just in case.

The pharmacy next to the house was seriously damaged and burning. Car alarms were shrieking, and barely a single vehicle parked within thirty metres of the house had any glass left in its windows. Terrified neighbours were emerging from their homes or peeking out through their curtains at the incredible carnage taking place right there in their sleepy little suburban street. The howl of police sirens was nearby and approaching fast as the backup units who'd been waiting in the wings now raced to the scene.

Ben's instinct was to leap out of the car and run to lend assistance to the stricken assault team. His hand was on the door handle and he was poised to fling it open when he spotted movement from the rear section of the house that hadn't been destroyed in the explosion. The solitary figure of a man scrambling from what looked like a small bathroom window, dropping to the ground and making a rapid escape across the garden. The intensity of the blazing fire was casting long, black, dancing shadows across the rear of the house and neighbouring properties. The running figure vanished into the darkness, then reappeared as he scaled a wooden fence into a next-door garden.

Moments later, Ben saw him dash along the side wall of another house and vault the front garden wall into the street and hit the pavement running. He was maybe eighty yards away but Ben caught a clear glimpse of him under the glow of a sodium lamp. Tall and leggy, dressed in a hoodie top with a sports logo, faded blue jeans and white training shoes. He threw a wild look back at the blazing house and the chaos happening outside, and kept running. Sprinting hard around the corner.

Roth had spotted him too. 'Sonofabitch! He's getting away!'

Ben said, 'No chance. He's ours. Hold on tight.'

The Alpina roared into action as Ben stamped hard on the gas, twisted the wheel and propelled them out of their parking space, slewing around in a doughnut to point in the direction of the escaping fugitive and then accelerating hard to catch up with him. Roth was already out with his pistol. The street behind them was suddenly lit up in a swirl of flashing red and blue and ululating sirens reverberated off the buildings as the police rushed in.

Ben screeched the car around the corner where the runner had gone, and the flashing lights and leaping flames were lost from view. So was their target. Side streets extended in all directions and he could have hot-footed it down any of them. 'Dammit, where'd he go?' Roth exclaimed.

Ben said nothing. They shot across the mouth of a narrow lane off to the left, and were almost past it before he caught a fleeting glimpse of the figure sprinting away from them down the pavement, trying to stay in the shadows of the buildings. 'There!' Ben braked to a screeching halt, slammed into reverse and backed up a few metres. Forward drive, foot to the floor. The tyres bit hard and the Alpina rocketed through the bend and down the narrow lane after him.

Now the chase was almost over, and the running man knew he had zero chance of escape. He threw a startled look back over his shoulder, blinking in the glare of the oncoming headlights. Ben saw his face clearly for the first time. It was Hasan Jafari, the Sudanese guy in Roth's picture and the prime target of the GIGN operation.

Jafari was twenty metres ahead when he gave up trying to outrun the speeding car and spun around with a pistol in both hands. He fired twice, missing with the first shot. The second yowled off the corner of the Alpina's roof. The third was liable to do worse. But Ben didn't give Jafari time to fire it. Without slowing down he mounted the kerb, smashed a litter bin out of the way and aimed the wing of the car at Jafari in a glancing impact that caught him in the side and spun him violently off his feet. He tumbled hard to the ground, still clutching his pistol.

Ben lurched to a halt and he and Roth were instantly piling out of their doors. Jafari was struggling unsteadily to his feet, staggering as he raised the gun to shoot at the two men striding purposefully towards him. Ben got there first, trapped his wrist, sent the weapon spinning to the pavement and put him on his face with the muzzle of his own gun pressed hard into the back of Jafari's neck.

'Nice takedown,' Roth said.

'I'll show you how it's done sometime,' Ben replied.

Roth looked down at Jafari with a shark smile. 'This is your lucky day, motherfucker.'

Three blocks away the mayhem from the aftermath of the explosion sounded like a ground assault. The burning house and red and blue lights of the emergency vehicles were lighting up the sky over the rooftops and the night air was acrid with smoke. Ben thought about the GIGN men who wouldn't be going home tonight, thanks to Jafari and his friends' little home cooking exploits. In another few minutes the police would have the whole area cordoned off. They needed to get out of here fast.

Roth turned to Ben and said, 'Crunch time, amigo. We either hand pretty boy over to GIGN and the cops, who'll tear him limb from limb, or we snatch'm for ourselves and dive into a pile of shit a mile deep.'

'I'm already in it,' Ben said. 'Might as well get in all the way. The authorities can have him after we're done with him.'

'Fine by me,' Roth replied, grinning fiercely. He seemed to be loving every moment of this.

'If you want to make yourself useful, pop the boot lid for me.'

'The what? Oh, you mean the trunk.'

'And get the roll of Gorilla tape from my bag.'

'Boy oh boy. This is just like the old days,' Roth said. Ben made his pistol safe and put it away, then pinning Jafari to the ground with his knee he tore off a length of the strong black tape and wrapped it three times around the prisoner's head to gag and blindfold him. Then he used two more lengths to bind his wrists and ankles before hauling him upright by the scruff of the neck and dragging him around towards the back of the car. The two of them dumped Jafari unceremoniously into the boot and slammed the lid down on him.

'Where to?' Roth asked as they got back in the car.

Ben had no desire to bring a kidnapped terrorist back to his own apartment, safehouse or no safehouse. What he had in mind was going to require a different kind of venue.

'It's time for you to meet a friend of mine,' he said.

'I can't wait.'

Chapter 38

It was after one a.m. by the time they rolled up to the tall wire mesh gates of Fred's junkyard. The headlights shone on the rusted corrugated metal sheds and workshops inside the compound. Roth peered up at the curly razor wire that topped the twelve-foot fence. 'Wow. How quaint. Our very own Guantanamo Bay.'

'Fred values his privacy,' Ben said.

'I can resonate with that.'

'Plus, not all the business he does on the premises is strictly legit. Let me do the talking, okay? He doesn't speak a lot of English, anyway.'

'Wouldn't be a problem, bro. I'm fluent in seven languages.'

'I keep forgetting what a genius I have for a partner.'

Alerted by their presence, the junkyard dog bounded out of the moss-covered hulk of a derelict Citroën that was his kennel, and came streaking across the yard to hurl himself against the gate, barking furiously, wild eyes and gleaming fangs flashing in the headlights. Moments later dazzling floods lit up the compound and the steel shutter door of the largest corrugated building rolled up with a clatter. The burly shape of Fred appeared, clad in the same greasy blue boiler suit that he apparently slept as well as worked in, and clutching the sawn-off shotgun that he'd tried to sell Ben on his last visit. Fred lumbered across the yard, squinting suspiciously at the unexpected visitors.

Ben stepped from the car. He called out in French, 'Tire pas. C'est moi.' *Don't shoot. It's me.*

'I can see that,' Fred said gruffly. 'Who's your friend?'

'That's my cousin Bob,' Ben said.

'Right, sure.' Fred waved the shotgun in the direction of the car, noticing the fresh dents and scrapes from that evening's escapades. 'Come to trade the Beemer in? Looks like it's seen better days.'

Ben shook his head. 'And part with a classic? Sorry to disappoint you, Fred. We need to use your place.'

'For what?' Fred didn't seem too delighted at being dragged out of bed at this uncivilised hour, but when Ben explained their purpose in coming here and what was in it for him if he agreed to help them, his sour expression melted into an amused sort of leer. 'I always knew you were into some kind of heavy shit. Never asked any questions.'

'Wise policy,' Ben said.

The deal was struck. Fred unlocked the thick chain that held the gates, and rasped a command to the dog that sent it back to its kennel. When the Alpina was through the gates he closed them and locked them in, then waved Ben over to the large shed.

The building housed Fred's main workshop as well as the grimy old touring caravan in which he dwelled like a troll in a cave. Ben parked up among the piled crates and assorted rusty bits of junk as Fred rolled the shutter down behind them.

Roth stepped out of the car and stood wearing his Delta face, arms folded. 'Cousin Bob, hm?' Fred said wryly, eyeing him. Ben skipped the formal introductions. Instead he showed Fred the pistol he'd taken from Jafari, which was

Fred's payment for letting them use his place. Fred gave the weapon the once-over and seemed satisfied. 'Not bad. I know a guy who's been looking for one of these.'

'I'm not even going to ask what he wants it for.'

'Discretion is the better part of valour,' Fred said.

Muffled stirrings were coming from the Alpina's boot. Ben opened the lid to reveal the gagged, blindfolded prisoner uncomfortably folded up inside. Fred didn't miss a beat. Apparently, people came here all the time with captive terrorists to interrogate.

'Bring him in here,' Fred said, motioning through a doorway. They hauled the struggling Jafari from the boot of the car and dragged him by the arms as Fred led the way into an adjoining shed.

'This is where we hack 'em up and dispose of the bits,' Fred said loudly, which Ben supposed was for the prisoner's benefit. The shed walls were sheet steel and the floor was compacted earth. They shoved him over to a wheel-less truck chassis that had been slowly returning to iron ore for a very long time, and tethered him to it using lengths of rusty chain, of which copious quantities lay about. Fred directed a bright work lamp to shine into his face. Ben tore away the tape, removing most of his eyebrows in the process. Jafari yelped and blinked in the dazzling light.

'He's not going anywhere,' Fred said, eyeing him like a hungry grizzly bear eyes a fat, juicy Montana elk hunter.

'W-who are you fucking people?' Jafari stammered in French.

Ben replied to him in Arabic, so that Fred wouldn't be privy to their conversation. 'Doesn't matter who we are. All that matters is what we're going to do to you if you don't start talking to us. You hurt a lot of people tonight, so don't be expecting too much mercy.'

Roth had found a large ball peen hammer to play with and was slapping it against the palm of his hand. His Arabic was even more fluent and less accented than Ben's. 'Now, you murdering little scumbag. I'm gonna start with your fingers, then your toes. Then I'm gonna beat your brains out. Squishing terrorists is my specialty.'

Hearing the two white foreigners speaking his country's official language made Jafari flinch, because he knew full well what the implications were.

'This doesn't have to be hard,' Ben told him. 'All you have to do is tell us where we'll find Nazim al-Kassar. Then you can take your chances with the police, who I can promise you will be a lot nicer to you than my sadistic friend here.'

From the look in his eyes it was instantly obvious that Jafari recognised the name very well. 'I know who you are,' he said defiantly. 'Government fucking agents. British, American, who gives a shit? You want to catch Nazim, but he's too smart for you. Nobody can catch him, inshallah! Nazim will fuck you all.'

Roth looked at Ben. 'Sounds like this guy has a real attitude problem.'

Jafari spat. 'You Yankee assholes are all the same. You think you're so smart. Look around you, smart man. Jihad is already victorious against the dying civilisation of Europe. Soon all of its people will be Muslim or live under our rule as dhimmis, our slaves. Nothing can stop that. And then the filth of America will be next. We'll overthrow your US government through jihad and the dominion of Sharia will cover all the world. Allahu Akbar!'

'Your Caliphate is finished, moron,' Roth said. 'You had a good run, but this man's army stopped it.' He prodded a finger to his own chest. 'It's over. You're done, get it? And your lunatic comrades need to rethink their plans for world domination because they're all gonna end up just like you.' He brandished the hammer.

Fred was watching from the sidelines, not understanding a word but anticipating a good show. Ben had no doubt that Roth would carry out every bit of his threat if he were left to his own devices. He had no intention of letting the American start laying into an unarmed captive. Though Jafari didn't know that.

The only problem was that Jafari didn't seem the least bit afraid of whatever the crazy American might be about to do to him. He looked Roth straight in the eye and screamed, 'I'm only a servant of Allah. You can beat me, you can break my bones, you can kill me, but you can't defeat me, because to die in the way of Allah is our highest hope!'

And Ben believed him completely. It was the reason why none of the aggressive foreign policies of the West in fighting jihad had had, or could ever have, any serious effect. Because how could you deter an enemy who wasn't afraid of death, one who actually embraced its prospect, who had been this deeply conditioned to believe that martyrdom in the name of their holy cause was their most glorious possible calling? Allied naval commanders had faced the same frightening truth when they'd first encountered the Japanese kamikaze suicide pilots in the Pacific campaign of World War Two. It was a whole new kind of warfare, and it changed the rules entirely.

Which called for a more subtle strategy than Roth's heavy-handed approach if they were to have any chance of success here tonight. Ben was quite certain that Hasan Jafari would have a big contented smile on his face while Roth gave him his ticket to Paradise by smashing his brains out.

However, Jafari was still a man. And men, no matter how resolute in their beliefs, were generally subject to universal, primal, archetypal terrors that penetrated far deeper than any book-taught ideology ever could. Fundamentalist religion was a powerful force, to be sure, but it couldn't undo millions of years of evolution stretching back to mankind's earliest ancestors. Lizard brain theory, it was called, and it was a concept that Ben happened to subscribe to. You just needed to know how to reach that profound psychological core.

Ben turned to Fred, and switching to French he said, 'Fred, go and fetch Milou, would you, please?'

Jafari frowned, caught off balance by this turn of events. 'Who the fuck is Milou?'

Ben replied, 'Your worst fear, Hasan. Literally.'

Fred was gone for a moment. When he came back he was struggling with the crazed, wild-eyed dog on the end of a leash as taut as a bowstring. Froth dripped from its jaws as it yearned to sink its snapping fangs into the flesh of a stranger, and it didn't really care whose. The human chained to the truck chassis would do fine. Ben stepped out of its reach. Even Roth looked afraid of the thing.

And so was Jafari, quite understandably. He backed away as far as he could, trying to cross his legs to protect his groin, which was at the perfect level for the dog's gnashing jaws and most exposed to attack. He might have been ready to die a glorious hero's death in the name of Allah, but nothing could quite prepare the most determined martyr for the reality of having one's testicles clamped between the fangs of a savage beast, torn off by the roots and messily devoured in front of his eyes. Ben had been fairly sure that the prospect of such violent, bloody castration would be enough to make even the most devoted believer quickly forget all about the teachings of scripture. And he'd been right.

Primal terrors. Crude, but unquestionably effective. Men were so vulnerable, deep down.

Hasan Jafari soon began to talk.

Chapter 39

Once the floodgates opened, they couldn't shut him up. All the while, Fred was hanging onto Milou's leash, and probably hoping that Ben would give him the signal to let go.

More often than not, a man will tell the truth when he's within moments of gory emasculation; and so when the prisoner desperately and repeatedly insisted that he had no idea where Nazim al-Kassar was, and that he, Hasan Jafari, was just a minion, a lowly footsoldier, and not privy to such top-level intelligence, Ben and Roth reluctantly had to accept that he was being sincere.

But that didn't mean Hasan Jafari had nothing to offer his tormentors by way of information.

'The woman,' he gasped, breathless with terror as the dog went on eyeing him with bared fangs. 'I know where she is. Please – please, don't let it bite my balls off!'

'Julien Segal's wife? She's alive?'

'I don't know her name. But yeah, yeah, she's alive, I swear. They're holding her because they don't trust him. It's all part of the big plan.'

Ben and Roth exchanged glances. 'What big plan?'

'I don't know! I'm telling the truth!'

'He knows,' Roth said. 'Let the dog go. Just one bite. A small nibble. Like a sampler.'

'No! Arrgh! Don't do that, please! I just know where they're holding her. Inside one of the old ghost Métro stations, Saint-Martin. They use the disused tunnels as a base!'

The underground ghost stations were part of Parisian urban legend. Ben knew about Saint-Martin, though he'd never been inside.

'It was taken out of service eighty years ago, at the start of the war,' he explained for Roth's benefit. 'The Salvation Army use it as a homeless shelter. It's even got a street entrance on Boulevard Saint-Martin that the public can just walk into. I can't believe anyone would think of making it their hideout, let alone to store a hostage in.'

Jafari shook his head. 'There's another way in. It takes you to parts of the system where nobody ever goes. They've been closed up so long, hardly anyone knows they even exist.'

'You've been down there?'

'Once. A couple of times.'

'You know where they're keeping her? Have you seen her?'

Jafari nodded reluctantly. 'I was with them when they took her there.'

'Piece of shit,' Roth muttered, shaking his head in disgust.

'Listen to me, Hasan,' Ben said. 'There's only one way you get out of this. That's by taking us to the ghost Métro station. Tonight. Now. You do that, I promise we won't hurt you.'

Jafari stared at him, as though he was thinking hard and working out his options. 'I'll get you inside,' he agreed after a beat. 'Whatever you say.'

Roth was looking deeply unhappy. Ben took him aside and asked quietly, switching back from Arabic to English, 'Do we have a problem?'

'Damn right we have a problem. This asshole is more than happy to show us the way. Because he's setting us up to walk into a trap. How many of your hardcore jihadis do you suppose are guarding her down there, packing Kalashnikovs and Uzis, or sitting waiting for us with their thumb on a goddamn detonator switch? Five? Ten? And two guys are gonna go waltzing in there alone, deep into enemy territory with no backup and nothing more than a couple of pistols? Forget it.'

'I agree, it's an uncertain proposition. But it's the only way we can get to Segal's wife.'

'So what? I mean, I feel for the lady, but you can't always save them all. Why take the risk?'

'Because she's the best chance we have of bringing Segal in,' Ben said. 'Once she's free, Nazim has a lot less hold over him. He might be willing to jump ship.'

'Hm. Long shot.'

'And because I'm not leaving an innocent woman down there with a bunch of trigger-happy maniacs,' Ben said. 'That's just how it has to be.'

'What are you, the white knight?'

'If you're not up for it, fine. You stay behind and I'll go alone. It won't be my first time.'

'I didn't say I wouldn't come along. I just don't like this jaws of death shit. Been through enough fucked-up situations to know best how to avoid them.'

'Whatever you decide,' Ben said, 'make your mind up fast. The clock's ticking. The GIGN raid is bound to have made Nazim jumpy and they're liable to move her to a new location, or maybe even kill her.'

Fred had been listening to their whispered conversation, and now came over to them. He said to Ben in French, 'You people speak more languages than the fucking United Nations, but I understand enough to gather that you have a need for armament. Correct?'

'Whatever gives us the edge,' Ben said.

'I think I can help in that department. Because I don't only deal in rusty sawn-offs to sell to third-rate stick-up artists. I have some other merchandise that could interest you.'

Fred put the dog away, much to the relief of the chained-up prisoner, then led Ben and Roth to his caravan where he reached under the bunk and dragged out a large metal case. 'You can't be too careful,' he said as he undid the four combination padlocks holding the lid shut.

Inside the case, wrapped in oiled cloths, lay a pair of gleaming black automatic weapons. Ben could have recognised them blindfold. They were MP5SDs, manufactured in Germany by Heckler & Koch and purposely developed for Special Forces. The 'MP' designation stood for *Machinenpistole* and the 'SD' for *Schalldampfer*, which was German for 'sound suppressor' and referred to the integral silencer tube that shrouded the machine pistol's short but highly accurate five-inch barrel. It was one of the best weapons ever devised for the kind of warfare in which Ben and Roth had once specialised. The Rolls Royce of submachine guns, reliable, efficient and exactly as deadly as it needed to be.

Roth whistled at the sight of the guns, and couldn't suppress the schoolboy grin that spread all over his face. 'Holy shit, I haven't handled one of those babies since Delta.'

Fred laid the guns on the bunk and hauled more greasy rags out of the trunk to reveal a nest of loaded magazines, long and curved and each containing thirty rounds of nine-millimetre ammunition, sitting on top of stacked cartridge boxes. 'Over five hundred rounds in total,' he said. 'It's my personal stash. But you're welcome to make use of it, for a fee of course.'

'This should even the odds a little,' Ben said. He turned to Roth. 'So are we happier now?'

Roth's grin had stretched from ear to ear. 'We're happier, all right. It's gonna be like the old days, except this time there are no bureaucrats to mess things up. No dumbass rules of engagement to get in our way. Just you, me and the bad guys. They won't know what hit 'em.'

Ben lifted one of the weapons off the bunk. It was the full-on military version with a four-way fire selector switch: safe, single shot, three-shot burst, fully automatic. One of the most illegal items for any civilian, in any country, to possess. It was like new, barely used, oiled and shiny. The bolt mechanism felt as slick as glass. 'Are you expecting a war to break out, Fred?'

'I get the feeling there's going to be one tonight,' Fred replied.

Things moved fast after that. Ben and Roth unchained Hasan Jafari and marched him outside to the car. This time he was allowed to ride up front with Ben, while Roth sat behind him with a pistol to his head. The two submachine guns were strapped up inside Ben's green bag on the back seat, together with all the loaded magazines and enough extra ammunition to lay waste to a regiment.

As they headed back across the city, Jafari told them that the way inside the abandoned ghost station of Saint-Martin was via its neighbouring working station, République. That destination took them right into the heart of Paris, north of the river.

It was after 2.30 a.m. by the time they parked up the Alpina in a nearby street and walked the rest of the way, with Jafari two steps ahead and Roth still discreetly pointing the pistol at him through the pocket of his jacket. Ben's heavy bag gave a metallic jinking sound at every step. Any gendarme who picked this moment to stop them would get quite a surprise.

The République station was almost empty at this time of night. Ben, Roth and their prisoner entered the breezy tunnel from the street like regular travellers, bought tickets at the automated kiosk and made their way down through the bright white-tiled corridors, heading for the Lines 8 and 9 platforms. The decommissioned station of Saint-Martin lay hidden between here and Strasbourg-Saint-Denis on the westbound line.

Roth was over his earlier reluctance and seemed cheerful, almost jaunty. Jafari was edgy and mostly silent as he walked two steps ahead of them, like any prisoner being forced to lead the enemy back to his own secret camp. Ben was watching him closely in case he tried to bolt or trick them, and a couple of times caught him secretly smirking to himself. Roth was right. Jafari was looking forward to steering his captors straight into a nice little trap.

A descending flight of steps came out at the left-hand end of the platform, near the mouth of the westbound tunnel. There were a few people scattered along the near-empty platform, waiting for the next train with the wee-small-hours look of tired urbanites who weren't much interested in the activities of their fellow subway travellers. Jafari glanced across at them to make sure nobody was watching, then turned to Ben and Roth. 'This way,' he hissed, pointing past the warning signs into the mouth of the tunnel. 'Hurry. Another train will be along soon.'

Following his lead, they quickly slipped off the end of the platform and jumped down onto a narrow walkway, about eighteen inches wide, that ran along the narrow space between the left tunnel wall and the tracks. Jafari set off at a jog, with Ben and Roth close behind. In stark contrast to the gleaming white brightness of the station the tunnel was dark and murky, lit every few yards by a wall light. The arched ceiling was streaked and crumbly. The curved walls were ancient brick, caked in the soot and dirt of over a hundred years and covered in new and old graffiti from where generations of street artists had sneaked into the tunnel to leave their signature. Snakes of wiring ran here and there, daisy-chained together by prehistoric electrical connection boxes. The ground between the tracks was gravel, dark with soot. They moved fast, in case a train came.

There was no turning back now, as Ben and Roth ventured into the unknown after their guide. Three men were going in. But not all of them would be coming out again.

Chapter 40

After a few dozen yards the walkway widened out into an arched opening in the side wall to their left, connecting with a parallel tunnel and more tracks. They paused there to open the bag and take out the MP5s. Jafari hovered uncertainly nearby while Ben and Roth spent a moment loading and checking. Ben flipped his fire selector to three-shot bursts. That would give him ten trigger squeezes before his thirty-round magazine was depleted. He slipped four extra loaded mags into his pockets. Enough firepower for most situations, barring the need for artillery and air support.

Roth said, 'I'm good.'

Ben slung his bag, much lighter now, over his shoulder and told Jafari, 'Lead on. We're right behind you.'

They kept moving at the same trotting pace. The mouth of the tunnel was a long way behind them now, just a white semicircle that vanished out of sight as they followed the curve of the parallel tracks. Moments after, Ben sensed the tunnel beginning to vibrate, a subtle tremor at first, then quickly building in intensity as the tracks started to thrum and the rumble of the approaching train grew louder. It paused to pick up the passengers from the platform, then accelerated into the tunnel. The rumble became a loud, breathy roar. First Jafari, then Roth, then Ben, made it to the next archway, and they hid behind the crumbly stonework as the train streaked by with a slap of wind and a deafening screech, its windows a blur.

Then the train was gone again, wending its way into darkness beneath the city. The three of them emerged from their hiding place and pressed on. Jafari motioned them towards the parallel tunnel to the left. By the glow of the wall lights it appeared older and dirtier and less used. He explained that this was part of the disused network. 'But be careful as we cross the tracks. The live rail is still connected to the grid and it'll fry you like an egg.'

'Thanks for the thought, Hasan,' Ben said.

Jafari shrugged. 'If I let one of you step on a live rail, I figure the other will shoot me in the legs, then take me back to that stinking fucked-up shithole place and turn the dog on me again. So I do it only for myself.'

'You're a man of remarkable perception. Now keep moving.'

They crossed the disused line to the walkway on the far side and walked on along the abandoned tunnel, which gently curved away until the other disappeared out of sight behind them. The glow of the wall lights was dulled by grime. It felt like a thousand miles below the earth, deep in the bowels of the labyrinth from which it was easy to imagine there could be no escape.

Roth whispered, 'How much further?'

Jafari replied over his shoulder, 'We're getting closer.'

After a hundred more yards, they came to a heavily graffiti-scrawled iron door on the left, fitted with a panic bar handle that had been recently used, hand marks visible against the dirt. Jafari said, 'Through here.'

Jafari pushed the door open and stepped through. Roth went next, Ben last. They had emerged into the abandoned station of Saint-Martin.

The silence and emptiness of the place were total and eerie. Almost every square foot of its smooth, curved wall tiling was covered in the work of the street artists who'd been venturing down here for decades to use it as a giant canvas. Some of the graffiti must have been thirty years old, undisturbed all this time. Older by far were the ancient advertising billboards from the 1930s and 40s, featuring slogans for products that had ceased to exist long before Ben was born, half-hidden beneath layers of dirt and cobwebs. It was like stepping back into the past. A deserted, dusty old museum. Or a tomb, haunted by the spirits of this strange subterranean world that the city dwellers above had mostly forgotten even existed. Ben wasn't superstitious but felt a shivery tingle up and down his spine.

'Oh man,' Roth said, impressed. 'You could shoot the most awesome zombie movie down here.'

'We're not here for zombies,' Ben said. He nudged Jafari with his gun. 'Hurry.'

'We need to go along the tunnel,' Jafari said. 'There are two stations, joined together. The woman is being held in a room near the second station.'

'Deeper into the deathtrap we go,' Roth muttered. He had his weapon at the ready, finger hovering close to the trigger. Jafari led them along the deserted platform and into the mouth of the next tunnel section. Dirt and debris littered the tracks. The smell of rats and mould was strong.

The second station was more extensive than the first, with broad stairways leading to different levels and corridors branching off here and there. Fewer urban explorers had ever ventured this far, judging by the lack of street art on the walls. They passed down some steps, heading deeper below ground. Then Jafari pushed through a personnel-only doorway marked ENTRÉE INTERDITE SANS AUTORISATION and led them down a tight, winding service passageway with big duct pipes overhead and more doors left and right.

Ben's tension was rising with every yard they progressed. He had a relaxed grip on his weapon, but every nerve of his being was alert and primed for instant action, and he sensed the same edginess coming from Roth. They were right in the heart of the labyrinthine complex that the terrorists had made their underground burrow. Anything could happen, at any moment.

Then it did.

Ben heard it first, and swung his MP5 towards the sound a fraction of a second before Roth did the same. Voices and footsteps, approaching from behind a closed steel door to their right. They were suddenly no longer alone down here.

The wall light above had a bad connection and was flickering like a strobe, creating a stop-motion effect. Ben grabbed Jafari's arm and stepped quickly to the hinge side of the doorway. Roth retreated into the shadows on the other side.

Now the footsteps and voices came closer, until they were just beyond the door. Ben nodded to Roth. He raised a finger to his lips, telling Jafari to stay quiet. Then he waited for the door to swing open.

The two men who pushed through it were having a conversation in Arabic. Which, as was immediately apparent, was their native language. The two other features they had in common were their straggly black beards and the short, stubby Kalashnikovs casually slung over their shoulders. One man was short and fat, the other tall and thin. They stepped out into the passage, their movements jerky under the flickering light. The fat one laughed at the joke the thin one had just made. Then the laugh suddenly died on his lips and their smiles fell as Ben stepped out from behind the open door and Roth emerged like a jungle predator from the shadows, with the stone-killer blank eyes of a Delta Force ninja assassin.

Jafari broke away from Ben and yelled in Arabic, pointing at his captors, 'They kidnapped me! Kill them!'

His colleagues would have been happy to oblige him, but the element of surprise was on Ben and Roth's side. The two terrorists barely touched their weapons before the brief muted chatter of the MP5s filled the passage. Ben's triple-stitch burst punched a tight vertical group of holes in the fat guy's heart. The first of Roth's rapid two single shots ripped into the thin guy's chest and the second to the head, before he even started to fall. The perfect double-tap, expertly executed. The two men slumped silently to the floor and lay still under the stop-frame flicker of the light.

'Nothing like slick teamwork,' Roth said.

'Nice double-tap,' Ben commented. 'Anyone would think I trained you.'

'Smartass.'

Jafari stood for a moment, staring in dismay at the corpses of his associates. Then he started to back away, but Roth grabbed him by the neck and dragged him down to his knees, grinding the fat silencer tube of his weapon into Jafari's neck. 'Now it's your turn, A-hole.'

Ben wasn't having that. He slapped down Roth's gun. 'No. We need him.'

'He has it coming.'

'We all have it coming,' Ben said. 'But it's not time for him to find Paradise just yet.' He asked Jafari, 'How close are we to where they're keeping the Segal woman?'

'Close,' Jafari mumbled, sweating.

'Lead us to her,' Ben said. 'Any more tricks, I'll castrate you myself.'

'And then we'll get to work on you,' Roth growled.

Before moving on, they quickly relieved the dead men of their weapons, unloaded the two Kalashnikov magazines and dumped the loose ammo down a ventilator shaft. Depriving the enemy of useful ordnance was a top rule of Special Forces combat operations.

Jafari muttered, 'This way,' pointing nervously into the doorway from which the two terrorists had appeared. Ben shoved him through it and they followed him down an even narrower corridor, which led through a crumbly stone archway into the wider open space of a maintenance bay where two ancient trains stood partially dismantled on a section of track that probably hadn't been used since before the outbreak of World War II. Only the scuffed tracks of footprints on the dusty concrete walkway by the tracks gave away that anyone had been down here in decades.

Jafari stopped at a grimy, riveted steel door inset into the wall of the maintenance bay. His eyes bulged nervously as he threw a look back at Ben and Roth, signalling 'This is it. What do I do?'

Ben set his MP5's fire selector to fully auto and heard the small click as Roth did the same. Then Ben took his left hand off his gun, made a fist in the air and mimicked *Knock, knock, knock.*

Jafari hesitated, swallowed hard and then knocked three times.

Chapter 41

Jafari's three knocks made a hollow clang on the steel door that echoed off the tunnel walls.

A gruff voice from behind the door called in Arabic, 'Who's there?'

Jafari called back hoarsely, 'Hasan Jafari. Nazim sent me to check on the hostage.'

Silence from behind the door. It was an anxious moment. If the men inside became suspicious and called Nazim to check, assuming they had any phone reception down here, then the jig was up. It could spell disaster for the hostage, if indeed she was still in one piece. Worse, Ben knew that he and Roth could easily become trapped inside the tunnels as Nazim mobilised his troops to block their escape routes. Roth's face, half-lit in the murky glow of a wall lamp, showed that he was thinking the same grim thoughts.

The silence dragged on for three long, painful seconds. Then the gruff voice from behind the steel door said in Arabic, 'Okay,' and Ben felt the relief melt through him.

Next came the grinding sound of a long, heavy deadbolt being drawn open from inside the door. The rusty hinges squealed as the door opened a crack, and a bearded face peeked out. Recognising the figure of Jafari standing there, the guy pushed the door open the rest of the way.

Brighter light shone out from inside, silhouetting the outline of a large, burly man with another stubby Kalashnikov hanging across his chest.

Now was the time to move, and Ben had to move fast. He was on Jafari in two long strides and thrust him violently through the doorway, sending him crashing into the burly guy and headbutting him under the chin. The burly guy sprawled on his back with Jafari on top of him, both of them stunned by the impact. With the doorway clear, Ben and Roth poured through it like liquid, guns raised and marking their targets as they entered.

The holding cell was some kind of storeroom or workshop, with a bare concrete floor and metal shelving stacked ceiling-high with dusty crates and boxes, tools and bric-a-brac. It had an old wooden table at its centre, and some chairs. Sitting on one of them, blindfolded, bound and gagged, barefoot and wearing the nightdress she'd had on when they snatched her from her home, was the woman whose photo Ben had seen on Julien Segal's office desk. She looked thin and frail and rigid with terror. Ben only gave her the briefest glance, because he had more immediately pressing matters to deal with first. Three of them, including the burly guy on the floor.

The room exploded with the sound of gunfire. Two of the startled guards managed to snatch up their weapons and get off a couple of wild shots before the twinned chatter of the silenced MP5s, like the sound of ripping cardboard, hosed them down with nine-millimetre bullets and sent them spinning off their feet. One of them cannoned against a wall and slid down it with his chin on his chest, leaving an oily smear of blood. Another crashed wildly backwards into the shelving and brought down an avalanche of tools and boxes as he slithered dead to the concrete. The execution was swift and ruthless. Last to die was the burly guy on the floor, who recovered enough from his shock to snatch a pistol from his belt and swing it halfway towards Roth before Ben shot him in the head.

After the violence came a sudden stillness, the only sounds in the room the frightened whimper of the hostage and the tinkle of a spent cartridge case rolling across the floor. Smoke drifted in the light. Ben looked at Roth and nodded. Roth nodded back with a wink. 'Thanks, buddy.'

Jafari was still lying on the floor, sprawled flat next to the body of the burly guy. Roth grunted, 'On your feet, scumbag,' and kicked him in the ribs. When there was no response, Roth crouched down and rolled Jafari over. One of the wild shots fired by his terrorist cronies had gone through his left eye.

'Whoops. Looks like he made it to Paradise after all,' Roth said.

Meanwhile Ben had made his weapon safe and gone over to the woman tied in the chair. She was trembling, and flinched at his touch as he gently removed her blindfold, then the gag. He said, 'Madame Segal?'

She blinked in the light and stared at him with fear-crazed, bloodshot eyes. Her hair was all awry and the nightdress was torn at the shoulder from her struggle against her kidnappers. Tendons stood out on her neck like cords. Her voice was croaky and full of emotion as she replied, 'I-I'm Margot Segal. Where am I? Oh God, I thought they were going to kill me.'

'Nobody's going to hurt you now. You're safe.'

'W-who are you? Are you the police?'

Ben hesitated a moment before replying. He'd been thinking about this for some time. Making a snap decision he flashed his fake ID. 'Inspector Jacques Dardenne, special antiterrorist division. This is my colleague, Mike Anderson, of the FBI Joint Task Force.'

'Enchanté, Madame,' Roth said graciously. His French accent was as bad as his acting.

There was a long carving knife on the table. Ben didn't want to imagine what the kidnappers had been planning on using it for in the event that they decided to murder her. Beheading was the method most beloved by these fanatics. He picked it up to slice the plastic cable ties holding her ankles and wrists. She gasped as her hands were cut free, and began rubbing her chafed wrists.

'Are you hurt? Did they harm you in any way?'

She shook her head. Trying not to look at the dead men and the blood everywhere. 'They didn't do anything to me, but my feet are hurting. They made me walk such a long way. And I'm so cold and hungry. They didn't give me a single thing to eat this whole time.'

Ben examined her feet. They were dirty and the soles were cut and abraded from the long march at gunpoint through the tunnels. The bastards must have smuggled her inside the République Métro station in the dead of night when nobody was around. He stripped off his jacket and wrapped it over her bare shoulders. She shivered and pulled it tight around herself.

One of the dead guards wasn't too large a man, with smallish feet that looked about the same size as Margot Segal's. He was wearing soft, cushiony Nikes that he wouldn't be needing any more, so Ben pulled them off him and knelt down to gently slide each in turn onto her feet. It was the best he could do for her for now.

She winced a little as he eased the shoes on. 'You don't know how happy I am to see you. Are the other officers coming too?'

'We're on an undercover operation,' Ben said. 'Top secret. You were kidnapped by members of a terror organisation who may have infiltrated the government and police. That's why it's just him and me, for the moment. We can't afford to take any risks with your safety. Understand?'

'Oh, my goodness.' She looked fazed, but seemed to believe him.

'We need to take you into protective custody. Can you walk?'

'I'll try. I'm a little weak. Where's my husband? Where's Julien? Is he all right?'

'We need to discuss that,' Ben said. 'But let's get you out of here first.' He took her arm and supported her as she stood shakily up out of the chair. 'I've got you. You'll soon be fine.'

Roth stepped over Jafari's corpse as though it were a garbage sack and headed out of the cell door, checking left and right. 'We're clear.'

'It's time to go, Madame Segal.' Ben helped her thread a path through the dead bodies and out through the doorway after Roth.

'It's a long way back, bud,' Roth said. 'She gonna be okay?'

'I'll carry her if I have to. Let's get moving.'

Chapter 42

It was indeed a long way back, and Ben did have to carry her. Exhausted after her ordeal, Margot Segal was soon asleep in his arms. Roth held onto both MP5s and walked ahead as they slowly retraced their steps. But with their guide now dead, tracing their way in reverse through the maze of tunnels and passages and doorways was a confusing business. After more than twenty minutes of progress, Roth halted in a dark passage that suddenly looked unfamiliar and said, 'Shit. I think I led us through the wrong door back a ways. This whole place all looks the same. Damn that asshole Jafari for getting in the way of a bullet.'

'That's a nice way of saying you've got us lost,' Ben said.

'Hey, put it on me, why don't you?'

'You're the point man, Captain. I have my arms full.' Which Ben did, literally. Margot Segal might have been slightly built, but she was becoming a dead weight. His wounds were hurting him again.

They doubled back and tried what Roth initially thought was the correct doorway. Except it wasn't. But the wrong turning had led to an important chance discovery.

'Well, well,' Roth muttered.

Back in the day, the large brick-built space in which they now found themselves might have been a power substation room, judging by the assortment of clunky old obsolete electrical equipment that had been mostly ripped out and piled to one side as junk.

Much more recently, it had served as something very different. Modern neon striplights had been crudely rigged up to the prehistoric wiring system, brightly illuminating the row of ten heavy-duty metal work benches that were arranged along its entire length. Six of the benches were bare, while the remaining four were covered with crisp new parcel-sized cardboard boxes printed with a company name, ETZ INTERNATIONAL, some of them sealed with packaging tape and others cut open.

'No prizes for guessing who put this little lot here,' Roth said. 'It ain't the public transport authority, and that's for sure.'

Curious, Ben rested Madame Segal in a corner, made sure she was comfortable, then joined Roth in examining the contents of the opened boxes.

'Food baggies,' Roth muttered. 'For what? Packing sandwiches?'

Ben popped open one of the sealed boxes. Inside were tightly-rolled cylinders of brick-sized, food-grade plastic bags like the ones Roth had found. The box easily weighed ten kilograms, which amounted to several thousand empty bags packed up inside. He checked two others and found the exact same contents there as well. A fourth box contained dozens of bobbins of sealing wire, pliers, tape and surgical rubber gloves and facemasks. A fifth was packed full of brand new digital weighing scales, still in their factory wrapping. Roth dug inside another and held up a plastic scoop and a funnel for Ben to see.

'Whatever they're doing with all this stuff,' Ben said, 'it's no cottage industry. All these empty benches were put here for a reason. There's enough material here to bag up at least fifty thousand packages, or more. Question is, of what?'

'It's a goddamn drug processing lab, is what it is,' Roth said. 'Got themselves a nice little production line set up, smack bang under the middle of Paris.'

'But without any drugs.'

'Let's find out.'

They checked every single box, and found no trace of illicit substances inside them or anywhere else. Roth studied the business name and logo on the packaging. 'ETZ International. No address, no web URL. Is that some kind of shell corporation, or what?'

'Remember Jafari mentioned some kind of grand plan he didn't seem to know much about?' Ben said. 'This has got to be it.'

'So what's the deal? Heroin? Cocaine?'

'You know as well as I do that's one of the ways terrorists have been funding themselves for decades.'

'Three billion dollars a year from the opium harvests of Afghanistan alone,' Roth agreed. 'Until our government clamped down on the fuckers so hard we choked off most of their supply. Now if they so much as bend over to blow out a fart or pick a poppy, the CIA knows about it.'

'Then they're getting it from somewhere else,' Ben said. 'And they mean business, obviously.'

Roth spread his arms wide. 'So where's the merchandise? This place is as clean as an anal retentive's butthole.'

'They're waiting for it,' Ben said. 'The shipment coming in from Tripoli. That could be what this was about, all along. It could be what Romy overheard Segal and Nazim al-Kassar talking about. It could be the reason they killed her.'

Roth lowered his voice so that Margot Segal wouldn't hear. 'If the shipment is drugs, what's our guy Segal's part in it? Why involve a freakin' antiquities expert in a major narcotics smuggling operation?'

'Good question. From what Françoise Schell told me, I thought Segal was helping Nazim trade in stolen historical relics. If it's really all about drugs, I can't understand how the two relate.'

Roth jerked a discreet thumb back over his shoulder in Margot Segal's direction. 'You think she knows?'

'I don't believe she's got the smallest clue what he's involved in. But I mean to find out.'

'I got another good question for you,' Roth said. 'How in hell did they manage to get all this stuff down here in the first place? Not to mention the container-load or two of dope they're apparently expecting to get their hands on any day now. Don't tell me they're fixing to lug it all through the tunnels. There's got to be another way in, right? One that our friend Jafari didn't know about. Dollars to doughnuts the morons guarding the lady didn't know about it either. Operational security. You don't trust footsoldiers with information above their pay grade.'

Ben knew that Roth had to be right.

And that was when he saw the leaf.

Chapter 43

Autumn in Paris. The stuff of romance. The explosive reds and golds of the capital's half-million trees at this special time of year had inspired lovers, dreamers and poets going back centuries. Songs had been written and movies made about it. To go strolling beneath the orange-hued canopies of the Tuileries Garden or wander the paths of the Parc Monceau with the crisp crunch of the magical golden carpet underfoot was to drink in the quintessential flavour of the City of Light. From October through November, the autumn leaves were everywhere. Though pretty much the last place one might have expected to find any was sixty metres below ground, in the deep dark recesses where the sun never shone, the rain never fell and nothing grew except mould, mildew and rodent populations.

The single dead leaf was lying on the floor a few steps from where Ben was standing. It was reddish-brown and curled up and brittle-looking. Just one out of countless millions, but the sight of it in such an incongruous setting made him stare. He walked over to it and picked it up, inspecting it between finger and thumb. Odd.

He looked around him and saw where it had come from. A few more steps away, hidden in the shadows away from the glow of the overhead neons, was another door. He could see a dim strip of light shining from the inch-wide gap below it. A couple more leaves were trapped in the gap, brown and curled just like the one he was holding.

'What's up?' Roth said. Ben made no reply. He walked over to the door and tried the handle. It was locked. He crouched down beside it and picked up one of the other leaves, and felt the gentle breath of a draught against his fingers.

'There's something behind this door,' he said.

It took both of them to shoulder it open with a crack of splintering wood. They stepped through the doorway into a concrete space some ten feet square, and for the first time in nearly two hours tasted fresh, cool air. The floor was covered in leaves.

Ben craned his neck upwards as another dead leaf spiralled down like a snowflake to meet him. High above, through the iron grid where the ventilation shaft opened up at street level, he could see stars twinkling. A metal ladder with safety hoops ran part-way up the wall to a grille platform, then another, and a third section extended all the way to the top. Alongside the ladder was a cable pulley system with an electric hoist for lifting equipment up and down the shaft inside a steel cage.

'There's your other way in,' he said to Roth. 'And our way out.'

'Well, I'll be damned. Those wily sons of bitches.'

The hoist system might have looked ancient and ropey, but it was a hell of a lot preferable to trekking all the way back through the tunnels. The big red Bakelite switch on the cage's rusty old control box still worked fine. Ben fetched Margot Segal from the inner room, and moments later the three of them were riding up the shaft as the cables creaked and the pulleys whirred. The hoist came to a juddering halt at the top landing, just a few ladder rungs below street level. They breathed in the fresh breeze from the ventilation grid, and could hear the sound of occasional passing traffic. Nearly four in the morning, Paris was at its quietest, oblivious of the battles that had been taking place below ground that night.

The grid was hinged like a trapdoor but secured by a heavy padlock, which offered little resistance to a couple of silenced gunshots before they dropped its mangled remains back down the shaft. Ben heaved the grid open, tossed his bag with the guns inside up onto the pavement, and pushed his head and shoulders out. The ventilation shaft opened up onto an alley off a narrow tree-lined side street he didn't recognise. The adjoining main street was just a few yards away. He pulled himself out of the shaft and ran over to it, and realised that by luck they were just a couple of hundred yards from where they'd left the car. He ran back to the shaft and helped Margot Segal clamber out. Roth was the last to emerge.

'Well, that was fun and games.'

Ben's jacket wasn't helping to protect Margot Segal much from the night chill, and she was shivering and looked faint. 'Wait here,' he said to Roth, gave him the bag and sprinted for the car. Less than two minutes later he screeched up at the mouth of the alley. They got Margot Segal into the back, and dumped in the bag with the guns.

She murmured, 'I've never been in a police car before.'

Ben thought, *And you still haven't.* He jumped back behind the wheel, Roth bundled into the passenger seat and they were away with the heater blowing on maximum.

'Where to?' Roth asked.

Ben wanted to take her to a hospital but was worried about all the questions that would be asked, especially when the real police turned up. A hotel was out of the question, because of the same inevitable suspicions when two tough-looking men turned up with an older woman in a nightdress who looked exactly like someone who'd recently been kidnapped and held hostage. The only option he had was to return to his place, and take his chances that it was still safe.

They were there within the hour.

Thierry had not returned. Ben wasn't expecting to see him again. The guy was a disappointment. Ben carried Margot Segal into the bedroom and laid her down on the bed. By then she was alert enough to be talking more as the feelings of relief began to hit home. 'Is this the protective custody you told me about, Inspector Dardenne?' she asked.

'It's only temporary, until we find something better,' he assured her. 'You'll have everything you need, I promise.'

'Couldn't I go back home?'

'The moment it's safe, you will. And you can call me Jacques, all right?'

'Thank you, Jacques,' she replied softly, and Ben felt like a bastard for deceiving her. As he removed her shoes and went to work cleaning up her feet with cotton pads and antiseptic cream, she described the terrifying moment when the kidnappers had attacked her in her home.

'At first I was certain they were robbers, or that they were going to rape me or something awful like that. Then they put something over my eyes and I realised they meant to take me away. I've never been so frightened in my life. I had no idea where they were taking me. We drove in a car for a long time through the night. Then they made me get out of the car and walk. They had a gun to my back. At least, I assumed it must be a gun. We went into a Métro station. I couldn't see but I recognised the sounds, the smells. Then they led me into a dark place that I knew must be a tunnel.

They made me walk for the longest time through the darkness, shoving me along, pulling me and pushing me this way and that, until my feet were so sore I could hardly go another step. I had no idea where I was any longer, where we were going or what would happen to me when I got there. I kept asking, "Why are you doing this to me?" but they told me to shut up, and eventually they gagged me to make me quiet. Then we came to the place where you found me. They tied me in the chair. I don't even know how long I was there. It all seems so distant now. Like a terrible dream.'

Ben assured her, 'If you'd like to see a doctor, I can get one to come and take a look at you.' As he said it, he was wondering how he could do that. A man of Fred's connections might know someone. Every city had its under-the-table medics, often vets, who treated crooks for gunshot and stab wounds for cash when regular medical assistance was too risky.

She replied, 'I don't need a doctor. I just want to know where my husband is, and what's happening. Why would those men have targeted me? You said they were terrorists. Then I heard you and Agent Anderson talking about heroin and cocaine, and something about a shipment. I'm not stupid. I understand a lot of English and I do have some idea of how things work. Is Julien mixed up in something bad?'

'We think that Julien was coerced into doing business with these people,' Ben said. 'That's why it's important that we talk to him before he gets himself into any worse trouble.'

She looked at Ben with alarm. 'What kind of trouble? Are they going to kill him?'

'Not if Agent Anderson and I can help it. But we need to act soon.'

'What will you do? Will Julien be put in prison?'

'If Julien helps us to catch the ringleaders,' Ben said, 'we can do a plea bargain deal with him that will keep him out of jail.'

Real-life detectives probably didn't use terms like 'ringleaders', but it sounded good and had the right effect on Margot Segal. 'My husband is a good man,' she said. 'We've been married for over thirty years. We've had our ups and downs but, well, he's all I have.'

'We know that, Margot,' Ben replied. 'And I truly don't want anything bad to happen to him. That's why I need your help to contact him. His office colleagues said he was travelling to some conference overseas. Do you know where he went?'

She looked puzzled at the mention of a conference. 'He never said anything about that to me. He often travels, but I always know exactly where he is. Except this time. When he got back from his last overseas trip, to Libya, he said he had to go away again for a few days. He was all secretive. He seemed nervous. He never used to act that way but he often does, these days. This time even more so.'

'Do you have any idea what he was nervous about?'

She shook her head. 'None. I seldom know what his trips are about as I don't know anything about archaeology. I asked him if something was wrong, but he just said not to worry, that everything would be fine, and he'd be home again soon. That was two days ago. I was going to call him on his mobile to check that he was all right, but I never got the chance because that's when those men suddenly turned up and—' Her eyes filled up with tears.

'You often call him on his mobile when he's away on business?' Ben asked.

'All the time. I know the number by heart.'

Ben took out his phone. 'Then call him now.'

Chapter 44

Margot Segal dialled the number and pressed the phone to her ear. 'What do I tell him?' she asked Ben, anxiously.

'Tell him the truth,' Ben said. 'I want him to hear your voice and to know that you're safe. Then I'd like to talk to him.'

She nodded. Waited for her husband to pick up. After a few more rings she whispered to Ben, 'It's gone to voicemail.'

'Leave a message.'

She nodded again. After the prompter bleep she said in a voice hoarse with emotion, 'Chéri, it's me. I don't know where you are, but I wanted to tell you that I'm all right. I'm safe. Please call me back. I so badly want to hear your voice.'

Her words were straight from the heart and touchingly sincere. She ended the call and passed the phone back to Ben. 'What do we do now?'

'Now we wait for him to call back.'

'What if he doesn't?'

Ben thought, *If he doesn't, it means he's probably dead already*. 'Let's just wait and see.'

It was a roll of the dice. The longer it took for Segal to respond, if he ever did, the harder it would be for Ben to keep up the pretence with his wife. He was prepared to give it a few hours, but after that he'd have no choice but to bite the bullet and pass her over to the real cops, for her own safety. And that would throw a spanner in the works of his plan.

But Ben didn't have to wait long. They were still sitting in the bedroom when, two minutes after Margot had left her message, the phone rang. The caller ID on the screen was the same number she'd dialled. He handed the phone to her. 'It's him.'

She sounded breathless as she answered the call. 'Julien?' Then, at the sound of his voice, she burst into tears. 'Yes, it's me, Chéri. I'm safe. I'm all right. Inspector Dardenne and his friend from the FBI rescued me . . . Yes, I'm here with them. In protective custody . . . Yes, they're here with me now.'

Ben held out his hand for the phone. She hesitated, then passed it to him. He stood up and left the bedroom, closing the door behind him. In the apartment's small living room Roth was lounging idly on the armchair with his eyes closed.

'Margot? Margot? Are you there?' Julien Segal sounded agitated and confused on the other end of the line.

Ben said quietly and calmly, 'Monsieur Segal, my name is Ben Hope. You don't know me, but I'd very much like to speak with you. Are you alone? Can we talk?'

After a long beat Segal replied, on the edge of panic, 'Yes, I'm alone. Are you the police? What's this about the FBI? Where's my wife?'

Ben glanced back at the bedroom door and kept his voice low. 'She's in good hands, Monsieur Segal. I promise you that. But we're not the police, which you should be happy about. I only told her that as a way to convince her to call you.'

Segal sounded even more confused and flustered. 'Then . . . who the hell are you?'

'I'm the man who found Romy's body,' Ben said. 'I know who killed her. I know that Nazim al-Kassar has been coercing you to do business with him. We can put a stop to that. Right here. Right now. But I need your help. Where are you?'

Silence on the phone. Ben could almost hear Segal's brain churning furiously. After another long pause, Segal muttered, 'I . . . I'm in Le Havre.'

Ben nodded. It all made sense to him. 'You're at the port. Waiting for the shipment to come in. You'll oversee the unloading of the cargo, then you'll call Nazim's people to come and take it away. They'll put it on a truck, maybe more than one, if my guess is right, and transport it to Paris. But it's not the last shipment they'll be bringing in. This doesn't stop, does it? Because these people own your whole life now.'

Segal's confusion had morphed into pure fear. He quavered, 'H-how do you know all this?'

'Never mind me,' Ben said. 'Let's talk about you. You don't have to work for Nazim any more. Margot is safe. The men who were holding her are dead. You're off the hook. But we need to act fast. Do you understand what I'm telling you?'

'They'll kill me.'

'We're not going to let that happen, Julien. Trust me. We can make all of this disappear.'

'That's impossible. I'm in so deep. When the authorities find out what I've helped those people do, they'll send me to prison for thirty years.'

'Maybe nobody needs to know,' Ben said. 'When this is over, maybe you and Margot can just go back to your lives like before.'

'The cargo ship is expected to arrive sometime around eight-thirty this morning,' Segal said. 'Things are in motion that can't be stopped.'

'Let's take this one step at a time,' Ben said. He looked at his watch. Le Havre was a couple of hundred kilometres from Paris. 'Give me your location and I'll be there as soon as I can.'

'With Margot?'

'With Margot,' Ben replied. 'And then you need to tell me what this is all about. There are some blanks to fill in.'

'And if I refuse?'

'I'll turn her over to the care of the police, and make sure that she tells them everything that I know,' Ben said. 'At that point, your life really is over. You won't be safe anywhere, not even in prison.'

'You're not leaving me much choice, are you?'

'I'm offering you a chance,' Ben said. 'The only one you have. You can thank me later. After you've hugged and kissed your wife who, in case you've forgotten, was a hostage until a couple of hours ago.'

Segal heaved the deepest sigh. 'No. I'm thanking you now. Whoever the hell you are, I owe you a debt I couldn't ever repay for taking her away from them. Margot means everything to me. And that evil bastard Nazim knows that. He told me he'd do to her what he did to poor, poor, sweet Romy.' His voice choked up as he said her name. 'He's a monster. I hate him more than I can possibly tell you.'

'That's why you're going to help me finish him, once and for all. Do we have a deal?'

Another pause. Then, 'Yes. All right. We have a deal.'

Segal gave Ben the address of a hotel near the Port of Le Havre. They agreed to meet in the lobby. Then Segal thanked him again, and the call was over.

Roth hadn't moved from the armchair, but one eye was open. 'Are we on?'

Ben said, 'We're on. Let's roll.'

Chapter 45

The 200-kilometre drive took them north and east towards the Normandy coast, almost exactly half the distance back to Le Val. It was motorway all the way, the A13 straightening out the sinuous, meandering path of the Seine River that connected Paris to the major port city of Le Havre.

Ben's watch was ticking towards 5.20 a.m. by the time he pulled up in the off-street parking at Julien Segal's hotel on a street named after some dead admiral, close to the sixteenth-century cathedral that was one of the town's only buildings to have survived the devastation inflicted on it during the 1944 Normandy invasion. But Segal hadn't chosen the hotel for its scenic view or luxury. It was a basic, no-frills establishment just a stone's throw from the docks, where he clearly wished to keep a low profile.

Dawn was some time away. A light rain was falling, driven inland by a gusty wind from the Channel. Ben shut off the engine and rolled his head around his shoulders to relieve the tension in his muscles. His eyes were burning and felt dry. He'd driven fast to get here in so short a time. Roth had remained silent the whole way, deep in his own thoughts, whatever those were. Margot Segal was still asleep on the back seat, lying curled up with a travel blanket over her and her head resting on Ben's bag. It couldn't have made for a very soft pillow, filled as it was with weaponry and ammunition, but she'd been so washed out by the last two traumatic days and nights that she didn't seem to care. Ben had given her some spare clothes he'd found in the safehouse, an old pair of jeans that needed to be rolled up at the bottom, a holey T-shirt and a baggy olive-green army pullover that draped over her like a tent.

He gently woke her, telling her they'd arrived. Her eyes blinked blearily open and then filled with excitement at the prospect of being reunited with her husband. The early morning dampness shrouded them with its sea-salty tang as they walked from the car towards the hotel lobby entrance. Roth carried the bag and Ben held onto Margot's arm because she was still weak and shaky.

As agreed, Julien Segal was waiting for them in the small, dimly-lit lobby. He was alone. Through the glass doors he looked old and shrivelled, a man worn to the bone with fear, worry and guilt. Margot let out a cry when she saw him, broke away from Ben and rushed inside to meet him. Ben and Roth hung back outside to let the couple have a minute or two in private. It was an emotional scene as they clung tightly to one another, both of them weeping.

But it was no unmitigated moment of joy either. By the time Ben and Roth stepped into the lobby, Margot had started firing the inevitable questions. 'Why is this happening, Julien? What have you got us involved in?' Her husband stood there looking utterly helpless and defeated with his head hanging. He muttered, 'I'm so ashamed.'

Margot stepped away from him and gripped Ben's arm. 'This is the police officer who rescued me, Inspector Jacques Dardenne. And this gentleman here is his colleague, Agent Anderson from America.'

Ben said, 'Why don't we go up to your room? There's a lot we need to talk about.'

Segal's poky single room was on the third floor and had a partial view of the docks in the distance, France's largest container port covering a broad expanse of coastline, a million lights reflecting on the water. He had a chair pulled up to the window and a pair of binoculars on the sill, as though he'd been sitting for hours scanning the horizon for the arrival of the cargo ship. The bed was rumpled, though he didn't look as if he'd been getting much sleep. He motioned to a coffee-maker on a sideboard and offered some to his visitors. It tasted like stewed compost, but both Ben and Roth had drunk a lot nastier brews when they were in the army.

Roth carried his cup over to the window and stood looking out through the binoculars. Ben sat the couple down on the rumpled single bed, and pulled a chair opposite them. 'First things first. Margot, I have a confession to make. My name isn't Jacques Dardenne, and neither I nor my friend here are police officers. If we were, your husband would be in handcuffs around now. As he knows very well. What matters here is that we are your friends. The only friends you've really got. So please listen carefully to what I'm about to say.'

Her outburst of surprise and consternation was understandable enough. Julien Segal clasped his wife's hand and said, 'Chérie, please, let him talk.'

Over the next five minutes, Ben told Segal everything that had happened since the moment of his chance encounter with Romy Juneau in the street: the visit to her apartment, the sighting of Nazim al-Kassar leaving the building and the discovery of the video footage on her phone. Tears returned to Segal's eyes and his chin fell to his chest as Ben described finding her dead.

'It's all my fault,' he muttered, struggling to contain his emotion, when Ben had finished. 'She was . . . I felt . . . that is to say, I had no idea she was there in the warehouse. Not until afterwards, as we were due to come back from Libya and she was acting so strangely around me that I had to ask her what was wrong. Then she told me what she'd witnessed. She was furious with me, threatened to resign, called me all kinds of names. I tried to explain myself, but she wouldn't listen and we argued for a long time. But I swear I knew nothing about a video. She didn't tell me she had filmed us.'

'Luckily for you, she didn't just take it straight to the authorities,' Ben said. 'Instead, when she got back home she tried to contact a reporter called Françoise Schell.'

'I know that name.'

'I'm not surprised. She wrote an article on terrorist organisations and the antiquities trade. Right up your street. That's how Romy found her, too. But unluckily for Romy, her closeness to your work made your little terrorist pals suspicious. She was being followed, and her apartment phone was almost certainly tapped. That's the only way they could have known about her call to Françoise, and the anonymous message she left her saying that she knew about a criminal conspiracy concerning a shipment and some kind of terror plot unfolding.'

'Oh, God,' Segal groaned. He wiped a tear. His hand was trembling.

'At which point, she needed to be eliminated, and fast, before she shared any more of what she knew with anyone. And Nazim al-Kassar was obviously happy to do the job himself. A highly motivated individual, our Nazim. It wasn't enough for him to kill Romy. The reporter is dead, too. And so would I be, if he'd had his way. Except I don't kill too easily.'

Segal was shaking his head in anguish. 'I don't understand. How is it that you know so much about Nazim al-Kassar?'

Ben said, 'It's a small world when you operate in certain circles. Let's just say there's history between us. The kind of history that makes him want me dead just as badly as I want to see him get what he deserves. But we're not here to talk about me, Julien. You have a great deal of explaining to do. Who exactly is Nazim to you, and what the hell are you involved in?'

'Tell them,' Margot Segal urged her husband. 'We need to know everything, Julien.'

'And I have nothing to hide any longer,' Segal replied, collecting himself. 'Not any more. So here it is. The whole truth.'

Chapter 46

Segal said, 'It all began years ago. Back in 2015, I spent some time working in Syria with a colleague called Salim Youssef. A wonderful man whom I loved and respected very much. He was really a mentor to me, almost a father figure. His passion for ancient art and treasures was one of the reasons I got into this business in the first place.'

Roth hadn't spoken a word until now, but he'd been listening carefully. 'Salim Youssef was murdered by Daesh forces, during their big push across Iraq and Syria in 2015, right before they established the new Caliphate.'

Segal frowned, and his eyes became misty and faraway as he relived the moment from his past. 'I was there, right at his side when it happened. We were in an ancient temple outside Palmyra. Everyone else had fled, knowing that the jihadist army was advancing closer every minute. Salim and I were desperately trying to evacuate as many artifacts as we could from the temple, because we knew all too well what those vandals would do to these priceless treasures in the name of religious supremacy. We had already managed to transport some in Salim's small truck to a hiding place nearby, in the hope that we could return afterwards to rescue them. A vain one, probably, but we had to try. Anyhow, we were too late. Before we could reload the truck, a group of Islamist soldiers arrived and entered the temple. Nine of them, heavily armed, the leader dressed in black. They understood exactly what we were doing, and demanded to know where we'd hidden the remainder of the artifacts.'

Ben could tell where the story was going. 'And Salim refused to tell them.'

'Oh, yes. He was the bravest man I ever knew. You should have seen the way he stood up to them right to the end, denouncing them as savages and betrayers of their faith. To my shame, I had no such courage. I was completely paralysed with dread.' Segal paused to reflect sadly, then went on: 'They made us kneel on the temple floor. The leader took out his knife. I remember it so clearly. He . . . he decapitated Salim.'

Margot was staring at her husband with wide eyes. 'Julien, you never told me any of this. You seemed upset when you came back from Syria, but I thought it was just because of the invasion.'

'I still can barely bring myself to talk about it,' Segal said miserably. 'That was the first time I ever met that murdering maniac Nazim al-Kassar. He was the leader. The man with the knife. He slaughtered poor Salim like an animal, as though it was nothing to him. The severed head fell on the floor right beside me. I truly, truly believed that mine would be next. When I heard the words "Now it's your turn" I almost choked with terror.'

Margot covered her face with her hands. 'Oh, God. Julien.'

'Nazim's had plenty of practice at slicing off heads,' Ben said. 'And worse things.'

'I can't imagine anything worse than what I witnessed that day,' Segal said. 'I still have nightmares. But the biggest nightmare is what has become of my life since. I've often wished that they had killed me, too.'

That was too much for Margot to hear. She burst into tears.

Segal went on, 'But I'm ashamed to say that I didn't have the courage to die the way Salim did. On my knees, I begged them to spare my life. Told them I'd do anything if they would let me go. I offered to lead them to where Salim and I had hidden the artifacts from the temple. Then I told them who I was, and about all the contacts I had across the world, and how I could help them to get their hands on a lot more. I truly didn't care what they did with them, whether they smashed them to pieces or took them as booty, as long as they agreed to let me go.'

'You sold out,' Ben said. 'Not just yourself, but the brave man who'd just died to protect what he believed in.'

'Yes, I was a coward,' Segal said. 'And I did what cowards do best. I survived. At first I was certain that Nazim was tricking me. But he was true to his word, because he suddenly had a use for me. The truth was that he had no intention of smashing up the artifacts. They were far too valuable for that.'

'And that's how you became his partner in crime.'

'God help me, it wasn't out of choice. I came home to Margot, and never said a word about what had happened in Syria, and got back to work, and prayed every day that it was over and I'd never hear from them again. Then a few weeks later, I got the call. Nazim al-Kassar was in Amsterdam and wanted to set up a business meeting.'

'That sounds real cosy,' Roth sneered.

'I was convinced I wouldn't return from Amsterdam alive. But I reasoned that they could kill me anytime they wanted, so what choice did I have? We met in a suite at the Pulitzer Hotel and he told me his plan. You see, whatever else Nazim al-Kassar might be, he isn't just some mindless idealist. Above all he's a businessman. A very serious businessman. He always kept an eye to the future, seeing ahead to the day when ISIL would be defeated in open warfare, and the jihadists would need to look to other tactics. Working from the inside, infiltrating lucrative trades like mine and using every penny to further their cause.'

Segal went on, 'And that was how it began. For the last four years they've been using me to bring illegally obtained antiquities into Europe for them to sell to raise funds for expanding their jihadist networks in France, Germany, Sweden, Denmark, Britain, everywhere. With my reputation and contacts, they were guaranteed a secure and steady trade route from various ports of the Middle East into Europe. I made sure that all the paperwork was always in order, but giving false destinations for the items, using straw buyers who were either bribed to take part in the fraud or were sometimes fictitious. Over the years I brought in over eleven million euros' worth of merchandise for them.'

'Taking a nice commission for yourself, I'll bet,' Ben said.

'I wouldn't have accepted a single cent of that money,' Segal protested. 'Not even if it had been offered. Which it wasn't. While they've been getting rich, the bastards have sucked me dry, like vampires. I'm close to losing everything I worked so hard to build. I can barely afford the rent on the Paris offices any longer. The house is remortgaged, too.'

Margot stared at him in horror. 'Our beautiful home?'

He shrugged. 'What else could I do? They made me their *dhimmi*, their slave. I was powerless to stop it. Don't you think I wanted to? Two years ago, I plucked up the courage to tell Nazim, "That's it, I'm done." Some days later an envelope arrived at the office, addressed to me personally. It had photographs inside.'

'Photographs?' she asked him. 'Of what?'

'Of you, my darling,' Segal confessed. 'One taken while

you were out shopping. The other at home, in the garden. There was no note, but none was needed. The warning was clear. If I didn't keep helping them, they would kidnap or kill you.'

Margot swallowed. A tear rolled down her face. She opened her mouth to speak, but she had no words.

Tears welled out of her husband's eyes, too, as he tried to make her understand. 'I couldn't tell anyone, least of all the police. These animals were ready to act on their threat at any moment. Nazim trusts nobody. I couldn't move an inch.' He turned to Ben. 'You saw what he did to poor Romy.'

'Go on,' Ben said.

'Then in August this year, Nazim contacted me again to tell me about his latest scheme. This was to be the start of a whole new venture, one that took a great deal of organising but promised to be the most lucrative for them yet.'

'The big plan,' Ben said. 'The cargo from Tripoli.'

Segal nodded.

'What's on the ship?'

Segal replied, 'Since it seems you've watched video footage of my meeting with Nazim inside the warehouse where the cargo was being stored prior to shipping, then you must already have seen it. We were standing right next to it as we talked.'

'Statues?'

Segal nodded. 'The biggest artifacts they've ever forced me to smuggle into Europe for them. Each inside its own shipping container, requiring two trucks to transport them by road. They're a pair of giant human-headed winged bulls, of the kind that existed long ago in ancient Mesopotamia.'

'Lamassu.'

'The guardians of the gateway. In the Akkadian language

their name meant "protective spirits". You seem to have more knowledge of this subject than I realised.'

'I saw them in the Louvre, years ago,' Ben said. 'Watching Romy's video brought the memory to mind. I went back there to check.'

'So you have some idea of what's involved. Similar examples are also on display at the British Museum in London and the Metropolitan Museum of Art in New York. Others haven't survived, such as the ones that were housed in the Mosul Museum before the filthy vandals of ISIL invaded the city and pounded them to pieces with sledgehammers. I'm quite certain that further magnificent examples are still waiting to be discovered beneath the sands of Iraq, Iran, Kuwait, Syria and Egypt, utterly priceless in value. However, I can assure you that you've never seen anything quite like the Lamassu on board the cargo ship, heading towards us even as we speak. These are quite different.'

Ben asked, 'In what way different?'

Segal said, 'Well, for a start, they're not real.'

Chapter 47

'Full of surprises, aintcha, Mister Segal?' Roth chuckled.

'In terms of size and scale, they're more or less identical to the exhibits you saw in Paris,' Segal explained. 'Otherwise, they're nothing more than crude, poorly detailed replicas that only a blind man or a complete fool could possibly mistake for the real thing from less than a few feet away. They're made of cheap plaster and were knocked together from moulded pieces in a backstreet workshop in Benghazi three months ago.'

Segal gave a bitter laugh at the looks on their faces. 'Oh, the deception is nothing particularly new. In 2015, when ISIL revealed their infamous video footage of the destruction of the artifacts in the Mosul Museum, archaeologists and historians the world over reacted in shock and dismay. What few people knew at the time, and only emerged later, was that about three-quarters of the pieces that the terrorists shattered with their hammers were modern plaster fakes.'

'So what happened to the real ones?' Ben asked.

'Some had already been relocated to Baghdad years earlier, after the Iraq War. In fact the authorities tried to claim that not one original piece had been left in the Mosul Museum by the time the jihadis took the city. That was untrue, and a cover-up of the fact that their attempt to protect the treasures was slipshod at best. Many genuine artifacts were still in place when the ISIL forces arrived. The majority of which were whisked off for sale on the black market, but not before they were used to mould plaster substitutes to destroy for the cameras.' Segal gave a dark smile. 'A fact to which I can testify, as it was me who fenced a large number of the genuine stolen items. As for the fakes, they only had to be good enough to look convincing on low-resolution video footage, fooling viewers into believing that they were seeing the demolition of the genuine item.'

'There's no business like show business,' Roth said. 'Those devious sons of bitches.'

'Not all the genuine pieces survived, however,' Segal went on. 'Among the priceless treasures they really did destroy in Mosul were the Lamassu winged bulls that were the museum's prize exhibits. It was their sheer size that doomed them. They were too big and heavy for the authorities to move to safety in time, and for the same reason couldn't be easily replicated, nor the real items sold off to rogue dealers. So the footage of their destruction was all too tragically real.'

'And yet, the ones on the ship are copies,' Ben said.

'When I said that Nazim al-Kassar was a serious businessman, I meant it. He's also far from stupid. The system for creating one-to-one scale plaster copies of such enormous statues was his idea. It was done by moulding separate plates which are then cemented together over a strong, light wooden frame and the joins plastered over to give the appearance of a single piece sculpted from a stone block.'

Margot Segal looked confused. 'I don't understand. You risked everything and put our lives in danger to help these maniacs make millions selling smuggled antiquities in

Europe. But those were always the real thing up until now, weren't they?'

'Yes, Chérie, I'm sorry to say they were.'

'And these fakes you're talking about, they were just decoys. Why would they go to the trouble of bringing in worthless plaster imitations that nobody would want to buy?'

'That's a good question,' Ben said. 'The answer is, because of what's in them. Statues cast out of moulded plaster plates are hollow. Something that large, it would have a lot of empty space inside.'

She looked at him.

'You told me that you don't know much about archaeology, Margot. But every kid I knew grew up hearing the legend of the Trojan horse. I'm sure you did as well.'

Her expression was blank. 'Yes, of course I know the story, but—'

'The Greek army spent ten years besieging the ancient city of Troy before they had the plan to create a huge wooden horse. When the Trojans came out the next day to find the Greeks had all sailed away, they thought they'd won and brought the horse inside the city as a trophy of war. Unknown to them, it was hollow inside, and filled with enemy soldiers who sneaked out the following night, threw open the gates and let in the entire Greek army.'

'He's right, Chérie,' Segal told his wife.

'But what's inside?' she asked, bemused.

'Not Greek soldiers, that's for sure,' Ben said. 'And not a jihadist invasion force toting automatic weapons, either, because they're already here. It's a shipment of drugs. A lot of drugs. I'm guessing that the world of antiquities import is too dully respectable a trade to have yet attracted the suspicion of Europol's narcotics division.'

Segal hung his head. He looked utterly defeated. 'So you knew.'

'We came across the processing plant in the hideout where they were holding Margot,' Ben told him. 'The place was empty, apart from a pile of boxes containing about fifty thousand plastic bags, waiting to be packaged up full of narcotics.'

'I have no idea where it is,' Segal said. 'You think Nazim would trust me with that kind of knowledge? But what I do know is that fifty thousand kilos is a conservative estimate. Nazim's target figure is actually more like sixty-five thousand, split over multiple shipments. Each of the fake Lamassu contains about four and a half thousand kilograms, which was the most weight they could hold without breaking up.'

Roth whistled. 'Holy shit. Nine thousand keys is almost ten US tons. A kilo brick of cocaine is worth about twenty-five grand, street price. Heroin costs even more, about thirty-eight dollars a gram. Times nine thousand kilos, which is nine million grams, that'd come to . . .' He paused for a moment as arithmetical wheels spun inside his head.

Ben got there first. 'Three hundred and forty-two million dollars.'

'Crap on a cracker. We're in the wrong goddamn business, amigo.'

'What you or I would do with the money is one thing,' Ben said. 'It's what Nazim would do with it that worries me. That much cash would pay for enough guns and bombs to declare war on Europe. And it's only the first shipment.' He wasn't even going to try to calculate the overall value of the whole 65,000 kilos.

Roth said, 'Man, he's looking at bringing in over seventy tons. The entire annual global heroin consumption is only about four hundred. Where's he getting it all from? Afghanistan? No fuckin' way. Pardon my French, Ma'am.'

Segal shook his head. 'I'm afraid you're wrong on both counts. It's not heroin. And it's not cocaine either. I almost wish it were. It's something much more sinister.'

Chapter 48

Ben and Roth exchanged glances. Roth's brow was crinkled in concentration, his eyes as sharp as a laser-guided weapons system locked onto its target.

Segal shifted to the edge of the bed, staring at the cheap hotel-room carpet as he came to the critical revelation. He'd finally managed to control the emotions that had been threatening to tip him over, and spoke calmly and mechanically.

'You obviously know, as everyone does, that Islamist terror organisations have been heavily involved in the drug trade for many years. You also know that their primary source, for a long time, was Afghanistan, where the cultivation of opium poppy and the facilities for refining the raw opium into heroin expanded enormously with the economic disruptions caused by the Soviet invasion. The Afghan government were unable to channel many resources into combating the growing illegal drug trade, because all their financial and technical aid was focused on fighting the insurgents. Worse, many corrupt Afghan authorities were willing to aid the drug traffickers, getting rich in the process. But the more enterprising elements within the insurgent factions were also very quick to get in on the act.

'As instability and war in the region went on and on,

so did heroin production. The continued American military presence only intensified matters, to the point where al-Qaeda and the Taliban became viewed as little more than glorified drug cartels. Which was a distortion of reality, since while actual drug cartels are only interested in personal gain, the Islamists saw themselves as engaged in a holy war that needed funding wherever it could get it. Moreover, if the fruits of the drug trade helped to weaken and destabilise the Western countries that were the ultimate target of their jihad crusade, so much the better. That's a crucial part of this. Drugs foster crime, violence, mental illness and social decay, and are one of the most effective means of rotting a civilisation from the inside out. And that's exactly what they want to happen, in Europe and eventually the USA.'

'We get it,' Ben said. Roth was staring intently at Segal and processing every word.

'I'm just filling in the background, so that you understand what this is really all about. Eventually, things reached the stage where enough was enough. After a 2017 UN report estimated that opium production had increased by eighty-seven per cent in just that year alone, the American military combined forces with the Afghan authorities in what was basically a CIA-guided mission to obliterate the opium trade. The ensuing air strikes were highly effective in destroying nearly all the country's refinement facilities. While they stopped short of reducing the poor poppy farmers to total destitution, they nonetheless absolutely hammered the supply of heroin available to the traffickers.'

'You know your shit,' Roth said. 'Not all of this is declassified information.'

Segal shrugged. 'Yes, well, you might say I have the inside track.'

'Go on,' Ben said.

'So, refusing to be deterred by such minor setbacks as the near-blanket destruction of the Afghan narcotics trade, the Islamists just switched gears,' Segal continued. 'Remember, they don't spend their ill-gotten gains on mansions and gold-plated Rolls Royces. Every penny goes into well-protected bank accounts, hidden behind layers of fronts, where it just grows and grows. They possess huge financial resources for developing new alliances and fresh ways of developing drugs that could replace the traditional heroin, allowing them to continue to accrue wealth while stepping up the attack on the moral and social integrity of the West. What might those new drugs be? They considered many options. Cocaine has always been the poor-relation, and its value has bottomed out in recent years. Other forms of recreational drug, like methamphetamine or marijuana, just don't have the same kind of market traction or profitability. Nor did the Islamists wish to truck with the organised cartels of Central and South America. So the question was, "Where do we go?"'

'China,' Roth said. Ben looked at him and wondered, not for the first time, whether the American knew more about all this than he was letting on.

Segal replied, 'China, exactly.'

'Why China?' Ben asked.

'Because,' Segal explained, 'China is the world's largest producer of a totally synthetic, lab-created opioid drug that is not only quicker, easier and cheaper to manufacture than its traditional competitors, but also infinitely more powerful. Rendering the likes of heroin and cocaine virtually obsolete in the modern age.'

'He's right, man, the times they are a changin',' Roth said. 'There's a new kid on the block, and its name is fentanyl. You don't have to cultivate it, you don't have to harvest it, and you don't have to refine the raw material into a finished product.

All you need is a basic lab, some beakers and whatnot, and some geek with a chemistry degree. Think of it as Heroin 2.0.'

'Fentanyl?'

'Technically, it's a painkiller,' Roth said. 'At least, that's how they envisaged it, when they invented it back in the fifties. Then, it was used solely as a medical drug. Before long they started putting it in patches, and fuckin' lollipops, and pretty soon after that it was all over the place. Over time the lines between medicinal and recreational applications became kind of blurred, like they are with morphine.'

'Except that fentanyl is between fifty and a hundred times more potent than morphine,' Segal said. 'Which is the main reason for its far greater popularity among the increasingly drug-dependent Western public. Fatal overdoses from prescription and non-prescription pain-relieving medications are outstripping the likes of heroin by a greater and greater margin each year. The modern synthetic opioid crisis is a fast-growing problem, with fentanyl emerging as its biggest contender. All the bans and regulations in the world can't stem the supply. Not with four hundred thousand manufacturers across China generating over a hundred billion dollars annually.'

'And it's toxic as hell,' Roth said. 'Drug squad dogs trained to sniff out heroin or coke all day long will die if they get just a tiny whiff of fentanyl fumes. Some addict who gets through thirty to forty bags of smack a day can use a single bag of fentanyl and drop dead on the spot. A quarter gram dose can be fatal. One pound of it is enough to kill two hundred thousand people. And one ton? We are talking major kick-ass lethality. A chemical weapon of mass destruction.'

'The maths are pretty simple,' Segal said gravely. 'One ton

of pure fentanyl is sufficient to kill four hundred million people.'

Ben looked at Roth, then at Segal. It seemed like an impossible number. His mind began to swim. 'That's more than double the population of Western Europe.'

'And they've got nine times that quantity,' Roth said.

'That's not all,' Segal said. 'It gets worse again.'

Chapter 49

'How can it get any worse?' Ben said.

Roth laughed. 'This guy's a hoot. I can't wait to hear the punchline.'

'It's worse for the simple reason that they're not doing this for the money,' Segal replied. 'Which means the fentanyl isn't going to be stored somewhere and drip-fed into the system like any other retail product the seller has invested in. When that shipment reaches France, just over two and a half hours from now, they intend to dump the entire quantity on the market all at once, for free. Gratis. It will create a tidal surge of chaos such as has never been seen in Europe before. Drug gangs will be slaughtering each other wholesale in broad daylight over who can gain the biggest slice of the cake. The police will be totally unable to contain the violence. There'll be stampedes and riots. The streets will be lined with comatose bodies and the hospitals will be choked with fatal overdose cases. Within weeks the number of hopeless addicts will multiply exponentially, and half the kids in France will be using. Within months, the effect on the whole society will be devastating, the state's resources strained far past breaking point. It's not hard to imagine what comes next.'

'The next generation of warfare,' Roth said. 'They can't

beat us on the battlefield. So this is how they take us down instead.'

'Using drugs to destabilise the enemy is nothing new,' Segal said glumly. 'It's what the CIA did to the American blacks through the nineteen-seventies and eighties, injecting drugs into their community to tear it apart and weaken potential resistance against oppressive government policy. A century and a half earlier, the same thing was being done to the American Indians, with cheap toxic alcohol, while in the mid-eighteen-hundreds the British were deliberately causing the Chinese to become addicted to opium. Now maybe the Chinese are getting their own back on Western Europe, using the jihadis as pawns in the game. And I'm afraid the strategy may succeed. Look at us. We're already on our knees. The signs of our decaying secular culture are all around, as the institutions collapse, traditions are erased and the population sinks into mindless degeneracy and nihilism, believing in nothing, living in an ideological void. One small push is all it might take to topple the whole crumbling edifice into total collapse. With the crusaders of the new holy war just waiting at the gates to come marching in and seize power.'

Margot Segal sat slumped in shock and dismay at what she'd been hearing. 'I just can't believe anyone could be so vicious and cruel. What have we done to them? What could make them hate us so much?'

'It's all right there in their book, Ma'am,' Roth explained. '"The infidels should not think that they can get away from us. Prepare against them whatever arms and weaponry you can muster so that you may terrorise them. They are your enemy and Allah's enemy." Qur'an surah eight, verse fifty-nine.'

'The terrible part is,' said Julien Segal, shaking his head, 'that sometimes I think it's not so hard to understand why they despise us so bitterly. The more our Western world loses its way, the more it only confirms their faith and motivation to press on to victory against an enemy that lacks the fire, courage and motivation to oppose them. There's a kind of purity to the way they think. Nothing we can do can deter or influence them. Their belief is absolute.'

'Sounds like you sympathise quite a bit with your terrorist buddies,' Roth said. 'Maybe you were happy to do your part helping them, so you can go on being their little dhimmi when they set up the new Caliphate of Europe, the House of War becomes the House of Islam and the black flag of ISIL is flying over Paris, Brussels and London. Maybe you're really a closet terrorist yourself, as well as a coward. Which makes me wonder if I maybe shouldn't just shoot your worthless ass, right now.' Roth took out his pistol. 'Sorry, Margot, but your husband is a prick.'

Segal put up his hands. 'Please! You can't—'

It was hard to tell whether Roth was joking or serious. 'Nobody's shooting anybody,' Ben said, pushing the gun away. 'You and I have better things to do.' He glanced at his watch. Six a.m. 'We still have some time to work out a plan of attack.'

'Jawohl, Herr Kommandant. So what do you have in mind?'

Ben turned to Segal. 'Tell me exactly what's scheduled after the ship comes into port.'

Segal was sweating, still staring at the gun in Roth's hand. 'Everything's set up to look completely legitimate. I have the paperwork, export licences and itemised descriptions of the cargo contents to show to the harbour master, who signs them over to the care of the Institute. Then the crates are to be unloaded from the ship onto a pair of flatbed trucks.'

'Whose trucks? Nazim's?'

Segal shook his head. 'They're rentals. The drivers are just a couple of men for hire who have no idea what they're transporting.'

'So Nazim won't have any of his people there except you?'

'Until the moment the ship arrives, it's just me,' Segal said. 'But he has a man on board. Ostensibly a crew member, but his real job was to supervise the loading of the cargo in Tripoli and keep an eye on it en route. His name's Zahran Azzam Yasin, a Libyan. He's one of Nazim's most committed and dangerous jihadists. A real fanatic.'

'Like the rest of his men are only touchy-feely semi-fanatics,' Roth said.

Ben asked, 'Where do the trucks go from there?'

'To a chemicals warehouse in Sandouville, about sixteen kilometres from Le Havre. Nazim and his crew will be waiting for it there. The drivers are expecting to unload the crates there, get paid and go home. That isn't what's going to happen, unfortunately for them.'

'Why unfortunately? What will they do to those poor men?' Margot gasped.

'Chérie, what do you think?' Segal replied sadly, then turned back to Ben. 'The warehouse is owned by ETZ International, which is a front for a variety of terror operations. The official owners don't exist. The real owners have arranged for it to burn down afterwards. Five hundred gallons of kerosene will make sure there's no trace left of the missing drivers, or anything that could link back to Nazim and his crew.'

'That'll do it,' Roth said.

'Meanwhile, the plaster Lamassu will have been removed from the crates and broken open. The fentanyl is contained inside two hundred sealed aluminium drums weighing forty-five kilograms apiece. Nine tons, to be divided into ton-and-a-half payloads aboard six smaller commercial vans driven by Nazim's men, which will then make their separate ways to Paris. They'll rendezvous at a secure location in the city and wait for evening. Come nightfall the processing plant will be getting into full swing, subdividing the fentanyl into nine thousand kilo bricks for fast distribution via the jihadist network.'

Ben asked, 'How the hell do they expect to carry nine tons of merchandise in two hundred metal drums underground through a ventilation shaft at street level without anyone noticing?'

'Haven't you been following the news?' replied Segal. 'Tomorrow night is Saturday. Every weekend the anti-government disturbances are getting worse. The whole of Paris is braced for another round of anarchy and violence. The police will have their hands full. It's the perfect diversion for Nazim to do whatever he wants.' He shook his head. 'If the authorities think the situation is falling to pieces now, wait until the effect of nine tons of lethal free drugs begins to hit the population of Paris. Things will degenerate very quickly. And that's just the first shipment. There will be more to come.'

There was silence for a few moments as they deliberated. Roth said, 'Way I see it, we have two options. Plan A, we hit them at the warehouse as they're unloading the crates. Plan B, we head back to the city, wait for tomorrow night and jump on them as they make the drop-off.'

Ben didn't agree. 'Either of those plans involves us getting into a battle with the full force of Nazim's men. There are only two of us, remember?'

'Then we call in the cavalry,' Roth said. 'The GIGN boys will be itching to get even after what happened last night.'

'All the more reason to keep them out of it. Striking back in anger makes for bad tactical planning. They'll roll in with the tanks and artillery, Nazim will see them coming from a mile off and there'll be a bloody slaughter. In the middle of which, Nazim himself is liable to slip straight out of our hands and disappear for ever.'

'Doesn't have to be the cops,' Roth said. 'You know people. I know people. We can do it right. There's still time to make the arrangements, if we act fast.'

Ben knew that he need make only one call to Jeff and Tuesday at Le Val, and they'd happily rush to Paris with enough personnel backup and weaponry to overthrow a modestly-sized dictatorship. But he had no intention of involving his friends in danger.

'No. There's a better way.'

'Which is what?' Roth asked.

'To strike where the weakest link in the chain is. Nazim can't afford to raise suspicions by posting twenty shifty-looking terrorist thugs at the docks. That's why he's leaving that job to Segal, because the transfer of the cargo has to look as innocuous as possible. So you and I will intercept the trucks with the crates on board before they even leave the port. The drivers will have to be bundled away somewhere they can't kick up a fuss. They might get banged up a little but that's better than having your head sliced off.'

'What about Zahran Yasin?' Segal asked anxiously. 'He'll be there dockside as they unload the cargo. He's supposed to ride along in one of the trucks.'

'Mr Yasin won't be making that trip,' Ben said. 'One man isn't going to be a problem, between two of us. Are you able to recognise him?'

Segal nodded. 'I remember him from the one time I saw him. A small man, very slender and wiry. He has a shaven head and a long black beard. He looks incredibly menacing.'

'Then stick close to me and make sure you point him out the moment you see him. Roth and I will do the rest. Nobody else gets hurt, and all being well we can pull this off without firing a shot or drawing the slightest attention to ourselves. Then we make for some alternative location where we can smash the Lamassu open ourselves and grab what's inside.'

Roth thought about it. 'And what do you plan on doing with nine freakin' tons of fentanyl?'

Ben replied, 'Two can play at the hostage game. If Nazim wants to try to get his drugs back, he's going to have to come and get them on our terms, alone. That's where we take him down.'

Roth frowned. 'He won't go for it. He'll know it's a trap.'

'Of course he'll know. But he'll go for it, because he has to. Nazim might be pretty high up in his organisation's chain of command but he's not the top of it. Not even close. He's just a soldier in an army. And whatever he might be risking if he takes our bait, he knows it's nothing next to what his superiors will do to him if he loses their fentanyl. Then it's him on the wrong end of the knife.'

'I like the sound of that,' said Segal, smiling for the first time. 'I hope they chop off his rotten head.'

Roth pondered the idea for a moment, then said, 'Okay. Sounds like a green light to me.'

Everything seemed to make perfect sense. If what Segal had told them was true, little could go wrong.

But there was just one possibility that Ben had overlooked. His plan was unravelling even as they spoke. He didn't know it yet, but he would realise his mistake soon enough.

Chapter 50

Ninety minutes earlier

As the last arrival rolled to a halt on the cracked, rain-slicked concrete outside the warehouse, everybody climbed out. It was just after 4.30 a.m., the time when the world was at its lowest ebb. The six vehicles that had driven through the night from Paris to Sandouville were a mixture of commercial panel vans, all different makes and models, some stolen, the rest cheaply procured for cash.

Their occupants totalled fourteen men. Two of them were white European converts who, after years of living the kafir life, had found deep comfort and enlightenment in jihadist ideology. Another seven were immigrants from Somalia, Nigeria, Libya, Qatar, Syria and Afghanistan. Four were French-born members of the main jihadist cell in Paris. All were utterly loyal to their leader, Nazim al-Kassar. And all were men with a hardcore criminal past that included rape, murder, terrorist plotting, gun running and bomb-making. There wasn't one among them who wouldn't gladly make the ultimate sacrifice for this sacred mission on which they were now embarking.

Nazim was wearing a black leather jacket and a black baseball cap. He walked up to the warehouse entrance, unlocked the heavy padlock at the foot of the steel shutter and stepped back as two of his men, the Syrian called Abbud and the Nigerian called Shaykh, heaved it up with a noisy clatter. Shaykh was possibly the most devout of the entire gang, diligently observing his five-times-daily prayers and the recitation of the Fatiha, or opening, prayer a full seventeen times each day, and was often muttering Qur'anic verses to himself; all this, despite the fact that he was black, and that his Arab fellows quietly considered his race to be born slaves, described by the Prophet as 'raisin heads' in the Hadith.

Nazim stood by and watched as they drove the vans single-file inside the warehouse, spreading out to leave room for the two larger flatbed lorries to park later. The transfer of the two hundred drums to the smaller vehicles would keep them all busy for a while. Nine tons divided equally to a ton and a half per vehicle, the vans' maximum payload. Until they had it, all they could do was wait. They had several hours before the container vessel was expected to dock at Le Havre, sixteen kilometres west of here. Nazim believed in punctuality, preparedness and staying well ahead of the curve.

The terrorist leader appeared outwardly calm and composed as ever, but beneath the cool facade he was feeling nervous as his anticipation of the impending shipment grew more intense and the complexity of the plan crowded his mind. So many small details, of which any could potentially go wrong – and if anything did, it was he, Nazim, who would be held accountable by the staunchly unforgiving men who headed up his organisation and had made such a sizeable investment in this enterprise. It was a great honour that had been placed on him, but it was also a heavy burden of responsibility.

While all this troubling stuff was buzzing through his head, it occurred to him that some time had passed since he'd last checked with the men guarding the Segal woman. It was important to him that she be kept in reasonable condition, in case she needed to be used as further leverage. By 'reasonable condition' Nazim meant some degree of consciousness and the ability to scream horribly into a phone to remind her husband of what was at stake here; her state of health or prospects of survival meant little otherwise.

While his men were opening up the vans and preparing the transit crates in which the two hundred precious drums would be transported back to Paris in a few hours' time, he took out his phone, dialled and waited.

No response.

Nazim cancelled the call, frowned at his phone and tried again.

No response.

Disrespectful. Unacceptable.

This time he left a terse message in Arabic: 'This is Nazim. You better call me back right away. What's the matter with you sons of whores?'

Two minutes went by, then three, and still the phone remained dead in his hand. Now Nazim was getting concerned. He made a third call, this one to another of the Mohammeds back in Paris, different from the Muhammad who was one of the hostage's guards. Even Nazim mixed them up sometimes.

This Mohammed answered promptly 'As-Salaam Alaikum', instantly deferent when he realised who was calling. Nazim said, 'I need you to get down to the *makhba* [which was what they called the hiding place in Arabic] and check things out. Take a couple of others with you. Call me the moment you're down there. Got it?'

'Got it, boss.'

He waited. And waited. Patiently at first, though every so often he would try the guards' number again, to no avail. Almost half an hour went by, and Nazim was becoming quite agitated. Then the phone finally rang. Nazim snatched it up and barked, 'Talk to me! Where are you?'

The phone signal was crackly and weak, barely there at all. Mohammed's faint voice said, 'We're down there now, boss. All that's here is a bunch of dead bodies and an empty chair where the kafir bitch was.' Which, as a concise description of what he and his companions had discovered down in the ghost tunnel, was perfectly accurate. But then it got worse, because before Nazim could start yelling at him down the phone, Mohammed added, 'We went in by the ventilation shaft, boss. Someone else has been down there before us. It's been disturbed, and the door to the storeroom has been broken open too. What do you want us to do?'

Nazim was actually unable to come up with any instructions at this moment, other than, 'Try and fix things up and get out of there as soon as you can.'

'What about the bodies?'

'Leave them,' Nazim said. Which technically was a sin, as under Islamic law every dead body must be buried according to the proper protocol, although the fact that these men had died martyrs' deaths in the service of Allah circumvented that necessity.

Nazim ended the call realising that the tunnel hideouts were now compromised and would not be used again. That was irksome enough, but worse was the knowledge that only one man could be thwarting him like this. The foreigner. The man with no name. Why, why, could they not be rid of him? Who was this *shuitan*, this demon in human form, who seemed to be able to evade and outsmart them at each turn while ever whittling down their forces?

That thought led to more, and worse, conclusions. Because logic dictated that if the nameless white *shaitan* could get to the Segal female, it meant that he could get to the bitch's husband.

Within seconds of that realisation Nazim was dialling Segal's mobile number. By rights the *dhimmi* should at this moment be asleep in bed in his hotel near the port. Nazim let it ring and ring until it went to voicemail, then he re-dialled twice more and did the same again, but there was still no answer. Nazim finally gave up, his suspicions now fully alerted and his mind whirling as he considered the potential chain reaction of events. Segal knew far too much. If Nazim no longer had a hold over him, the infidel could cause their whole scheme to founder. Not only by spilling their secret to the foreigner, but by leading him right here to the warehouse.

Or something even more unsettling. Nazim felt a cold shiver as he realised his greatest vulnerability was the cargo itself, the moment it was unloaded on the dock. If Segal had betrayed him, the place could be swarming with police by the time the ship came in.

Mind racing, he looked at his watch. 5.14 a.m. The vessel was still a long way out to sea. He still had time to avert absolute disaster, but the sand was running fast out of the hourglass. He must act immediately. He would catch up with the traitor Julien Segal soon enough.

Nazim turned to his men and said, 'Stop what you're doing, all of you, and get back in the vans. We're aborting.'

Chapter 51

As the six vans sped away from Sandouville, heading back eastwards through the rainy, misty darkness towards Le Havre, a desperate new plan was fast coming together in Nazim's mind. He made another phone call, this time to his accomplice Zahran Yasin on board the ship, whose role in all of this was about to take a dramatic new turn.

Abbud the Syrian was at the wheel of the lead van as Nazim, next to him in the front passenger seat, told Zahran what would be required of him. When the call was finished Abbud looked perplexed. 'I don't get it. We're already headed for the docks, so why can't we just hang around and wait for the ship ourselves? If Segal has betrayed us to the foreigner, we just kill them and take what's ours, inshallah.'

Nazim replied calmly, 'And if the foreigner has brought the GIGN and a thousand gendarmes with him, are you going to kill them and take what's ours then?'

'Allah is our objective. The Prophet is our leader. Qur'an is our law. Jihad is our way. Dying in the way of Allah is our highest hope.' Abbud was reciting from the official doctrine of the Muslim Brotherhood, words that he'd venerated and repeated for most of his life.

'I have no fear of death,' Nazim said. 'But this plan must succeed, Abbud. I won't die having failed.'

Twenty minutes from Sandouville, just after 5.35 a.m., the van convoy arrived at the docks. The Port of Le Havre was a huge sprawl of industry with multiple terminals and wharves that could accommodate the largest cruise liners in the world, like vast light-spangled starships that glided on the waves. Its series of canals connected the sea estuary to the major shipping lane of the Seine River. Giant cranes stood tall against the pre-dawn sky and a million reflections were shimmering on the blackness of the water.

Using his smartphone to navigate, Nazim guided Abbud through the port's complex road system to the marina where private shipping came and went 24/7 and over a thousand vessels of all shapes and sizes were moored.

'This is it. Stop here.' Nazim jumped out. The five other vans pulled up behind them on the quayside and the terrorists crowded around their leader in the cold, pattering rain to hear the new plan. Nazim pointed across the dark water at the forest of masts bobbing on the swell.

'We are going to steal a boat. Something fast and strong that can bear carrying nine tons of cargo. Spread out among the piers and search. Surely we can find the one we need.'

It took them eighteen precious minutes to come up with the goods. Nazim was inspecting the moorings on Pier 7 when his phone buzzed. It was Dariush, the other of the two Afghans, sounding excited. 'Come quickly, boss. I think I found just the thing.'

Dariush's discovery was a twelve-metre, twin-engined cruiser that certainly looked the business and even had its own onboard hydraulic cargo loading crane. Abbud, who had studied mechanical engineering at the University of Damascus before taking up his career in international terrorism, reckoned it was up to the job. The decision made, all fourteen men clambered aboard with the automatic weapons and long-handled sledgehammers they'd brought from Paris. Abbud soon figured out how to hotwire the diesel Cummins motors, and within minutes they were cast off and away. Nazim had piloted boats before, during gun-running operations back home, but this thing was faster than any he'd known. They sped out of the harbour with their bows high in the air and slapping the waves, throwing out a foamy wake behind them.

By now it was edging towards six a.m., just two and a half hours or so before the cargo ship was expected in port. At a speed of some twenty knots, that meant it was still about fifty nautical miles from the coast, give or take. The stolen vessel with its powerful diesels and Rolls Royce waterjets could cover the distance in less than half the time. Nazim called Zahran again, who gave him the ship's current GPS coordinates.

Nazim estimated that they would intercept the ship's course within an hour, perhaps less. He would strike fast, get the job done and escape before anyone even knew what had happened. He was smiling. He was winning again. Nothing could stop him.

Meanwhile, on board the ship, Zahran Azzam Yasin was getting ready to do his part. After receiving his orders from his superior, he bided his time awhile on deck and then headed for his cabin. He shared his crew quarters with three other seamen, all of whom were currently either on work shift or drinking coffee in the mess canteen. Zahran opened the locker by his bunk and took out his prayer mat and qibla compass, which pointed permanently towards Mecca. He laid the mat on the floor, prostrated himself and said his prayers, then carefully rolled the mat up and put it away. Next he took out a sports bag and laid it on the floor to unzip it. Inside, wrapped up in a couple of T-shirts, was the stubby AK-47 that he'd had little difficulty smuggling on board in Tripoli.

Zahran was extremely familiar with the weapon, having undergone extensive training in an ISIL terrorist boot camp in his native Libya. He clicked in a loaded magazine, racked the cocking bolt and set the safety, then put the weapon back in the holdall, slung the bag over his shoulder and left his cabin. It was 6.30 a.m. precisely. Nazim and the others would be here in about thirty minutes, which gave Zahran all the time he needed.

He strolled nonchalantly through the ship's passages and corridors until he reached the bridge, the vessel's highest point and the domain of the captain and officers. As an ordinary seaman Zahran's tasks seldom required him to perform watchstanding or helmsman duties, and so his sudden appearance on the bridge was unexpected. The captain was in the midst of a conversation with the radio officer when they saw him and turned. Without a word Zahran set down the sports bag and, before anyone could react, yanked out the AK.

The captain froze, but the officer made the mistake of lunging towards the radio console. Zahran blasted it apart with a deafening burst of gunfire, then pointed the weapon at the officer and said, 'Next time, I shoot you. Now get the crew up here. And remember, I know every man on board. Do not try to trick me, or everyone will die.'

All six officers and the fifteen crewmen were soon all hostages on the bridge and made to kneel with their hands on their heads. Some of the seamen who had been on morning shift were wearing yellow waterproof overalls; others had been roused from their bunks and were dressed in shorts and T-shirts. All of them were staring at Zahran with a mixture of rage and disbelief that one of their own guys, albeit one who'd just been taken on and whom nobody really knew well, could be doing this. But if anyone was toying with the idea of trying to disarm him, the steely, determined look in his eye soon persuaded them otherwise.

Zahran was completely calm and in control. On his command the engines were shut down. Now the ship was dead in the water, drifting aimlessly and wallowing on the waves. The radio console was completely shattered and in pieces, but the radar was still working fine – and within minutes it was showing an approaching vessel that Zahran knew was his leader. Pointing the gun at the kneeling hostages with one hand he took out his phone and called Nazim with the good news. 'The ship is ours. Allahu Akbar!'

'What is this outrage?' the captain demanded. 'Are you hijacking us? You want money?'

'Keep your money, kafir,' Zahran replied.

It wasn't long before the stolen boat was tethered up alongside the cargo ship, dwarfed next to the gigantic hull and in danger of being crushed by its roll. 6.52 a.m. Nazim had made excellent time. Zahran ordered three crewmen to descend to the deck and lower ladders, so that Nazim and the rest of the men could board. 'Do it now. Or I shoot the captain.'

One by one the terrorists clambered up the ship's side. Nazim had never set foot aboard such a huge vessel. When he reached the bridge he congratulated Zahran on his excellent work. 'Allah be praised!'

The captain was less impressed. He was a large, square-built man in his late fifties, with a red complexion made redder with anger, and he was growing less intimidated by the minute. 'This is bare-faced piracy and you'll never get away with it,' he blustered at Nazim.

'We're not here for your ship, infidel filth,' Nazim replied. 'We are here to take what's ours. And to liberate you from your ways of ignorance.'

And before the captain could say another word, Nazim's knife was in his throat. The captain let out a shrill gasp and fell to his knees. The officers and crew started screaming and yelling. The rest of Nazim's men shoved them back at gunpoint. One of them tried to resist, and Zahran shot him in the face. Nazim slowly stepped around behind the captain, the blade still buried deep in the flesh and gristle of his neck, slicing and sawing as blood pumped down the man's white shirt and spattered over the floor of the bridge.

'Murderers!' screamed the radio officer.

Nazim or any of his men could have explained to him that this was not murder. The ship's personnel were *kuffar harbi*, infidels at war with Islam; therefore they were enemy soldiers who spread corruption throughout the face of the earth; therefore it was not only permitted but mandatory under Sharia law to kill them, and in fact it would be a punishable offence to let them live. But why bother explaining anything to infidels?

The horrific act was over in seconds. Nazim held up the captain's severed head by a hank of greying hair, then flung it away with contempt and spat on the decapitated body slumped at his feet. A lake of blood spread around his feet as he turned to the seamen. 'Who among you can operate a forklift truck or the ship's cargo crane?' Their faces were pale. They were too terrorised to protest and too appalled to speak. A couple of uncertain hands went up.

Nazim turned to Zahran. 'Can you vouch for them?'

'I can't say for certain,' Zahran replied. 'I think I've seen that one drive the forklift.'

'They'll have to do,' Nazim said.

'What do we do with the others?' Dariush asked.

Nazim smiled. Once again, the holy scripture provided the answer. *When you meet the unbelievers in battle, smite their necks.*

He said, 'Cut off their heads.'

Chapter 52

The screams were drowned out by the crash of the waves as Nazim led the way down from the bridge, followed by Abbud and Zahran with the two spared crewmen stumbling along at gunpoint. Outside in the murky first light of dawn, the wind was lashing the ship with rain and salt spray. They descended the clattering metal gangways to the deck, feeling the heave and roll of the vessel beneath their feet. Mountains of containers were stacked up to form neat aisles along the length of the deck, like walking through a gorge.

Zahran led the way to where their two containers were kept. Every day of the voyage he had been making secret visits to them, making sure they were securely lashed in place, checking every inch and marvelling at the power of what was inside. He knew only that it was some kind of weapon that could bring the *kuffar harbi* to their knees and bring glory on the world.

Nazim had to shout to be heard above the roar of wind and sea. 'Let's get to work.'

The two surviving seamen were pressed into action. By the time the rest of the terrorists joined their leader on deck, the containers had been opened and their precious contents brought out. The ship's massive Hyster forklift truck could handle loads of up to thirty tons and had no problem ferrying the wooden crates across the deck. Nazim pointed out where he wanted them set down, side by side near the stern railing above where their stolen boat was moored like a limpet to the container ship's hull. A powerful floodlamp lit up the deck. Shaykh, Zahran, Abbud and Jamshid prised the crates open with crowbars and pulled their sides apart to reveal what was inside.

The pair of huge Lamassu were a weird, surreal sight on the deck of a modern container ship. Very few of Nazim's men had had any clear idea of what to expect, and were gaping at the statues in amazement.

'Fetch the hammers,' Nazim commanded. 'Smash them open.'

The men obeyed enthusiastically, a gang of them standing beneath each monster statue and swinging away with gusto. For Nazim, watching, the moment was a nostalgic reminder of the glorious days of the ISIL conquest of Syria. The first few pounding blows did little more than crack the thick plaster. Then the cracks began to widen, and fragments began to rain down, exposing the internal wooden frames. More chunks of plaster fell away and the first dull glint of the aluminium drums inside became visible. A few more blows, and the two hundred drums began to spill out of the shattered bellies of the Lamassu. As each one thumped to the deck it had to be quickly propped up on end to prevent it from rolling dangerously around. Jamshid was bowled off his feet by one that crashed into his shins. Another almost burst through the railing.

7.08 a.m. Nazim was acutely conscious of the time going by. He had no idea how these things worked, but it was likely that the French coastguard would be alerted if a ship in their waters fell out of radio contact for any length of time. Every minute counted.

Then it was time for the next phase, transferring the nine tons of drums onto the small boat. This was the hard part. Nazim turned to the crewman who'd claimed to know how to use the crane, and said, 'Your turn. Get moving.'

The guy had gone bluish-white with fear. 'I . . . I . . . can't . . .'

'You told me you could operate it. That's why you're alive.'

The guy fell to his knees, cringing on the deck like a supplicant at Nazim's feet. 'Please! I have a wife and child.'

'Then they're better off without a liar for a husband and a father,' Nazim said, and he drew his pistol and shot the guy in the back of the head. The crack of the shot was snatched away by the wind. At the sight of his shipmate's bloody execution, the crewman who'd been pressed into operating the forklift truck let out a wild yell and tried to make a break for it. Nazim took aim at the fleeing man and shot him in the back. He pitched face-first to the deck and lay still.

'What do we do now?' Jamshid said anxiously, looking at the two hundred drums. Their boat seemed very small and distant, a cockleshell at the foot of a cliff. 'Lower them down the side one at a time on the end of a rope?'

'We don't have time for that,' snapped Nazim.

'I think I can work the crane,' Zahran volunteered. 'I'm smarter than any of those kuffar morons.'

'Then hurry, and don't mess this up,' Nazim warned him.

And Zahran went running off to the crane, to clamber up the tall ladder to the operator's cab and start figuring out what all the levers and switches did. The rest of the men got to work rigging up a makeshift lifting sling using a large, heavy canvas sheet attached by chain hooks. Using the sling, fifteen or twenty drums at a time could be lowered down to the boat, where a team of men would unload them and stow them safely in the hold.

Or that was the idea, at any rate.

Zahran's crane operating apprenticeship didn't start well. The whole thing was swaying so badly that the first trial batch of only three drums fell out of the sling halfway down the side, narrowly avoided smashing straight through the bottom of their boat, and fell into the sea. Nazim ran a hand down his face and tried to control his frustration.

They all watched as the empty sling came back up, swinging like a pendulum with the ship's motion. For Zahran's second attempt, they risked ten drums. Nearly a thousand pounds of product, enough to wipe out one hundred and ninety-eight million people, soon to be headed for the bottom of the sea if he let them fall. Zahran must have been sweating up there inside the crane. Nazim ordered Shaykh and two of his other more dispensable men to clamber into the sling along with the ten drums. If they died, they'd at least die for Allah.

But after his initial failure Zahran now seemed to be getting the knack. A few tense minutes later, all ten drums were successfully aboard the boat. Nazim sent Abbud, Dariush and another man called Mahmud down with the next batch to help with the loading. It took another twenty-eight minutes to complete the transfer of the remaining 187, every second of which strained Nazim's patience to the maximum while the six men on the boat laboured like maniacs to stow the cargo securely aboard.

At last, the job was finished. Zahran returned from the crane, penitent for having lost three of their precious drums. Nazim was willing to forgive him. 'With what we have, brother, our enemies are doomed to total defeat and humiliation. You will be rewarded for your part in this great conquest.'

The glow of dawn was beginning to infiltrate the murky

darkness in the east. Nazim faced south in the direction of land and carefully scanned the horizon and the sky in search of approaching coastguard boats or helicopters. He saw nothing, though his instinct told him they'd be here soon. He was prepared to do battle with them if necessary, but he much preferred to avoid them altogether.

At 7.42 a.m., less than an hour since their arrival, Nazim and the remaining terrorists on deck scrambled down the ladder to the boat, which was sitting somewhat lower in the water with nine tons of cargo aboard. The engines roared into life, the ropes were cut and the cruiser sped away from the drifting hull of the cargo vessel, now just a ghost ship. Keeping the boat's lights turned off he set a wide, sweeping course back towards land. By the grace of Allah, they would not be spotted.

The Normandy coast wasn't far away. And there, the ultimate victory awaited him.

Chapter 53

By 7.42 a.m., Ben, Roth and the Segals had already long since left the hotel. It had been Ben's decision to check Margot into a cheap guest house across town, where Nazim's people couldn't find her while the three men headed for the port to meet the ship. Once she was safely ensconced in her room and her husband had said his reluctant goodbyes, they jumped back into the Alpina and hustled over to the docks with a few minutes to spare before the ship was expected to come in.

Even before they got there, it was becoming clear that something was wrong. Police sirens were wailing all over Le Havre and they were overtaken by several Gendarmerie cars that were obviously in a great hurry, heading in the same direction as them. Roth said, 'Hello. Wonder what's up?'

Ben didn't like it. 'Something tells me we'll find out soon enough.'

And they did. The Port of Le Havre was teeming with police. Sirens were whooping and screeching and flashing lights everywhere illuminated the greyness of the dawn with swirling reds and blues. 'What do you suppose has happened?' Segal asked anxiously from the back seat.

Ben parked the Alpina a discreet distance away from the action, killed the engine and said, 'Wait here.' He stepped out into the drizzling rain and walked from the car, mingling with the crowds of dock workers and police. The port was a fairly frenetic place at any time, but now there was an electric tingle in the air that told him something serious had happened.

As a docker in orange overalls and a hard hat came past, Ben stopped him and asked in French, 'Excuse me, but do you know what's going on?' The guy was about sixty. He gave Ben a bemused look as if he couldn't quite believe it himself, and replied, 'A ship was attacked offshore earlier this morning. We've only just heard. The coastguard patrol found it dead in the water about twenty minutes ago. They say it was pirates.'

'What?'

The guy nodded in amazement. 'Word is that they murdered the captain, the crew, every poor bastard on board. Cut their heads off. That's the rumour, anyhow. It's crazy. I never heard of such a thing happening here. This is France, not Africa.'

Ben thanked him and let him go on his way, then ran back to the car to relay the news to Roth and Segal.

'It's got to be our ship,' Roth said. 'What are the odds, right? No way it can't be. This is not good, guys. Not good at all.'

Ben's whole strategy felt as though it was unravelling at an alarming rate. 'If it's Nazim, it almost certainly means that he's found out that Margot's free. Which tells him that he's lost his hold over you, Julien. He'll have a pretty good idea who's responsible, and he knows we're a step ahead of him.'

'Or were,' Roth said. 'He's just pulled a killer move on us.'

'He's resourceful,' Ben said. 'I'll give him that. Damn it.' He shook his head.

'Yeah, well, looks like we're wasting our time here, boys. The sons of bitches could be anywhere by now.'

'Perhaps there's still a chance,' Segal suggested. 'What if we were to revert back to the idea we talked about earlier? Instead of intercepting the cargo here in Le Havre, we can return to Paris and surprise them tonight as they deliver it to their secret processing plant.'

'Forget it,' Ben said grimly. 'If Nazim even suspects that his plans are blown, he won't touch those tunnels again with a pole a mile long. He probably already had an alternative location lined up as a contingency plan. And that leaves us back at square one, because we have no idea where to start looking for him now. None.'

'In short, folks, we are royally screwed,' said Roth, master of the understatement.

'Not just us,' Ben said. 'If Nazim's fentanyl hits the streets.'

Defeat. It was a hard word to say. An even harder reality to admit to. But right now there was no way past it.

Ben sank into his seat and watched the raindrops gather and trickle down the windscreen glass like tears. In moments like this, there wasn't much else to do but pull out your cigarettes and lighter. He bathed the tip of a Gauloise in comforting orange flame and drew in the smoke. The three of them sat gazing in the direction of the port, watching the big ships and smaller boats in the distance. Maybe if they sat staring at it long enough, their ship would come in and everything would be okay.

Or maybe not.

It was 8.25 a.m. Police response vehicles were still rolling up and armed officers running everywhere like ants. What exactly they hoped to achieve with all this frenzied activity, Ben couldn't say. Perhaps they were on the lookout for men in frock coats and eye patches, with cutlasses and flintlock pistols stuck through their belts, while the real pirates were far away laughing.

'Look on the bright side,' Roth said. 'Somewhere down there among all the chaos are a couple of truck drivers who'll never know how close they came to getting iced.'

'What are we going to do?' Segal said helplessly as the reality of the situation began to bite. 'And what am I going to do? If Nazim thinks I've betrayed him, he'll kill me.'

'And your wife, too,' Roth supplied helpfully. 'Cost of doing commerce with terrorists, my friend. They don't make for the most trustworthy or sympathetic of business partners.'

'But that means I can never go home again! They know where I live!'

'You have the option of disappearing voluntarily,' Ben said. 'It's preferable to being whisked away in the middle of the night and ending up in a hole in the forest.'

'And what about my business? I spent years building it and now it'll be totally finished!' Segal glared at Ben. 'You told me you would put an end to this. You promised it would all be over. "Trust me. We're not going to let that happen." Your very words. Why did I listen to you? I was better off before!'

Ben said nothing. Maybe Segal would have preferred for his wife to remain a hostage, too.

'Think I'll stretch my legs and get some air,' Roth announced with a sigh, clapping his palms on his thighs and unlatching the passenger door. He got out of the car, turned up his jacket collar against the drizzle, and Ben watched him walk off in the direction of the docks. Before he vanished from sight behind some wharf buildings, he took out a phone and appeared to be dialling a number.

It wasn't the first time Roth had decided to go for a

spontaneous little stroll. And not for the first time, Ben wondered what the hell the American was up to.

Segal was still prattling on in Ben's ear. 'Are you listening? I'm talking to you and I demand an answer.'

Ben ignored him, leaned back in the driver's seat and closed his eyes, considering his options. He was good at improvising. But it wasn't so easy to improvise when you had nothing whatsoever to go on. He took another long puff of the Gauloise and blew out more smoke. Behind him, Segal started to make that truly irritating theatrical kind of spluttering, as though he was suffocating on sarin gas.

Eyes still shut, Ben told him, 'If you don't like it, then get out of the damn car.'

'It's raining. You want me to get soaked?'

'I wouldn't be doing this, if I were you.'

'Doing what?'

'Annoying the hell out of me. Under the circumstances, not advisable. Unless you want to be chewing on your own teeth sometime in the near future.'

Segal huffed, then rocked forward the empty passenger seat and clambered out of the car. 'I'm going back to the guest house to be with Margot.'

'Suit yourself.'

Ben went on smoking. A couple of minutes later, he heard the passenger door again and opened his eyes. Roth was back from his walk, hair slicked with rain. He asked, 'What's up with Segal? I just saw him slinking off with a face like a grizzly shitting a pine cone.'

'Never mind him,' Ben said irritably. 'Did you have a pleasant little stroll?'

'Inspiring,' Roth said as he bundled into the car. 'You might even say educational. Time to haul ass, buddy.'

'Where to? Back to your island?'

'Nope, not just yet. I was thinking of a scenic little Normandy seaside spot called Plage de Vaucottes. It's about forty klicks up the coast from here.'

'Don't tell me. It was right after Paris on your visiting France bucket list.'

'Wrong again. I never heard of the place in my life before. But it so happens that what you Brits might call *a bit of a flap* happened there within the last few minutes, and is still ongoing. One that the cops don't even know about yet. But they will pretty soon, so I'd suggest we get moving.'

Ben stared at him. 'What kind of a flap?'

Roth answered, 'One that involves a buncha badass dudes doing badass shit, and more gunfire than the locals have known since June 1944.'

Chapter 54

Nazim's sharp ears had picked up the faraway thump of the helicopter not long after their departure from the dead cargo ship. Guessing it was a coastguard patrol aircraft coming out to investigate the loss of radio contact, he'd pressed on fast into the night to avoid being spotted. His course had taken him in a wide parabolic arc that made landfall some way up the coast. The north-easterly sloping shape of the coastline meant that he'd been closer to land than the ship had been to the port. By 8.02 a.m., just twenty minutes since making their escape, they were already approaching the shore.

Which was when the first real problem presented itself, because there seemed to be nowhere for them to land. Nazim closed the throttle and tacked along the coastline, peering impatiently through the curtain of mist and rain but seeing only sheer, craggy cliffs. After a couple of minutes he spotted a cove with a stretch of open beach. There was no kind of harbour or pier, nothing to moor up to, but Nazim didn't give a damn. He whacked the throttle wide open and steered right for the cove. He braced himself for impact. Three . . . two . . . one . . . *Now.*

The boat grounded itself with a thumping, rending, grinding crash that shuddered the vessel from stem to stern and jolted two of his unwary men off their feet. Their momentum carried them right up out of the water and onto the beach, the deep-draught aluminium hull ploughing a V-shaped furrow through the loose rock and shingle. The propellers bit down hard against solid ground and buckled, stalling the engines. The boat slithered to a halt at a diagonal angle to the beach. It wouldn't be taking to sea again in a hurry, but so what? They were on land, and ready to move to the next phase.

The terrorists clambered out onto the sloping deck and jumped down to the ground, clutching their weapons. There were a lot of grins and high-fives. Only the more intelligent members of Nazim's gang, like Abbud and Zahran, seemed to be aware of the new problem that now faced them. Namely, the fact that they were fifteen heavily armed men in possession of nine tons of illicit drugs, stranded in the middle of nowhere miles from their vehicles, and even further from their destination. Abbud frowned and asked, 'So how do we plan on getting out of here?'

But the redoubtable Nazim al-Kassar wasn't about to allow such piffling concerns to deter him. By the light of the rising sun he could make out some houses and buildings in the distance, a few hundred yards inland from the beach where verdant hills and fields rose up high above sea level.

He pointed. 'This is a rural area. The people are all peasants, and look how green the land is. Which means there'll be farmers everywhere, and farmers have large trucks and tractors and trailers for carrying all kinds of loads like manure and livestock. Those weigh a lot more than nine tons.' Nazim's confidence was authoritative, his knowledge of this place he'd never seen before absolute. He turned and swept his pointing finger across the beach. 'The ground is all rock and shingle. We'll have no problem getting a heavy vehicle down here to the boat. Then we'll just load up the barrels and be on our way. All right?'

'Whatever you say, boss.'

'Shaykh, Jamshid, Mahmud, Dariush, hurry up to those houses and find a suitable vehicle while the rest of us stay here and guard the cargo. Steal it and bring it back here as fast as you can. If anyone gives you any trouble, kill them, but do it quietly.' Nazim thought for a moment, then added, 'In fact, bring back two suitable vehicles. We also need a car capable of carrying six men.'

'Why do we need a car as well, Nazim?'

'Because,' Nazim explained as patiently as possible, 'we can't drive all the way to Paris in some shit-covered tractor. We wouldn't make it halfway down the motorway before we were stopped. And none of us wants that. So our first priority is to get the cargo off the beach and transport it somewhere safe, not too far away, while six of us slip back to the port and collect the vans, so we can carry on to Paris like before. Hence the need for a reasonably large car that can carry two men up front and four in the back. Do you understand?'

They understood. It seemed like a fine plan.

Until they started trying to put it into action.

As instructed, Shaykh, Mahmud, Jamshid and Dariush shouldered their AK-47s and set off at a sprint towards the distant houses. A track from the beach connected with a narrow road that wound upwards through the hills and fields. They had only the vaguest notion of what a French farm might look like, but even so the very first property they came to looked promising. It was a pretty black-and-white traditional Normandy cottage with a neat garden filled with flower beds, a picket fence and a few scattered barn-sized outbuildings, one of which the four men were certain must contain the large truck or tractor and trailer they were looking for.

‘Be on your guard,’ Shaykh warned the others. ‘Any sign of trouble, we must end it fast.’

‘Don’t be stupid,’ Jamshid replied, pulling a face. ‘You heard what Nazim said. These people are just weak peasants. They won’t give us any problem.’

Unslinging their weapons they hopped over the fence and began hunting through the property. The first outbuilding they came to was a lean-to garage in which a tiny, bright red Citroën was parked.

‘Look, guys, the keys are in it,’ said Dariush, peering in the driver’s window. ‘We can steal it, easy.’

‘I’m not getting in that thing,’ Mahmud said, pointing disdainfully at the chromed ichthys Christian emblem stuck to the back. ‘Besides, we’d never get six of us inside.’ Which was a fair point, since the car could seat only four large adults at a pinch.

‘We could always steal this one and another as well.’

‘Then we’d have to steal three vehicles, not just two,’ Shaykh said. This was getting complicated.

Jamshid, who seemed to have assumed leadership of the group, shook his head and said, ‘Let’s do this properly. Keep looking.’

The second outbuilding was a large wooden shed that turned out to be a chicken house. No trucks, no tractors, no trailers. Scouting further, the terrorists spotted another property half a field away, which they suddenly realised looked much more like an actual farm than the black-and-white cottage. The blocky stone house was rather run-down and rough around the edges, surrounded by a dirty yard and a collection of much larger, purposeful-looking barns. Two chunky hardtop pickup trucks with jacked suspension and bull bars stood parked outside the farmhouse, hinting at the presence of more useful vehicles inside the barns.

'We should check that place out instead,' Jamshid declared.

But the moment he said it, they heard an angry yell from behind them. All four whirled around to see a middle-aged, overweight white man in a dressing gown and slippers, storming towards them from the cottage clutching a double-barrelled shotgun in his fists. Apparently, it wasn't every day the locals woke up to find three Middle-Easterners and a Nigerian armed with assault rifles lurking in the garden. The guy seemed quite worked up about it, red in the face and shouting at them in French. 'What in God's name are you people doing on my property?'

At the sight of their weapons, the householder started yelling even more angrily, and levelled his shotgun at them. A loud blast split the morning air. Whether the guy had let the shot off accidentally due to nerves, or intentionally missed in the hope of scaring the intruders off, nobody would ever know. A fencepost four feet to Dariush's left splintered in a hail of birdshot. The terrorists looked at one another. Nazim had said to keep it quiet, but it was too late for that now. All four of them raised their AK-47s, aimed at the old fat white guy and opened fire before he could get a second shot off. The simultaneous bursts of full-automatic gunfire were much, much louder than the shotgun boom. And much more accurate. A dozen or more high-velocity rifle bullets tore into the man's chest, killing him instantly and hurling him flat to the ground.

'I told you these peasants could cause us trouble,' Shaykh said to his companions.

'What do you expect from a Christian?' Dariush sneered.

Before anyone else could reply, a woman burst out of the cottage. She was about the same age as the fat guy, wearing a nightdress. And screaming at the top of her voice as she ran a few steps and faltered at the sight of her dead husband lying in the dirt covered in blood.

They shot her, too. Bullets ripped at her nightdress and she tumbled backwards into a flower garden with a muted squawk.

By now the tranquillity of the rural Normandy morning was well and truly shattered. The sharp reports of rifle fire could easily be heard from the beach, where Nazim and the others were guarding the grounded boat. And they could certainly be heard from the house half a field away from the cottage.

The terrorists had been right in supposing that this was the home of real, actual farmers. Seven of them: four brothers called Jean-Luc, Jean-Étienne, Jean-Claude and Jean-Pierre Pasquinel and their three cousins Léon, Noah and Axel. All strong, rough-hewn and brawny country boys, aged between eighteen and thirty-one. The Pasquinel land covered twenty-nine hectares, enough to keep them busy, and had been in the family for eight generations. René Pasquinel had died some years back, leaving his sons to work the place and look after their mother. The cousins had joined them a while later; the most recent arrival was twenty-three-year-old Axel, currently on the lam after skipping bail over a petty misdemeanour.

Like all farmers the Pasquinel boys and their cousins had been up early that morning, and were finishing breakfast around the long farmhouse kitchen table when they were startled by the sound of gunfire coming from the Simonot place next door. 'What the—?' said Jean-Luc, the eldest, spilling his coffee as he jumped up from the table and went to the window to look.

Moments later, they were grabbing the hunting rifles that hung on racks near the door, and running outside. Jean-Luc and his brothers leaped into one of the pickups and went tearing out of the farmyard and across the field that separated their property from that of Maurice and Suzette Simonot. As they approached the cottage they stared in horror at the torn, bloodied bodies on the ground: Maurice sprawled out on his back near the barn, Suzette crumpled in the flower bed. Stunned shock quickly gave way to speechless anger as the brothers spotted four strangers, clutching what appeared to be Kalashnikov rifles, piling into the Simonots' little bright red Citroën C1 and taking off in a hurry.

Jean-Luc whipped out his mobile phone to tell his eldest cousin Léon back at the house the barely believable news that a bunch of crazed killers with machine guns had just murdered their friends next door and stolen their car. Moments later, Léon, Noah and Axel were arming themselves with another rifle and two shotguns, leaping into the second pickup truck and hammering across the field to join the four brothers.

By the time the pickup trucks reached the road the killers had vanished. It took a couple of screeching wrong turns on the maze of country lanes before they realised that the fleeing perpetrators had been heading for the beach. 'I see the fuckers!' roared Jean-Pierre, pointing down the hillside at the little red dot of the car hammering along the rocky path. He skidded and turned back, the second pickup truck following right behind.

To their astonishment, as the pickup trucks hurtled down the track in pursuit, they saw there was a whole boatload of the bastards on the shore. The four killers had just got there, joining a group of at least another ten who were all similarly toting automatic weapons. There was no other possible explanation: this was surely the vanguard of the long-awaited invasion force, the one they'd been reading about on various websites, set to sweep through Europe and spread death and destruction. And the Pasquinel boys were the thin line of resistance.

Neither the brothers nor their cousins were the kind of people who were inclined to call the police at such moments of crisis. For generations the Pasquinel family, stretching back in time from their late father to his father to his father before him, had been used to sorting out their own problems. And the way France was going now, nobody trusted the authorities any more. Acquaintances in Paris had been shot at, batoned, tear-gassed, hospitalised and jailed in the riots. The Pasquinels and their cousins all harboured the same grievances against the police and the state as the protesters. No goddamned way were they going to call for help. Not to mention there was the fact that Axel stood to be arrested if the law caught up with him.

'Lock and load, boys,' Jean-Luc said, cocking his hunting rifle. 'These motherfuckers are going down.'

It was 8.24 a.m. and the cool, misty October morning was about to warm up considerably.

Chapter 55

The Alpina blasted out of Le Havre and stormed up the D940 coastal highway at blistering speed. It was a route Ben knew well and had travelled often in the past, because the road would take them within a rifle shot of Étretat where he sometimes went kayaking and climbing the sheer white cliffs. He was so close to home, and yet he couldn't remember the last time he'd felt this far from his objective.

Next to him in the passenger seat Roth was playing it cool and lounging in silence with his feet up on the dash. Ben had left the port without asking the American any more questions, but plenty of them were swirling around his head as he drove and he couldn't hold them back any longer.

'I'm going to need some answers, Tyler. Who were you talking to back there? Where are you getting fed this information?'

'Now ain't the time to go into all that,' Roth said dismissively. 'Oh, and don't even thank me for getting you out of a hole just now. Didn't your momma teach you not to bite the hand that feeds you?'

'She also taught me not to trust people who keep too many secrets. You seem to make a habit of it. And get your feet off the dashboard.'

'Touchy,' Roth said, and straightened up in his seat with

his head towards the window. The conversation appeared to be over. Ben was resolved to get the truth out of him later. For now, though, they had some distance to cover in as little time as possible and he needed to lay down all of the Alpina's four hundred horsepower on the twisty coastal road without getting them killed. Big wide open fields zipped by on both sides, the hazy grey sea in the distance; now and then a village that forced him to scrub off some speed before he put his foot back down hard and the Alpina's gauge needles soared in the dials. Every few minutes Roth was receiving a new text message from some mysterious source, and was reading them with a frown on his face and the phone angled away from Ben like a poker player's cards. Ben bit his lip, fixed his eyes determinedly on the road and said nothing.

The Alpina rocketed past his old haunt of Étretat. He took the D11 and raced for the home stretch, through the pretty village of Bénouville and then jumping onto a minor road through a valley called the Fonds d'Étigue, running parallel with the coastline. It occurred to him that Roth must have received his tip-off from the same person who'd alerted them to the GIGN raid in Villejuif. But then, how did this person apparently know things the police didn't even know yet?

At last, they were coming into Vaucottes. Ben had covered the thirty-eight kilometres from Le Havre in just over eighteen minutes, which would have been closer to fifteen if he hadn't had to slow down for built-up areas. He cut through the narrow country lanes past the scattered homes and farms, heading towards the beach with still no idea of what Roth was leading them into. The bag of guns and ammunition was a reassuring presence on the back seat, ready for action in case they were about to stumble on a war zone. It certainly didn't look like one. It looked exactly like a quiet little corner of the world that had existed trouble-free for the last seventy-odd years, ever since the final shot of the Battle of Normandy had rung out over the landscape.

But whatever had been happening here earlier that morning, it was all over now. As the Alpina hit the rough track down towards the sea and the beach came into view, they saw that it was empty.

Empty, apart from the Gendarmerie Airbus H-135 helicopter sitting on the shingle, a few metres away from a large boat that was grounded and lying at a tilted angle on dry land.

Roth said, 'Shit.' Ben braked the car to a halt on the track, tyres pattering on the rocks.

The police chopper seemed to have only just arrived on the scene, its fast-spinning rotors slowing to idle speed. The pilot and five passengers had climbed out and circled the grounded boat. Four of them were clambering aboard and crawling up the sloping deck to check out the contents of its hold.

'These cops are worse than Texas yellowjackets,' Roth grumbled. 'Always buzzing around your head when they're not wanted.'

The gendarmes were too far away and too preoccupied with what they'd found on the beach to have noticed the car on the track. Ben slammed into reverse and backed up a short distance to where they'd passed a sandy lane off to the left, which looked to him as though it climbed and snaked upwards towards the clifftop overlooking the beach. His guess was right. The rise of the land kept them hidden from below as they made their way up the incline. The track petered out and Ben went bumping and lurching through long yellowed grass and rocky ruts, coming to a halt a short distance from the cliff edge. He turned off the engine, grabbed the binoculars from the glove compartment and stalked from the car to find a good vantage point.

He didn't have to search for long. About a million years ago part of the cliff had subsided to form a V-cleft and a long, jagged mound of rubble sloping down to the western end of the beach, like a staircase for giants. Flattened on his belly in the reedy grass of the cleft Ben had a perfect sniper's view of the goings-on below. The chopper's rotor blades had slowed almost to a standstill. The same four gendarmes were still at the grounded boat and seemed extremely interested in what was inside.

Roth joined Ben, moving through the stiff grass without making a rustle. He lay flat next to him and produced a mini-pair of binocs of his own, apparently out of nowhere.

'Bet your ass, that there's our pirate vessel. Looks like she's been run aground. I can't believe they had it all planned out this way. More likely they stole her from the port, right while we were sitting talking to Segal in his goddamned hotel room. Can you believe the fuckin' audacity of these guys?'

Ben was seriously contemplating pointing his pistol at the American and forcing the truth out of him. But he was too intent on what was happening down there to look away. The four cops had lifted out some of the contents of the hold and were obviously in a hurry to unload the rest. Ben could see why. The tide was coming in, each new wave rolling and foaming a little further up the shingle than the last. They didn't have a lot of minutes before the water's edge would be lapping at the boat.

As he watched, the cop down in the hold lifted up a shiny aluminium drum to pass to his colleague. It was obviously heavy. The second cop passed it along to a third, and the fourth set it down on the shingle next to the boat hull. Ben counted eight drums, with more to come. They looked like brewer's beer kegs. Except as he and Roth both knew, what was inside them wasn't beer.

'And there's our fentanyl,' Ben muttered. 'All nine tons of it, with any luck.'

Roth smiled one of his shark smiles. 'It won't be long before the cops figure out they've just made the largest drugs haul in history. As for Nazim, his bosses won't be too pleased with him that he's lost their merchandise. Looks like we derailed their plans, big time.' He frowned. 'The only question is, where'd the sonofabitch go?'

The remaining two cops weren't at the boat. Ben scanned across to observe them. That was when he saw the unmistakable dark shapes on the beach and knew he was looking at dead bodies. Three of them. One lay curled up among the rocks about thirty metres from the boat, the other two a little way further up the beach. The binocs didn't magnify enough to give much detail, but Ben was able to make out that two of the dead were Caucasian males, not old, maybe in their twenties. One of the gendarmes was examining the third body, which belonged to a dead African guy, lying face-up with his head thrown back and a beard like a bird's nest jutting into the air. Lying on the shingle next to the corpse was a firearm with the unmistakable shape of an AK-47. A short distance away, the other cop was busy setting up a row of cones from the chopper and stretching police tape to cordon off the scene.

A moment later came the chorus of approaching sirens. The officers on the beach turned to look, and Ben scanned the binoculars across to see four police cars and two ambulances bouncing down the track towards them. Reinforcements had arrived. And now Ben decided he'd seen enough. He lowered the binoculars and turned to face Roth.

'Okay,' he said to the American. 'Explanation time. Let's have it. The whole truth, right now.'

'You should be happy, man. The cops have the dope. Nazim's getting his butt kicked big-time and we're winning on points. Fortune's on our side. What's to explain?'

'Not good enough, Tyler. I'm getting tired of your bullshit and secrecy. First you're going to tell me what the hell happened here. Then you're going to tell me how you knew, and who you really are.'

'I don't know as much as you think I do,' Roth said, acting falsely accused and stung. 'All I was told was there'd been a disturbance. Hey, I'm on the level, man. And you know who I am. I'm your old compadre from back in the day, right? Who else could I be?'

'You'll have to do better than that, Roth. You've been keeping me in the dark from the moment I turned up on your island.'

Roth was silent for a moment. Ben was waiting for him to start talking when he caught a movement out of the corner of his eye. He turned to look, and then he saw it.

Among the rocks of the cliff subsidence was the figure of a man. He was making his way towards them.

Chapter 56

Ben's deeply instilled instinctive reaction was to snatch out his pistol to point at the unknown potential threat. But even as his hand began to reach for the weapon he could see that the man clambering up – trying to clamber up – the rocky giant's steps from the western end of the beach wasn't in a condition to be much of a threat to anyone.

Roth's explanations would have to wait a little longer. Ben sprang to his feet and began scrambling down the rocks.

Immediately Ben could see the guy was a local, and not one of Nazim al-Kassar's jihadists. He was maybe twenty-two or twenty-three, in jeans and a hoodie top. Spiked hair, ruddy outdoorsman's features, broad shoulders, a lot of muscle. And a wound in his left deltoid that was bleeding profusely all over the rocks, leaving a slick trail behind him as he struggled to inch his way upwards with his one good arm. He'd managed to drag himself halfway up the face of a big craggy boulder that blocked his path, but now he was in trouble, clinging on single-handed and in danger of slipping all the way back down. From the look on his pain-contorted face he wasn't going to be able to hang on much longer. If he fell, it was likely that the cops on the beach would notice him. That was obviously an outcome he was desperate to avoid.

Ben reached the flat top of the boulder and reached down to grab the injured guy's arm. He said in French, 'You're okay. I've got you.' The guy was heavy. Solid stock, raised on milk and prime beef. With a lot of effort Ben managed to grapple and haul him up onto the boulder to safety, and out of sight of the police who were now appearing on the beach in greater numbers. Blood was leaking everywhere. Ben's hands were red with it. He examined the gunshot wound. The bullet had gone right through the left shoulder, punching a smaller entry hole above the collar bone and a chunk of flesh ripped out where it had exited an inch from the shoulder blade. As far as Ben could tell, nothing was broken. It could have been a lot worse. But it wasn't particularly good. He was going to need medical attention before long.

'You got me,' the young guy wheezed in resignation, too weak to put up any resistance. 'So arrest me.'

This time around, Ben decided it wasn't the smart play to impersonate an officer. 'I'm not the police. What's your name?'

Visibly relieved despite his pain, the young guy replied, 'Axel. Axel Roux.'

'Okay, Axel. I'm guessing you're not one of the bad guys. Tell me who shot you and what the hell happened here.'

Axel coughed, and the movement made him screw up his face in agony. He gasped, 'They killed Léon and Jean-Étienne.' Tears of more than just physical pain leaked down his ruddy cheeks. 'They killed Maurice and Suzette, too.'

'Who killed them?'

'I don't know who they are. Scouts for some kind of fucking invasion force, or something. They came in on a boat. About fifteen of the bastards. Armed with machine guns.'

'There are three bodies on the beach. Two white, one black.'

'The black guy, he's one of theirs. We shot him. But they started it.'

'Who's we? How many of you?'

'Seven of us, four brothers and three cousins. We live at the farm, up the hill. Maurice and Suzette were our neighbours. Those fuckers murdered them and stole their Citroën.'

'And you all decided to come down here and shoot it out with them like the O.K. Corral,' Ben said. 'Not a wise move.'

Axel tried to nod his head, but the pain was too much. 'We had to do something. I think they were trying to steal a truck, to get away from the shore. That's why they were snooping around. We got in the pickups and chased them down to the beach. We hadn't realised there were so many of them. When we turned up they started shooting at us. Léon, he got hit first. Then Jean-Luc, he shot the black guy. Then Jean-Étienne got hit, too.' Axel screwed his eyes shut and wiped the tears with his good hand, making blood smears on his face.

Léon and Jean-Étienne accounted for two of the bodies on the beach, and the dead jihadist for the third. Ben listened as Axel went on:

'We didn't have a lot of ammo. Just what was in our shotguns and rifles. They kept firing and firing at us. Then I felt myself get hit too. I went down. Jean-Luc grabbed me and we ran and hid behind some rocks. We couldn't move, they had us pinned. There was so much shooting going on, it was like a war. I don't remember everything. I was so scared. I was feeling faint and bleeding like crazy. Thought I was gonna die. Last thing I remember is the bastards getting into our pickups and taking off.'

From Axel's incoherent account Ben was gleaning that three of the brothers and one cousin were still alive and out there somewhere. It sounded like Jean-Luc was the leader of the gang. Maybe the eldest brother. Ben asked, 'Did Jean-Luc and the others go after the shooters?'

Again, Axel tried to nod and groaned aloud at the pain in his neck and shoulder. 'I think so. I must have been unconscious. Maybe they thought I was dead. When I woke up they were gone, and so was the C1.' He added, 'They're gonna kill the bastards if they catch them.'

Ben glanced back and saw Roth winding his way down the rocks towards them. Then he looked again at Axel's gunshot wound. Still bleeding heavily and showing no signs of stopping. 'You're going to have to get to a hospital. There are two ambulances on the beach. They'll look after you.'

Axel tugged urgently at Ben's sleeve with his good hand. 'Please, dude, don't tell them I'm here. They'll arrest me. I skipped bail in Orléans, see? I didn't do anything wrong but they'll put me in jail. I don't want to go to jail!'

Which explained why Axel had been crawling away from the police. Axel had been a bad boy. Ben said, 'Maybe the local morgue would suit you better.'

The tugging caused a mobile phone to fall out of Axel's hoodie pocket. Ben caught it before it could go tumbling down the rocks. A cheap Samsung, sticky with blood. And it was giving him an idea. 'Do you have Jean-Luc's number on here?'

'What do you want it for?'

'To talk some sense into him before he gets himself killed, too. I'm going to borrow this phone, Axel. Are you okay with that?'

'Do I get it back?'

'Unless we're all dead,' Ben said. 'Which is a possibility, given who we're dealing with. You've no idea how lucky you are. Most people don't tangle with Nazim al-Kassar and live to tell the tale.'

'Léon and Jean-Étienne weren't so lucky,' Axel groaned. 'Take the phone. I don't care if I don't get it back.' He clutched his shoulder. More blood leaked out from between his fingers.

'What's your other cousin's name?'

'Noah.'

'What colour is Maurice and Suzette's car?'

Axel stared at him. 'Why would you ask?'

'If I'm going to go after it, I need to know what it looks like. There are an awful lot of Citroën C1s on the road.'

'It's red. With one of those fish badges on the back. The Simonots were Christians.'

Roth had reached them. He seemed to have taken his time coming down the rocks. Maybe he'd been making more of his mystery phone calls, Ben thought. Roth squatted on the rocks a few feet away and gave Ben an inquisitive look. He asked, 'What's up with this guy?'

Ben showed him the bloody phone. Switching back to English he said, 'This is going to lead us to Nazim. We're moving on. That little discussion we were about to have, we'll have later.'

'Whatever you say, chief. Taking him with us?' Roth said, pointing at Axel.

Ben shook his head. 'He's going to hospital.' Which in English sounded enough like the French word 'hôpital' for Axel's face to fall in dismay.

'Don't do this to me, dude! I'm barely hurt!'

'Désolé, Axel. I'm not having you bleed to death on my account.'

Ben led the way back up the rocks towards the V-cleft in the cliff. He waited until they were three-quarters of the way up before he took out his pistol and squeezed off two rounds into the bushes. The sharp reports echoed across the beach. By the time the police came running to investigate and found the injured man, Ben and Roth would be gone.

Chapter 57

Returning to the car, Ben rolled down the cliff path and made a discreet escape back along the narrow country lanes. They weren't leaving a moment too soon, as the police were descending en masse upon the once sleepy village of Vaucottes that was now experiencing its bloodiest day since the Wehrmacht's defences had collapsed in the face of the Allied invasion, and tank battalions rumbled over this picturesque landscape. More sirens were screeching and wailing from further inland, a few hundred yards from the beach, and Ben could see flashing blue lights among the scattered properties up there. It looked like they'd found the bodies of Maurice and Suzette, adding to the death toll.

Police cars zipped by in the opposite direction as Ben sped away from Vaucottes. If it had been him, he'd have ordered every car in the vicinity to be stopped and searched. He was glad that the local police commander didn't think the same way he did.

He had cousin Axel's phone in his pocket, and when they were far enough from Vaucottes to be sure they'd got away clean, he pulled over in a grassy layby, killed the motor and took the phone out. He wiped the blood off the screen, then checked the contacts menu. It held a list of names, of which four were the initials J-L, J-C, J-P and J-E. Ben reckoned that if the eldest brother was called Jean-Luc and his late sibling's name had been Jean-Étienne, the other two were most likely Jean-something as well. Nothing like having imaginative parents.

Ben brought up the number for J-L and held it for Roth to see. Roth knew what to do. He took out his own phone and got to work as Ben dialled the number from Axel's phone. He put the call on speaker so Roth could hear.

The number rang, and rang, and was on the verge of going to voicemail when the call was picked up. The sound of a hard-pushed car engine was audible in the background. In the foreground was a strained and urgent male voice saying, 'Axel? Axel?' Jean-Luc had probably thought that his cousin was dead.

'I'm not Axel,' Ben said. 'But he's alive. He's going to be fine, Jean-Luc. And I need you to listen to me very carefully.'

There was a stunned silence. Just the rasping engine noise and someone else's muffled voice in the background yelling in French, 'What's happening? Is he okay?' Jean-Luc yelled back at him to shut up and drive. Then asked Ben, 'Who the fuck is this? Why are you calling on Axel's phone?'

'Think of me as your best friend in the world right now,' Ben replied. 'And your only chance of coming out of this alive. What you're doing is very stupid.'

Jean-Luc's voice was cracking up with stress and barely audible over all the noise. 'What the fuck are you talking about? You don't know me.'

'I know that you're with your brothers Jean-Claude and Jean-Pierre and your cousin Noah, driving a red Citroën C1 belonging to your neighbours Maurice and Suzette Simonot, who are dead. You're in pursuit of your own two pickup trucks, which are being driven by a gang of armed and dangerous men who will murder you all without thinking twice if you get any closer to them. I repeat, this is not a wise action. I strongly recommend that you stand down, right this minute. Am I making myself clear?'

There was a silence on the phone. For a few seconds all Ben could hear was the background buzz of engine noise resonating around the cab of the speeding Citroën. Then: 'Who the fuck *are* you?'

'I'm sorry about your brother and your cousin,' Ben said. 'I understand what you're feeling. I'd probably feel the same. But if I was going to do something about it, I'd do it the smart way. Not like this.'

'I'll fucking kill those bastards. Every last one of them.'

'No, you won't,' Ben assured him. 'You'll end up just like Jean-Étienne and Léon. Or worse. You don't know these people. I do.'

While they were talking, Roth had been entering Jean-Luc's number into a GPS mobile geolocation app and now he was staring intently at his phone as he waited to get a fix on the target. Ben was impatient to get moving. There was more muffled shouting on the line as Jean-Luc had an exchange with the others in the car with him. Ben caught the words 'go faster', and the driver yelling back, 'I told you, it won't *go* any fucking faster!'

'Jean-Luc? Are you there? Hello?'

'They're getting away. There's something wrong with this car. It's overheating and losing power. I think it caught a bullet in the radiator. The temperature gauge is right in the red.'

'How close are they? Are they still in sight?'

'Just about,' Jean-Luc replied. 'But we're gonna lose them,

damn it. Who are these fuckers anyway, since you seem to know so much about them?'

Ben replied, 'Trust me, you don't want to know.'

'Why should I trust you? You won't tell me who you are. How do I know you're not one of them?'

'If I'd been one of them, your cousin Axel would be lying on the beach right now with his head sliced off. Instead of being on his way to a nice comfortable hospital. And a jail cell, too, but at least he'll be safe there.'

'Are you the cops?' Jean-Luc asked suspiciously.

'No, I'm someone who wants to take these people down just as badly as you do,' Ben said. 'But I won't let you get killed in the process.'

Jean-Luc considered that point and seemed to accept it. Then he said, 'Okay, then what's in those drums?'

Ben suddenly had a bad feeling. 'Drums?'

'Drums, barrels, kegs, whatever you want to call them. While they had us pinned down they grabbed all they could off the boat and loaded them into our trucks. First I thought the bastards were some kind of invasion force. Now I'm thinking it's all about what's inside those things. They're drug dealers, right? Or gun runners. Shit, we're losing them. Can't this car go any faster?'

Now Ben's bad feeling was growing worse. So the police didn't have all the fentanyl after all. With a chill in his heart he asked, 'How many drums did they take with them?'

'I wasn't exactly counting,' Jean-Luc said impatiently. 'I was too busy trying to keep low behind the rocks and not get shot. As many as they could fit in the back of our trucks along with their guys. Maybe a dozen, maybe more. Shit! We're falling right back here. Now I can't see them at all.'

Ben did the maths. Twelve drums, forty-five kilos apiece,

was 540 kilos, nearly twelve hundred pounds. And if one pound of the stuff was poisonous enough to kill two hundred thousand people, Nazim still had the means to murder over two hundred and forty million of them. The entire population of France, three times over, with enough change to wipe out everyone in Luxembourg into the bargain.

Not good. His palms felt clammy and his mouth had gone dry.

Then Roth held up his phone for Ben to see as the GPS mobile tracker got its fix on the Citroën and flashed it up on a map with a little red inverted teardrop pinpointing its position. 'Target acquired,' he said with a fierce grin.

Roth was enjoying this far too much.

Ben was surprised by the tracking result. Now that he knew that Nazim had managed to salvage a quantity of his loot, he'd have expected the terrorists to waste no time at all in heading for Paris, so that they could press on with what remained of their plans. But Paris lay some two hundred kilometres to the south-east, heading past Rouen on the A13 motorway. Nazim was bearing almost due south and a little to the west. He was already nearly forty kilometres from Vaucottes, hustling fast as the crow flew. Sticking to the minor D-roads, but looking as though he was intending to pick up the A28 motorway further south.

In which case, he was going nowhere near Paris at all. So what the hell was his plan?

'Still there, Jean-Luc?'

'I'm still here. But we're fucked. We'll never catch them in this shitbox.'

'Hang in there, Jean-Luc. We're on our way.'

Ben had a lot of ground to catch up. But that was what the Alpina was made for. He was pointed in the wrong direction. He fired up the engine with a throaty blast, spun the wheels as he pulled a tight U-turn in the road and accelerated away so hard that the car fishtailed and the rev counter needle was swallowed in the red. He said to Roth, 'You wanted to find out what two hundred miles an hour feels like? Buckle up.'

Chapter 58

This was the one chance they had of ever catching up again with Nazim al-Kassar, and Ben wasn't about to let it slip between his fingers. He blew through the country lanes at 130 kilometres an hour and jammed it to over 160 as he hit the network of broader, smoother D-roads in pursuit of the target. Roth's phone hung cradled in the holder on the dashboard and the little red inverted teardrop was still moving steadily southwards ahead of them, moving at a decent pace.

Ben went faster. As they skirted back past Le Havre he wondered if Julien Segal was still with Margot at the guest house, but Segal didn't remain in his thoughts for long. They hit the D579 and signs flashed by for Lisieux and Le Breuil en Auge. Then onto the D406, speeding towards Hauteville. Thankfully little traffic was travelling on the minor roads that day. What there was, the Alpina slammed past as though it was accelerating backwards. Ben was holding steady at 220 kilometres an hour whenever and wherever he could, burning wild amounts of fuel and triggering speed traps all over the place. All it took was one police car to flag them and take up the chase, and then there'd be a whole world of trouble because Ben would have no intention of slowing down for anyone or anything, short of an anti-tank barrage. But that was a risk he had to take.

Shooting a glance sideways at Roth in the passenger seat he noticed that the American had strapped himself in tight and was gripping the door handle, the muscles in his jaw tight as piano strings. It gave Ben a certain fiendish satisfaction to know that Roth was crapping his pants and doing all he could to hide it. Ben rocketed towards the tail of a lumbering goods truck that filled the lane up ahead and waited until the last millisecond before he swerved around it towards the oncoming traffic, then blasted through the narrow gap with the needle at the 170 mark and hammered it back up past 200 on the straight. Just to scare Roth a bit more. It was either that, or punch him in the head.

The Alpina's throaty engine drone filled the cabin and would have made it hard to have a conversation, even if Ben hadn't been so intent on driving that he had nothing to say. But his mind was crowded with one troubling concern after another. It was bothering him that he couldn't figure out where Nazim was going. There was a plan at work here. If only he knew what it was.

Almost forty-five minutes had passed since leaving Vaucottes. Towns and villages, farms and forests and sign-posts flashed past in a mad blur. They were cutting due south straight through the heart of Normandy. Getting closer to the point where they'd pick up the motorway just beyond Gacé, and catching up fast with the target. Too fast, Ben thought. The little red teardrop was still moving in the same direction as before, but it seemed to have slowed right down. Then, speaking for the first time in a while, Roth said, 'They've stopped moving.'

Sure enough, a few kilometres before the motorway, Ben spotted the little red Citroën C1 with a chromed fish on the back, parked up in a layby at the side of the road. He braked hard and pulled into the layby in front of them.

The Citroën's bonnet was up, and there was smoke rising from under it. A pair of young guys were standing looking inside the engine bay, one of them scratching his head and the other with his arms folded in obvious disgust. Another two were sitting inside the car, smoking cigarettes and looking glum, frustrated and angry. All four were hefty country boys like Axel Roux, in jeans and denim and check shirts.

Ben and Roth got out of the Alpina and walked towards them. The two country boys in the car got out too, and stood defensively with their fists bunched. The two standing by the open bonnet turned around and scowled at the approaching strangers. It looked like the preliminaries to a bar fight, but Ben understood that it was just a bunch of angry, grief-stricken and deeply frustrated young blokes posturing as a way of working off their emotions. He said, 'Which one of you is Jean-Luc?'

'That'd be me,' replied the one with folded arms.

'That's what I thought,' Ben said. Jean-Luc was the eldest and the biggest of the bunch, and he had the most aggressive scowl. Behind all the angry expressions Ben could make out some facial resemblances among the three surviving brothers. Which made the fourth fellow Noah, the cousin who'd managed to escape unscathed.

Jean-Luc asked, 'Are you the guy who phoned?'

Ben took out Axel's phone and tossed it to Jean-Luc. 'You can give it to him when you visit him in jail.'

Jean-Luc frowned at the smears of dried blood on the casing. 'How's he doing?'

'He'll survive. But he might not have, if he hadn't been persuaded to turn himself in.'

'Then I suppose I should thank you. What's your name?'

'You can call me Ben,' Ben said. 'No thanks are necessary.'

'And who's this guy?'

Ben jerked a thumb at Roth. 'Him? He's just a hitch-hiker I picked up.' He nodded towards the smoking engine bay of the Citroën. The little red car wasn't going anywhere. 'Looks like you were right about the bullet in the radiator.'

'Yeah. Fuck this piece of crap.' Jean-Luc spat angrily at the car and lashed out a savage kick, smashing a headlamp.

'Easy,' Ben told him. 'This car just saved your lives. Because if you caught up with Nazim, you wouldn't last a minute.'

'We can handle ourselves,' said one of the brothers, pointing inside the car. A shotgun and a scoped hunting rifle were propped against the back seat, fairly incongruous in a jaunty little urban runaround. The breakdown recovery crew were going to love it when they got here.

'Everybody thinks that until they find themselves eating a bullet,' Ben replied. 'Which way did they go?'

A lorry sped past with a slap of wind that made the little car rock on its springs. Jean-Luc pointed sullenly in the direction it was heading. The rumble of the motorway could be heard in the distance.

Ben asked, 'Any idea where they're going?'

One of the other brothers said, 'How the hell should we know?'

'Wherever it is, they've got a hell of a head start on you,' Jean-Luc said.

Ben thought, *He's beating us. He's going to get away.* He raked his mind for ideas. Nothing much was coming to him. He asked, 'What kind of trucks do you have?'

'*Did* we have,' said Cousin Noah.

Jean-Luc said sourly, 'Mine's the black Toyota Hilux. Jacked up and tuned to the max with a full performance upgrade kit. You'll have a hard time catching it. Even in that thing.' Pointing at the Alpina. One of his brothers said, 'Mine's the silver Nissan Navara.'

Ben was in the realm of guesswork now, and it wasn't a place he liked being. He turned to Roth and asked in English, 'Any more magic tricks up your sleeve?' But Roth was acting evasive and Ben was in no mood to waste time.

He carried a detailed map of Normandy in the glove compartment. Fetching it from the car he spread it out over the bonnet. The metallic blue paintwork was filmed with dust and the metal was hot to the touch. He leaned over the map and studied the familiar road layout in the hope that something would come to him. He quickly found Vaucottes, an almost unnoticeable dot on the northern coastline. From there, his eye traced two descending, diverging routes. The one he'd first expected Nazim to take, and the one they were following instead. The former tracing a line south-eastwards towards Paris, the latter breaking further and further away the more it edged towards the west. The two lines formed a lopsided inverted V with the starting point at the top, Paris on the end of the bottom right fork, and Nazim's unknown destination somewhere on the bottom left. That was assuming that Nazim kept to his current course and hit the A28 motorway heading further south. If he continued on that path he'd eventually reach Le Mans, the home of Ben's reclusive billionaire acquaintance Auguste Kaprisky.

Ben couldn't understand why Nazim would want to travel so far south. Maybe he didn't. Maybe his destination lay closer. Just a few kilometres after the road merged with the motorway lay the northern edge of the Normandie-Maine Regional Natural Park, a huge area of protected forest, pastureland and Alpine meadows covering over half a million acres. It was a haven for trail walkers, climbers, canoeists and nature lovers. Perhaps it could offer sanctuary to escaping terrorists carrying enough deadly pharmaceuticals to eliminate the entire population of the country. Ben pictured Nazim in a canoe, paddling through some scenic river valley, cackling with glee as he emptied gallons of fentanyl into the water. The image was ludicrous.

Ben sighed and stared at the map, trying to put himself in Nazim's shoes, to get into his mind. Which was relatively easy to do, in some ways. He and his enemy had much in common. Like him, the Iraqi was a dedicated and uncompromising warrior who wouldn't turn away from his objective once his intention was set. A man for whom failure was not an option. When challenged by the failure of one strategic plan, he would do what any clever tactician does: adapt, improvise, overcome that challenge by whatever means possible and form an alternative strategy that the enemy hadn't anticipated. And when presented with a golden opportunity to strike a punishing blow against the opposition, he would use it with great intelligence and ruthless efficiency.

Yet in so many other ways Ben could no more get into Nazim's mindset than he could relate to an extraterrestrial being. Nazim was a terrorist. Probably the most natural-born terrorist Ben had ever known. His whole *raison d'être* was to cause havoc against innocent people. He had been responsible for a great many deaths in his lifetime, but never until now had he had the means to wreak such mass destruction on the hated West. As his options diminished, the pressure mounted and time turned against him, all his energy would be focused on coming up with the quickest and most effective new method of carrying out genocidal murder.

And now Ben had to go against his own nature and try to think like that himself.

What would he do, in Nazim's place? Possessed of the means to rub out the lives of millions of ordinary, unsuspecting civilians, what would be the most rapid and direct way to launch his strike? You wouldn't waste time and energy depending on middlemen to distribute the fentanyl onto the streets. That opportunity had come and gone. No, instead you'd focus on deploying that weapon directly against its targets. As many of them as possible, and all at once. Causing maximum damage, instantly, like detonating a nuclear warhead over a population-dense area.

Ben stared at the map until its little lines and squiggles seemed to float in front of his eyes and lost all meaning. Willing it to yield up its secret. His mind churning so hard that his brain ached. He flashed back on the image he'd pictured, of Nazim in his canoe, polluting the clear sparkling river water with his poison.

And that image led to another. One that made sudden and terrifying sense. He looked again at the map, and traced Nazim's route downwards with his finger, and landed on the spot, and understood.

When the realisation hit him, it made his guts twist.

He turned to Roth.

'I think I know what they're going to do.'

Chapter 59

From the moment he'd heard the first crackle of gunfire coming from the village, even before the skirmish on the beach with the idiot locals who thought they could stop him, Nazim had known that he was going to have to abandon his strategy. The new one hadn't been long coming. As he and his remaining men hurriedly loaded as many barrels as they could aboard the pickup trucks, piled in and took off, he'd already decided what he must do next. And he liked it.

Nazim was in the jacked-up black Toyota Hilux, sitting up front next to Abbud at the wheel. Mahmud, Dariush and two other men were jammed in the rear crew cab seats, and another pair were riding in the hardtop load bed with the eight drums of fentanyl salvaged from the boat. The remaining six drums were aboard the silver Nissan following close behind, driven by Zahran. The trucks hammered up the shore, hit the track and set off on their winding high-speed journey through the maze of country roads.

Nobody had as yet mentioned anything about poor Shaykh, lying dead on the beach with the two infidels they'd killed. He was on his way to Paradise now, or whatever attenuated form of it the Prophet had reserved for raisin heads. If the police found the body before it was claimed by the tide, they'd almost certainly identify him from their terror watchlist and connect him with known associates, including some of the present company. Nobody much cared about that, either.

As they hurried away from Vaucottes Nazim took out his phone and did an internet search, which led him to a list of links, which in turn led him to a specific website, which he spent a few moments studying with great interest. It was perfect. Not too far away, just a couple of hours' drive. If possible, they would ditch these vehicles en route and switch them for something less conspicuous. Perhaps pick up a hostage on the way, too.

The four-wheel-drive Toyota was a macho boy's toy with all the bells and whistles, including a fancy inbuilt sat nav system. Abbud was fiddling with it as he drove. A text input box popped up on the screen, prompting him to program their destination. Abbud punched in the letters P-A-R-I-S and the winding route towards the capital instantly appeared. 'Looks like we can get there in less than three hours via the A13,' he said, looking pleased that the temporary glitch in their plans was now behind them and they were back in the game.

Nazim didn't answer right away. He was thinking about the Islamic State's call to all believers in the West to attack all infidels by whatever means possible. '*If you are not able to find a bullet or an IED, then single out the disbelieving American, Frenchman, or any of their allies. Smash his head with a rock, or slaughter him with your knife, or run him down with your car, or throw him down from a high place, or choke him, or poison him.*'

With those last inspiring words resonating in his mind, Nazim felt his fate being sealed. He smiled to himself. Then more words came to him, this time from a verse of the Holy Book, one he'd memorised a long, long time ago:

'If there are twenty among you with determination they will vanquish two hundred; if there are a hundred then they will slaughter a thousand unbelievers, for the infidels are a people devoid of understanding.'

Nazim didn't have as many as twenty men, let alone a hundred. But the sacrifice they'd make would bring about the slaughter of many more than a thousand unbelievers. And for that, Allah would smile upon them and take them to His bosom for all eternity.

A feeling of great peace and serenity washed over Nazim. The dull, grey morning sky was gradually brightening and a pale October sun twinkled through the clouds. Today would be a fine day to die.

He calmly told Abbud, 'We're not returning to Paris. Our future lies along a different path.'

Abbud looked puzzled. 'Then where are we going, Nazim?'

'To Jannah,' Nazim said, with the solemn reverence that was due when speaking of the final abode of the righteous and devout. 'But first, to this place.' He reached across to the sat nav screen and tapped in a new destination in place of Paris. The revised route instantly showed up on the display. A completely new set of directions heading in a totally different direction. The alternative location was the city of Alençon, 189 kilometres south of the coast and 173 kilometres west of Paris.

'What's there?' Abbud asked, having never even heard of it before.

'Our destiny is there,' Nazim replied. 'Allah, in His infinite wisdom, intends a special new purpose for us. A short distance away from that town is a certain high-security facility. One that we are going to attack, invade and capture, and use to launch a death blow against the infidels.'

A glow of excitement came into Abbud's eyes. The prospect of an early arrival in Paradise didn't faze him in the least. If today was to be his last day on this earth, he welcomed his fate. 'A military base?'

Not just Abbud. The men in the back of the crew cab were listening intently to the conversation. This was the moment they'd spent their lives dreaming of. They had utter faith in their leader and would follow him to whatever end Allah had in store.

'Better than a military base,' Nazim said. 'It's the biggest water treatment plant in Northern France and one of the largest in Europe. It pipes water to millions of homes across the region. Countless people, every minute of every day, drink that water. They cook their stinking food with it. Make their coffee with it. Brush their teeth and clean their clothes, wash themselves and bathe their infants in it. Allowing us to deliver our weapon straight into the bodies of the infidels. We're going to poison them all.'

Allahu Akbar! The men were delighted. If they'd been riding in an open-top vehicle, they'd have started firing their weapons in the air out of sheer exuberance. The guys in the crew cab repeated the glorious message for those in the back, who might not have heard.

In fact this was nothing entirely new, since waterborne attacks were a familiar and well-tried terrorist tactic. In 2003 Iraqi agents in Jordan had been arrested for trying to poison water supplying US troops near the Iraq border. Yet nothing remotely on this kind of scale had ever been attempted, or even dreamed of, before. It was as ambitious as 9/11 and could even eclipse it. If they could pull it off, they'd be heroes for the rest of time.

Only Abbud wanted to know the specifics of Nazim's scheme. 'How are we going to do this?'

'It's very simple. I expect that we will meet a significant security presence as we push our way inside. We kill as many as we can find, as quickly as we can, until there's no more resistance. Then we find the right pipe, or reservoir, or whatever, and dump in all fourteen barrels.'

'You're talking about thousands and thousands of cubic metres of water pumping out every day,' Abbud said, putting his engineer's hat back on. 'What we have will be as dilute as a drop in the ocean.'

'But still concentrated enough to make a great many infidels very, very sick,' Nazim replied with supreme confidence. 'It takes only a small amount of the poison to be effective. The young and the elderly will be most vulnerable to the toxic effect. They will die in large numbers. Inshallah, we can kill hundreds of thousands of healthy adults too. Not to mention the terror it will strike into the entire country as people become afraid to drink, or splash even a single drop on their skin. Fear will be as effective a weapon as the weapon itself. The authorities will overreact by cutting off the water supply. Without water, even a strong nation is brought to its knees. Businesses and factories will shut down. Agriculture and food production will be crippled. Their whole economic infrastructure will collapse, and there will be rioting and crime as the survivors of the attack begin to starve and fight among themselves. The shockwaves will continue for months afterwards.'

'Much will depend on finding the right part of the system to dump the contents of the barrels into,' Abbud said.

'You're the engineer.'

'I am. But these facilities are complex. One mistake, we could end up pouring the whole lot into a sludge tank, or any number of useless places, and it would never even make it to the public water supply.'

'Then we find someone there who can tell us where to put it. A senior manager, a chief technical officer, someone like that.'

'What if they refuse to play ball?'

Nazim shrugged. 'Who refuses?'

'Someone who wants to play the hero. They'll have a pretty good idea of what we're about to do. Few infidels would want to be responsible for helping to kill thousands of their own kind. Unless we ran into a Hitler, but that would be too much to hope for.'

Ah, Hitler. What a champion. If only he'd been one of theirs.

Nazim pondered the problem and saw an easy solution. 'This senior manager or chief technical officer is most likely to be a man, yes?'

'I'd say so. The infidels like to pretend they strive for gender equality, but theirs is still a man's world, mashallah. One of the few things we have in common with them. Why do you ask?'

'Because if it's a choice between facilitating the deaths of a thousand strangers or being directly responsible for a pretty young woman's brains being blown out right in front of his eyes, no kafir will play the hero for long.'

'I understand what you're saying, brother. But how do we know there'll be any pretty young women at the facility?'

'We don't,' Nazim replied. 'So we'll find one en route and take her hostage. That won't be a problem. There's always some slut around for the picking.'

Abbud thought about it and slowly nodded, warming to the plan. 'I think it can work.'

'Of course it can work. Allah's knowledge has no beginning or end, and He is with us. We can't lose, brother.'

The terrorists changed course and sped southwards. Soon, very soon, the final phase of their plan would kick into action.

Chapter 60

The facility was owned by Keres Holdings International, one of the oldest and most established multinational corporations in Europe, with fingers in every pie from public utilities to media and telecommunications. The industrial giant's interests in water, electricity and natural gas supply and waste management had been spun off into a separate company, K.H.I. Environmental, in 2008, which had invested over three billion euros into the development of its state-of-the-art water treatment plant in the scenic hills of the Alpes Mancelles near Saint-Léonard-des-Bois, a few kilometres west of the commune of Alençon.

Discreetly blended into the landscape of a pretty river valley, from the air the hundred-acre site looked like a NASA space centre. The plant's management prided themselves on being able to comfortably handle over half a million cubic metres of water a day, using the latest eco-friendly technology to remove nitrogen, carbon and phosphate, neutralise odours and eliminate organic matter. The result was beautiful, crystal-clear and sparkling bright water that rivalled the finest mountain spring for purity. K.H.I. even had its own patented thermal treatment process that enabled six hundred metric tons of sludge a day to be converted into renewable energy. The green revolution had arrived.

Two hours after setting out from their landing point on the coast, Nazim al-Kassar and his terrorist gang were about to arrive, too.

As intended, they had paused en route to switch vehicles, in case the two pickups had been reported stolen to the police who must now be swarming all over Vaucottes. Nazim found the perfect replacement transportation at a quiet little truck stop soon after leaving the motorway. The articulated haulage lorry with some generic company name emblazoned along its trailer was sitting on its own in a weedy layby. While Nazim and his men descended quietly from the pickups and stalked up to the lorry with their weapons in their hands they could see the fleshy, round-shouldered shape of the driver sitting in his cab. He didn't seem to notice them approaching; the brightening morning sunshine reflecting off the glass made it hard to see what was distracting his attention. Nazim signalled to Zahran to take the passenger door while he strode up to the driver's side. He quickly hoisted himself up the cab steps, wrenched open the door and jabbed his AK-47 in the face of the shocked and terrified driver. Zahran simultaneously did the same thing on the other side.

The piercing woman's scream that sounded from the cab solved the mystery of what had been preoccupying the driver before he was interrupted. Not that Nazim or any of his gang would ever know or care, but the lorry driver's name was Henri Boudin, he was forty-seven years of age, still lived with his mother and had never had a girlfriend. He was kind of hoping that the nineteen-year-old hitch-hiker named Roxane, whom he'd picked up eighty kilometres ago and had spent every moment since trying to impress with his scintillating personality, might consent to becoming the first. He'd pulled into the layby as a last-ditch attempt to work his seductive charms on the poor girl, who had been on the verge of giving him the finger, jumping out of the cab and making her escape when the doors were unexpectedly yanked open and Roxane and Henri each found themselves staring into the barrel of an automatic weapon.

Nazim was pleased. Not only had they just procured themselves the ideal form of transport to carry them and their cargo the last few kilometres to their destination, they'd also acquired the hostage he'd been looking for. Such serendipity was a sure sign that Allah was indeed looking over them.

By contrast, Nazim had no interest in the lorry driver, who was dragged screaming from his cab, beaten to the ground and had his throat swiftly and bloodily cut. After they'd transferred the fourteen drums of fentanyl from the pickups to the artic trailer they hefted his body into the back of the Toyota.

The lorry had been empty, presumably on its way back to base from making a drop-off. The hostage, now bound and gagged and too petrified to even try to resist, was bundled into the trailer where twelve armed terrorists drooled over her with hungry eyes and strict orders from Nazim not to rape her. It would not be appropriate to enter Paradise sullied by contact with a Western kafir whore; she could be useful to them in other ways.

Then Nazim, Abbud and Zahran clambered up into the tall cab and rumbled away on the final leg of their journey, leaving the abandoned pickup trucks in the layby. After getting off to a shaky start the operation was now back in full swing. They skirted the edge of Alençon and headed west into the pleasant green Alpine countryside with the blue sky above them and their hearts full of blissful thoughts of hatred and destruction. Some time afterwards, they reached their final objective.

A smooth private road wound its way into the scenic river valley to the water treatment plant. The terrorists halted the lorry a hundred metres from the gated entrance, sat in silence and observed. Beyond the gates the main office building looked like a slick modern airport terminal in miniature, with signs for reception and staff and visitor car parks. A small fleet of industrial utility vehicles, modified golf carts with load beds attached, stood parked outside. Visible in the background were the Olympic-pool-sized circular reservoirs and elevated bridges and gantries, giant ducts and pipes and pumps and all kinds of other installations and equipment whose purpose even Abbud, the engineer, could only guess at. Everything was sparkling clean and state-of-the-art. Somewhere among all that high-technology layout, they supposed, was the crucial spot in which they needed to dump their toxic cargo in order to inflict maximum damage on the population.

But they had to get there first. Blocking their way was more mesh fencing than in a medium-security prison. The perimeter stretched for ever and stood twelve feet high, topped with coiled razor wire. A glossy billboard reading K. H. I. ENVIRONMENTAL gleamed in the sunshine, and below it the wire was festooned with PROPRIÉTÉ PRIVÉE and ACCÈS INTERDIT AU PUBLIC warning signs. Despite the obviously high security concerns, the only guard they could see for the moment was a solitary uniformed attendant working the barrier from his hut at the main gate. As they watched, a car approached the barrier, its occupant flashed an ID pass and the barrier glided open and shut to let it through.

'Looks like you need authorisation to get inside,' Abbud said.

'Our authorisation comes from God,' Nazim replied. 'Let us prepare.'

Everyone descended from the lorry, leaving the hostage helplessly bound and gagged in the trailer alone. The fourteen men gathered on the vehicle's blind side, where they were blocked from view of the office building and security hut. They faced east towards Mecca and prostrated themselves on the ground to utter their final heartfelt prayers. There was no turning back now. They had no expectations of leaving this place alive, and they didn't care. Their faces were filled with pride at the prospect of being chosen for this glorious moment.

Nazim reached into a little backpack he'd brought from Paris, and took out a tattered ISIL battle flag. It was the very same one he had carried with him all through the war, back in the day. It had seen a lot of action. He hung the black banner from the side of the lorry behind the praying men, set up his phone to video record and propped it on the ground a few metres away to film them.

When the prayers were over, making sure he was in the camera shot, he addressed them. 'Brothers, the moment you have all prepared for all your lives has now come. I know that you will fight bravely for glory against our enemies. This is likely to be our last stand, as the police will soon send an army to surround us and there will be no escape. Be assured that if we are slain in the Way of Allah, He will never let our deeds be lost.'

One of the younger men began to cry as lip-trembling pride gave way to emotion. They clapped his back and hugged and comforted him and said, 'Jafar, my brother, don't be afraid. When you are scared, think of Allah.' Jafar wiped his tears and replied, 'I'm only scared that I won't succeed in doing my part in our victory.'

Nazim then picked up the phone and pointed it towards himself, with the black flag of Jihad nicely framed in the background. He jutted out his chin and said fiercely into the camera, 'I am a soldier of the Islamic State, a slave of Allah, and these are my last words.'

For the next minute or so, he calmly described what they were about to do. On behalf of the Islamic Ummah worldwide he took responsibility for the imminent deaths of all the infidels soon to be slaughtered. 'This is our sacred duty and the wish of Allah. For He is all-wise and most merciful. Allahu Akbar!'

Nazim saved the video and emailed it to his contacts who would know how to plaster it all over the internet after the glorious attack was over, perfectly timed to set the world media on fire. Then the West would know exactly who had done this to them, and be afraid.

They all took their places back inside the lorry. The three men in the cab nodded to one another. Abbud slammed the stick into gear, veered towards the gates and accelerated hard.

The security guy in the little hut by the gate was a man close to retirement age, with a white moustache. He looked round, then stared open-mouthed as he began to realise that the eighteen-wheeler roaring towards him wasn't going to slow down.

Less than two seconds later, the security guy became the first official casualty of the water treatment plant attack. The lorry hit the barrier and went tearing through with a crash of rending steel and wire. It flattened the security hut with the man inside it and rolled on through the debris, trailing bits of crumpled wreckage that scraped and sparked on the concrete.

Nazim yelled at Abbud to keep going, which Abbud did, aiming straight at the reception building. A woman dressed in a trouser suit, maybe an administrator, was running out of the building in shock at what was happening outside, joined by a couple of other personnel. She froze in the doorway, unable to move, paralysed by disbelief. Abbud did not steer away from her or take his foot off the accelerator. *Slaughter him with your knife, or smash his head with a rock, or run him down with your car.*

She was still standing directly in their path and seemed to lock eyes with Nazim half an instant before the lorry ploughed into the building and mowed her down under its wheels. The glass doors and windows caved violently inwards and forty tons of eighteen-wheeler forced deep inside, crushing and pulverising everything in its path before it came to a grinding halt. Then Abbud crunched the gears into reverse and backed out. The windscreen was opaque with cracks and blood spatter. Nazim grabbed his weapon and said, 'Let's go.'

The three of them kicked open the dented cab doors and jumped out into the carnage. Nazim shot one of the screaming employees who'd been crushed only half to death. Not out of mercy, but because the screaming grated on his ear. The terrorists inside the trailer rolled open the shutter and a few leaped out, the rest staying inside with the cargo and the hostage.

More security personnel, who had been enjoying a mid-morning coffee break when the attack began, now came running. They took one bewildered look at the crashed lorry and the armed terrorists and flew into disarray. One of them gamely stood his ground and even managed to snap off a round or two with his pistol, but his shots were wildly off target. Dariush pinned him in his sights and gunned him down like scything weeds.

As easily as the first line of security had collapsed, the

second was unable to offer much resistance. After a few moments of sporadic gunfire the security men fell back and took to their heels. Not one of them made it more than a few steps before they were taken down by full-automatic fire. Dariush was yelling ALLAHU AKBAR! ALLAHU AKBAR! over and over, his eyes wild with glee and blood lust.

The young female hostage had come to her senses after the initial paralysing shock of fear, and was screaming and struggling like a wild animal. There was blood running from a cut on her brow where the crash impact had sent her flying. Nazim pounced up into the trailer, grabbed her and knocked her cold with a punch to the jaw. Jumping back down to the ground with the unconscious girl hanging limply in his arms like a rolled-up rug, he delegated his orders to his men.

'Abbud, Zahran, Dariush, Jafar, with me. The rest of you, take the barrels from the lorry and load them onto those things.' He pointed at the fleet of utility golf carts. 'Make for the water reservoirs on the other side of the building. We'll meet you there. Move, move!'

Fire had broken out inside the wreckage of the entrance foyer, which was filling with acrid black smoke. Alarms began to jangle. Nazim strode inside the building with the hostage slung unconscious over his left shoulder and his gun in his right hand.

His men followed. Their boots crunched on broken glass and left prints in the blood of the dead. At the far side of the smoke-filled reception area was a corridor with open-plan offices either side. Those employees who hadn't already fled in panic were making their desperate escape. The terrorists shot a couple of them and stepped over their bodies without a second glance. Nazim told Abbud, 'Your idea was a good one. If we see someone who looks like a senior manager or chief technician, don't shoot them. We need them alive.'

Nazim seemed icy cool, but inwardly he was flushed with the thrill of battle. So much had changed since their near-disastrous start that morning. Then, he had felt the looming presence of failure so close that he could smell it. Now, victory was just inches from their grasp. It seemed that nobody had the force to oppose them.

But that, too, was about to change.

As Nazim was leading the way deeper into the building he paused and cocked an ear, listening past the shrilling of the fire alarm to the unexpected thud of a helicopter outside.

The very loud, very close thud of a helicopter.

Nazim looked up. 'What's that?'

Chapter 61

At times of pressing need, it sometimes pays to call on a friend for help. And that was exactly what Ben had done. Not just one friend, but specifically three.

The moment Ben had realised what Nazim was planning, he'd called Jeff Dekker at Le Val and outlined the urgent situation. Jeff's instant response: 'Are you kidding, mate? We're on our way.'

And wherever Jeff went, the irrepressible Tuesday Fletcher was sure to follow. But Le Val was more than a two-hour drive from where they needed to be, and there wasn't time for that. Which was Ben's reason for appealing to help from the third friend. Someone who could make things happen much more quickly.

Not so very long ago, Ben had rescued Auguste Kaprisky's beloved great-niece Valentina and her father from some bad men in Russia. The octogenarian billionaire would do anything for Ben. And Ben didn't know too many other people who possessed a private collection of some of the world's fastest civil aircraft, kept on permanent standby with a team of pilots. Within minutes of his call to Kaprisky at his estate near Le Mans, the old man's Learjet was in the sky and whooshing northwards at 858 kilometres an hour towards Cherbourg, the nearest airport to Le Val.

Meanwhile, Jeff and Tuesday were piling towards Cherbourg in Jeff's souped-up Ford Ranger, a journey of just twenty-odd kilometres that Jeff broke every rule in the book to cover in record time. They met the jet at a private terminal and were immediately back in the air heading south for Le Mans, where an Airbus H155 helicopter capable of over 320 kilometres an hour was waiting to fly them to their destination. Total time in the air: just under forty-seven minutes, plus the short while it had taken Jeff to drive like a bat out of hell to Cherbourg. The ever-resourceful Kaprisky had even supplied an arsenal of weapons from his personal bodyguard retinue, to save Jeff and Tuesday having to tote the hardware from the Le Val armoury into a public airport. The old man was thoughtful like that.

While all this was going on, Ben and Roth had been screaming southwards in the Alpina and somehow managing not to get pursued by the traffic police. They arrived at the water treatment plant outside Alençon just before the helicopter appeared. With every passing minute Ben had been getting increasingly worried that he might have misjudged the whole situation. What if his instinct was wrong? What if he couldn't read Nazim's intentions as well as he thought he could? What if Nazim was somewhere else, far away, laughing?

But Ben's fears were grimly put to rest when he saw the thick black smoke belching from the main building and rising over the facility, and the mangled hole where the front gates used to be. Fire alarms were going off inside the building. It wouldn't be long before the police and emergency services got here. Ben wanted to be in, out and gone before that happened.

Roth nodded. 'Good call, bud. This is it, all right.'

Ben said nothing as he rolled the car to a halt a distance

from the wrecked gate and surveyed the scene. Other than the flames and smoke he could see nothing moving within the facility compound. The thought flashed through his mind that Nazim could have already achieved his purpose and left. Then he heard shots from inside the building and knew that wasn't the case.

There was little time for introductions as the helicopter landed and Ben's friends met Roth. The American's Delta Force credentials were good enough for them. 'Looks like the party started without us,' Tuesday said, gazing across at the burning building. Having been thwarted in his ambitions to become the first ever black Jamaican soldier to serve in the SAS, he was the only one of the four without a Special Forces background. But his skills were on a par with anyone's, and there wasn't a comrade whom Ben and Jeff trusted more completely with their lives.

Now they moved fast. Two heavy holdalls were unloaded from the chopper, containing four Swiss-made Brugger & Thomet MP9 submachine guns, tactical vests with spare magazine pouches, and radios. They kitted up as the helicopter took off, blasting the ground around them with its rotors. Then the four jumped into the Alpina. Jeff took Roth's place up front next to Ben at the wheel. Roth rode in the back with Tuesday. It was going to be a short journey. Nobody spoke. They knew what they were going into, and what was at stake.

Ben sped through the smashed gates, roared past the wreckage of the security hut and saw what was left of the man who'd been inside. Only a very large vehicle, travelling fast, could have wrought such destruction. Like a tank or an armoured personnel vehicle. But as the Alpina cut through the smoke wreathing the front of the building he could see no tank or APC inside the grounds of the treatment plant. Just a crash-damaged articulated lorry with its cab doors hanging open and the shutter rolled up on its empty trailer. Dead bodies littered the compound. None of them were Nazim's men.

Roth leaned through the gap in the front seats and pointed a finger beyond the building towards the heart of the treatment plant. 'The motherfuckers are already in. Keep moving, bud.'

Ben didn't reply. He put his foot down and tore through the curtains of smoke and across the compound, rounding the side of the burning building.

'Watch it!' Jeff said.

Ben had seen it, too. He braked to avoid the industrial utility cart a few metres ahead. It looked as though it had been making its way towards the complex of reservoirs and ancillary buildings when it had broken down. The bullet holes in its plastic bodywork were a clue as to why.

But it wasn't the bullet holes Ben was fixing on as he swerved to a stop. On the cart's rear load bed stood two shiny aluminium drums. The same exact kind that Ben and Roth had seen aboard the beached boat at Plage de Vaucottes that morning. And standing beside the cart were three armed men. An instant earlier they'd been kicking it and jabbering curses at it in loud Arabic. Now they whirled their weapons around to aim at the Alpina and opened fire.

Bullets raked the car's bonnet and windscreen. Jeff, Tuesday and Roth leaned from the windows with their MP9s and let rip. Their combined fire was devastatingly more accurate than that of the terrorists, and all three targets crumpled and hit the ground. Two instantly dead, the third badly injured. But the pure fentanyl spouting from a perforated drum and spattering over his face and chest would soon finish him off.

'Just what the doctor ordered,' Roth quipped.

Nobody replied. Ben went to drive on in pursuit of the others. The moment he pressed the accelerator he knew one of the terrorists' high-velocity rounds had hit something critical under the bonnet and the car was in bad trouble. It limped a few metres then ground to a halt. A loud mechanical rattle from the engine compartment getting rapidly louder. Smoke already beginning to leak out from the edges of the bonnet. He pressed the pedal all the way down. No power. No response. Useless.

He kicked open his door. 'Everyone out. We're on foot from here.'

Chapter 62

'Someone's out there.'

'The police?' Abbud said, creasing his brow as he peered up at the ceiling and listened hard to the thump and clatter of the rotor blades not far away. 'So soon?'

'Maybe,' Nazim said. He hadn't anticipated them turning up this fast. But he didn't have time to worry. 'It's not important. We do this, no matter what.'

They pressed on. The hostage had come to and was squirming and struggling on Nazim's shoulder. He thumped her again. Outside, the helicopter sounded as though it had landed. Then, just moments later as the terrorists pushed on deeper into the building, kicking open doors as they went, they heard it taking off again.

Nazim thought that was extremely odd. A police helicopter wouldn't just touch down momentarily and then fly off. It would be joined by a whole mass contingent that would surround the building, seal off every exit and prepare for an armed siege.

His puzzled thoughts were cut short as he picked up the muffled and distant-sounding reports of shots being fired somewhere outside in the compound. Something strange was happening out there. He couldn't believe that the security guards were trying to remount a resistance. This was somehow connected to the mysterious helicopter. Nazim didn't like not knowing, but the pressure only made him more determined to succeed.

They burst into an office. A plump black woman in her forties, wearing a pink dress, froze in wide-eyed horror by the window she'd been unsuccessfully trying to climb out of. Nazim let the hostage slip from his shoulder and kept a tight grip on her arm as he pointed his gun one-handed at the woman in the pink dress. He demanded, 'Are you a manager? A technician?'

Her words tumbled out in a breathless gasp, 'No, I'm just a secretary. Please, don't—'

Nazim shot her twice in the chest before she could finish, and watched impassively as she slid down the wall by the window. 'Just as I thought.'

He swept out of the office, dragging the hostage along behind him. The girl was unsteady on her feet, traumatised past the point of dumb shock. Abbud followed, then young Jafar, then Dariush and Zahran bringing up the rear. Further down the same corridor they reached another office. Nazim smashed the door open so violently that it nearly came off its hinges, and stormed inside the room to see a middle-aged white man cowering on all fours under a crowded desk, as though trying to shelter from a bomb attack. Suit, crooked tie, greying hair, and a large slab of a belly that hung down to the floor. This one seemed a more likely proposition. The blood drained from his face and he showed his palms in supplication. 'P-please! I don't want to die!'

Nazim repeated the question, 'Are you a manager?'

The fat man's head pumped up and down, shaking his jowls. 'I-I'm Daniel Lebrun. I'm CEO of this facility. Who are you people? W-what do you want?'

At Nazim's nod, Abbud and Dariush dragged the company

director out from under the desk and forced him into a chair. He was wheezing and clutching his chest, and his face had flushed from ghastly pale to purplish-red. 'Oh, oh! I think I'm having a heart attack. My pills!'

'You can have your pills if you help us. I'll even get you a doctor.' Nazim could lie with great sincerity when needed.

Lebrun could barely take his eyes off the gun in Nazim's hand. 'Help you do what?' he croaked.

'You're going to show us where we can access the public water supply from your facility. I want to see blueprints. Maps. Or else you take us to it personally. I don't care which. But you'd better make it quick.'

Lebrun babbled, 'I d-don't understand. Access it for what?'

'To spike it with poison and kill all the infidel pigs like you,' Dariush said fiercely.

Lebrun seemed to suddenly forget his imminent heart attack, and now the redness in his cheeks was a flush of anger. 'You're insane if you think I'd help you with a terrorist act. I'll die first. And who is this poor young woman? What are you animals doing to her? It's an outrage. Hear me?'

Playing the hero. Nazim glanced at Abbud, who shrugged as though to say, 'I told you so.'

They could have tortured Lebrun into compliance, but torture takes time and has its limitations, especially when dealing with chronically ill subjects who are liable to drop dead from sudden cardiac arrest, defeating the object of the exercise. The alternative method was much more effective. Nazim threw the female hostage roughly to the floor, pinned her down with his boot and pressed his rifle muzzle to her throat. Her eyes were rolling and she made a gurgling sound. Nazim said, very calmly and evenly, 'You will help us, or you will watch this female's blood spray across your face, and you will die knowing that you could have spared her life. Your choice, kafir. Which is it to be?'

Lebrun boggled up at Nazim, then down at the hostage, then back at Nazim. Sweat poured from his brow, ran into his eyes and made him blink. 'A-all right. I'll . . . I'll take you there and show you. Don't hurt her. Please! I have a daughter the same age.'

Nazim took the gun away from the girl's throat. She was spluttering and holding her neck, tears rolling backwards from the corners of her eyes. He yanked her harshly to her feet. He would kill her afterwards anyway. 'Good. Then lead the way. And no tricks, or you'll see what happens next.'

Lebrun was yanked up from his chair, shoved out of the office and made to lead the way through the building, one thick arm held tightly in Dariush's grip. He muttered, 'What are you going to put in the water?'

'That's not your concern,' Abbud said.

'Okay. Okay. We have to get to the main reservoir tanks.' They came to a fire door and Lebrun gasped, 'We can go out this way. It's quicker.' Dariush shouldered the door open. It led to a fire escape with a heavy outer door fitted with a panic bar. There were large windows either side, facing out onto the rear of the building and a view of all the large circular reservoirs, gantries, bridges and pumping stations stretching out far and wide.

Still holding onto Lebrun, Dariush grabbed the panic bar and shoved open the outer door. Nazim was standing three or four feet behind with the female hostage, Jafar and Abbud to his sides and Zahran hovering behind. Nazim felt he could trust Lebrun to lead them to the right place. They were close now. Triumph was inevitable.

And then it all suddenly fell apart.

As the outer door swung open Nazim caught a glimpse of someone standing there. Someone he'd seen before. Someone holding a pistol. Then, before anyone could react, the loud detonation of a gunshot filled the fire escape. The back of Dariush's head blew out like an eggshell. Blood spattered across the side of Lebrun's face. The hostage screamed. Dariush folded at the knees and slumped dead to the floor.

For a fraction of a second, all Nazim could do was stare. The shooter was a tall man, about the same height as him. Thick blond hair hanging across his brow. Blue eyes as hard and cold as the mountain glaciers of Afghanistan. The weapon in his hands looked like an extension of his arms. As though he'd been born holding it.

The foreigner. The white *shaitan*. The man with no name.

He wasn't alone. A darker-haired man Nazim had never seen before was standing at his side with a submachine gun and the steely expression of a combat-hardened veteran.

Then in the next split second, everything erupted into chaos. Abbud fired at the doorway, in such haste that his bullets stitched a ragged line of holes up the wall and a pane of reinforced fire glass. A return chatter of full-auto fire spat from the doorway and Abbud staggered backwards, dropping his weapon, crimson flowers blooming on his shirt. Jafar never even got the chance to open fire before a lightning double-tap from the blond *shaitan*'s pistol punched through his forehead and chest and snatched the life out of him before he even began to drop. Zahran rushed in front of his leader to defend and protect him. He raised his weapon and yanked the trigger, but the AK had jammed. He hurled it down. Whipped out his knife, still wet with the blood of the lorry driver. Charged towards the doorway with the blade raised high and a furious bellow of 'ALLAHU AKBAR!' bursting from his lungs.

Nazim heard the ensuing gunfire, but he saw no more. Because by then, he was already retreating at a wild sprint down the corridor, dragging the hostage along with him.

Chapter 63

The surviving jihadist was only a young guy, barely in his twenties, but his short life would soon be over. He was moaning pitifully and reaching out for help with a red-slicked hand. Not everyone who thinks they're willing to die for their beliefs still feels that way when the moment actually comes.

The blood pumping from the several bullet wounds in his torso was the least of the dying man's worries. Clear liquid fentanyl was still spouting from the holes in the shot-up drum, spattering and splashing over him where he lay unable to move. Ben was standing at a distance to avoid breathing the toxic fumes. What Roth had said about the sniffer dogs dropping dead from just one whiff had been enough to make him very cautious.

'You've had it, son,' Ben told him in Arabic. 'There's nothing anyone can do for you. But you can make it right by telling me where Nazim is.'

The young guy's eyes rolled in fear and confusion. He pointed a bloody hand towards the main building. Whether it was the effect of the drug scrambling his mind or he was genuinely contrite in the face of impending death, Ben neither knew nor cared. Then the young guy's body convulsed and a geyser of dark blood spouted from his mouth. After a violent seizure, he was dead. Ben turned away. Jeff, Tuesday and Roth were looking at him with grim faces, waiting for his lead.

Roth said, 'You can't know Nazim's in there.'

Ben replied. 'I aim to find out. But first we have the others to deal with. Split up. Two teams. Tuesday, you go with Roth. Jeff, you and me. Keep in radio contact.'

Tuesday and the American set off at a fast trot towards the complex of reservoirs where three dead terrorists had been heading. Ben and Jeff hugged the side of the building, working their way around. Ben was favouring his pistol over the MP9 that hung behind his back on its sling. Jeff muttered, 'So, this Roth guy. What's his role in all of this?'

'That's a good question, Jeff. I haven't quite figured that one out myself yet.'

The front of the building was still burning fiercely. The wind had changed and was blowing the smoke their way, making the air acrid and bitter. Ben could no longer see Tuesday or Roth. He and Jeff stalked along a few steps apart on bent knees with weapons up and ready, constantly covering one another's movements, eyes flashing left and right for the slightest glimpse of the enemy, totally focused, each man utterly confident in the other.

It was the lull before the storm. Nothing could root you more fully and consciously in the present moment than the knowledge that, any time now, conflict and violence were about to explode all around you. Whatever negative truths were spoken about the stress of combat, it was the time when true warriors felt most alive.

It was as he and Jeff were scouting the rear of the building that Ben thought he sensed a movement on the edge of his vision, and turned quickly to look. Nerves could play tricks on you, but he hadn't imagined it.

Figures flitting past a window.

Heading for a fire exit door.

The door beginning to open.

Ben and Jeff ran to take up position. And then the door swung open the rest of the way, and the lull before the storm was over.

Two men were framed in the doorway. On the left, a darker-skinned man of Middle Eastern blood, clutching an AK-47 with the stock folded and his finger on the trigger. On the right, a greying fat man in a rumpled suit and a crooked tie, who looked as if he was having the worst day of his life. It was like a shoot/no shoot target on a firing range. Take out the hostage, you lose the game. Take out the bad guy, you win. A no-brainer, but all the same a supreme test of lightning fast decision-making and reflexes, when split seconds mattered. Ben lined up his pistol sights on the guy with the AK and fired. One shot, one kill, centre of the forehead. The guy went down like a tree. The fat man stayed standing, blood spattered across one side of his face, eyes blinking in shock. Suddenly Ben could see four more men and a woman inside the doorway behind him. The woman didn't appear as though she wanted to be there.

And the person holding her by the arm was Nazim al-Kassar.

The exchange of fire that followed was fast and furious. A full-auto burst rattled from inside the doorway but just strafed the entrance. Jeff fired off a string from his MP9. One more down. Then Ben fired again with his pistol. One more down, before he could get off a shot. Then a wild man with a shaven skull and a long black beard and a knife in his fist came flying at them, screaming like a demented maniac. Ben and Jeff's bullets found him at the same time, a ragged quick-fire series of blasts that hammered into his chest and shredded his heart and lungs. The wild man staggered but somehow stayed on his feet and kept coming. Ben and Jeff shot him again, and he crunched down on his face at their feet.

Four down.

One gone.

Nazim was suddenly nowhere to be seen. He'd escaped back inside the building. Taking the female hostage with him.

In the next moment, they heard more gunfire coming from the reservoirs at the far side of the plant. Tuesday and Roth had encountered the rest of the terrorists. Ben's instant response was to go to their aid. But Jeff shook his head, shoved Ben's arm and pointed inside the doorway, yelling, 'Go! Get him!'

Ben hesitated. Torn between going after Nazim and helping his friends. Jeff yelled again, 'Go! Move it! Don't let him get away. We can deal with the rest.'

Then, slamming in a fresh magazine, Jeff was off at a sprint in the direction of the battle.

Ben hesitated just a moment longer. Thought, *Fuck it.* Pushed past the bewildered fat guy in the suit still standing there, and ran into the building after Nazim.

Chapter 64

The smoke became thicker and more choking the deeper Ben ran into the building. For a minute it seemed as though Nazim had just vanished into thin air. Or had he made it to another exit and rejoined his men?

Then Ben saw the blood spots on the floor. Small star shaped splashes, spaced a few paces apart. Nazim had taken a hit. Or else his hostage had.

Ben followed the trail, pausing every few instants to listen hard, but he could hear nothing except the tireless jangling of the fire alarm. He rounded another corner and found himself looking down a long passage filled with smoke. And he stopped, looking down. Because the blood trail had suddenly stopped, too. Like a path leading nowhere.

Or one that had doubled back on itself to deceive him.

His sixth sense suddenly tingling like an electrical field. Sensing a presence close by. Then his ears picked up a sound behind him. The scrape of a footstep. He turned quickly.

Nazim al-Kassar was standing there with his young girl hostage. Her hair was all awry, her eyes wide and rolling from side to side like a spooked horse's. Nazim held her pinned against his body, his left hand clamped tightly over her mouth, the right pointing an AK from over her shoulder. His finger was on the trigger and his face was livid with hate.

Ben was already ducking back into the smoke. Nazim lost his aim at the last moment, but the trigger was already breaking under his finger. The rifle shot was sharp and loud in the confines of the corridor. Ben raised his pistol to fire back, hunting for an aiming point. His target was small. He didn't dare go for a headshot, for fear of hitting the hostage. So he aimed a little wide, going for the shoulder.

And missed. But it was a lucky miss. Instead of the shoulder, his bullet caught Nazim in the wrist. Nazim let out a cry and the AK clattered from his hand. Ben moved in closer, looking for another shot. Then stopped short when he saw the knife in Nazim's good hand, held to the girl's throat. She wailed, 'Mister, don't let him kill me!'

'Drop the pistol or she dies!' Nazim said tersely.

'Then you die too, Nazim.'

'You think I'm afraid of dying? Your choice, *shaitan*.'

Ben lowered his pistol and let it slip from his hand. He could still hear shooting from outside. He was desperately worried for his friends out there, but he had to close his mind to it and stay focused.

'Let her go, Nazim. Let it be just you and me.'

'Me and you? And who *are* you?'

'Just a man,' Ben said.

Nazim spat. 'I don't think so.'

Now Ben could see the blood dripping from Nazim's right thigh, the leg of his combat trousers soaked black with it. He must have caught a stray round during the exchange in the doorway. It explained why he'd chosen not to run, but to stay and fight.

'Think what you want,' Ben said. 'Just let her go.'

Nazim smiled. 'I think she must die.'

'There's been enough blood for one day.'

'That's where you're wrong, *shaitan*. There is never enough blood.'

As though in slow motion Ben watched the muscles in Nazim's hand holding the knife start to tighten. The fingers clenching, knuckles whitening. The sinews in the forearm squeezing as the blade's pressure on her throat increased and the cutting edge began to draw horizontally across her soft flesh. She screamed. She was already as good as dead. So Ben no longer had anything to lose by taking a crazy chance. In one smooth, superfast motion he swung out his other weapon. The MP9 that was slung behind his back where Nazim couldn't see it. Not until this moment. Not until the submachine gun was in Ben's hands and spitting flame from its short muzzle. Ben actually saw the girl's blond hair flutter, like meadow grass in the wind, as his bullets passed within two inches of the side of her head and punched into Nazim's chest. The knife dropped. Nazim staggered back two steps and let her go, and stumbled away up the passage. He crashed through a door and disappeared from sight.

Ben hurried over to the fallen girl. Another second, and Nazim would have slashed her from ear to ear. The cut was bleeding but not deep. She'd probably live to a very old age, with a little white scar on her throat to remember this moment by.

'What's your name?'

'Roxane,' she whimpered, hardly able to speak for emotion.

'Roxane, I'll be right back. You sit tight, okay?'

She gave a tremulous nod, gazing into his eyes. 'Okay.'

Ben left her and chased after Nazim. There was a bloody smear on the door that the injured terrorist had crashed through, below a sign for TOILETTES. Ben batted the door open and stepped inside the staff bathroom, smelling the scent of ammonia mingling with the harsh tang of smoke. The fire alarm had stopped jangling and the lights had begun to flicker as the fire spread through the building and slowly melted down its electricals.

Ben stood rock-still in the bathroom and looked around him. The walls were tiled white. A line of sinks and mirrors covered one side, a row of cubicle stalls the other. One of the cubicle doors was open. There was another oily red smear of blood all down the door. And a leg sticking out from inside. A leg clad in combat trousers, with a black high-lace boot on the end of it.

Ben walked slowly towards the cubicle where Nazim lay curled up and bleeding heavily. Just then the radio fizzed into life. Jeff's voice crackled, '*All clear here. Target secured, seven combatants down. Repeat, seven combatants down. No casualties on our side. Talk to me, Ben. Over.*'

With intense relief flooding through him Ben thumbed the talk button and radioed back, 'Copy that. Be with you in a minute. Out.'

He stepped closer to Nazim. The man was alive, just about. His breath was coming in gasps and the pool of blood around him was spreading fast and thick, reflecting the flickering lights.

Nazim raised his head and tried to prop himself up as Ben crouched near him. Ben spoke in Arabic. 'The great Nazim al-Kassar, dying alone in a toilet. Not exactly the glorious end you'd envisioned for yourself.'

Nazim coughed blood. Mortally wounded, but not quite dead yet. In a croak he asked again, 'Who are you?'

'Someone from your past,' Ben replied. 'You remembered me, didn't you?'

'All these years. You still had to come after me. Your kind will always hate my kind.'

'I don't hate you, Nazim. We're all locked in a war that nobody can ever really win. That just makes me sad.'

Nazim's eyes were beginning to cloud with death, but a flicker of surprise passed through them. 'Then why did you risk your life to stop me? Have you any idea what we would have done to you, if we had caught you?'

Ben was surprised, too. 'You're asking me this, now?'

Nazim spluttered up more blood. He managed a nod. 'I need to understand what drives a man like you.'

Ben had nothing against indulging a dying man's final wishes. He replied, 'I do what I do so that more innocent people don't have to suffer and die. People like Salim Youssef. People like Romy Juneau and Françoise Schell and the Simonots. People like Samara.'

Nazim blinked, trying to remember even as his life ebbed away. 'Samara?' His voice had faded to little more than a whisper.

Ben's mind flashed back once again to the woman in his dream. The same dream he'd had so many times. He saw the Iraqi dusty roadside checkpoint from sixteen years ago. The young woman in black, clutching her pregnant stomach as she approached the unsuspecting group of Coalition soldiers. The sudden white flash and deafening percussive blast of the explosion. The grisly aftermath of the suicide bombing. Her poor dead face looking up at him.

He said, 'You probably never even knew her name. Neither did I. Samara was just what I called her, to make her seem more real to me, not just another piece of torn-up meat. She was an ordinary person caught up in that hell, like the rest of us. She didn't have to die like that. Men like you made her die. Her and many others. There's a Samara in every village, in every town and city, vulnerable to falling prey to you and your kind. That's why I had to end this. Not for politics, not for religion or ideology, and damn well not for country.'

Nazim sank back to the floor and gave a gasp. 'And you had your wish,' he murmured softly. 'It is over.'

'Yes, it's over, Nazim. For you and all your men. You failed. But at least you can die knowing that you gave it all you had. Maybe there's still a place for you in Paradise, if Allah can forgive you.'

Nazim smiled. 'He is most forgiving.' Then the life washed out of his eyes, his head rolled limply to one side and he was dead.

Chapter 65

Ben was on his way back to attend to Roxane when the whole building was suddenly swarming with black-clad GIGN troops. They'd come ready for a full-scale war: battle armour, helmets, respirators, goggles and military weaponry bristling in all directions.

Finding himself rapidly surrounded, Ben put down his gun and made no attempt to resist arrest. He was tempted to say something clever like 'What took you so long?' but kept his mouth shut as, with admirable thoroughness and no small amount of yelling, they put him down on his face and trussed his hands behind his back with a plastic tie. Then he was marched outside with dozens of cocked assault weapons poking at him. The police had closed in hard and fast, stealthily and in large numbers. The water treatment plant compound was awash with personnel and vehicles. Four ambulances were rushing to the scene, though they'd probably need more. A fire crew were busy dousing the flames that had consumed much of the front portion of the main building. Black armed response vans were still arriving, pouring yet more boots on the ground as though it was going to take every armed cop in France to contain a situation that was already over.

Ben's escorts led him across the compound towards a

waiting unmarked police van with smoked-out windows. In the midst of the melee he spotted Jeff and Tuesday, likewise cuffed and surrounded by hordes of anti-terror troops in black who were herding them into another pair of identical plain vans. As happy as he was to see his friends unscathed, it upset him that he'd brought this trouble on them. He should never have called on their help.

There was no sign of Tyler Roth anywhere.

Then Ben lost sight of Jeff and Tuesday as he was bundled into the windowless rear of the van, caged behind steel mesh and accompanied by several officers who no doubt had orders to shoot him dead if he tried to escape. If Nazim al-Kassar had received this much care and attention from the US military, back in the day, things might have turned out differently.

The van took off at speed. Ben settled down for the ride and said nothing to his captors. He guessed they were taking him back to Paris, and wondered if they were in convoy with the vans carrying Jeff and Tuesday. Whatever lay at the end of the road – terror charges, murder charges, incarceration – he could only wait and see how it played out.

Two hours and twelve minutes later, Ben felt the van come to a stop. His guards were on their feet and pointing their guns at him as the doors opened and he was marched out into a secure underground parking space where more police were standing by with shotguns and machine carbines. If he'd been travelling in tandem with Jeff and Tuesday, they'd been taken to a different location.

From the underground parking facility Ben was hustled up several floors in a steel lift with more armed escorts, and then to a bare holding cell with no windows and a door like a vault. They cut the tie away from his wrists, took his shoes and his watch, and then left without another word and locked him up.

At times like these, you try not to let yourself speculate too much about what's in store. Ben had been a prisoner before, and he knew how to empty his mind and remain utterly still and quiet for many hours. The cell had a single bunk bolted to the floor, a metal toilet and a sink. He sat on the bunk, closed his eyes and sank into a meditative state.

He'd been sitting like that for over four hours when they finally came for him. Hearing the door unlock, he opened his eyes and turned. A different pair of guards, this time accompanied by a silent, severe-looking man in a dark suit, gave him back his shoes and walked him from the cell and down a passageway to a door. The guy in the suit knocked, and opened it. The guards motioned Ben inside. He stepped through the door and found himself in a plain, institutional office with beige walls, no carpet, a single window and a large desk with two chairs.

Sitting at the desk, dressed in a smart blazer and chinos and looking as if he owned the place, was Tyler Roth.

Chapter 66

Roth didn't get up. 'You have no idea how much I hate this part of my job, man. I'm a field guy, always was. That's what I keep telling them, but do they listen?'

Ben would have been amazed if he hadn't already half-expected this to happen. He replied, 'That's funny. I thought you were retired.'

Roth laughed. 'Oh, you know, once you're in the club they never really let you out of their clutches. One thing leads to another.'

'In your case, those things being Delta leading to the CIA.'

'We prefer to call it the company,' Roth said. 'Sounds cosier, don't you think?'

'To me, it just sounds like you've been playing me for an idiot this whole time.'

'Oh, you're no idiot, my friend. Don't do yourself down. In fact, you've probably got most of this figured out already, a smart dude like you.'

'It all goes back to the very beginning,' Ben said. 'You knew Segal was being coerced by Nazim's people. And you had a tap on Romy Juneau's phone, because you thought she might be involved, too.'

Roth shrugged. 'We didn't really know about that, for sure. But we did know that we weren't the only ones listening in. Which kind of suggested that she wasn't working for the bad guys, and they suspected her. One thing about terrorists, they're almost as cautious and paranoid as we are.'

'So you were waiting to see if she'd get hit,' Ben said. 'How charming. Whereupon you'd have moved on the hitters.'

'Or at least known more about who was involved,' Roth said. 'Although we already had a pretty good idea. We had a bunch of agents watching her day and night. We were watching when she bumped into you in the street. Your face got twigged instantly. Gave some folks quite a shock, until they decided it really was just a crazy coincidence and that the Brits didn't have their own spooks on the case. Then, when you turned up at her place and blundered right into the middle of our operation like some damn fool white knight riding in to help the damsel in distress, we were watching that too.' Roth shook his head. 'You could have walked face-first into a fucking bullet, you asshole.'

'I'm so glad we're having this conversation at last,' Ben said.

'Absolutely. What a fabulous rapport we're having. Why don't you take a seat, make yourself comfortable?'

'No thanks. If I get too close I might want to crack this desk in half with your face.'

'Nice way to speak to the guy who just sprung your ass out of jail.'

'Keep talking.'

Roth eased back in his chair and put his feet up on the desk. 'So now we had an unwanted witness, and definitely not someone we wanted mixed up in our business. The initial response was that we should intervene to remove you.'

'As in, kill me.'

'Sure, but "remove" sounds better.'

'Good luck with that. It's been tried plenty of times before.'

'Oh, I know you're a tough motherfucker. But the company has manuals on covert assassination thicker than a phone directory, and ways and means like you wouldn't believe. Nobody sees them coming. Not even you.'

'Seems I had a lucky escape there. So why the change of plan?'

'Because when you contacted Keegan wanting to talk to me, of all people, some bright spark inside the company figured that maybe there was another angle here, one we could use.'

'Keegan?'

Roth chuckled. 'Getting it, aintcha? Yeah, Keegan was part of the setup. Most of the PMC assignments that he handles are really just fronts for covert CIA operations in countries where the US government can't openly operate. He's one of us, or as good as.'

'Small world,' Ben said.

'Getting smaller every day, that's for sure,' Roth replied.

'The island. Is that really your house or is it some kind of CIA station?'

'No, the island is the real deal, home sweet home. We wanted you well out of the way, so we figured, why not bring you over to my place? While you were enjoying my hospitality a couple of our Parisian assets were sent in to snatch your pal Thierry and his friend from your apartment and take them into protective custody. Turns out to be a talented fellow, that Thierry. Once he had access to some proper resources to help him decrypt the audio track on the Juneau video recording, he started getting much better results. The audio was very interesting.'

Ben didn't know whether to marvel at the cynical ingenuity of Roth and his associates, or just reach across the desk and break his nose in a couple of places. 'And where is

Thierry now? Or was he "removed" once you had what you wanted?'

'Oh, don't you worry about your little forger buddy. Like I said, quite the talented individual. He'll be kept plenty busy working for us from now on, with a whole new identity and a pleasant life somewhere far, far away from all the people he pissed off back home.'

'That's very sweet of you. And as for me, my whole involvement in this was to use me to get Nazim. You knew how dangerous he was, and you didn't want to risk the lives of your own agents. Correct?'

'Kind of like the old fable about the monkey using the cat's paw to get a roasting chestnut out of the fire,' Roth said. 'It's all about plausible deniability, my friend. You becoming involved turned out to be a golden opportunity for us. It meant we didn't have to do anything much except watch from the sidelines. Anything bad happened to you, so much less embarrassment for the company. Plus, as a special bonus, it so happens that you're better than any of our people. You proved that. You've got some useful friends, too. Of course, I did give you a helping hand now and then.'

'Like the spy satellite that was watching the coast and spotted the boat coming ashore at Vaucottes,' Ben said. 'That's the only way you could have known about the attack before the police did.'

Roth gave a chuckle. 'Guess I gave myself away there, huh? Anyhow, credit where credit's due. You did a pretty darn good job, my friend. Maybe you'd consider quitting that deadbeat shooting gallery you call a training school, and coming to work for us, too.'

'That's the second wonderful job offer I've had this week. I think I'd rather go off shooting rebels in Ethiopia for Ken Keegan.'

'Think about it, man. Seriously.' Roth grinned. 'Let me tell you what you're missing, though. See, this was never really about Nazim. He's out of the picture, whoopee. But the guy was just middle-echelon. Small fry, in the great scheme of things. No, the real target all along was Nazim's boss.'

'And that would be who?'

'His name is Ibrahim Mohammed al-Rashid. Iraqi, born on a little farm somewhere north of Damascus in 1949. To look at him, you'd think he was a sweet old grandfather. In reality he's the meanest, most perfidious sonofabitch who ever lived, not to mention the smartest. We've been trying to nab him for years. Suspected mastermind of an endless parade of jihadist terror atrocities, but the wily old fox always seemed to be a step ahead of us. Try as we might, we just never could nail him down. Until now.' Roth looked at his watch with an air of satisfaction. 'As we speak, our dear Mister al-Rashid is on his way to a secret facility where he's gonna spend the rest of his miserable life being very useful to us. Thanks to you, and Thierry Chevrolet.'

It took Ben a moment to understand. 'The audio track.'

Roth nodded. 'Segal was getting cold feet about the whole fentanyl thing. Nazim was worried he was going to screw up, so he mentioned the name al-Rashid to scare the living daylights out of him. That's all it took to give us the solid connection we'd been trying to establish between the old man and the known bad guys.'

Ben said, 'But Nazim already had his threat against Margot to keep Segal in line.'

'Sure, in theory. Only when Nazim had Margot kidnapped he didn't know that her husband had been wishing her dead for years. Literally. Because Margot was the one with the wealth. Her father made a ton of money in cement when she was little. She was an only child and inherited a few million bucks when he died. Whereas Julien has been squandering cash hand over fist all the time they've been unhappily married, and depending on her to keep him in his glory. He spends more than he earns, has run up heavy debts and is technically broke. Margot getting kidnapped by a bunch of murderers was the best thing that could've happened for him, because if they'd killed her he'd have gotten rich on her fortune and the life insurance. With her out of the way, he was planning on running off with the new love of his life. Sadly, not to be.'

Ben blinked. 'Romy Juneau?'

'You got it. The guy was madly infatuated with her. Our agents found a whole stack of love letters in her apartment. Whether she felt the same way about him, I guess we'll never know. Personally, I have my doubts. Anyhow, now that Romy's gone and Margot's back in the picture, I guess Segal will be the perfect lovey-dovey husband for a while longer.'

Ben's head was spinning from all the intrigue. 'Enough of Julien Segal. What happens to Ibrahim al-Rashid?'

'Use your imagination, man,' Roth said casually. 'The usual. What else?'

'Torture?'

'And then some. But we prefer the term "extraordinary rendition". You should be proud. We never woulda got the bastard without you.'

Ben pictured a seventy-year-old man being systematically taken apart by CIA spooks in some dingy cellar in a nameless foreign country, and he felt sickened. 'You're a real piece of shit, Roth.'

Roth spread his hands. 'Yeah, well. You know how it is. But don't be too rough on us. I mean, we're buying you a nice new car. The very latest B3 Biturbo model, to replace the one that, needless to say, was never anywhere near the water treatment plant in Alençon.' He smiled. 'Least we can do by way of a reward, right?'

'Stick your reward up your arse,' Ben said. 'Am I free to go now?'

'Free as a bird. Consider yourself and your two compadres officially off the hook. Actually, you never would've gotten onto it, if the cops hadn't come charging in and fouled everything up. Same old.'

'Good enough,' Ben said. 'Just a few loose ends, before I walk out of here and you never see me again. First, Roxane. How is she?'

'Being well cared for and doing just fine,' Roth said. 'She kept asking about the good-looking blond hero dude who saved her. Guess she must have imagined it. Shock does funny things to the brain.'

'Then there's Michel Yassa. Wherever he is now, I need to know they won't pursue him for the murder of Romy Juneau.'

'That won't happen. You have my word. Next?'

'Next, there's the matter of Axel Roux, his cousin and the three farm brothers who I wouldn't like to think were in any trouble either.'

'Won't be easy getting past the skipped bail issue. Axel might pull a little jail time there. But I'll see what I can do.'

'You do that.'

Roth looked amused. 'This is what I always admired about you, Ben. You're such a goddamn saint. Always looking out for the little guy. Is there more?'

'No, I think that concludes our business.'

'Don't forget the job offer. Still on the table, anytime you feel like reconsidering.'

Ben turned to leave. 'See you in hell, Tyler.'

Roth laughed. 'If I get there first, I'll be waiting for you, bro. Otherwise, you keep a seat for me.'

The guards were waiting for Ben outside. They led him to another room where he was given back the rest of his things. Then he was shown out of an exit, and found himself standing alone outside the grand Police Prefecture building on Place Louis Lépine, smack in the middle of Paris, opposite the roofless remains of Notre Dame Cathedral.

Not quite alone.

Jeff and Tuesday had been magically released from police custody a little sooner than him, and were waiting on a nearby bench, enjoying what little sunshine the October day had to offer. As they spotted him coming out they stood and came over with big smiles.

Ben hugged them both. He said he was sorry for what he'd had to put them through.

'We've been through worse,' Jeff said. Which was pretty much the kind of thing Jeff always said.

'So what just happened in there?' Tuesday asked. 'It's not every day you're handed a "get out of jail free" card.'

'Roth,' Ben replied, lighting a Gauloise.

Jeff grunted. 'I knew there was something funny about that bloke.'

'I could tell you,' Ben said.

'But you'd have to kill us,' Tuesday finished for him, with a face-splitting megawatt smile you couldn't look at directly without sunglasses.

'Who gives a shit anyway?' Jeff said. 'Let's go home, eh?'

Ben smiled, too. 'Yeah. Let's go home.'

Read on for a sneak preview of the
next Ben Hope thriller

The Pretender's Gold

Coming May 2020
Available to pre-order now

PROLOGUE

Loch Ardaich
Scottish Highlands

'Can you believe this crap?' Ross Campbell muttered to himself as he stared through his rainy van windscreen at the narrow, winding rural road ahead, carving onward for endless miles into the murk. The December cold and rain were showing absolutely no sign of letting up, and he had the prospect of a good soaking to look forward to when he reached his remote destination.

What a bummer. What a drag. Of course, this job would have to land on him on the dreichest, dreariest and most depressing day imaginable. Today of all days, marking exactly twelve months since Katrina had left him to run off with that rich bastard cosmetic dentist from Inverness.

Ross strongly felt that he should instead be slouched in his armchair at home, nursing his smouldering resentment in front of the TV with a few bottles of Broughton's Old Jock at his elbow. Yes, he was still feeling sorry for himself. Yes, he was taking it badly and allowing his chronic anger to get the better of him. And anyone who had a problem with that better keep their opinion to themselves. Got that, pal?

But however Ross felt he should be spending this miserable

winter's afternoon, his duties as partner in the firm of McCulloch & Campbell, Chartered Building Surveyors, obliged him to be here. His task: to scout and assess the western perimeter of the development site within the Loch Ardaich pine forest, right out in the sticks thirty miles north of Fort William. Like it hadn't already been scouted and assessed a dozen times already, but what was the point of complaining?

The closer he got to his destination, the more aggressively the rain lashed his windscreen. The road narrowed to a single-track lane in places as it followed an endless series of S-bends along the forested shores of Loch Ardaich. The heather-covered hills rose high all around, their tops shrouded in mist and cloud. Now and then he passed a lonely cottage or deserted stone bothy. On a clear day you could sometimes spot an osprey circling over the waters of the loch, or even an eagle; and it wasn't uncommon for a red deer to suddenly burst from cover and leap across the road right in the path of oncoming traffic, scaring the wits out of the inattentive motorist. Ross had lived here all his life, though, and for him the scenery and fauna of the remote western Highlands that drew thousands of visitors each year from all around the world held little wonder or fascination.

At last, the wire-mesh fence and main gates of the development site appeared ahead. The adverse weather conditions had kept most of the protesters away, but the diehards were still grimly hanging on. Ross gave a groan as he saw the small crowd huddled in their rain gear by the gates, ready to wave their sodden banners and scream abuse at any vehicles entering or leaving the fenced-off construction zone. Ross would have bet money that Geoffrey Watkins was among them. Come up all the way from England to stir up as much trouble as he could, Watkins was the most militant of the lot.

Ross personally didn't have a lot of time for the environmental nutters in general, though he had to admit they might have a point on this occasion. It had certainly been one of the more contentious projects his firm had been involved in, and he'd often wished that his senior partner, Ewan, hadn't agreed to take it on. The plans for an eighteen-hole championship golf course and gated community estate with million-pound homes for wealthy retirees had attracted no small amount of anger from locals. Two hundred acres of ancient pine forest had been earmarked for destruction under the scheme, sparking furious resistance and attempted legal action by one of the larger and more organised eco-warrior groups. The environmentalists had lost their legal case in court months ago, but in spite of the ruling against them were still gamely doing all they could to disrupt the development. Their methods had been creative enough to cause protracted and extremely expensive delays. The company who'd initially landed the contract had been brought to a virtual standstill by the legion of protesters who had invaded the site, chained themselves to trees, lain in the path of bulldozers, harangued the foresters and generally made it impossible to get the excavations underway. When the company had built a scale-proof fence worthy of a prison compound and brought in security personnel to eject the protesters, the ecowarriors had simply sharpened up their game by sabotaging construction vehicles, slashing tyres and setting an awful lot of valuable machinery ablaze, until in the end the company execs had been forced to cut their losses and give up.

Three more construction firms were now in competition to decide which lucky crew would take their place. All the while, persistent rumours abounded of a lot of dirty money changing hands and palms being greased for the project to be greenlit. If you believed the gossip, certain local officials were going to do well out of the deal – if and when it actually got completed. The situation was a mess.

Ross was driving his company van, a little white Peugeot Bipper with the chartered surveyor firm's logo proudly emblazoned on its side, a magnet for trouble. Not much wanting his vehicle to be attacked and pelted with missiles, he slipped away from the main gates and detoured around the site's western perimeter to a small side entrance the protesters had, mercifully, chosen to leave unguarded today. He parked the van and listened to the rain pounding the roof. The ground was turning to slush out there, appalling even by the normal standards of a Scottish winter. Beyond the fence stood the thick, dark forest, ancient and forbidding. Local folklore held spooky old tales of bogles and sluaghs and other evil spirits and hobgoblins that lurked in the woods, preying on the hapless. What a load of shite, Ross thought, but he still didn't much fancy having to venture inside.

He changed into his wellies and tugged on his raincoat before getting out of the van, then took the plunge. Moments later, he'd undone the padlock holding the side gate and let himself through the fence, closing it behind him before setting off at a trudge towards the trees.

The forest was very dense and hard to walk through, and Ross was certainly no hardened outdoorsman. He tripped and stumbled his way for nearly a quarter of a mile using a GPS navigation device to orient him towards the western boundary. Without the GPS he'd soon have been hopelessly lost, probably doomed to wander forever. Overhead the tall trees swayed in the wind and their branches clacked and clashed like the antlers of fighting stags in the rutting season. Deep, deep in the forest he swore out loud – who the hell could hear him, anyway – as he had to clamber over a slippery, moss-covered fallen trunk that blocked his path with no other way around except through a mass of brambles that would have stopped a tank. He cursed even more vehemently a few metres further on, when he was forced to negotiate a steep downward slope where part of the ground had been washed away by floods of rain, exposing tree roots and a great deal of centuries-old rotted and richly odorous vegetable matter.

Damn and blast. Why'd this have to happen to me? At least, if it was any consolation, the rain had stopped.

He was halfway down the slippery incline when he lost his footing. He windmilled his arms to try to regain his balance, to no avail. Next thing he was tumbling and slithering through the gloopy mud, desperately grasping at roots in an attempt to halt his descent but unable to stop himself until he'd rolled and somersaulted all the way to the claggy, squelchy bottom.

'Oh, for God's sake!' he yelled as he managed to sit upright, caked from head to toe in wet, cloying, dripping, freezing cold filth that dripped from his fingers and matted his hair. 'I don't bloody believe it!' Followed by a stream of much more profane invective.

But then his words abruptly died in his mouth as a very strange and unexpected sight caught his eye.

He reached out and raked in the dirt to uncover the rest of the shiny, glinting object whose corner was peeking up at him from the ground next to him. Something hard and small and thin and round, which he picked up and held up to look at more closely. As he wiped dirt off it, a stray beam of sunlight penetrated through the pine canopy above. It reflected off the object in his fingers, and it was as though someone had shone a golden light in his face. He gasped in astonishment.

Then, moments later, he was finding more gold coins in the mud. Dirty, but perfect and beautiful. Six, seven, eight, nine, ten of them. The torrential rain flood that had washed away part of the bank must have disturbed them from their hiding place. How long had they lain undiscovered in this remote and little-travelled neck of the woods?

Suddenly, Ross Campbell's unlucky tumble and getting clarted up to his oxters in muck had become the best thing that had ever happened to him. As fast as he could stuff the coins into his coat and trouser pockets, more kept appearing all around. Within minutes he'd collected dozens of them. It was so incredible he was laughing and hooting to himself like a kid. When finally he could find no more, he struggled back up the slippery bank with his booty weighing down his pockets. The return journey to the van seemed to take him about half the time. He was so dazed and ecstatic that he barely noticed the brambles and treacherous terrain, and didn't think for a single moment about his filthy, wet clothes or the fact that under them he was soaked to the bone.

Back at the van, he piled into the driver's seat and dug some of the coins from his pocket to re-examine more closely. They were old, really old. He was no expert, but he was certain they must be worth a ton of money. A bloody fortune, lying there in the mud for hundreds of years, just waiting for him to come and find it.

Ross could hardly contain himself. The day's task was almost completely forgotten. He'd just tell his business partner Ewan that the weather was too awful to get the job done, and promise to return as soon as possible. Which he certainly intended to do, to have a more thorough search in case there might be a whole load more of this beautiful treasure buried in the same spot. He had the exact location marked on his GPS device.

In the meantime, he needed to get home as fast as he could. A hot shower and a cup of tea, before he caught his death. Then he'd spend the rest of the afternoon, and probably the evening, cleaning up, counting and re-counting his glorious loot. What might the coins be worth? Five thousand pounds each? Ten? The numbers made him dizzy, and fantasies were already forming in his mind. He could picture himself quitting his job, for a start, then getting out of this godforsaken shithole and making a beeline for somewhere with warm sandy beaches, palm trees and beautiful bikini-clad girls, maybe never to return. Fuck Katrina and her dentist! He'd show them.

He'd need to get the coins independently valued, of course. The internet would only tell him so much. But it would have to be discreet. And preferably done by an expert in another part of the UK, maybe in Edinburgh or London. Someone who'd never be told the precise location of the discovery. Nor would anyone else, certainly nobody local. As it seemed that he alone knew about this, he meant to keep it that way. The last thing Ross wanted was for others to come searching. And with the Loch Ardaich development project so conveniently put on hold, he'd have plenty of opportunity to come back here as often as he liked to hunt for more treasure.

With a trembling hand Ross started up the van engine, then took off in a rush. He couldn't wait to get home. This was, beyond a shadow of a doubt, the most wonderful and exciting day of his entire life.

It would also prove to be one of the last. He didn't know it yet, but he would never live to see his fantasies come true. Nor did he have any idea of the chain of events his strange discovery was about to set in motion.

If Ross Campbell had not found the gold coins that had lain hidden all this time in the forest, people would not have been hurt or killed. None of the things that were about to happen would have taken place. And the men who were soon to be drawn into the web of danger would not have become involved.

One man in particular. A man Ross Campbell would never meet. A man called Ben Hope.

But Ross Campbell had found them, and now the storm was coming.

Chapter 1

Eleven days later, the clouds were gone and the sky was bright and blue. But none of the assembly who had gathered at the cemetery in the village of Kinlochardaich to watch the interment of the coffin was smiling.

What an unspeakable tragedy. Ross Campbell had been a much loved member of the community, even if he had been going through some personal ups and downs in the last year and not always the cheerful and carefree soul he'd once been. It was hard to keep secrets in this close-knit community, and everyone knew that his former long-term girlfriend, Katrina Reid, was now living with someone else in Inverness. Then again, those who had spoken to Ross in the few days leading up to his untimely death reported that his mood had radically improved all of a sudden. For reasons that remained unclear he'd seemed strangely happy, even jubilant, as though he'd finally broken free of the emotional troubles that had plagued him since his relationship breakup. It seemed so ironic that, just as his life appeared to have turned a corner, he should fall victim to such an awful accident.

It was "Patch" Keddie, the one-eyed bird watcher who was one of the community's more colourful fixtures, who'd discovered the body floating face-down among the rushes at the edge of Loch Ardaich while on his solitary wanderings in the countryside with backpack and spotting scope, four days earlier. Shocked and upset by the grisly discovery, Patch had hurried to a spot where he could get phone reception and called for an ambulance, but it was already far too late.

It appeared as if Ross must have been exploring the loch-side when he'd slipped and fallen into the water. His surveyor's van was later found quite a distance away, parked by the fence of the golf course development site. This had sparked much puzzled debate about what Ross was doing down at the water's edge, a good quarter of a mile or more from the location he'd been surveying. Perhaps he'd wandered over there just to enjoy the magnificent views. In any case, having never learned to swim he had little chance of escaping the freezing cold water. He wasn't the first victim to have been claimed by the depths of the loch.

Among the mourners at the graveside was Ross's partner in the firm, thirty-four-year-old Ewan McCulloch. Head bowed and grim-faced, Ewan was visibly shaken to the core by the loss of his business associate and friend. Though they'd only worked together for five years, like most folks in this close-knit community with relatively few incomers they'd known each other for nearly all of their lives.

Other attendees at the funeral included Ross's stricken parents, who now lived near Inverness. Mrs Campbell had wept bitterly throughout the gruelling church service and was so crippled with grief that she could barely remain upright to watch her only child's coffin go into the ground. Her husband bore his agony in stoical silence, but the expression in his eyes was ghastly to see.

Katrina Reid, the ex-girlfriend, was conspicuous by her absence. Nobody was terribly surprised that the untrust-worthy little cow had not bothered to show up. Also present were Mairi Anderson, the surveyor's office administrator; William and Maureen Reid, who ran the Kinlochardaich Arms, the village's one and only pub; Rab Hunter, the local mechanic who'd known both Ross and Ewan since primary schooldays; Patch Keddie the bird watcher who'd found the body, tears streaming from his one eye; and Grace Kirk.

Grace was a couple of years younger than Ewan, had attended the same primary and secondary schools and then left for a time to pursue a career as a police officer in the big city. She'd returned to her birthplace a few months ago and was the only female officer in the area. Today she was off duty and out of uniform, hiding her reddened eyes behind dark glasses as she stood in the back of the crowd with her hands clasped and shoulders drooping.

When at last the gut-wrenching ceremony was over, there were solemn handshakes and hugs and commiserations and more tears before the assembly began to disperse. Poor Mrs Campbell had to be virtually carried away to the waiting car. Ewan had been hoping to say a few words of thanks to Grace Kirk, but when he turned away from the grave he saw she'd already gone. He shared a quiet moment with Rab Hunter, who clapped him on the arm and said, 'Rough times, man. You okay?' Once you got past the intimidating muscles and the piratical beard and earring, Rab was a big softy at heart. His eyes were full of tears and he kept blinking.

'Yeah, I'm okay,' Ewan lied.

Rab shook his head and blinked once more. 'I still cannae get my head aroond it, you know? He was here with us, and now he's gone.'

'I can barely believe it either,' Ewan replied, truthfully this time. He, too, was having a hard time adjusting to the reality of Ross's death. They parted, and he walked slowly back across the cemetery grounds and past the old grey stone church to where he'd parked his van. It was a little white Peugeot with the company name on the door, identical to the one Ross had been driving. Ewan didn't have a car of his own. His only personal vehicle was a rundown old camper, currently off the road and somewhat neglected. Maybe one day he'd get around to it.

As Ewan headed homewards he was asking himself the same question he'd been asking for days: What on earth was Ross doing down there at the lochside? He couldn't have been lost; he knew the area as well as anyone. Ewan didn't believe he was admiring the scenery, either. Ross couldn't have given a damn about such things. Had he been drinking? A couple of times in the months since Katrina had left, Ewan had thought he could smell alcohol on Ross's breath during work hours. Maybe he should have reached out to his friend, offered support, but he'd said nothing at the time. Now he feared that Ross's emotional state might have been more serious than anyone had supposed.

At the back of Ewan's mind was the unmentionable thought that wouldn't go away.

Suicide. Was it possible?

Surely not. Ross wasn't the type to top himself. But then, every man has his breaking point. What if Ross had simply reached his? What if the apparent uplift in his spirits during his last few days – and yes, Ewan had noticed it too – was really just a desperate man's last-ditch attempt to disguise the bleak despair that was consuming his heart and soul?

If that was true, then Ewan had truly failed his friend.

'Oh God, Ross. I'm so sorry.'

When Ewan got home to the small house in which he lived alone, he went straight to the kitchen and poured himself a stiff whisky from a bottle a client had given him the Christmas before last. He wasn't much of a boozer, but this could be a good time to take up the habit. He sat down heavily in a wooden chair at the table, gulped his drink and then poured himself another. Mixed up with his grief was the bewildering issue of how the business was going to continue with just him as a solo operator. There was already too much work for two partners, especially if the massive undertaking that was the golf course project went ahead. Ross's sudden absence left a gaping hole that threatened to swallow Ewan up, too.

He had been unable to do any work since receiving the news of the death four days ago. He had no plans to go into the office tomorrow either. Nor the next day, most likely. Let's just sit here and drink, he thought. By the time he'd finished the second whisky the edge was coming off his pain and he decided that a third would help even more. He knew he'd probably regret it, but what the hell.

Ewan woke up in the darkness. The phone was ringing. What time was it? He must have been asleep for hours, and had no recollection of having moved from the kitchen table to the living room couch. His head was aching and his mouth tasted like the contents of a wrestler's laundry basket. He should never have drunk so much. Bleary-eyed and disorientated, he managed to get up, turn on a light and stumble across the room to answer the phone. Who could be calling?

He picked up. 'Hello?' he croaked.

There was silence on the line. Ewan repeated, 'Hello?'

DON'T LET THEM GET INSIDE YOUR MIND.

A young girl is abducted from her rich and powerful family. And only Ben Hope can find her . . .

DEATH FOLLOWS IT. NOW BEN HOPE MUST FIND IT.

An apparent home invasion leads to a savage murder – and the hunt for the killers will lead Ben Hope to a shocking historical secret . . .